I wasn't even in the room when she was killed, how could I be a suspect...

I was almost out the door when I turned to take one last look around. Tina's travel bag was sitting on the bed, and the vodka bottle was still on the table. Even if it wasn't my liquor of choice, I could see no sense letting it go to waste. I walked over, grabbed the bottle, and put it into the shopping bag that held my belongings. Just then I heard a cell phone ringing from somewhere in her bag. I looked over my shoulder at the door. No one seemed to be in the hallway. The phone rang again. I dug into her bag and found the phone. The display read "Puddy." It rang again.

I know I shouldn't have, but I answered it. "Hello?"

"Who's this?" the voice on the other end asked. "Let me talk to Tina."

"Um, Tina can't come to the phone right now."

"Bullshit. Put her on," the voice demanded.

"Yeah, well, you know Tina's been drinking, what with all that's happened. Why don't you come on over to the hotel, Puddy? We can talk."

"Who the hell is this? How do you know my name? Is that bitch talking? You tell her she says anything to anyone that gets me in trouble, she's a dead woman."

"You're too late, Puddy. Someone already killed her. You want to tell me anything about it?"

"She's—dead. Oh shit, oh shit—"

The phone went dead.

"Hey, what are you doing?" a voice asked from behind me.

I turned. It was the young officer who had stood guard at my door.

"Um, just checking for messages," I answered.

"Yeah, right. You're under arrest and coming to the police station with me."

So much for the Evergreen Motel. Seemed I found other accommodations.

Wes Byrne has lost his wife to cancer and his career as an investigative reporter is in a free-fall because of a decision to investigate the powerful drug company that contributed to her death. Now, after losing another, and what may have been his last, chance to revive his career, he arrives in his old hometown to attend the funeral of a murdered childhood friend before continuing on the road to oblivion. Despite his repeated denials, however, his reputation as a reporter leads people in the town to believe he has actually come to find his friend's killer. Wes soon stumbles upon more dead bodies and becomes a "person of interest" to police in those murders. He has no choice but to go against his better judgment and, fueled with more than a few tumblers of Powers whiskey, expose the murderers to avoid becoming the next victim.

KUDOS for *Last Respects*

In *Last Respects* by John Essick, Wes Byrne is a failing investigative reporter whose life is in a down spiral since his wife died of cancer. Now has just been fired from his latest job at the *Providence Sentinel*. But when he goes to his old hometown to attend the funeral of a murdered friend, everyone thinks he is there to investigate the murders, even though all Wes wants to do is to attend the funeral and leave town. Then his car is stolen and an old friend from high school is murdered in his hotel room. Wes is now a person of interest in the newest murder and being drawn into the investigation whether he likes it or not, though he is just as likely to be the next victim as he is to find the murderer. Essick's character development is superb and the mystery intriguing, with a number of subplots equally as compelling as the main one—a highly entertaining read. ~ *Taylor Jones, The Review Team of Taylor Jones & Regan Murphy*

Last Respects by John Essick is the story of a man who has lost everything important in his life—his wife, his career as an investigative reporter, and his self-respect—and who just wants to continue his downward journey in peace. Just as Wes Byrne is fired from his latest job, he gets a phone call telling him that an old friend has been murdered. Since he has nothing else to do, Wes packs his belongings into his twenty-year-old car and heads for his hometown to attend the funeral. He barely arrives in town when his car is stolen and everyone he meets thinks he is there to investigate the murder of his friend since the police don't seem to care. Wes tries to explain that he is no longer employed as a reporter, and he is just there to attend the funeral, but no one believes him. Then when another old friend—who returns his stolen car on the condition that he take her with him when he leaves town in the morning—is murdered in his hotel room, Wes is arrested for her murder. Since the police have no evidence to hold him on, he's released but told not to leave town. Now that he has to stay, he decides to do what everyone thinks he is already doing and find out what he can about the murders—a decision that soon has the killer targeting him too. *Last Respects* is a suspenseful mystery/thriller that will keep you on the edge of your seat from beginning to end, turning pages as fast as you can. *~ Regan Murphy, The Review Team of Taylor Jones & Regan Murphy*

ACKNOWLEDGMENTS

To Joanne Dobson and The Hudson Valley Writers' Center, Sleepy Hollow, New York, for nurturing the birth of my idea;

To family and friends for reading through early drafts and providing their honest feedback throughout the revision process;

To the talented Colleen Ragusa for the creation of this wonderful book cover art;

To Black Opal Books, and, in particular, Lauri for saying yes and Faith for the patience to work with me through the editing process

To June Prager for her meticulous proofreading and editorial suggestions; and

To the guys at the Civil Armory, Pleasant Valley, New York, for expert advice on firearms.

LAST RESPECTS

JOHN ESSICK

A Black Opal Books Publication

DEDICATION

*For June and for those who believed that I would,
but are no longer here to see that I did.*

CHAPTER 1

The reason I'm showin' ya the door, Byrne, is, despite whatever great reputation you may believe you have, I think your writing's crap."

I had to hand it to Rollie. There were so many other ways he could have told me the paper was letting me go. After all, it was no secret the newspaper industry was dying and jobs were being eliminated every day. I was one of the newest hires at the *Providence Sentinel*, the city's first, now only, and, if things continued the way they were, last newspaper, so he could have taken the old lack of seniority tack. Or he could have trotted out the old standard about changing demographics and the need for the paper to attract new, younger readers. Either would have displayed a touch of decency. However, if I had learned one thing during my brief tenure at the *Sentinel*, it was that Roland "Rollie" Deeple, Features Editor, was one of the biggest sons of a bitch I ever had worked for.

I looked across his cluttered desk and couldn't help noticing the smug look of satisfaction on his face. He was enjoying this. He had never wanted me on his staff in the first place. The decision to hire me had come from above, and I was given my column in Features over his strenuous objections. Now, here was an opportunity to not only kick me to the curb but also send a shot upstairs to remind the powers that be that no one tells Rollie Deeple what to do.

"Does Tom Hawkins know?" I asked.

"Yeah, and he agrees. All I had to do was show him this," he said, waving two pages of my latest copy. "No one wants to read another depressing column about death and loss and whatever sad sack shit is happening in your life."

A little meatball of a man, more bread crumbs than hamburger, Rollie represented everything I loathed in this business, what I'd come to call "tenacious mediocrity." It made me angry to contemplate that this foul-tempered, mean-spirited hack had back-stabbed and manipulated his way to becoming an editor of a fairly important newspaper. Day after day, I watched him dash the ambition of every young reporter who possessed a modicum of the talent he knew he himself didn't have, or crush the career of a good writer who he thought posed a threat to the power he had schemed so hard to attain. It further angered me to realize that, in my case, this horrid little fat man was right. My writing stank.

Rollie waited for my reply, but all I could do was stare at the stain on his shirt. Every day that I had worked at the paper, Rollie managed to have a stain somewhere on his shirt. As I sat there, I sadly realized the thing I was probably going to miss most about the paper was not the camaraderie of fellow reporters or the rush I once got from seeing my name in an article's byline, but instead throwing my dollar in the office pool each day and making a guess as to what Rollie had managed to spill on himself that morning. Today I went with raspberry from a jelly-filled donut. Wonder if it was too late to change it to blood, my blood.

"I want you packed up and your desk cleared right away. When you're ready to go, security will escort you out," he said, interrupting my thoughts.

"Security? That won't be necessary."

"Paper policy. We wanna to make sure you're not walking off with any state secrets and make sure you leave the building like you're supposed ta. We've had nuts hide out in a bathroom and sabotage the next edition after the day-staff had gone home. We've learned to take precautions."

I stood to leave. So far, I thought I'd handled myself

with dignity and kept my emotions in check. "I'm not the saboteur type," I replied. "Besides, I couldn't do any more damage to this newspaper in one night than you do on a daily basis."

"Get the hell out of my office, you loser," Rollie screamed.

So much for dignity, but sometimes dignity was overrated.

☙❧

As I left his office, I could see from the faces of my now former co-workers that word about my dismissal had spread. Made sense, of course, since it was a newspaper staffed by professionals trained to be on top of the latest events. Some gave me a wry smile and a shake of the head. Others averted their gaze lest whatever I had that caused my firing be transmitted by eye contact.

I walked over to my desk and was surprised to see an empty file box already waiting for me there. Rollie didn't waste time.

He needn't have worried. It wouldn't take me long to pack because I'd never really settled in. The *Sentinel* never felt like home, although I'd be hard pressed to say exactly what home felt like anymore. I had it once, really had it all, forever ago. Then everything seemed to crumble so quickly, and here I was packing up my stuff just like I had everywhere I'd been since everything...well, actually the only thing that mattered...had washed away.

Margie the office manager—a short, slightly plump woman in her mid-forties, with her hair cut short with jagged bangs and her reading glasses hanging from a chain around her neck—was also there. She had a file with my name on it in her hands, no doubt with my marching orders inside.

"Wes, I'm so sorry, really. Just a few papers to sign…"

she said, putting her reading glasses on. "God, I hate this part of my job."

"It's okay. It's not your fault," I said just as my smartphone began to vibrate on my desk, where I'd tossed it when I came in. With my luck, it was my landlord calling to tell me my place was infected with bedbugs.

No, the call was from out of state. I didn't recognize the number, but it had an area code I hadn't seen for a long time. I hesitated for just a moment then answered it.

"Wes Byrne."

"Hey, Wes, It's Tim. Tim Brewer," a voice replied.

Tim didn't have to give me his last name. I recognized his voice immediately, even after so many years.

"Hi, Tim. Long time. How'd you track me down?"

"I've got my ways. Listen, I know you're probably busy, but I just thought you might want to know. Someone killed Stevie."

Suddenly I couldn't breathe and the room seemed to press in on me from all sides.

"Wes. You still there?"

I needed space. I found my distance by stepping back into the safety of what I did best, or once did best. I became a reporter. I picked up a pen that was on the desk and grabbed a notepad out of the desk drawer. I wrote *Stevie dead. When? How?* "Any idea who did it?" I asked Tim.

"No, not yet—and to tell you the truth the police aren't exactly tripping over each other trying to find out. Anyway, the funeral's on Friday. Thought you might wanta come down for it."

I didn't answer, just pressed my pen down hard as I underlined the words I'd written on the notepad.

Suddenly, I heard a loud thumping and looked up to see Rollie standing and banging at his office window that looked out over the newsroom.

He was glaring at Margie and pointing at me with his left hand while fanning at his ear with his right hand the way a dog that's got fleas does.

"Tim—hold on a moment," I said. I looked at Margie. "You don't suppose Rollie wants you to tear my ear off, do you?" I asked.

She sort of smiled. "No, I think he wants me to take your phone," she said with a please-don't-blame-me shrug.

I put the phone back to my ear and turned to avoid looking at Rollie.

"Tim, listen things are a little crazy for me right now. Let me call you back in a little bit when I'm alone."

"Sure, no problem. Whenever it's good for you,' he said.

I wrote down Tim's number from the screen readout, ended the call, and handed the phone to Margie. I signed the papers she pulled out of my file. She put them back in the folder, patted me comfortingly on the arm, and left me to my packing. "I'll need your ID card too. You can leave it at the front desk when you leave. Sorry. I hope things work out," she said before walking away.

I started putting the very few possessions I had in the box while trying to collect my thoughts. Elaine from Accounting came walking up to my desk.

Elaine was probably in her late-twenties, although whenever we talked she mentioned yoga and weekend hikes and bike rides, so she might have been older and just in great shape. She wore her blonde hair short, cut above the ears, parted on left with the top hair sweeping across her forehead. She was probably the nicest person I'd met at the *Sentinel*.

"Gee, Wes. Real sorry to hear the bad news. Looks like it was quite a shock."

It took me a moment to realize she was talking about me being fired, not Stevie's murder.

"What? Oh, the job. No, it's not a big deal, just goes with the territory sometimes."

She handed me my last paycheck. "I've got some other bad news."

"Really, what's that?"

"You just missed out on Rollie's stain pool. You were

close, but it turns out that today he had a few slices of cherry pie for breakfast, so it's a cherry stain, not raspberry. Pretty close, though."

"Pie for breakfast?" I asked absently.

"Probably how he keeps that boyish figure. Anyway, good luck," she said with a smile and a pat on my upper arm as she turned and walked away.

I finished packing the file box and put the lid on it. I looked up and standing in his open doorway was Rollie, watching me, a smug look on his jowly face. I looked at the stain on his shirt. That about summed up my sad-sack life. A guy like Rollie pigged out on a pie full of cherries while I got a large slice of the humble variety.

CHAPTER 2

A little early, ain't it? Even for you?"

I recognized the voice well before my eyes adjusted to the dark interior of the Ink and Pen, the preferred watering hole of Providence's newspapermen and women since type was set by hand. Liam Dooley, a slight trace of an Irish brogue in his speech, which I'd always viewed with a reporter's skepticism seeing as how he was born and raised in Providence, was at his usual place behind the bar.

"Ah, shit," he said, and I realized he could see me clearly enough and must have noticed the tell-tale file box I carried into the bar with me. "Not you too? How the hell am I supposed to stay in business if that damned paper keeps firing my best customers?"

"I guess you'll just have to water your whiskey down even more," I replied as I approached my usual seat at the bar. Of course, I could've sat anywhere. The bar was empty at that early hour.

"Hold your tongue. An Irishman would no more water down whiskey than a Hindu would eat a steak."

Slowly I began to distinguish Liam's bulky figure manning his post. If ever a man was born to own a bar, it was Liam. He had a knack for remembering the name of every customer who ever entered his place and could make even the most miserable human being on the face of the Earth feel welcome. I was always amazed how he seemed to know enough about everything to keep a conversation going, but not so much as to appear an expert. He let the customer fill that role. He had an easy-going manner and a natural gift for telling jokes and stories. Despite his size—he was easily over six foot three and must have weighed well over 250 pounds—he moved behind the bar with the grace of Fred Astaire, and I swear he could hear an empty glass touch down upon the bar top, no matter how loud the bar crowd, and swoop in with a refill before a patron could call out for another round. Yet congenial as he was, he made it known, in his way, that he'd countenance no monkey business in his bar, and an unruly customer would find himself flying ass over heel into the street quicker than lager turns to piss.

I sat down and placed the box on the stool beside me.

"Well, just in case, pour me a double. And so I won't be drinking alone, pour one for yourself and one for my late, lamented career at the *Providence Sentinel*, here," I said, gently tapping the lid of the file box.

"Well, it is a bit early for me, but seeing as to the occasion, I'd be a poor friend to say no," he answered.

Liam placed three shot glasses on the bar and poured some Powers whiskey into each right to the peak. The two of us raised our glasses, and then clinked them against the one sitting in front of the half-filled file box.

"To lost jobs and broken hearts," Liam toasted.

We knocked back our shots and slammed our glasses on the bar with a loud thud.

"Your friend here doesn't appear to be too thirsty," Liam said, wiping some whiskey off his mouth with the back of his hand.

"Yeah, well, he's taking it pretty hard. I think it's his first time." I sat for a moment remembering mine. "I, on the other hand, do not have that problem," I said and slid the full whiskey glass over in front of me.

"Well, you know, Wes, and forgive me if I'm sticking my big Mick nose where it doesn't belong, but Jaysus, you must have seen it coming. I mean, some of the stuff you wrote was depressing enough to make Little Orphan Annie slit her wrists."

"Everybody's a critic," I said. I polished off the remaining shot of whiskey. No sooner had I returned the glass to the bar than Liam refilled it for me.

"So, what are your plans? I can't imagine, much as I'd miss you, that you'll be staying around Providence. Not much, besides my dear friendship, to keep you around, is there?" he asked.

That was one of things I'd come to love about Liam. He would stick his big Mick nose wherever he thought it needed sticking and his honesty was refreshing. We'd hit it off pretty well the first time I came into the place and, once he found out we both had ancestors in County Donegal, he'd practically adopted me as a brother. I was going to miss him.

"Ya know, I did a little research on ya, seeing as how I'm the curious sort and like to know a little about my customers, especially those running a tab. I read some of your old stuff, from where was it…Boston? You were once a pretty good reporter—broke some big stories."

I ran my finger around the top of my shot glass, eyeing Liam warily. "Yeah, and stepped on a lot of the wrong toes. So what?"

"So, I was wondering what happened."

I raised the glass to my lips but only took a sip this time. It wasn't yet noon after all.

"Nothing I really feel like talking about."

"Yeah, well, unless you want to kiss your newspaper career goodbye entirely, you better start talking about it, and it might as well be with me."

To hell with the hour. I finished off the rest of the whiskey in one quick swallow. I put the glass back on the bar and covered it with my hand to stop Liam from pouring me another.

"Okay, you want to be my psychologist. Well, here's the road version and then we go back to you being the bartender and me being the soon-to-be drunk. Once upon a time, I had a good career and a great marriage. My wife died, my career went up in smoke, and I ended up getting a job here only because the father of a friend happened to be one of the bigwigs at the paper. Ever since I got here, I've written crap and got canned. End of session." I moved my hand from atop the glass. "Pour me another drink…please."

Liam was silent for several moments. Then he shook his head sadly and filled my glass. He poured one for himself.

"Sláinte!" he toasted and we drank our shots. We were back on familiar turf.

"So, what are ya going to do now?" he asked.

"Well, believe it or not, getting fired was actually the bright news of the day. Seems a friend from long ago days was murdered in my hometown a few nights ago. I'm debating going back for his funeral."

"Why wouldn't ya?"

"Well, before I left years ago, I broke a story for the local newspaper that pissed off some very important people and hurt someone I cared about deeply. I don't think I'd be welcomed back with open arms," I explained.

"You think those people are still mad at you?"

"People in my old hometown hold grudges the way folks in other places hold Fourth of July celebrations. Everybody's just waiting for the fireworks."

"How'd your friend die?" Liam asked.

"Haven't gotten all the details yet."

"Police catch who did it?"

"No, and knowing my friend's reputation with the local constabulary, they aren't going to knock themselves out trying to find the culprit. Stevie—that was his name—had a way of pissing people off."

"You're a reporter, or at least you once were. Don't you want to know what happened?"

"Of course I do. We haven't been close for years, but there was a time we were as close as brothers, but I am not going down there to get involved. Those days are over."

"Tough situation," Liam said, pouring each of us another round. "You can do the wrong thing and go back and try to the find the killer, or you can do the right thing and go back and find the killer—or you can be a horse's arse and do nothing."

I shook my head and chuckled. Leave it to Liam to make me laugh at a time like this. "Yeah, I think it's what they call a conundrum."

"Ya know what I think you should do?" Liam asked.

"You mean other than start lining up a liver transplant donor?" I asked, eyeing the full shot glass in front of me.

"I say to hell with the people you might piss off. Maybe if you go back you find your friend's killer, you start to find your old self as well."

"I'm a reporter, or at least was, not a detective. Besides, I thought I said the shrink session was over," I answered.

"I'm not saying that as a psychologist. I'm saying it as a friend." He lifted his glass. "To old friends and new beginnings."

We drank.

CHAPTER 3

Callous as it might seem, Stevie was the one person I knew that I could easily understand being murdered. In fact, when we were growing up, I sometimes thought I would be the one to do it. He just had a way of pushing people's buttons, and I swear he could have made a Buddhist want to slap him silly. So it was strange that the news of his death, his murder, was such a shock to me.

"The police seem to think it had something to do with drugs," Tim explained to me when I called him back on Liam's cellphone after sufficiently numbing myself with James Powers's gift to civilization. I had slipped into a back room at the bar to get away from the raucous lunch crowd to where it was quiet enough to talk. For further privacy, I installed myself in an old wooden phone booth with a sliding glass door that Liam had somehow managed to keep in the bar. Legend had it then when a guy from the phone company came to take it away, Liam got the guy so drunk he forgot all about it. Having it here, even though the phone was no longer connected, was just another of those things I loved, and would miss, about the Pen and Ink. I placed a coaster on the writing platform in the booth and placed the beer I had brought with me on it.

"Did he have any drugs on him when he died? Did he have any drugs in his system?" I asked.

"Hell if I know. I get my facts the old-fashioned way— gossip at the Town Crier Diner with my breakfast and no one there seems to have any information—just opinions," Tim answered.

The mention of the Town Crier brought back warm memories of teen-age nights spent languishing in the comfortably upholstered booths and sharing tall tales of sexual exploits—or, in my case, lack thereof—over plates of steak fries with gravy and onion rings, our selections from the jukebox mixing with the voices of waitresses barking out orders to the cook. It was odd to think of Tim now being one of the regulars we used to crack jokes about and swear we would never become. Still, I had to admit feeling a slight twinge of envy as I pictured him sitting at the Formica counter arrayed with condiments, sugar packets in their holders and salt and pepper shaker stations and discussing the high school football team's chances in the upcoming season or the need for a traffic light on Main Street with the usual crowd that gathered each morning.

"Well, did they find the murder weapon?" I asked.

"What's with the all the questions? Thinking of poking around where you're probably not wanted when you come down for the funeral?"

"No, no, of course not. You know me. I just like to know what's what is all," I answered. And I meant it, despite what Liam had said about finding the killer in order to find myself. I had decided to go to the funeral somewhere between my last shot and my first beer, since I really had nothing else to do or anywhere else to go. Just for the funeral, that was all. I planned to get in and get out of my old hometown before moving on to the next phase of my life, whatever that might be.

"Well, if you are, you should know that I hadn't seen Stevie for years, but from what I heard he was running with a pretty rough crowd. I'm glad you're coming but you should be careful. The last thing you need in this town is more enemies."

I took a swallow of my beer and imagined the type of people Tim was talking about—a gauntlet of drug dealers, bikers, and other small-time hooligans. I could picture them all lined up, just waiting for the chance to bash in my thick reporter's skull with their chains, clubs, and baseball bats. And that was just the women. The men would rip me apart with their bare hands.

In and out—nothing more, I promised myself.

"Don't worry, I'll behave. No one will even know I'm there. By the way, how's Sue Ellen taking Stevie's death," I asked, deciding to change the subject.

"About what you'd expect, seeing as he was her kid brother. Wouldn't be surprised if she blames herself a little, although she did everything she could to help Stevie straighten out," he answered.

"Yeah, she always looked out for him. Can't tell you how many times she beat up one of the older boys for messing with Stevie when we were growing up. Nobody wanted to mess with her."

"Right, up until high school and then there wasn't a guy in town who wouldn't of stood in line for a chance to wrestle with her."

We laughed and then were both silent for a few moments. I knew that Tim, like me, was remembering how things used to be. You think things will never change, can't imagine life being any different and then next thing, you see people you thought would be your friends forever in the supermarket or at the dry cleaners and they're almost total strangers.

"Guess she's still married to Tony," I said.

"Yeah, though rumor has it things aren't so great between them—just more Town Crier gossip, mind you."

I had to admit I was a little glad to hear that. I never liked the guy, even before all the trouble I stirred up, and it was mutual. I wasn't that surprised that Sue Ellen married him, because she'd always, even when we were kids, made it clear that she was going to marry money, and Tony came from the richest family in town. He married her, I always thought, just to prove he could, because every guy in town was after her. Of course, he was one of those bastards that always seemed to get what he wanted, even when he didn't deserve it. Sue Ellen was another case in point. I always thought she was more of a trophy to him than a wife.

"She runs with the horsey crowd these days, so I don't see too much of her. Got a couple of kids—daughters—both pretty like her. She raised them right, didn't let them get spoiled, despite all the money."

We were silent again. The thing about old friends, and I still considered Tim a friend, despite the years and the distances I put between us, was how you could know just what the other was thinking and it was just a matter of time before it came out.

"Do you think she's still mad at me?" I asked. "I'd hate to come down to the funeral and cause some kind of scene."

"No, to tell you the truth, I don't think she is. Last time I saw her, she even asked about you. I think maybe being married to Tony, she understands how things really were. Now would Tony be thrilled to see you? That's another story altogether."

"So you still think I should come?"

"You kidding? You owe it to Stevie and, hell, if there is some dust up between you and Tony, well, no one would be happier than Stevie, wherever he might be resting. He'd hate having a boring funeral."

CHAPTER 4

At one time, each small town in America had a unique identity, a way for a traveler to know whether they were in some backwoods burg in Rhode Island or Connecticut or New Jersey. That time had passed, and it seemed these days it was impossible to distinguish one strip mall of fast food restaurants and retail chain stores from any other strip mall anywhere along any road in our country. America seemed to have blended into one endless stretch of commercial conformity. I wondered if the same thing had happened in East Hastings.

It felt more than a little macabre to rush to see someone placed in a hole in the ground, so rather than take Rte. I-95 south I decided to drive along the less direct back roads down to Stevie's funeral. Not that I really had that much of a choice. There wasn't much chance my reliable, old 1989 Toyota Camry was up to competing with SUVs and tractor trailers on the interstate for the more than six-hour drive south. I didn't mind, really. It only seemed appropriate that neither my car nor I seemed capable of driving in the fast lane anymore.

The Camry was the first, and only, new car I had ever bought. When I got it, I thought I'd hold onto it for a few years before I traded it in for a newer model, probably something a little sportier. I used most of my very first paycheck for the down payment, but seeing as how I was single and renting a studio apartment, I didn't mind the expense. It suited my needs. It was dependable transportation, good gas mileage, and so what if it wasn't a chick magnet? It wasn't that bad-a-looking car. I'd take good care of it, keep it clean. The women could wait a year or two to fight over me.

What's that old saying? If you want to make God laugh, tell him your plans? Well, my sportier car never happened. I made good money at the paper and had actually built up a little bit of a savings account when I met Jan. Things moved fast. Next thing I know we're living in an overpriced two-bedroom apartment in downtown Boston on my salary, while Jan was working her way through med school. We could've found a cheaper place outside of the city, but she had to be close to school and the hospital where she spent extra hours volunteering, and I figured, since I was going to be the *Boston Herald*'s next great investigative reporter, I should get to know the sinister back streets and alleys of the city I was going to clean up. Any extra money we happened to scrape together went toward saving for the house we intended to buy after she graduated. We would get something real nice with the extra income, once she was working and had paid off all her tuition debts. We'd need room for the kids, after all. Nice plans. I think comedians call it the set-up.

Instead, Jan got ovarian cancer and even though she was surrounded by the best medical minds and technology and had access to the very best treatment available in the entire country, the cancer won and took her away from me. I got a little bitter. I guess I started looking for a bad guy. There had to be a bad guy. Beautiful, bright, full-of-life people like Jan just didn't die.

I found my suspect—PharmaHeal, one of the largest pharmaceutical companies in the country. Rumor had it the cancer drug they developed, the one prescribed for Jan during her treatment, was about as useful against her cancer as a fly swatter against a swarm of locusts. And they knew it.

I went after them. Man, did I go after them. But I guess I

got a little stupid, lost a little perspective on who I could trust and who I couldn't. There was a lot at stake. I didn't listen to the warnings because I was going to take them down. I didn't care that PharmaHeal was big and powerful—ex-governor, an ex-presidential candidate, and a member of one of the most powerful families in Massachusetts on the board of directors powerful—to say nothing of being the *Herald*'s biggest advertiser. My story got squashed and I was not-so-delicately told to keep quiet and consider how much I treasured my career as a journalist.

Why didn't I listen? I'd keep asking myself that for a long time to come. I would listen today, no doubt about it. But back then…well, every time I closed my eyes I saw my lovely Jan fighting against that damned disease, and I saw how strong she was trying to be for me. For me! So I got a lot of stupid. I gave the story to a rival paper and waited for the fireworks.

Well, they came, and they were all directed at me. Sources recanted or completely disappeared. PharmaHeal—with plenty of help from the *Herald*—portrayed me as an out-of-control, angry, —okay, so I did tend to end my days with my butt plastered on a bar stool—and unprofessional opportunist with an axe to grind. I guess I was lucky not to end up in jail or sued for libel. I think everyone was just happy to see me go away.

So I packed the Camry, left Boston, and started driving downhill.

Still, I loved this old car. It was one of the few vehicles that my six-foot-three-inch frame comfortably fit into, and now after twenty years, the driver's seat felt as cozy as a living room recliner. A lot of forty-one-year-old men probably wouldn't feel the same affection for a car with dried out cracks on the dashboard; mysterious rattles from inside the door frames; and a smell that seemed like a mix of rotting banana peels and stale, spilt milk. Throw in the fact that every personal belonging I owned was either stuffed into the trunk or piled on the back seat, and my situation sure didn't scream "success." I didn't care. It was the one thing I owned, and it was full of memories from better times.

I drove along my back roads of America, hoping to find a down-home tavern along my route, a no-frills place where I could get a quick lunch, a mid-day eye opener or two, and maybe play some darts or long board. No such luck. It would probably be easier to find a gas station with attendants that squeegeed my front window than a tavern.

I gave up and the best I could do was a bright, whole-some-looking place with a name that I knew had been cooked up in a boardroom by a bunch of advertising executives who would never set foot in the place themselves. Upon entering, I was met by a twenty-something, cute, bright and wholesome-looking hostess who seemed just a little too glad to see me.

"How you doing today? You're all alone?" she asked.

Damn, was it that obvious? "Yeah, afraid so," I answered.

"Right this way," she said, snatching a menu the size of a placemat, only razor thin and laminated, out of a holder by the front desk. She turned and began to lead me into a dining room filled with tables covered with checkered tablecloths and chairs with metal heart-sculptured backs. A few booths lined the walls. The room was filled with mid-day light that streamed in through the large windows at each booth.

There was a decent lunch crowd, with the noise level somewhere more than a murmur and less than a buzz.

Using the sharp skills honed over years of investigative reporting, I looked around and noticed that nowhere was there a person sitting alone, by themselves, at a table or in a booth.

"Excuse me," I said before the hostess took me too far into the dining room, "do you have a bar I can eat at and maybe get a drink?"

"Of course, right this way," she said, turning around, and

leading me out of the room. As we passed back by the hostess station she grabbed a different, but just as large, menu from a holder by the front desk.

"These are our drink specials and bar appetizers," she explained. "We offer over fifty fabulous cocktails for you to choose from—Sex on a Beach, Fuzzy Nipple, Mai Tais—"

"That's all right. I just want a Powers or two?" I interrupted.

The hostess slammed on the brakes, and I nearly ran into her from behind. She wheeled around, almost slicing my neck with the edge of the menus she was cradling in her arms.

"A Powers?" she asked. "Is that some kind of energy drink?"

"Depends on the time of day," I answered.

She scanned the large drink menu.

"We have one with Red Bull, vodka, and cranberry juice—called a Molotov Cocktail—but not a Powers. How do you make it?"

"You don't have to," I answered. "It comes premade right in the bottle."

"Oh, then I doubt very much that we have it. Our bartenders make all our drinks fresh while you wait. That's what makes them taste so good."

I didn't bother asking about darts or long board. No need to, because I knew, up in heaven, God was busting a gut.

CHAPTER 5

I couldn't shake the feeling almost as soon as I crossed into the East Hastings town limits that I was being followed. Pure paranoia because, despite my initial apprehension that I would be tarred and feathered upon my return, the more I saw of the town I left behind, the more I realized that it was doubtful anyone in this town even remembered that I had ever lived there.

East Hastings had changed, but not in the let's-build-some-strip-malls-and-call-it-a-town way that so much of America had. No, East Hastings, it seemed, had grown up, from a small, sleepy college town into a prosperous, chic, very happening place. The adults had taken over—or at least what passes for adults these days—and from all appearances, the adults had quite a lot of money.

Of course, there had always been money in East Hastings. Old money, that owned acres and acres of farm land and pastures for horse breeding, and new money earned through law practices and political favors because East Hastings was the county seat of Hastings County. Everyone knew the money was there, but when I was growing up the working class never really saw it, unless they worked at the country club or one of the exclusive, historic restaurants which had been serving the well-heeled and rich heels since the town's founding in the late 1700s. That's the way the old rich wanted it.

Now it was on display, in front windows of jewelry

stores and fine art galleries and places to eat called bistros, ristorantes, and cantinas that didn't just serve food but cuisine. Back in the day, East Hastings was a town of Fords and Chevys, though the moneyed set drove Lincolns and Cadillacs. Now the street was lined with Saabs, Volvos, and BMWs. At least I didn't feel too out of place with my import, even if it was twenty years old.

Since I was a few hours early for the funeral, I thought I'd park and stretch my legs and see how many memories I might stir up by taking a walk along High Street and, hopefully, shake the silly sense that someone was watching me. I'd known the feeling before, back in Boston when my investigation of PharmaHeal somehow got back to the company. However, then it wasn't just an odd sense. I was actually being tailed. I saw them because they wanted me to see them. They wanted me scared and, if I hadn't felt so damned righteous, I should have been. Instead I made it all into a game, giving the two guys who followed me everywhere nicknames—I called them the Hound Brothers, Bassett and Harrier—and paying the booth attendant money for their tolls when they trailed me through toll booths on the Mass Pike or over the Tobin Bridge.

This time, though, I saw no one. Maybe deep down I think I was actually hoping I might be tailed. How sad was that? I wanted to be noticed, have someone remember who I was, so bad that I would create an imaginary stalker.

If that didn't call for wallowing over a drink, I don't know what did, but out of respect for Stevie rather than find a bar, I instead opted to kill time at Bean Me Up Espresso, a place I hoped wasn't near as cute as the name implied. Actually, it was just your basic coffee house—palpable, thick aroma of coffee in the air, cushy sofas with coffee tables, wooden bistro chairs and square tables, recessed ceiling lighting—with the only bow to kitsch being the photographs from *Star Trek* hanging on the walls all about the place. Looking around, it was pretty ironic to see a picture of the space-traveling Kirk talking into a hand-held communicator and notice that most of the patrons were either speaking or texting into a similar device at their seats. East Hastings—the final frontier. Who'd have known?

I ordered and took my coffee to a corner chair and table at the far end of the place in order to have a good look around, at the comings and goings. I've often wondered if I became a reporter because I always felt more comfortable on the outside looking in, always on the perimeter and never part of the action or if that's just where I always found myself.

Bean Me Up Espresso was doing good business. In addition to a steady stream of take-out orders, there was a nice crowd for the late afternoon and a pleasing mix of ages huddled around tables. Those who weren't talking on cell phones or texting were working on laptops or poring over college text books. I seemed to be the only one who wasn't doing anything. Then I spied a relic, or soon to be relic, sitting on an empty, nearby table—a newspaper. And not just any newspaper! *The Daily Chronicle*, the paper where I launched my career as a stringer covering township and borough meetings that were more boring than a Saturday night in Utah.

It's also where a chain-smoking, hard-boiled newspaperman named Hoppy, short for Hopkins Brewster Weatherly, gave me my big shot and had the balls to stand by me when the flak was coming at me hot and heavy. I was embarrassed to realize that I hadn't contacted him since everything started going downhill after Jan or to even let him know I was coming back for Stevie's funeral. Of course I'm not sure I could explain how everything went so sour to him.

Besides, it had been so long since I'd talked to him I wasn't even sure he was still at the paper, or even still living in East Hastings.

I opened the paper to check. Yep, there it was at the top of the masthead. Hopkins Weatherly, Editor. The best editor I have ever known. Why did he still do it? How could someone as good as him spend an entire career at such a small-time, one-horse—

"Is anyone sitting here?"

I looked up from my newspaper to see an attractive redhead standing at my table, holding a large ceramic cup of creamy coffee. Her long hair was styled in bouncy waves and, though she may have had overdone it with a bit too much eye shadow and mascara, she had lovely light green eyes. She wore a breezy light-yellow Victorian-lace peasant blouse that highlighted those eyes and a knee-length denim skirt. Her open-toed, high-heeled wedge sandals accentuated a pair of very shapely legs and showed off brightly painted green toenails.

I did what I usually do in the presence of a beautiful woman—acted like a spaz. In my attempt to appear gentlemanly, I dropped the paper and sprang up from my chair. Rather than appearing suave, however, my thighs caught the underside of the table, rocking it and the coffee sitting upon it.

I saw the smile on the woman's face turn to horror as both table and hot coffee tumbled her way. However, I was quick enough to lunge across and save both the table and cup from tipping over. I then stood erect, gave what I'm sure was my goofiest smile, and swept one hand toward the empty chair beside the now still table. "Be my guest," I said.

To my surprise, she sat down. "That was quite a show. A simple yes would have been enough," she said. I sat down and pulled my coffee over carefully to avoid any further mishaps. "I don't think I've seen you here before," she said. "I'm a bit of regular, you see, need a caffeine fix or two to get me through the day. Are you a big coffee drinker?"

That was, of course, my cue to say something but instead I sat staring at her. There was something familiar but I couldn't place it.

"Are you okay? Did you hurt yourself on the table?" she asked.

I got it! "Tina Sanders, right? Graduated from high school, class of 'eighty-two?" I said.

She looked a little taken aback, thrown a bit off balance. "Well, my last name is Stewart now, but yes I—" She looked at me a little more closely. "Oh my God. Wes? Wes Byrne? I can't believe it. I haven't seen you in, like forever. I thought you left town."

Tina Sanders, now Stewart, was one of the many young vixens who had tortured my adolescent soul from grade school to high school graduation. Unfortunately for me, her tastes seemed to run toward the "bad boys" in school and, since the baddest thing I ever did was cutting class to go to an all-day Marx Brothers film festival in the city, I never made a blip on her radar.

"I did," I answered. "Went away to go to college and haven't been back since. I came into town for a friend's funeral—Steve Darby—I don't know if you remember him."

"Oh, of course, I knew Stevie, saw him around once in a while. I'm going to his funeral too. Poor Stevie! I can't believe someone would kill him like that, stabbing him in the back and all. I hope they catch the guy who did it."

"I haven't seen him for years—heard he didn't change much though." I said.

"Yeah, we useta…um…go out once in a while after my husband died," she replied, glancing down briefly at her coffee. "Moe Stewart, remember him?" she asked, looking back up. "A coupla years older than us, his brother Tommy was a junior when we were seniors? Died in a truck accident."

"Sorry to hear that. I remember him, I think. Tall, kind of lanky—didn't he have a nickname?"

"Slo-Moe, cause he did everything real slow, never in a hurry. Kinda nice in the bedroom, if you know what I mean," she said, giving me a quick smile, and I'm sure I blushed, "but anytime we had to go somewhere, it'd just drive me crazy. I used to always be after him. 'Hurry up, will ya, we'll be late,' but he would just always take his old sweet time. Lost control on an icy road—rushin' home from work to be with me on our first Christmas Eve—only time I think he ever hurried in his life."

She paused and I could tell the memories were flooding back. She picked up a napkin, daubed at her eyes to stem the beginning of a tear, and then, as someone who's grown accustomed to living with grief, turned the conversation away from the pain.

"How about you? I see you're married?" she said, indicating the wedding band I still wore on my finger. "First thing a single woman looks for on a good-looking man is a ring."

I'd never been able to take the damned thing off, seemed like betrayal, though I always wondered if there'd come a day.

"Was married. My wife died a few years ago. Cancer," I answered, as always avoiding eye contact whenever I had to say it out loud to someone.

Tina reached across the table and touched my hand. "I'm so sorry."

It had been a long time since a woman had touched me like that and I hated to admit it, but it felt nice. I looked up and there was a sweetness in her eyes, a shared knowing. Maybe I wasn't ready to move on from Jan entirely, like everyone kept telling me to, but I thought I could share a night with someone like Tina, a fellow survivor, a first small step and not feel too guilty.

"So much death around us—my Moe, your wife—what was her name?" she continued.

"Jan." I answered.

"Your Jan, and now Stevie. Of course, with a traffic accident and cancer, a person doesn't have much choice. In Stevie's case…well, he sure knew how to piss people off. I remember one time, he was playing darts over at the Circle Bar, and old Cooty Lewin was riding him pretty hard, saying he was no good and all, that he might as well give up and let the next person play. Well, Stevie just starts throwing like you wouldna believe and scores out with three darts to the bull eyes—never seen nothin' like it. So he struts on over to where Cooty's sittin', spins round, pulls down his pants, and shoves his ass right in Cooty's face. He says, 'How do like this bull's eye?' I swear I thought old Cooty was going to kill him right then and there." She laughed, a sweet laugh, and I couldn't help but join in.

"Sounds like Stevie," I said.

"Yeah, well, like you said, he didn't change much over the years. Guess none of us really have around here," she said, taking a sip out of her large coffee cup.

"Must be a lot of theories floating around about who killed him. Have you heard anything about why someone would do it?" I asked. I regretted the question as soon as it came out of my mouth.

"What?" she asked, a sudden defensiveness, a trace of anger in her voice. "How the hell would I know who would do a thing like that? Why would you ask me such a thing?"

"Sorry, must be the reporter in me. Always asking inappropriate questions," I answered.

Tina straightened up sharply and her eyes narrowed. "Reporter? Are you a reporter?"

"Yeah—or at least I used to—"

"That's right," she said. I could see the past working itself back up, see her working through the years. "You caught those people dumping crap into the Kithane a long while back."

Suddenly Tina seemed a little nervous, started fidgeting with the coffee cup.

"Yeah, but that was a long time ago. See, I ended up working for a paper in Boston."

"Those people went to jail, didn't they?" she asked.

"Well, yeah, for a couple of years, nothing like what I thought they deserved."

"Now you're back here asking about Stevie?" she said.

"Just idle curiosity is all. Like I said—"

Tina quickly looked at her watch, then grabbed her

purse, and started digging through it. "You know, I just re-membered I've got to call my sister. She was…um…food shopping out at Acme and wanted me to meet her," she said, pulling a cell phone out of her purse. It rang just as she was starting to dial, startling her a bit. She looked at the number and then looked at me quickly before answering it.

"Oh, hi, Terri, you wouldn't believe who I'm having coffee with. Wes Byrne. You remember Wes Byrne, doan ya, the reporter?" She smiled as she listened to the caller. "That's right…that's the one…" She pulled the phone away from her ear and covered the front microphone with her hand. "My sister remembers you," she said. Then put the phone back to her ear. "Yes, back for Stevie Darby's funer-al…says he just got into town. Isn't that a coincidence that I would run into him? He's asking questions about Stevie's murder, though I don't have anything to tell him, of course. Um, are you done with your, um, shopping yet? You are…good…okay, I'll come right over and meet you."

Although I couldn't make out what the caller was say-ing, the person was saying it loud enough that Tina pulled the phone a little way from her ear. I wouldn't swear to it, but it sure didn't sound like a woman's voice on the end of the line.

"Yeah, yeah. I'm leavin' right away," she said. She end-ed the call and tossed the phone back into her purse. She stood up hurriedly, leaving her coffee half-drank, pushing her chair in. "It was real nice to see you again, Wes. I really gotta get going."

"Let me walk out with you. I was just about to leave anyway," I said. I started to get up but Tina reached across and put her hand on my shoulder, keeping me in my seat.

"No, don't go on my account," she said.

"No, I really should get to the hotel," I said, rising up, despite her firm pressure. "Check in time at the Hearthstone is two o'clock, and I want to shower and change before the funeral. I'll walk you to your car."

"No!" she answered brusquely, though she tried to

quickly compose herself. "I'm parked at the garage and it's a bit of a walk—and besides you're parked in the opposite direction."

"I am? How would you know where I'm parked?"

"What?" she asked, backing away from the table as if it there was a bomb sitting under it. "Oh…um…oh, aren't you? Just a lucky guess, I guess. Listen, I've really got to go."

With that, she turned and was gone, almost careening into a patron carrying a full cup of coffee in her rush.

I watched her go. *Well*, I thought, *I certainly haven't lost my way with East Hastings women.*

I took both of our cups over to the dirty dish bin and then stopped at the counter to buy a copy of the *Chronicle* for later reading.

I left the Bean Me Up and started walking back to my car, running the whole thing through my head. Everything had been going so nice until I asked her about Stevie's murder—me and my damn questions. It was odd, though, her reaction.

Stop, I said to myself. *I mean, c'mon, there was no way Tina could be involved in Stevie's murder? Okay, so she did say she and Stevie hooked up once in a while—maybe there was a jealous boyfriend. Nah, that was crazy thinking, that the very first person I speak to in East Hastings was involved in Stevie's murder.* I really needed a quick nap and a shower.

I turned into the parking lot where I parked the Toyota and couldn't believe what I saw—or didn't see. My car was gone.

CHAPTER 6

I'd finished filling out all the paperwork and had spent the last twenty minutes waiting in the lobby in case the police officer assigned to the case had any more questions. Good thing I had brought the *Chronicle* from the Bean Me Up because, with the exception of wanted posters and community announcements hung about the walls, the police station was sorely lacking in reading material. I wasn't expecting rat-eared copies of *Crime and Punishment*, but you'd think they'd have old issues of police magazines, with names like *Badge and Siren* or *Patrol Beat*, lying about.

I gathered from reading the *Chronicle* that, aside from the high school football team's chances for a title once the season started in September, the big issues were increased traffic due to new home development out along Route 83, several home fires suspected to be arson in neighboring Harrisville, and—well, what do you know, a rash of car and farm equipment thefts that authorities believe to be the work of a local criminal ring.

It seemed that for over the past two years, throughout East Hastings and local neighboring towns and communities, tractors, harvesters, and other large farm equipment had been stolen from farms and automobiles had been disappearing from parking lots and garages, off streets, and, in some cases, right out of people's driveways. At first, authorities attributed the rise in car thefts to young kids stealing the cars and driving them into Philadelphia where they either traded them for drugs or just abandoned them. However, as more area farms began to report missing farm equipment, police and criminal investigators began to believe that the thieves were much more sophisticated than a bunch of kids.

Down the hallway a door, over which a sign reading *Criminal Investigations* stuck out from the wall perpendicularly, opened and a uniformed policeman came out, carrying a clip board. He glanced my way and began walking toward me. His black shoes were polished to a scuffless sheen, his dark-brown trousers sharply-creased, his light brown, short-sleeved shirt neatly pressed, and his star-shaped badge shined to a bright luster. As he approached, his lips started to curl up into a sneer and, when he got close enough, I understood why. It was Danny Sullivan.

"Well, well, I just couldn't believe it when I read the report but I'll be damned—Wus Byrne, crime victim," he said. He held the document I had filled out earlier that was attached to his clipboard up for me to see. "Says here someone went and stole your nineteen-eighty-nine Camry. That can't be right, can it—a hot shot reporter like you driving a twenty-year old car?"

Danny Sullivan was one of the members of the "Fearsome Foursome," who along with Randy Smith, Glen Poppy, and, of course, Tony Augustino shared a common mission of making my life a living hell from elementary school up until the day I graduated from high school. The four had taken bullying to a whole new level where I was concerned. If there was a way to humiliate and degrade a fellow human being that these guys missed, I really wouldn't want to know about it.

I endured "purple nurples," wedgies, noogies, pantsings, towel snaps, and swirling, as well as the very hilarious strip-a-guy-down-and-toss-him-into-the-girls'-locker-room stunt. There was no end to the enjoyment those four could find in tormenting me.

I had a feeling this wasn't going to go very well.

"When did you become a cop?" I asked.

"That's police officer, Wus."

"The name's Wes."

I could see he was a little shocked by my come-back, maybe expecting the same old "Wus," and, to tell the truth, I was a little surprised myself. It felt good.

He stepped closer and looked down menacingly at me in my chair. "Once a wuss, always a wuss, and—" he continued, pointing to his badge, "—this here means if I want to call you Sally or Betty, I damn well can."

"Okay, right, sure. Listen, I just want my car back. Everything I own was in it. Can you put out an APB or whatever you can to find it?" I answered, not wanting to give him any chance to escalate things.

"Oh, of course—whatever you say. Why don't I just call every officer off every case they're working so we can find your piece of crap rice burner?" he replied, taking another step closer, now practically standing on my toes.

I took a deep breath. "Look, I just think that the sooner you all start looking for it, the better the chances of finding it, is all."

His neck muscles tightened, his face reddened and his eyes became little piercing arrows. "You trying to tell me how to do my job, you god-damned son of a—"

"Is there a problem here, Officer Sullivan?"

We both turned to see a policewoman approaching us, and, based on the way Sullivan suddenly morphed from my tormentor into the friendly cop on the beat, I knew instantly that she was the one in charge of the show.

"No problem, Chief," he said, reaching out and patting me chummily on the shoulder. "Me and Wes here went to school together back in the day. We were just…ah…fooling around…um…catching up…"

"I understand his car has been stolen?" the head honcho asked, giving Sullivan a dubious glance before turning to me.

"Yes, that's right. Out of a public lot on High Street." I reached out my hand. "Wes Byrne, Officer…"

"Chief—Chief Roark," she said, taking my hand. "Sorry to hear that."

She was stout, not fat but solid. At first blush, I would have said she was ex-military. Her brown hair was cut short, neat, and conservative, and she had the general bearing of a soldier or marine.

She had serious, penetrating brown eyes, and I suspected she didn't miss much.

She took the clipboard from Danny and studied it. "So you just got into town. Visiting?" she asked, not looking up.

"Yes, well, I grew up here but I'm in town for an old friend's funeral. I stopped for a cup of coffee and came out to find my car missing."

"I see. That friend of yours happen to be Steve Darby?" she asked, now looking up, her eyes growing a little bit more penetrating.

"Yeah, and um…I'm afraid I'm going to be late for the service," I said, glancing at my watch. I didn't know what she was after and didn't want to stick around to find out, my car be damned. "Maybe I can call a cab or something and Danny—er, Officer Sullivan—can finish filing my report while I wait for it."

"No need for a cab. I was just heading over myself—out of respect for the family. Give you a lift." It was as much an order as an offer. "You about done here, Sullivan?" she said to Danny.

"Yes, sir. Got pretty much everything I need right here," he said, taking the clipboard back from Chief Roark. "I was just about to put a description of the car out over the wire, in the hopes someone might spot it. Figured the quicker I got the word out, the better our chances of finding it."

"Well, get to it."

"Yes, Chief. Right away." He smiled his best apple-polishing smile at her before heading off down the hallway.

Chief Roark watched him go and then turned to me and

cocked her head in Sullivan's direction. "So, you two old friends?"

I looked over the captain's shoulder to see Sullivan turn and give me a glance that could melt a glacier before he disappeared through the hallway door.

"I wouldn't exactly say that," I answered.

CHAPTER 7

Driving to Stevie's funeral with Chief Roark, I was visited by the same thought I always had over the years whenever I did ride-alongs with cops, namely that it is so much nicer to sit in the front than in the back of a police car. Never liked the back, without door handles or even a way to roll down a window. And they all have that thickly-screened, or in this case Plexiglas, panel running across the top of the front seat, a clear demarcation of power. Of course, my feelings may have been influenced by the time, on my very first ride-along with the Boston cops, I was left in the car for hours after their shift—some sort of initiation I guess. They sat and drank in a cop bar while I endured stares from passer-byes and taunts from neighborhood kids.

Roark let the silence rest between us as she pulled out of the station parking lot and into traffic. She waved to a few pedestrians walking along on the sidewalk and they waved back.

I guess it was up to me to break the silence.

"I appreciate the ride to the service, Chief, but I could have just called a cab," I said.

"Not a problem. I was going myself. Besides, this ain't Boston where you just step out and hail a cab down," she answered.

It had to be a coincidence that she mentioned my old city. "Have you been to Boston?"

"No, never have, but I know you used to work there, while ago," she said.

No, not a coincidence, and I suddenly sensed her offer of ride wasn't one either, though I had no idea why. I mean, I'd only been in town a few hours, and I was the victim here. I glanced quickly at my door. It did have a handle, but the door was locked and I didn't see any button or switch to open it. "Danny, er, Officer Sullivan, tell you that?"

"No, just good old police work. We found one of your old business cards in Steve Darby's wallet. I called the number. Wondering if it was a lead of any sort. They said you hadn't worked there for a couple years," she answered.

We were driving out to the cemetery on Route 5, a road I'd driven along a thousand times, as a kid with my mom and then as a teenager once I got my driver's license. It struck me that, although the buildings hadn't changed, the businesses they housed had. Hansen's Hardware Store was now Emilia's Vintage Boutique, and The Five Point Pharmacy was now The Five Points Kitchen and Bath Design Showroom.

The signs for the shopping center entrances along the road were cleaner, somehow brighter, cheerier, and the small islands of dirt and shrubbery were all neatly landscaped.

"Your card doesn't say what you did at the paper—just your name and phone number. You didn't happen to work in the accounting department or sales, by chance?" she asked, darting a quick, sort of knowing glance my way.

"No, I was a reporter," I answered.

"Really? But you're not a reporter anymore?" she asked, this time not taking her eyes off the road.

"Actually, most recently I was a columnist, at a couple different papers," I said.

"Ah, well, a columnist. Funny that you keep saying 'was.' Does that mean you're not one now?" she said.

"Well, no, I'm sorta between jobs at the moment. That's why I hope I get my car back soon. Going to explore some possibilities a little farther south," I said, hoping to change the subject.

"South is nice. I was stationed at Camp Lejeune in North Carolina. Nice country, great barbecue." She was quiet again for a minute or two. "So you've become a bit of a drifter, huh?" she asked in an easy-going manner, although the way she said it made me sound like I had just jumped off a freight car and would be back on the rails as soon as I grubbed a few meals and earned a little stake sweeping floors or washing dishes.

"Wouldn't say a drifter—like I said, just between jobs," I answered, a bit defensively perhaps. "About my car—"

"Oh, we'll sort that all out. You didn't say where you're staying while you're in town?" she asked.

"No, I didn't, but it's in the police report," I answered, turning to face her. "You know, I have a feeling there's a question you want to ask. In my experience, the direct approach works best."

"Is that experience as a columnist or a reporter?" she asked.

Again she became quiet. It seemed to be taking an awful long time to get to the service.

"No, nothing in particular," she finally said. "It's just that, well, I guess police and reporters are a little like bears and dogs, you know, where it's something in their instinct to just not get along very well. The dog doesn't seem to like the fact the bear is bigger, and the bear doesn't like having a dog sniffing around it and nipping at its heels, trying to prove how tough it is."

"Sounds like you have experience—with bears and dogs, that is," I said, looking out the window, hoping to see a church spire or graveyard, any indication that we were almost at the service.

"I do," she said with an emphatic nod. "See, I do some hunting—mostly small game—occasionally go bow hunting for deer. Well, one time I was out hunting with some other marines during leave and one of them had a dog. We turned a bend and there was a black bear, wasn't a big one, maybe 350 pounds. It didn't look happy to see us. You should have seen the hackles on its back raise up—like happens when they sense danger. The dog, well, it went nuts at the sight of the bear, tore at the leash, and got free, went right after that bear—no regard for its safety."

I turned back to look at Roark. "Dog sounds kind of stupid."

"That's what I've always thought. Better to just turn tail and get on out of the bear's way, but it's that bear and dog thing I guess. Dogs just don't seem to know better," the chief said. "So anyway, we can't get a shot at the bear, what with the dog nipping and jumping at it. Besides, we were only carrying for small game. We had nothing to bring it down, probably just get it madder."

"And let me guess, the dog didn't win." I said.

Roark shook her head. "No, it didn't. At some point, the bear seemed to just get fed up and swatted the dog away with one of its big old paws. Sent the dog flying. It didn't die though, just knocked silly."

At last, I saw the large field stone columns at the entranceway to the church. I didn't know what was going on here, but I was glad the ride was finally ending. "That's a fascinating story. I guess it had a happy ending, with the dog living, and all," I said.

"Yeah, we actually took it hunting again, but it wasn't the same. Seemed to only want to get the scent of that bear again. Didn't learn a thing. But I guess that's the way dogs are."

"I guess so. I don't know much about dogs, to tell you the truth," I answered.

"You didn't ask about what happened to the bear," Roark said.

"Well, what happened?" I asked.

"It just went on about its business, marking out its territory. Way I imagine it, bear never gave that dog another moment's thought. More important things to do, probably."

We pulled into the drive, between the two columns, and along the road that led to the entrance of the church. There was a hearse at the base of the steps that led to the church doors and a few people, dressed solemnly, most smoking cigarettes, milled about. The chief pulled the police cruiser in behind the hearse and turned off the engine. I noticed she didn't unlock the doors, though.

"I'm glad we had this chance to talk," she said, turning her body to face me. "See, it's nothing personal, but when I find a reporter's business card in a murder victim's wallet and then suddenly that reporter shows up in my town…well, let's just say it tends to get my hackles up a bit, speaking metaphorically. Could be nothing—hope it is nothing," she said, looking me directly in the eyes.

"I'm just here for Stevie. Paying my last respects—and once I get my car back, I'm gone," I said.

"Well, that's good to hear. Sure you'll be off to bigger and better things. I do promise you we'll do everything to get your car back. In the meantime, don't you go chasing off after any scents, if you know what I mean. You leave the police work to the police."

With that she touched a switch on the driver's side arm-rest and the door locks popped up.

"You don't have to worry about me," I said, opening the door. "This dog's got no more hunt left in him, speaking metaphorically."

I quickly climbed out of the car. Seemed a ride in the front of a police car wasn't that much fun either.

CHAPTER 8

I thought I had made a clean get-away, but after I entered the church, pausing to look over the crowd to find someone I might possibly know, Roark came through the doors from behind and sidled up next to me.

"I forgot to ask you how you're getting back to your hotel after the service. I could give you a ride."

I scanned the gathered mourners with a little more urgency and was relieved when I saw Tim Brewer turn his head around in his seat about halfway up the right aisle. He motioned for me to join him and indicated an empty space beside him.

"That's very generous, but I see an old friend over there," I said, pointing to Tim, "and I'm sure I can catch a ride with him after the burial."

"Okay, then. Enjoy your time in East Hastings," she said before walking off down the aisle, pausing to shake a hand or two along the way, before sliding into a pew close to the front on the left side of the aisle.

I proceeded down the center aisle toward where Tim was sitting with his family—his wife Ellen and their two kids. As I neared them, I noticed that Tina Sanders was sitting about two rows in front of them and was watching me. I gave a small wave, but she quickly turned back to the front. A balding, sausage-headed man sat beside her, some flab from his neck spilling out over the tight collar of his dress shirt. Tina's sudden turn caused him to look first at her and then to turn and look at me. He whispered something to Tina, and she nodded her head. His beady eyes sized me up, and then he turned his attention back to the front, again whispering to Tina, this time a little more animatedly.

Tim's family all slid over to give me a little more room in the church pew. I shook Tim's hand and nodded my greeting to Ellen, his wife, and the two kids, trying to remember if their names were Glen and Kathy or Gary and Karen. I only knew them from their pictures on the Christmas cards I'd received from Tim over the years. Ellen smiled briefly, sufficiently somber. The offspring glanced up momentarily before bowing their heads, returning their attention to their electronic game devices held low, at arm's length, on their laps.

I was amazed to see that Tim had spent the last twenty or so years growing to look almost exactly like his father—the same receding hair line with a bit of gray beginning to show, his face still youthful, a little paunch that hung over his belt. The eyes were Tim's though—bright, friendly— unlike the stern, hard disciplinarian eyes of his father, who, quite frankly, always scared the hell out of me.

"You won't believe what happened to me just now, really strange. The chief of police—" I began to say.

Tim turned to look at me, his eyes giving me the once over. "Nice of you to get dressed up," he said, and I realized that I was still wearing the Bermuda shorts, polo shirt, and sandals I had on when I got into town. Damn, just the impression I was hoping to make.

"My clothes were stolen," I said to him in a low voice.

"What? Why would anyone want to steal your clothes? I mean how many six-foot-three-inch thieves are there running around?"

"They were in my car. Somebody stole my car," I answered, perhaps a little too loudly because Ellen cast me a disapproving glance.

I also couldn't help notice that Tina sat up a little straighter in her pew and, again, the guy next to her leaned

over and whispered something to her. Again, she only nodded.

"Well, welcome back," Tim answered.

"Yeah, it's been a pretty weird day."

I looked around at the assembled masses. There was about a hundred people, give or take a few.

"Pretty nice turn out. Hate to say it but I thought there might just be Sue Ellen, you, me and a few of the old crowd," I whispered to Tim.

"Well, actually, I'm not sure how many of these people even knew Stevie. Think most of the crowd showed up either out of respect for Sue Ellen or to kiss Tony's ass."

Ellen shot Tim a look that would freeze lava. "Tim, we are in church!" she scolded with a hush.

"Sorry," he replied to her, "it's true, but I'll watch my language." He turned back to me. "That's the family up in the front there," he said, indicating with a nod of his head the first pew in the church. "Sue Ellen's the one wearing the hat. Those are her kids next to her, she's got two—I think I told you that—and then, of course, there's Tony."

I craned to get a good look at them, but could only see backs of heads and Sue Ellen's hat. I was still working up what I would say to her, had been ever since I heard the news, and was actually wondering if I was right to come at all when the minister approached the pulpit and things got under way.

捦捦捦

It was a pretty nice service, as far as they go, although it seemed like there was someone else in the casket that sat to the one side of the pulpit, the way the speakers talked about Stevie. Loving son—okay, I'll give him that. He seemed to get along with his dad, whenever he wasn't on the road. His mom was a nice woman who thought the world of her Ste-vie and he always did his best to shield her from most of his escapades. Loyal and loving brother…well, that might have been a bit of a stretch. There was the time in junior high when he was selling naked pictures of Sue Ellen. Of course, the pictures weren't actually of her, but of Nancy Holligan. They had been taken from behind, through a bedroom curtain and pretty much out of focus so it really could have been anyone, so I guess it was no crime, no foul, but still…

And I couldn't really say as far as him being a generous and doting uncle, although I imagine he was the type to shower his nieces with gifts when he was flush but also let birthdays and holidays pass without a note.

No, the real bullshit was all the stuff about him always being willing to help neighbors and working hard to overcome his demons. Or about the way he put family first and could be counted on most when things got a little rough. Of course, I really didn't expect the truth, about how you knew deep down you couldn't trust Stevie as far as you could throw him but how, regardless of anything he did, you could never stay mad at him or really—okay, I'll say it—stop loving the guy.

As the service ended, we all rose and stood as Tony and a few other guys—some who I recognized from high school, others who I didn't and none who were probably friends of Stevie—escorted the casket as it was rolled up the center aisle on a draped cart, Sue Ellen, her kids, and family following behind. I hated to admit it, but Tony still looked good—handsome with just a tinge of gray at the temples, trim and powerful, and sharply dressed in a tailored black suit, white shirt, and gray tie with matching handkerchief. Tony saw me, and we locked eyes for a brief moment. Not the friendliest of looks. He turned his head to say something to the guy behind him, who nodded and then looked me over as they passed.

Sue Ellen was as beautiful as I remembered her, although behind the slight veil that covered the upper half of her face it was difficult to make out her features clearly. Tears slowly streaked from beneath the veil and she dabbed at them absently with a handkerchief as she followed the casket up the aisle. I thought she was going to pass by without noticing me, when, with a slight start, she turned her head to look at me. A sad smile appeared and she silently mouthed the words, "Thank you," before moving on.

The rest of the mourners filed out of the pews, starting at the front and emptying, in order to follow the family. So since we were near the rear, it took a little while for me, Tim, and his family to get out of the church. We stepped out into the midday sun. I stopped at the bottom of the steps to watch the back doors of the hearse close while Tim and family continued along the sidewalk that ran to a parking lot, stopping to talk to a family with children about the same age as Tim's kids.

The sun was bright and I was feeling my pockets to see where I'd put my sunglasses when the guy who had been walking behind Tony with the casket approached. He was a pretty good-sized gentleman, hair slicked back, black suit, white shirt buttoned at the collar, no tie, big chest, and no doubt big biceps. He had shark-like eyes that scanned me up and down. My attire appeared to amuse him. He leaned in close.

"Tony wanted to tell me that he can't stop you from coming to the cemetery, but that you are not to go near his wife or family and, by no means, are you to come to the house with the other mourners afterward." He paused to let the message sink in. "Got it?"

There wasn't really much to say. "Got it," I answered.

Tim, who had seen everything, left his family and came over to stand next to me as I watched the guy walk away.

"Like I said earlier," Tim said with a little laugh, "welcome back."

CHAPTER 9

I stood on the outer fringe of mourners as Stevie's body was lowered into his grave. Over everyone's heads, I could see Sue Ellen sitting in a metal folded chair beside her two girls—pretty, like Sue Ellen was at their age—and Tony standing on her other side. Sue Ellen held the hand of the child sitting nearest her, most likely her eldest daughter, probably fourteen, although she could have been older, tightly in her lap. It might have been my imagination or perhaps just a result of the way I was feeling about Tony at the moment, but it seemed that at one point he reached his hand over to rest it on Sue Ellen's shoulder and she imperceptibly shifted her body to slide out from under it.

The service ended and I remained back as the crowd lined up and moved along to offer their condolences to the family. Any thought I might have had about joining the line was quelched by the sight of the large man from the church service standing quietly behind the family with his eyes fixed upon me, a slight sneer on his lips. At one point, Sue Ellen looked up my way and tilted her head slightly, as if wondering why I wasn't coming forward. Then she looked over at Tony, busy shaking hands with someone I didn't recognize, then over her shoulder at that sneering big guy and then back toward me. She seemed to nod in understanding, although I might have been seeing things that weren't really there.

I couldn't believe what I was doing, letting those two

keep me from speaking with Sue Ellen. Sneer be damned, I was going to go up to her. And I would have, really, if at just that moment Tim hadn't come over to me, along with three other guys who, after a moment, I recognized as Denny Lucas, Bob Keith, and Dom D'Annunzio. We had all hung out with Stevie back in the day, and they might have been the only ones at the funeral, besides Sue Ellen of course, who really knew him. By the time we had all shook hands and I answered their initial questions about how I was and I had told them about my car to explain why I was dressed the way I was, I looked up and saw that Tony was leading Sue Ellen away from the grave toward their limousine. As I watched, she stopped for a moment and turned back to look first at the grave and then up at me. Tony turned as well, and when he saw she was looking my way, turned her back in the direction of the car, a little too forcibly for my tastes, made a comment to her that I'm sure was at my expense, and walked her away.

"Any chance you've come to get your old job back at the *Chronicle*? Maybe you can take over for old Hoppy now that you've had all that big city experience," Denny said, bringing me back into the conversation. Denny had been a pretty good athlete in his day, and I was always sort of amazed that he had hung with us back in high school. Of course, his sport was gymnastics, at which he excelled, but that probably wasn't macho enough for the guys like Danny Sullivan and his jock friends. Denny still looked good, tanned, and confident. It turns out he had done pretty well starting an exercise club in East Hastings and now had three others in the county.

"Now why would Wes want to get on board a dying ship? The *Chronicle's* become nothing more than a tabloid, running down the accomplishments of this town with its stories about thieves running amok and murderers. It may have had its day, but times are changing. Wes probably has big plans," Bob said, taking my hand and shaking it firmly. "Of course, if you are thinking of settling down, I've got a few places listed that would be perfect for you."

Bob had started selling houses right after college and, from all appearances, was doing pretty well. He was heavy and with a notable stomach, but he was wearing suspenders over his pressed white shirt so there wasn't a roll hanging over the waist. His well-fitting, I would guess tailored, black wool-blended suit hung well on his frame. His yellow tie was still knotted tightly at his neck, although I think the heat was beginning to get to him a bit, sweat forming around his collar. He wore a yellow gold Oyster Rolex watch on his left wrist, which I noticed when he pulled a neatly folded handkerchief from his suit coat's right inside pocket and dabbed at the beads of sweat on his forehead and back of his neck.

"Well, I have no plans of working at, let alone taking over, the *Chronicle*. Hoppy is a great editor, no one could run it like him. I'm just here to pay my last respects and then move on," I continued. "Been thinking about checking out points south, never been south."

"Wait a minute," said Dom, turning to Tim. "I thought you said Wes was thinking about looking into Stevie's murder, and we were supposed to convince him to do it."

Ah, good old Dom, He was always honest, even if he had a habit of saying the wrong thing at the wrong time. The thing about Dom was that, on the surface, he didn't appear to be anything really special, average height, a little bulky, and he'd never been—and there was no use arguing the point—the sharpest tack in the carpet. But he was just such a good guy. People trusted him, they liked him, and he treated everybody, and I mean everybody, straight up.

"That's not what I said, Dom," Tim quickly interjected, giving me a quick look of mea culpa before turning back to Dom. "I said that Wes was coming down for Stevie's funeral and that, if he had any questions about the murder, we should tell him what we know."

"Well, whatever you said, I think it's a good idea," Dom said to Tim. "Nobody else is doin' nothin'. It ain't like you're gonna find Stevie's killer sitting up there in your ivied tower."

Sometimes, I now remembered, it took a moment or two to decipher exactly what Dom was talking about.

"Ivied Towers," Bob guffawed. "You're mixing up ivory tower which means out of touch and ivied walls, which sometimes means a college. There's no such thing as an ivied tower."

"And besides that there is not a speck of ivy at East Hastings University," Denny joined in.

"Ah, you know what I mean. Bob sells houses, I sell plumbing supplies, Denny's got his clubs, and Tim's teaching all day. What do we know about getting to the truth about Stevie? Wes does. He did it before."

There was a bit of silence. I checked out the neatly mowed grass at my feet.

"Hey, if Wes wants to go, who are we to stop him?" Bob finally said. "In the meantime, it's getting a little hot out here for me and I've built up a bit of an appetite, standing around out here in the fresh air," he added, patting his ample belly, "and think it's about time we headed over to Tony and Sue Ellen's place. It's air conditioned and I heard Costello's is catering."

"Well, er, I—" I started.

"Actually," Tim said, giving me a look that let me know he'd handle everything, "I didn't really see anyone other than Sue Ellen that I wanted to talk to, so I thought Wes and I would just pick up a case of beer and head out to one of the places we used to hang with Stevie, kinda hold our own private wake. You guys are welcome to come."

Good old Tim. Not only did he save me the embarrassment of telling the others that I was persona non-grata at Sue Ellen's, but he actually came up with a much more favorable alternative.

"That sounds like a good idea. How about the old spot out at the Kithane?" Dom replied. "I haven't been out to the Kithane in years."

"Sounds good," said Denny.

We all looked at Bob. It was obvious he was weighing the offer against what was sure to be an opulent spread at Tony and Sue Ellen's gathering.

"Okay—okay. I guess I'm in, but we also have to stop and pick up some hoagies to go with the beer. I'm starving."

"Great," said Tim. "Let me run over and tell Ellen. Denny, do you think her and the kids can get a ride over to Sue Ellen's with Holly? That way I can drive us in the CRV."

"Sure. I'll go make sure she doesn't mind," Denny answered.

"Yeah, I'll let Marcie know," added Dom, "she probably won't mind, seeing as it's Wes." He smiled at me. "Of course, you'll have to come over to the house for a dinner before heading off to wherever you're going. I know she wants to catch up."

"I'll get my car and follow you over," said Bob.

And with that they all headed off to their families, who I could see were waiting impatiently by their respective cars. Left alone, I walked over at last to Stevie's grave.

Workers were dismantling the tent that covered the immediate grave area and were rolling up the green tarp that had surrounded the grave. Nearby a small bulldozer idled, waiting to push the nearby pile of dirt over Stevie's coffin.

I slid a single rose out from one of the many floral arrangements left behind by the mourners and stood over the grave, looking down at the box that held Stevie's body.

On a small brass plate on the lid of the casket was Stevie's date of birth and his death and a quote from Ralph Waldo Emerson.

Do not go where the path may lead,
go instead where there is no path and leave a trail.

"'Don't go where the path may lead.' That's you in a nutshell, Stevie. I'm so sorry I didn't keep in touch. I don't know if it would have mattered, but at least—"

I stopped, the words catching in my throat, and a single, salty tear rolled down my cheek and over my lip. I looked up and noticed the workers had stopped to watch me.

"You guys take good care of this grave. He was a pretty good man, all in all," I said to them.

They turned and went back to work.

I threw the rose into the grave. "I really wish there was something I could—" I caught myself again. Sometimes words were just so worthless.

CHAPTER 10

As it turned out, now I was the one appropriately dressed. While I sat in the shade of river birches in my Bermuda shorts and polo shirt, sipping my cold beer by the side of the Kithane River in the mid-day August heat and humidity, my old friends, even with their suit jackets off and ties loosened, could not have been more uncomfortable in their oxford shoes, long pants, and collared shirts. I felt particularly bad for Bob. He had been expecting a feast of crab stuffed mushrooms, imported salamis, chilled shrimp, and a host of other artery-clogging hors d'oeuvres while swilling expensive wines in the air-conditioned comfort of Sue Ellen and Tony's house. Instead, he sat balancing a half-eaten roast beef hoagie—it was his second—on his lap and nursing a domestic beer as sweat turned his once neatly pressed shirt into a soggy layer of clinging cotton.

It had taken us about half-an-hour to drive around town to pick up the beer and hoagies and another half hour or so had passed while we ate. We spent the time catching up. They expressed their sympathy for Jan's passing. I quickly turned the subject to the changes East Hastings had gone through, and they took turns filling me in on their families. One thing that hadn't come up was probably the one thing that was foremost on all of our minds—Stevie and what the hell had gone on in his life for him to end up with a knife in his back in a dive bar.

We sat in silence and watched a group of young teenagers frolicking in the river a little ways up stream. "You guys remember the time Stevie likely saved me from drowning in this river?" Dom asked.

"Yeah," Tim answered. "When was that…seventh, eighth grade?"

"Pretty sure it was just after eighth grade, summer before going into ninth," Dom answered. "I remember because Kathleen Havery had developed the most amazing pair of tits I'd ever seen and I promised myself I was going to cop a feel before the end of summer."

"Yeah, I remember those. Magnificent!" Denny said. "The rest of her wasn't bad either, if I recall."

"I always thought she was a little stand-offish," added Tim.

"Well, with that rack, she had to stand-off a bit, didn't she?" Dom replied.

We all groaned. I shook my head, but couldn't help smiling—it was seventh period study hall all over again.

"So anyway, I was out here with Stevie, Tim, I think we were all there. Some girls were with us. I don't think you were, Wes," Dom continued.

"Probably at the library, after all, it was summer," Denny piped in.

"I think he had a crush on old Mrs. Linders, the librarian," Tim added.

"What was she…like eighty or something? Just Wes's type," said Bob.

"Hey, can I finish my story here? I don't care if you'd heard it before. It's about Stevie, the kind of guy he was." Dom looked at Bob, who graciously bowed his head, reached out his right hand, and rolled his wrist and hand to palm up, deigning Dom to continue.

"So, anyway I remember, it's a hot, humid day and it's great to be at the river with these girls. We're in our cut-offs and no shirts and the girls were wearing bathing suits. Kathleen was wearing a two-piece and looking real good soaking wet."

Bob pulled a cold beer from the cooler and held the iced bottle against his forehead. "Jeez, I'm gonna sweat off like thirty pounds by the time you get through this story."

"Hey, if you didn't keep interrupting—so Stevie, he knows I've got this thing for Kathleen and he pulls me aside and tells me that if I really wanted to impress her, I should do a flip offa this tree branch that's hanging out over the river. I wasn't too sure, but Stevie, he says it's a piece of cake and to prove it he shimmies up the tree and does this terrific flip offa the branch and into the river. I look at Kathleen and I can see she's impressed, so I figure, 'what the hell' and up I go. Course, I was a little bigger than Stevie and as I get out on the branch, the damn thing snaps, and down I go and the back of my head slams hard against the water and I go under. Luckily, Stevie was right there and managed to pull me out and get me to shore. I can't remember who, but someone ended up taking me to the hospital and I spent the night there. Man, I was close to really impressing her and, ya know, Kathleen didn't even bother to visit me." Dom took a long swallow of his beer. "Still, if it wasn't for Stevie, I'da probably drowned."

I noticed Denny, Bob, and Tim sharing a look between them as they tried to stifle laughter.

Dom noticed too. "What?" he asked. "What's so funny about me almost dying?"

Tim looked at Denny, Denny looked at Bob. "You tell him," he said.

"Tell me what?" asked Dom.

"Well, you see," Bob said, "since Stevie's gone, I guess I can tell you. One of the reasons Kathleen didn't visit you in the hospital that night was…um…well you see, we all went back to Stevie's house after dropping you off at the hospital, 'cause his mom was at work and there was some beer at the house, and, um, well…"

"Well, what? What happened?" Dom asked.

Bob looked at Denny and Tim. Both nodded for him to continue.

"Stevie and Kathleen disappeared into his room at some point, and they were still there when we all left," Bob finished.

Dom sat looking at Bob then at Tim and finally Denny. You could almost hear the wheels in his brain turning. "You mean," he started slowly but his voice quickly rose. "You're telling me that Stevie copped *my* feel?"

"Actually, a little more than that, according to Stevie," added Bob.

"That bastard! That son-of-a-bitch! I never woulda gone up that tree if not for him and then he—"

Tim, Denny, Bob, and I looked down momentarily to avoid eye contact, but it became impossible to hold the laughter in. As one, we roared. Even Dom saw the humor in the whole thing and started laughing along with us.

"Fucking Stevie," he said with mixture of admiration and sadness.

The laughter passed and each of us seemed to drift off for a moment with our own memory of Stevie and sat in silence.

Finally, Tim turned to me. "So, Wes, you're really just going off again?" he asked. "Aren't you just a little bit curious about what happened?"

"Yeah, sure. Of course, I'm curious, but c'mon, guys, it really is like I told you," I answered quickly. "I'm not here to poke around. Hell, I wouldn't even know where to start. I met the chief and she seems like a good cop. I'm sure she'll do all she can."

"I think we all agree the chief may be good, but the deck is stacked against her. Some people in town didn't even want someone from the outside brought in after Chief Close retired. Certain people even wanted Danny to take over," Tim answered.

"You mean Tony?" I asked, though I had a feeling I already knew the answer.

Denny, Dom, and Tim waited for the others to speak up. They were quiet for a minute or two.

"Yeah, Tony, those two were always thick as thieves, from way back," Tim said. "But not just him—same old families, just different generations. The Heards, the Abernathys…"

I'd worked in enough places now to understand that, big city or small town, a select few always seemed to call the shots, whether it involved zoning regulations, liquor licenses or who did or did not go to jail for their crimes.

"Now, they want it to just go away," Denny said.

"Oh, sure, the whole town's involved in this. And of course you all bring up Tony, the guy who got this town back on its feet?" Bob quickly interjected. "It was the drugs. Stevie was selling drugs, everybody knows it, and he pissed off the wrong people. Drug dealers should expect to be killed."

"So you're saying Stevie deserved it? Is that what you're saying?" Tim answered Bob and his voice had an angry edge to it.

"No, I'm not saying that, just that the town doesn't need a bunch of dirt being dug up. Who's gonna move to East Hastings if they think a bunch of drug gangs are running around killing each other—" Bob answered.

"It could have been a jealous husband," Denny said, interrupting Bob and Tim. "Not that I know anything, but Angie says she's heard stories from some of the women at our clubs. You know Stevie, he didn't exactly have boundaries when it came to who he slept with—single or married."

"I heard he was mixed up with the Crawfords," Dom said.

The other three looked at Dom as if he was conjuring up the devil.

"The Crawfords? Are they still in business," I asked.

"Yeah, yeah, of course. They're like cockroaches—stomp on one, there's always plenty more," Tim said. I couldn't help but notice the stone-cold look he sent Dom's way. "Not even Stevie would be stupid enough to mess with them."

"Well, you say that but I saw Stevie earlier this summer down at the marina in Sea Isle where I keep my boat," Dom continued. "Said he was in the market for one himself, asked me questions about the other boats docked there—how much would that cost, how much for that one? It took me years to save up to get my boat, and I know Stevie don't got that kind of money. So I ask him if he won the lottery, but he says, all sort of confidential-like, that he's expecting a big pay day, gives me that big grin of his. Well, there's only one way to get that kind of money in this town over-night and that's to do something for the Crawfords."

"Stevie wasn't mixed up with the Crawfords…" Denny said, and it might have been a coincidence but a large cloud moved across the sun and its brightness dimmed. It also felt, and this might have been my imagination, that the tempera-ture seemed to drop a few degrees.

"So, there you go, Wes, everybody's got a theory," Bob said after a moment, shaking out the final crumbs from a bag of potato chips into his palm. "You know, you guys really amaze me, and see there what you'd be getting into, Wes? It would all be a huge waste of time."

He licked the crumbs off his hand and crinkled up the empty bag. "What it all comes down to is that no one has any idea why Stevie was killed, let alone who did it. It coulda been anyone for any of a dozen reasons, and I'm not saying that outa any disrespect for Stevie, but we all know how he could push people's buttons."

Tim turned to Bob. "Sure he could, but the owner of the place he was stabbed was working the bar and said Stevie hadn't talked to anyone the entire night, said he was just sitting at the bar, checking his cell phone, sipping his beer like he was waiting for someone."

"Like he was watching him the whole time. Somebody coulda slipped in, someone holding a grudge, knew Stevie would be there," Bob answered.

"Owner said Stevie hadn't been in the place for months," Tim responded.

"Christ, Tim, what are you? Frickin' Sherlock Holmes or something? The owner said this, the owner said that."

"I've been following the case in the newspaper," Tim answered defensively.

"Here we go with the *Chronicle* again. Where are they getting their information? You know how it is with news-papers—if they can't find any facts, they just make things up to sell papers." Bob turned to me. "No offense, Wes."

I didn't realize I should be offended.

"And, yeah, like the owner's gonna tell the police—or the newspaper—the truth," Bob continued. "Like he'd have any customers if word got out he was putting suspicion on any of his regulars. Hell, most of the people who hang out at that joint have a lot to hide from the police, from what I've heard about the place. But no, don't blame some guy livin' in a bottle or some druggie. Instead, point the finger at the most successful guys in town, screw with people's marriages. So frickin' typical."

"Look, all I'm saying is that there are some people in town who have a lot of money invested in and around East Hastings, and you know, like you said, having a murder continue as front-page news probably isn't the best thing for business." This time Tim glanced quickly at me. "We just don't think the police are doing all they can to find the mur-derer."

"Ah, enough of this," Bob said as stood up. "You guys heard Wes. He doesn't want to get involved, has bigger fish to fry somewhere." He turned to me. "Good luck, Wes, wherever your travels take you, but right now I'm hot, sticky, and I think I've got ants crawling up my leg. I want to go home and take a shower—now."

He opened the top to the cooler and waited while we took last swigs of our beer and threw the empty bottles in-side it. We all stood.

"Guys, you know, I'm really sorry. I hope they catch the guy and all but—" I started.

"No, Wes, it's okay," Dom answered, but I could tell it really wasn't.

They just didn't understand. Not sure I did either.

"C'mon," Tim said. "I'll give you a ride to your hotel, maybe see if we can get you some new clothes." He fell in behind Denny and Bob as they headed back to the cars.

"And maybe some deodorant," said Dom, waving his arm with a playful smile, as he approached me. He took my hand. "Wes, if I don't see you before you go, I'm glad you could make it." He followed the others off.

I was alone. I turned and took one last look at the river. It really hadn't changed at all.

CHAPTER 11

M r…uh…" The hotel manager glanced at my credit card. "Mr. Byrne, perhaps you'd be happier at a motel up the road."

I guess I didn't look like the type of guest the hotel usually catered to. Instead of luggage I had two shopping bags, one from Thatcher's pharmacy which contained a new set of toiletries and the other from the Army/Navy Store where I purchased underwear, a pair of jeans, and a couple of shirts. I hadn't shaved for twenty-some hours, I'd been sitting in East Hastings humidity drinking beer, and, though I was not sweating at the moment, patches of stains still splotched my shirt. My breath must have been a nearly lethal combination of beer, salami, onions, and hot peppers. I also didn't think the manager was the one gently swaying side to side.

"No. I've always wanted to stay in this hotel. Can you believe I grew up here and this is the first time I've been here?" I answered.

The manager looked me up and down disapprovingly again. "Actually, I can," he said.

"Of course, living in East Hastings, why would a person stay here? I mean, you'd only need a place if you were from somewhere else—which is what I am now."

I didn't drink a lot of beer as a rule but when I did I often got an irrepressible urge to make small talk whenever I'd had a few too many. Thing was, I was awful at small talk.

"I'm sure I don't know," the manager answered, not looking up as he searched the data on his console. "Ah, there is a reservation." He didn't mask his disappointment. "Would you like a smoking or non-smoking room?"

"Non-smoking please. Of course, I always thought I'd be staying there, but I didn't, so when I knew I was coming back to East Hastings I thought, great, I can stay here."

"I see. Exactly how long are you expecting to stay with us?" the manager asked, eyeing my "luggage" suspiciously.

"Well, that's sort of up in the air. You see my car was stolen this morning, and I'm hoping the police will find it, but until they do I really can't leave town, at least until my insurance kicks in."

"I see," he said.

I think what he really saw was the last thing he needed— a character.

The reservation sheet stopped printing. The manager tore it along its perforated edge and slid it, along with two key cards, across the reservation desk. "I'll need your home phone please and your signature."

"Oh, yeah, well see I lost my job and thus my phone, which the job provided, so I don't have a number I can give you. I am planning to get one, of course, as soon as I'm settled," I added as some sort of consolation.

The manager wasn't consoled. He looked at the reservation screen.

"Mr. um…Byrne…"

"Yes."

"Well, I don't want to seem…well, too harsh, but you see we cater to the tour bus crowd, people coming to visit the museums and historic sites. They tend to be a bit older, like things quiet. We provide our guests with an ambience of understated elegance. We're not used to people simply wandering in off the street—"

He didn't finish his sentence because at that moment the first wave of one such tour group burst in through the front doors, led by a frazzled looking woman carrying a clip board. She was obviously the tour director. "Peter, daaarling, thank goodness," she said as she approached the front desk.

"You wait here," the manager muttered to me before turning his charm toward the tour director.

"Della," he answered her, moving out from the behind the desk to greet her, taking her hands in his cordially. "I was beginning to wonder what happened to you."

"Well, we had a little problem when some members wanted to stay longer at the vineyard, which made some of the others feel shortchanged with their time at the mushroom museum gift shop, and they were insisting we go back, which would have thrown us way off schedule—none of them seemed to care at all about the schedule. I mean what's the point if we don't have a schedule?"

"I understand completely," Peter the manager sympathized, "there's always a few bad apples," he said, and I couldn't help but notice the quick, derisive look he threw my way.

"—except when it comes to meal time," Della the tour director continued, gripping her clip board tightly and shaking it at no one in particular. "Heaven forbid, we're off schedule at meal time. You should have heard all the griping when we couldn't find the TGIF. We were only fifteen minutes late."

"I understand completely. It's not always easy, is it? Well, we do our best, don't we? We do our best. However, you may now put yourself in the hands of the Hearthstone. Why don't we have your group wait in the lounge before I check you in? Come this way," he said, leading her off toward an open set of French doors at the far end of the lobby. "They can get a drink at the bar and, if they are still hungry, perhaps an appetizer or two."

She leaned in close to him and spoke softly, but loud enough for me to hear.

"To hell with them, *I* want a drink." She turned and put on a big smile for her group. "Everybody, this is Peter and he is the manager here. He'll get everybody all settled in as quickly as possible. In the meantime, why don't we all go to the lounge and get comfortable."

"Right this way," Peter said, also putting on a big show of hospitality as he led them off.

I took the opportunity to discretely sign the reservation sheet, take my room key cards, and slip away. All I wanted was a hot shower, a clean shave, and a quiet night.

CHAPTER 12

*I*f *I'm going to get the bum's rush out of the place, at least I'll be a clean bum*, I thought as I left the bathroom to answer the rather insistent knocking at my room's door. I had no idea how long someone had been knocking while I showered and shaved with the bathroom door closed. Tossing the wet towel onto the bed, I slipped on some clean underwear and my new pair of jeans and then pulled on my new T-shirt that read "Property of Hastings University."

I had a feeling I had gotten away a bit too easily at registration and was expecting Peter to pay me a visit. I'd met a thousand guys like him, the type who protected their little fiefdom with the fury of a Doberman pincher. He lived for the chance to flex his authority over a person he deemed "undesirable." A bribe to let me stay through the night was probably out of the question, only contributing to his sense of superiority when he turned me down. Still, if I wasn't so tired and running low on money, I might have tried anyway, if for no other reason than to bring a little joy into his life.

I opened the door. It wasn't Peter. It was Tina, and she was looking even better than she had at the Bean Me Up. She wore little or no make-up and let her beautiful features do the talking. Her green eyes seemed to glow, accentuated by emerald earrings and a matching stone set in her gold necklace.

She had on the simple black dress and high-heel ankle

boots I had seen her wearing at Stevie's funeral. A large purse hung from her shoulder.

"I guess you're surprised to see me," she said with a mischievous little smile.

Stunned was more like it, and even now I can't remember exactly what I said, probably something profound like, "Um, yeah."

"Well, I remembered you saying you would be staying at the Hearthstone, and I have something I wanted to give you. But first you have to promise me—no questions."

No problem there. She had me so enchanted I couldn't even form a complete sentence. "Sure," I answered.

She reached over to grab something just out my sight in the hallway, lifted it, and dropped it at my feet in the doorway. It was my packed nylon duffel bag.

"I thought you might be needing this. I found it in your car," she said. "I brought the car back too."

"My car? Where did you find my—" I started to ask.

"No questions. You promised," she said, placing her forefinger to my lips. "Can I come in? Someone might see me out here."

"Sure, of course," I said, picking up my duffel bag, and ushering her in.

She took a quick glance both ways down the hall before entering. I closed the door behind her.

"I think you might be able to see your car out your window, if you want to take a look," she said as she tossed her handbag onto the bed.

I went to the window, looked out, and, sure enough, there was my old Toyota sitting in a space a little way across the lot. It looked no worse than before, though of course, it wasn't exactly in mint condition when it was stolen. I turned back to Tina.

"I know I promised, but I've gotta know. How did you get my car back? I mean, at some point I have to tell the police I've gotten it back and I can't just say I looked out the window of my hotel room and there it was."

Tina sat down on my bed, tossing my wet towel onto the carpet beside it. Maybe I was imagining things but she seemed to be getting sort of comfortable, the way she smoothed the bed covers and pushed down on the mattress to check the firmness. Maybe she was just thinking things over.

"Look, I want you to know, I'm through with everything—but I can't—I won't tell you any names. If I do tell you how I got your car back, can you just call me…what is that they call a person who provides information but the newspapers don't say who it is?"

"An anonymous source?" I asked.

"Yeah, that's it. I'll be an anonymous source because these people—who I will not name—they're awful scary, and I don't want them finding out I helped you with your story. God, of all the cars around town, I can't believe we go and steal *your* car—"

"Tina, there is no story, but tell me, what scary people exactly are we talking about?" I asked.

"Why the people who stole your car, silly, the ones you're here to write about."

"Who said I was doing a story about stolen cars."

"Well, why else would you be here? It's big news, isn't it," she answered, looking at me like I was a two-year old. "'Course I don't know that much anyway. I just helped Pud—er, someone—out once in a while."

I had to sit down. I pulled a chair out from a desk across from the bed and lowered onto it. First the police chief, then the old gang, and now even Tina—it seemed like I was the only one who thought I didn't have an agenda for coming back to East Hastings.

"Tina," I said, "I appreciate what you've done, but I think you might have put yourself in a lot of danger. I'm not doing any sort of story. In fact, I don't even work for a newspaper anymore. If you know something, I think we should call the police."

"No! No police, not yet. Don't tell them anything until

I'm gone." She grabbed her purse and stood up from the bed. "If you're going to call the police, I'll leave right now."

"Okay, okay, no police," I said against my better judgment.

Waiting until morning probably wasn't going to hurt. It wasn't like I believed the cops were wasting precious manpower out scouring the countryside looking for my car.

Tina sat back down and flashed me a smile. "That's good, 'cause to tell you the truth, I really don't have anywhere else to go. I was kinda hoping you'd let me stay here, with you, for the night."

"Stay? Why…um…yeah, sure, of course," I answered, trying to sound cool and calm although the temperature in the room seemed to shoot up about sixty degrees and it felt as if my shirt collar was tightening around my neck. "Do you…um…have any bags in the car you want me to get for you?"

"No. I've got everything I need for tonight right here," Tina said, patting her purse.

"In there?" I asked.

"Yeah, sure. After all, I won't be needing that much," she answered with a playful giggle. She reached into her purse and pulled out a very sexy looking negligee and held it up against her body. "I've been saving this for a special occasion."

This was incredible. Could it be that all my high school prayers were finally being answered? The saying is that God works in mysterious ways. No one ever said he or she took their sweet time about it. Of course, I wasn't complaining.

It was definitely not the time for complaining. Just a good time to go along and let my dreams come true. That was why I couldn't believe it when I heard the words come out of my mouth.

"Um, Tina, before we get too far along here, there's something I've gotta know. Was Stevie mixed up in this whole car theft thing? Was it one of these scary guys that killed him?"

Tina's lovely lips pursed into a pout. "You always were so serious. You know, I had a bit of crush on you back in high school, but you were always so busy with the school paper and everything you never even noticed me."

"I noticed you, Tina. Hard not to, you were the prettiest girl in school."

She smiled, leaned back a bit, rested her hands on the bed, gave her hair a quick toss, and crossed her lovely legs. Her ankle-booted right foot hypnotically flexed slowly, toes pointing toward the ceiling and then straight out at me. "And now?"

The room seemed to be running low on oxygen. Either that or I'd forgotten how to breathe.

"Even prettier, and I can't believe you're here—"

"Then why are you sitting all the way over there?" she asked.

I wish I knew. "Well, it's just…just that…well…"

She took a deep breath. "No, Stevie wasn't involved in the car ring, at least as far as I know. He wasn't the stealing type, you know, more interested in making the big score. I think he wanted to prove that he was smarter than everyone else, especially that brother-in-law of his."

That sounded right. Stevie might have been wild, and very willing to live life according to his own rules, but I never thought of him as a thief.

"Does it really matter? You promised no questions and, besides, you said you weren't doing a story anyway," she asked.

"I'm just curious, comes with the job—or at least the old job—and the police are going to ask me a few questions. I can't lie to them if I don't know the truth," I answered. "My car—how did you manage to get that back?" I continued, changing the subject a bit.

Tina hesitated, and it was obvious she was a little scared. "You promise not to tell the cops until I'm gone?"

"I do, in fact, I promise no one will ever know you were here," I said.

"Okay," Tina said, ironing out non-existent creases in the bed spread with her hand before looking up at me. "The way it worked is that whenever, Pud…uhm…what should I call the person whose name I'm not going to tell you?"

"I don't know, how about Mr. X?" I answered.

She laughed, and I had the feeling she was getting a kick about the part she was playing. "Okay. See I'd drive around with Mr. X—" She laughed again. "—in his tow truck a couple days a week. He had a list of cars to be on the look-out for and whenever he saw one on the list heading into town, we'd follow it to see where it parked and where the driver was going, like into a store or a bar…"

"Or the Bean Me Up," I added.

"Yeah," she said with a smile, "like the Bean Me Up. He'd drop me off and if it was a woman and she was shop-ping, I'd compliment what she was wearing or her jewelry or hair and ask where she bought them or had her hair styled. If it was a man—"

"You'd captivate them with your smile," I said. I was enjoying this too.

"Yes," she said and I noticed a slight twinkle in her eye. No man would stand a chance.

"So, anyway you can imagine how I feel when I find out it's you I'm supposed to stall, especially once I remembered how you got those people sent to jail for what they were doing to the river. I was going to call Mr. X and tell him to leave your car alone but he called me first and said he al-ready had it."

"So that wasn't your sister who called you," I said. "I thought the voice sounded a little deep."

"See, I knew you were on to me," she said. "That's why I rushed out."

"So what happened next?" I asked.

"A little later I met up with Mr. X and I told him all about you. He said to just keep quiet about it, that you'd never link me to the theft. No one ever did the whole time we'd been doing it."

Mr. X was right about that. I hadn't given it the slightest consideration that Tina had anything to do with the car being stolen.

"He said, even if you did, he'd take care of you himself. Well, then I see you come into the service for Stevie with the police chief, and I'm sure you're going to point me out, but you didn't." She gave me a lovely smile. "That was sweet of you, but I thought Pud—er Mr. X was going to crap in his pants when he saw you, though," she added with a little laugh. "After the service—we didn't even go to the funeral—we went back to Mr. X's place, where he had your car stashed to wait for—" She paused and tilted her head slightly. "What do I call someone else whose name I don't want to give you?" she asked.

"How about Mr. Y," I said.

"Oh yeah, that makes sense. So we were waiting for Mr. Y, who was supposed to help Mr. X strip your car for parts, but he didn't show up. Now Mr. X started getting nervous and he got a bottle of bourbon and poured a drink to calm his nerves. That's when I got the idea of bringing the car back to you, so I kept pouring. He never could hold his liquor, and eventually he passed out. I hot-wired your car, went by my place to collect a few things—and here I am."

"You know how to hot-wire a car?" I asked, amazed.

"Sure, Mr. X showed me how. It's really pretty easy, especially an old car like yours."

I know she didn't mean it as a put down of any sort, but for the first time ever I felt a little embarrassed that I'd held onto my old car for so long, never got that flashy new car I once promised myself.

"And this Mr. X, he's the one you're afraid of?" I asked.

"Him, oh no. He'd never hurt me. He just talks big is all," she answered.

I had a pretty good idea who Mr. X was. It must have been the sausage-headed guy she was sitting with at the church service. I wasn't really sure why it mattered in the first place. I wasn't going to get involved. Guess I just didn't like loose ends.

"So, does that answer your questions?" she asked with an air of finality.

"Just one last thing. How did you find me?" I answered.

"I told you. You said you were staying here when we were at the Bean Me Up," she answered, the playfulness returning to her eyes.

"Okay, but how did you find my room? There are quite a few in the hotel," I answered.

She sat up and crossed her hands on her lap. Again, she gave me that look like I was a two year old. "That was easy. I just asked the very sweet guy at the front desk and he told me. I said we were old high school sweethearts and I hadn't seen you for years. He was more than happy to help," she answered.

"Peter the manager—sweet, more than happy?" I asked softly, almost to myself.

"The manager? Oh no, not that old stick in the mud. This was a younger guy. I think he might be new," Tina answered.

"Wait, you know Peter?" I asked.

For the first time since she'd entered my room, it seemed I had knocked Tina a bit off-balance with my question.

"What? Know him?" she said a little nervously. Her posture straightened. "Of course, I don't know him."

"But you said he was a stick in the mud, and he definitely seems to be," I answered.

"Well, um, you see my sister stays here when she comes to visit—my place isn't big enough—and…well, I remember the last time she was in town that the manager gave us a little grief for being too loud late at night."

She got up off the bed and walked over to me. She leaned over, put her left hand on my right shoulder, and gently pushed me back a bit into my chair. With her right forefinger, she began slowly tracing my lips. She brought her face close to mine.

"You know, Wes. It almost seems like you really don't want me here," she said, again giving me that pouty look.

"No, no, I'm glad you're here. Really," I said, meaning it completely.

"Are you done asking questions?" she asked.

"Yes, most definitely. No more questions," I promised.

"Okay, well, I have one for you. Will you do me one—no, two favors?" she said.

"Sure, of course anything," I said.

I could smell her perfume and her face was so close to mine that a few strands of her luscious red hair brushed atop my right and left clavicles.

"Tomorrow, in the morning, will you drive me to my sister's house in Carlsbad? She said she'd put me up for a few weeks," she said.

"Yeah, no problem. Now that I've got my car, I can get on the road too," I said, my eyes captive to hers. "What else? You said two favors?"

She moved her forefinger to gently rub the tip and bridge of my nose.

"Before we get on the road, will you take me by my place? I want to pack a few more things and pick up my cats," she said.

"Of course," I answered.

"Good, and just so you don't go getting all serious on me again—" She stood, turned around, and reached into her purse that was sitting on the bed. She pulled out a three-quarters full bottle of Smirnov vodka. "I brought this with me so we could have a little fun on my last night in East Hastings. You do drink, don't you?" she asked.

"Only when I'm conscious," I answered.

"Good," she said, walking over to the table next to the chair I was sitting in.

A small plastic tray on the table held a few small translucent twelve-ounce plastic cups wrapped in plastic and one of those square plastic containers with a lid for ice. She put the bottle on the desk and picked up the container, holding it out to me.

"We're going to need ice—lots of it—and something to mix with the vodka. I can't drink the stuff straight," she said.

"Right," I answered, standing and taking the container out of her hands. "Ice and mixer coming up."

"And, Wes," she said, reaching her hand up and around the back of my neck, pulling me down to her, "don't be long. We've got some catching up to do."

She kissed me deeply. I kissed her back. My arms slipped around her, and I pulled her close to me. I'd almost forgotten how great a woman's body could feel, but sensed Tina's would bring it all back to me.

I reluctantly pulled away from her, turned, and headed for the door. On my way out, I grabbed the *Do Not Disturb* sign off the inside door handle. Let the stick in the mud manager be damned. I wasn't going anywhere tonight.

CHAPTER 13

Why wasn't the vending machine stocked with cans of tonic water? That would have made life so very simple.

Before I met Jan, I dated a girl a few times and she drank vodka, mixed it with tonic. I've heard the Russians have a saying, something like "There are no ugly women, only not enough vodka!" Well, it turned out the same held true for tall, geeky guys. The more vodka and tonics the girl drank, the wittier, interesting, and, dare I think it, desirable I became. Maybe lightning would strike twice.

Tonight, however, no tonic, so while Tina waited for me in my bed back in the room, I stood in front of the damned machine completely at a loss as to what soda she would like to mix with her vodka. So many choices and I wanted to get this right.

Jan drank wine, white wine, and very little of it. In fact, I don't think I ever saw her tipsy, let alone drunk. She always seemed to have studying to do, an early class the next morning or was on call at the hospital. She drank so little, in fact, that I had no idea how such a beautiful woman ever found me attractive enough to want to sleep with me.

The hell with it! I fed dollar after dollar into the machine and worked my way down from the top of the choices. One of the reasons this all seemed to be taking so long was my need to stop at the front desk and get change for my twenty. The machine only accepted one dollar bills. I found out Tina was right though. The young guy at the front desk was much nicer than Peter the manager. First he asked me if my visitor had found my room and after he handed me my change, he gave me a knowing look and wished me a good night. I told him I wished me a good night too. He laughed.

So now I was making my choices—7-Up, of course, Mug Root Beer, sure. Pepsi, sure. Mountain Dew, sure, Iced Tea, sure, why not? I was bound to be right with one of them. Once down the column, and then—spare no expense—another round.

I looked down at the collection of ten soda cans at my feet and realized I now had to carry them back to the room. There were no bags in sight. Of course, I could make a couple of trips but there was no way I wanted to leave that hotel room once I returned. There was, it seemed, no other option for me but to put my faith in the work quality of a Sri Lankan sweatshop worker and carry my load in my newly purchased "Property of Hastings University" T-shirt.

I pulled the bottom of my shirt out and began piling the cans into the pouch I created. I had to keep pulling the bottom up more and more with each can I deposited, so that by the time I had them all loaded, the shirt bottom was up to my chin. I realized I probably looked pretty silly, but no one was going to see me. I just hoped the shirt would hold out.

I had forgotten about the ice, so I had to slowly lower into a crouch to pick the ice bucket up off the floor. The cans shifted and slid toward the outer edges of my pouch, but I managed to keep any cans from falling out while I grabbed the bucket, placed it under the ice dispenser, and pushed the button that released ice a few times until the bucket was full. Life shouldn't be this hard. Then I thought of Tina. It was all worth it. In a matter of moments, I would drop the brightly colored cans at her feet like some kind of pirate's booty of sparkling gems.

I left the beverage nook and turned to return to the room.

"You there. Hold on a minute. I want a word."

I recognized the voice right away—Peter the manager. I

sped up as much as I could. The weight of the cans forced me to bend forward a bit and I couldn't move too fast without having them swing out and then back against my chest. I couldn't let him catch me. Paradise lay just around the turn at the end of the corridor.

"Mr. Byrne. Stop." I did. He came up alongside me. He was breathing like he'd just run a fifty-yard dash. "Didn't you—" He gulped some air. "—didn't you hear me calling you?"

"You were calling me? Is there something I can do for you?"

"Yes. You didn't finish filling out your reservation sheet. I need a phone number and license…what the hell is that?"

He eyed my pouch suspiciously. This wasn't turning out well at all.

"This? Ah, well…um…you see, I'm not supposed to tell anyone. It's supposed to be a secret."

"A secret, huh? Know what I think? I think you're some kind of junkie—heard junkies get massive sugar cravings. Why else would someone be carrying…what have you got there?…a dozen cans of soda?"

My room was only a few doors away down the hall. I couldn't let him stop me now. Time for a little creativity.

"Well…um…you see…um…I could get fired for telling you." The look on his face didn't show much concern. I had to come up with something and it had to be good. "Have you ever heard of Zagats?"

"Zagats, the restaurant reviewer? Sure. What's that got to do with anything? We don't have a restaurant here, just a lounge."

"Well…um…you see, there hasn't been any sort of announcement yet, People at corporate are keeping things pretty hush-hush, you know how they can be."

If he did, old Peter wasn't sharing his knowledge with me. The skepticism was clear on his face. I'd never been a good liar and expected to break out in a beady sweat at any moment, in spite of having cold soda cans pressed against my body in the air conditioned hallway.

"So—now you promise not to say anything, right?—well, we're branching out, you see, going to start rating hotels the way we do restaurants. I'm one of the reviewers."

"*You*?" he asked, "You don't look like any hotel reviewer I've ever seen."

"Yes, ah, that's the point. My bosses wanted me to base my experience at the hotel from the average joe's perspective—"

Peter frowned.

"Not that that's the type of clientele this hotel attracts," I quickly added to avoid any perceived insult and pander a bit to his pride. "It's just that if a hotel treats someone looking like me with great service, well then…you get the point."

It seemed to be working. He was listening, appeared to be mulling it over. "So what are all the soda cans for?"

"The cans…well, um, I'm checking for dust."

"Dust?"

"Yeah, we're very thorough. You'd be surprised how often the finest hotels have vending machines stocked with stale chips, candy with expired sell-by dates or dirty soda cans—really quite appalling. It's going to cost more than one hotel a five star rating when we launch our service later this year, I can tell you."

His face showed the slightest hint of concern. He seemed to be buying it. No doubt that first thing in the morning he'd be directing his staff to check every vending machine in the place. I saw my opening to get away.

"Well, if that's all, then I really should get back to my room and finish my work, although I must say at first glance these cans look just fine. Sure, they'll be no problem," I said, starting off to my room.

I was almost away when the manager caught up to me once again. This time he was all charm.

"I'm terribly sorry if there was any inconvenience. I mean we do have to be careful—the welfare of our guests and all. I want you to know that should you need anything, please don't hesitate to ask. Not because of the Zagat review, of course, but just because that's how we treat all our guests. No request is too great. And I do want to apologize, if there was any perceived abruptness on my part, it's just that when you showed up without any luggage or a car, well that's very unusual."

"Oh yeah, about the car. I'm afraid that was part of the undercover bit. I do have a car, my assistant brought it here and parked it in the back, outside my room—a red Toyota Camry—just in case you get suspicious. Massachusetts plates." Last thing I needed was him calling the cops to report a strange car sitting in the parking lot all night. As far as they knew, it was still stolen.

"Glad you told me. We do have a man who patrols the grounds, checking for anything unusual, security you see. After all, the hotel does everything it can to make sure our guests are safe and sound," he said with an ingratiating smile.

We'd just about reached my room and I realized that, with Peter standing next to me, it might be better to use my key than to knock and have a scantily-clad Tina open the door. Problem was, my hands were tied up holding the soda cans and ice bucket. I turned to him.

"Would you mind taking these cans for a moment while I fish for my room key?"

"Not at all. I'd be glad to."

He probably would have washed and waxed my car if I'd asked. He held out his arms as I poured the cans into them. Amazingly, he didn't drop one of them.

We reached my door just as I pulled my key from my back pocket. Turned out it wasn't needed. The door was slightly ajar.

Damn, I thought. *Tina must have given up on me.* I pushed the door open and entered the room. I didn't know it at the time, but Peter was following close behind me.

"Tina?" I called out, moving farther into the room. I

heard the sound of soda cans hitting the floor behind me. I turned and saw Peter dashing to the bathroom and then heard the sound of him retching into the toilet. I turned back and looked at my bed. Tina lay on her back, eyes vacantly looking up at the ceiling, a stain of bright red blood growing larger on the negligee she had put on for her special occasion.

CHAPTER 14

I want him arrested. He said he was checking our cans for dust!"

Peter had recovered from his episode in the bathroom by the time the police arrived and apparently cornered one of the officers in the hallway, pleading his case to have me dragged away and locked up.

"Instead, I find that...that prostitute sprawled out on his bed. I bet they were doing drugs. I knew he was up to something the moment he showed up."

I could hear, but not see Peter. The police had placed me in a room across the hall from mine and placed a guard at the door. I couldn't see directly into my old room but could only catch glimpses of what I assumed were forensic and coroner personnel moving about in the hallway beyond the guard.

"How soon will this all be cleaned up? I have a hotel to run and don't want to see my guests disturbed," I heard Peter say.

I wanted to get up from my chair and beat some compassion into him. I looked down and realized both my hands were clenched tightly into fists, and they were shaking.

This room was exactly like the one across the hall—same floral patterned curtains, same beige contemporary scroll design wallpaper, same plum plush carpet, same mahogany armoire. It even had the same beige and burgundy striped fitted bedspread on the king-sized bed, although, of course, this one didn't have the dead body of a beautiful woman lying on it.

The air conditioner had just been turned on, so the room still felt a little stuffy. I don't know why it is, but hotel rooms seem to have two temperatures—too hot and too cold. What I needed was fresh air to clear my head, but of course like all buildings these days, the windows wouldn't open to allow a breeze, if there was one on this humid August night, to waft in. I knew there was no way the young officer at the door was letting me take a stroll outdoors. He was all business.

Even at this early hour, his uniform was smartly pressed and his shoes shined to a polished sheen. He had a disconcerting habit of looking at me and tapping his fingers on his gun holster, as if he might have to pull his weapon out any second to keep me from making a getaway.

I'd seen murdered bodies before—came with the job of being a crime reporter. This was different though, very different. What struck me most, above all else, was the look in her eyes, those once sparkling eyes. Disappointment. That's what I saw. Disappointment in me, for not being there, for letting her life end the way it did.

"I had you figured for being a total loser, but not a murderer." Danny Sullivan was at the door. He was smirking again. Maybe it was a permanent condition, maybe he reserved it for me. Regardless, I couldn't help but sense that he was enjoying this.

He turned to the officer guarding the door. "You can leave us alone. If he tries anything, I think I can handle him."

"Yes, sir," the officer answered.

He looked at me, tapped his holster one more time, and left us alone.

Danny came into the room, closing the door behind him. He gave me a quick look-over. I don't think my East Hastings T-shirt impressed him.

"So what happened? You were all set for your big moment and she changed her mind when she took a good look at you?"

"You know, Danny, I always knew your tires were a little low on air, but even you can't think I would murder Tina."

Dumb thing to say. Door closed and only me and him in the room. He could beat me to a pulp and tell everyone I went after him trying to escape. I didn't care, though. I was angry, real angry, and while a killer was slipping away this jerk was standing there accusing me.

Danny's face tightened, his eyes hardened, and he took a few steps toward me. I should have been scared but wasn't. Maybe I wanted someone to hit me. Maybe I deserved it.

"I told you before, Wus, it's Officer Sullivan, and yeah, I think you killed her. Prisons are full of pathetic assholes like you, guys who think they're big shots and then snap when they realize what a failure they really are. I did some checking up on you. How many jobs you lose over the last few years? How many times you been fired? What happened? Tina laugh at you when you couldn't get it up, finally pushed you over the edge?"

"Christ, Danny," I answered, putting extra emphasis on his name. "You are such an idiot."

That did it. He was at me quickly and I did nothing to prevent the right hook that landed squarely on my jaw and sent me tumbling back into the table and onto the floor. Danny stood over me, breathing hard.

"Get up, asshole. C'mon get up. I'll show you who's an idiot."

The door opened and the officer who had been standing guard looked in.

Danny turned to him. "Get out of here," he ordered.

The guard glanced at Danny and then at me, lying on the floor. He didn't seem concerned in the least, actually seemed to like what he saw.

"Thought you should know. The chief just got here. Wants to talk to the suspect."

He closed the door, leaving us alone again.

Danny took a second to compose himself, get his breathing under control. "Get up and sit in that chair—and believe me, this isn't over."

I did as I was told. I felt my jaw and could feel a welt growing, but it seemed I still had all of my teeth. I shook my head, trying to clear the cobwebs. This wasn't the first time Danny had hit me and, despite the years passing since high school, he could still pack a punch.

"He's in here, Chief," I heard the young officer say out in the hallway. The door opened and Chief Roark entered. She looked me over and then turned to Danny.

"What happened to him?" she asked him.

"He tried to get past me and out the door and I had to hit him," he said.

She looked at him skeptically. "Okay, you can leave us alone," she said.

"What if he tries something again?" he asked.

The chief looked at me. "Are you going to try anything?"

"No, I'm not," I answered.

"Officer, you can go," she said, not looking at Danny.

"Yes, Chief," he answered and left the room without looking back.

Chief Roark came nearer and took a good look at the growing welt on my jaw. She wasn't dressed in her uniform. Instead she had on a partly zipped up black nylon taffeta windbreaker with EHPD silkscreened on the left chest over a sweat shirt, a pair of clean, neatly pressed blue jeans and a pair of lightweight high-topped boots. A nine millimeter Glock was holstered on her hip.

"What he said true?" she asked, though I'm sure she had a pretty good idea.

"The part about having to hit me is," I answered.

"You want to press charges," she said.

"Would it do any good? No witnesses and the word of a police officer against mine."

"Probably not," she answered.

I appreciated her honesty.

"Tell me what happened tonight with the girl," she asked.

"Tina," I answered. "Her name is Tina."

"Okay, tell me what happened to Tina."

"Nothing to really tell. She showed up at my room, I went to get something to mix with the vodka she brought with her, got back to my room, and—" I took a deep gulp of air and was surprised that my eyes were getting a little misty. "—there she was."

"What about your car? The manager said it's in the lot," Roark asked.

"Yeah, she brought my car back to me."

"Say where she got it?"

"No."

"Say who stole it."

"No."

"Big-time reporter like you didn't ask?"

"I told you, I'm not a reporter. I'm nothing," I answered.

"That's right. You're just passing through. Still, weren't you curious?" she said.

"Of course I was, but she made me promise not to ask any questions. She was scared."

"Say who she was scared of?"

"No, only that she was leaving town in the morning, wanted to spend—to spend her last night in town with me. I was going to take her out of here."

"You two have something going? What she was wearing, looked like you were more than just friends."

"No. I hadn't seen her for years, ran into her at the Bean Me Up this—er, yesterday morning—right before my car was stolen. Saw her at Stevie's funeral service but we didn't talk. Then she showed up here."

"You have any idea who killed her?"

"No, only that she was scared of someone."

"You know the hotel manager wants you arrested for

impersonating a hotel reviewer? Says you told him some kind of story about being from Zagats. Why'd you tell him that?"

"I thought he was going to throw me out. Came up with the first thing I could think of so he'd let me stay. You going to arrest me?"

"For lying to a hotel manager? I'd have half the husbands in town behind bars if that was an offense. Still, I want you to stick around, in case anything else comes up."

"Sure. Got no place to go. Speaking of which, can you recommend a good place to stay. I have a feeling the hotel manager isn't going to want me staying here."

"Think you're right. I'd suggest the Evergreen Motel up the Route Two-Twelve. It's pretty clean, from what I hear. Not sure how you're going to get there, though. We're going to impound your car, see if there's any prints or other evidence we get from it. Probably get it back to you in a day or two."

"What about my stuff in the room? Can I take that with me?"

"Yeah, I don't see a problem with that. Let me check, though." Roark got up to leave. She turned back to me as she reached the door. "Remember what I said about not liking coincidences? If I find out you've been lying to me or holding anything back…well, I'm not going to look too favorably on that. Understand?"

I nodded. "Sure do, and believe me, I'm completely in the dark here."

"Yeah, well any light comes on, you let me know."

Roark left the room and I could hear her talking to someone out in the hallway, though I couldn't make out what was being said.

Alone in the room, I suddenly realized how tired I was. It had been over a day and a half since I'd had any sleep. I didn't care if the Evergreen Motel was a complete dump, as long as my room had a bed.

"Okay, we've removed the body, so you can collect your

things, but don't touch anything else. Our people are going to check for prints," Roark said, poking her head back in the door for a second.

I raised my weary bones off the chair, left the room, and crossed the hall into my old one. Tina's body was gone, though there was a slight trace of blood on the bedspread. Other than that, no one would have any idea that a murder had taken place in the room only hours before. My stuff was right where I had left it, and it didn't look like anyone had disturbed it. I went into the bathroom to collect my toiletries. It had a faint odor of vomit and I resisted the impulse to call the front desk to remind Peter to have it freshened up. Let sleeping dogs lie.

I was almost out the door when I turned to take one last look around. Tina's travel bag was sitting on the bed, and the vodka bottle was still on the table. Even if it wasn't my liquor of choice, I could see no sense letting it go to waste. I walked over, grabbed the bottle, and put it into the shopping bag that held my belongings. Just then I heard a cell phone ringing from somewhere in her bag. I looked over my shoulder at the door. No one seemed to be in the hallway. The phone rang again. I dug into her bag and found the phone. The display read "Puddy." It rang again.

I know I shouldn't have, but I answered it. "Hello?"

"Who's this?" the voice on the other end asked. "Let me talk to Tina."

"Um, Tina can't come to the phone right now."

"Bullshit. Put her on," the voice demanded.

"Yeah, well, you know Tina's been drinking, what with all that's happened. Why don't you come on over to the hotel, Puddy? We can talk."

"Who the hell is this? How do you know my name? Is that bitch talking? You tell her she says anything to anyone that gets me in trouble, she's a dead woman."

"You're too late, Puddy. Someone already killed her. You want to tell me anything about it?"

"She's—dead. Oh shit, oh shit—"

The phone went dead.

"Hey, what are you doing?" a voice asked from behind me.

I turned. It was the young officer who had stood guard at my door.

"Um, just checking for messages," I answered.

"Yeah, right. You're under arrest and coming to the police station with me."

So much for the Evergreen Motel. Seemed I found other accommodations.

CHAPTER 15

A re there interior designers who specialize in police interrogation rooms, who scour the ends of the earth to find the drabbest paint colors, most uncomfortable furniture, and harshest lighting available? If so, the one hired by the East Hastings Police Department earned their money.

I'd been sitting in the interrogation room for more than an hour and a half, alone, and had plenty of time to consider the design concepts necessary to create the perfect ambiance for the space. I think the look would be called something like early-Inquisition. Paint the walls a corpse-pallored gray, something with a name like Confession or Purgatory. Furnish the room with a chair from the Marquis de Sade collection, selected with an eye toward inflicting immediate soreness and eventual unbearable pain. Then pick a ceiling light fixture that produces the most unrelenting lighting possible, one that gives off a brightness that penetrates even the most tightly closed eyelids, unforgiving in its glaring persistence. This fixture should also produce an almost imperceptible, yet constant and inescapable buzzing that weaves through the brain like a needle and thread. Top it off with the paranoia-inducing wall length mirror which, as anyone who had ever watched a cop show on television knew, was actually a one-way mirror, behind which interrogators studied a suspect like bacteria under a microscope.

The interrogation room door opened, and Danny Sullivan entered. He seemed very happy to see me, the way a hyena must be thrilled when it comes upon an injured zebra. He was followed closely by the chief, now in uniform. She carried a manila folder and I could see my name typed neatly on the folder's label—a very meticulous person, this chief. I might have been mistaken, but it seemed she actually smiled reassuringly at me as she sat down. Danny waited for her to sit then took his seat at her right side. If they were going to play good cop/bad cop, it wasn't difficult to determine who would play which role.

"Okay, before we get started, I want to make it clear that this is strictly an interview. No one is charging you with anything. Now, is there anything you want to tell me?" the chief asked, her eyes examining me. She opened the file folder, pulled a pen from her left breast pocket, and clicked it with authority.

"You know, being in the newspaper business, I've done my share of interviews—never needed to lock someone in a room to do one, though." I shifted in my seat to try to get the feeling back in one of my buns, knowing it would only be moments before the other one became numb. "Just for kicks, if you were going to charge me with something, what exactly would it be? I'm wondering what laws I broke."

"First, of all, I want to make clear that, since we never charged you with a crime, the door to this room was never locked, and you were free to leave anytime you'd like to. And as far as any charges, well, it's still early in our investigation."

"So you're saying I'm only a suspect or what's that term used these days…person of interest? That's just crazy, why would I want to kill Tina? She brought my car back, we were going to have a few drinks." I had to shift again, this time to alleviate the sharp stabbing pain that shot into my lower back. I tried to be inconspicuous so they couldn't see the effect the chair was having, but I noticed Danny's lip curl sadistically every time I moved. His chair probably had a cushion, the bastard. "What about that guy who called her on her cell phone, what's his name…Puddy?"

"Ah yes, Puddy," Chief Roark said, glancing down at the folder. "His real name is Patrizio Salvatore," she answered. "For some reason everybody calls him Puddy. Any idea where we might find him?"

"You know, for a moment there I was quite impressed that you've found out who he is so quickly, although I imagine there aren't a lot of guys named Puddy running around, but then you have to ask someone who's been in your town for one day where to find him. I mean, how the hell would I know where he is? I don't even know who he is."

"Well, you did talk to him. We thought maybe he told you."

"I've already made a statement about everything he said. He only asked for Tina then hung up when I told him she was dead."

"Why exactly did you answer Tina's phone?"

"I don't know. I wasn't thinking too clearly. I heard the phone ringing, I answered it. Bad habit, I guess."

The chief looked down at the folder, lifting the top page, reading. "That's right. That's exactly what you said in your statement—you heard the phone in the bag." She looked up, tilted her head slightly and locked her eyes onto mine. "Any other reason you reached into her bag? Were you looking for something, was there something you were after?"

"No, just the phone," I answered.

"C'mon, admit it," Danny broke in, leaning forward. "You were after the thirty thousand dollars in cash she had in there, weren't you?"

"She had thirty thousand dollars in her bag? And her killer left her bag behind? So maybe it wasn't a robbery. So someone wanted to kill her because—oh, shit, my car."

Danny sat back in his chair and facetiously clapped his hands. "Very good, oh that's very good." He turned to the chief. "Isn't it a treat to watch a great mind at work? You could almost hear the wheels in his head spinning." He turned back to me. "Of course, it's about your car. You think we're stupid? How many times do you think someone has their car stolen and then has it returned that same night? And then the person who returns it ends up dead—oh, and to top it off, the guy whose car gets stolen is a down and out reporter who really needs to break a big story, might just be hard up enough to do anything—and we hear that once up- on a time you got fired for being a little too fast and loose with the facts. That's right, we checked you out, know all about Boston," he continued. "So how did it work this time? You pay a guy to steal your car, say Puddy Salvatore, and plan to write a story about some made-up car theft ring? But then what happens? You decide to double cross Puddy, or Tina does. Sees you as her ticket out of town, takes the money you paid him and your car, and meets you at the ho- tel. But Puddy finds out and kills her. So sad how the mighty have fallen. You were such a big shot when you left here—"

"That's enough, Officer," the chief broke in.

I stared at Danny then looked at the Chief. Forget bad cop/good cop, I was hoping for bad cop/smart cop. "You don't actually believe any of this, do you?" I said to the chief. "I hadn't seen Tina in over twenty years, have no idea who this Puddy Salvatore is, and before I got here I had no idea anyone was going around stealing cars. Besides, if I knew she had thirty thousand dollars, don't you think I would have taken it?"

"Well," the chief answered, "there are a lot of things that don't make sense. It is strange that your stolen car was re- turned to you, and that Tina knew where you were staying, and that she had thirty thousand dollars in her bag. As far as we can find out, she didn't have a job or visible means of support—"

"But for your theory to work, that thirty thousand dollars would have been mine, the money I paid Puddy Salvatore to steal my car, which, by the way, is about thirty thousand dollars more than the damn thing is worth. As Danny here just mentioned, I'm a down-and-out reporter. Where am I going to get thirty thousand dollars?"

"Maybe you just didn't have time to get it back," Danny said. "Officer Collins probably caught you with the phone before you had a chance to get the money."

"C'mon," I said. "Getting her phone was more important than getting that money? That doesn't make sense."

The chief shrugged. "Like I said, a lot of things don't make sense. Still, we'd like to check your phone records to see if you made any calls to Tina or Puddy before you came to town. Where's your cell phone? It wasn't with your things at the hotel."

"I don't have a cell phone," I answered.

"You don't have a phone?" Danny asked incredulously. "Everybody has a cell phone. Geez, my eight-year-old son has one."

"Mine was the *Sentinel*'s. I had to turn it in, when I left."

"When you were fired," Danny added pointedly. "We talked to your editor at that paper too. Wasn't very happy to be awakened at this hour of the morning, but once he found out we were calling about you, he was more than happy to help. He said your days working for newspapers were probably just about over.

"You spoke with one Roland Deeple?" I asked, picturing the little bastard taking special delight in handing out that bit of information.

"Name sounds about right," Danny said with a smile.

"Okay, we'll contact the newspaper again, ask about the cell phone," the chief said, more to Danny then to me, who nodded. "Oh, and ask for any calls from land lines to this area code, just in case he used the newspaper's phones."

"You'll have to take my word on this. Newspapers are pretty hesitant about turning over records to the police."

Danny smiled. "When I spoke to your old boss, he said anything I wanted, just let him know. He doesn't seem to like you very much."

"Yeah, well it doesn't matter. You won't find anything. The only person I've talked to in East Hastings was my friend Tim when he called me about Stevie," I answered.

"So maybe you arranged it through Tim. I remember you guys being good friends," Danny replied.

"C'mon, this is getting tiring. You don't have any proof of any of this and you could probably be using your resources a little better than trying to uncover some vast conspiracy that started in Rhode Island. Any fool can see Tina's death has to do with something that's happening right here in East Hastings."

"Are you telling us how to do our jobs? You think we're a bunch of fools?" Danny asked through a tightened jaw.

"No, not at all. It's just that any fool could see I had nothing to do with this," I said, looking directly at Danny. "And since you seem to think I did, well, I guess that would make you a—"

I was tired, uncomfortable, and digging a deep hole for myself. Fortunately, a knock on the door interrupted me before I could finish. Good thing. I probably would have said something to really make Danny mad, and I had no idea about the chief's views on police brutality.

"Come in," the chief ordered.

One of the officers I had seen at the hotel opened the door a crack and stuck his head into the room.

"The suspect's attorney is here," he said.

The chief gave me a quizzical look.

"When did you call an attorney?" she asked.

I was just as surprised as she was. "I didn't."

The door opened fully and in walked a short plump woman who looked like she just crawled out of bed. Considering the hour, she probably had. She was wearing ratty looking tennis shoes, jeans, and a one-size too large sweatshirt with "Grand Canyon National Park" printed on it. Her brown hair was pulled back in a bun, though she must have done it in a rush because a few strands of her hair dangled loosely.

"Good morning, Chief, Officer. I've been asked to, um, check in on Mr...um..." She looked at the palm of her hand, where she had apparently written my name. Just the sort of attorney I would get, I thought. Who needs files when one has body parts? "Mr. Byrne." She looked at me. It seemed she was as impressed with me as I was with her. "That you?" she asked. I nodded. She turned her attention to the chief. "Has he been charged with a crime?"

"Morning, Gloria. No, he hasn't," the chief answered.

"So he is free to leave, if he so desires," she asked.

"Yes, he is," the chief replied.

She turned and smiled at me. "Do you want to leave?"

"Yes, I most certainly do."

"Then why don't we go?"

I stood up. Too fast, it seemed, because me my left leg had fallen asleep and turned into silly putty from sitting too long in that chair. It crumpled beneath me.

"My leg's asleep," I yelped as I began to fall forward.

I reached out to try to catch myself on the table. Danny leapt to his feet across the table and reached out to steady me. Or so I thought. Actually, he grabbed a chunk of my shirt in his left hand and pulled his right arm back, his hand forming into a fist. I looked into his eyes. There was a twinkle of delight in them. He could finish what he started at the hotel.

"Officer, stop," I heard the chief yell.

I thought it was too late, but Danny froze, still holding tightly to my shirt front, arm still poised.

"He lunged at me," he answered, not taking his eyes off me.

"Let him go—now," the chief ordered.

Danny did—reluctantly—pushing me back up straight and releasing his grip on my shirt.

I steadied myself on the table, moving my leg around to get the feeling back.

"Based on this little episode, I suggest you call me first if you have any desire to speak with my client. I think I should be in the room with him when you ask him questions," my new attorney said to the chief. "You have my number."

"I do," the chief answered. "Oh, and by the way, how did you come to be representing Mr. Byrne here?"

I was as interested in her answer as the Chief was, not that I minded her coming.

"Hoppy called me," she answered.

"Hoppy?" the chief and I said at exactly the same time.

"Yeah, the man thinks nothing of getting people out of bed in the middle of the night. 'Course he has to pay a little extra."

The chief turned to look at me. "I thought you said you weren't working for the newspaper?"

"I wasn't. I'm not. I have no idea why Hoppy would get involved. I haven't even spoken to him since I've been in town—for years, in fact."

The chief turned to my attorney. "How did Hoppy know we had him in here? Was it one of my people?"

"You know Hoppy will never reveal his sources," Gloria answered before turning to me. "You ready to go yet? I'm tired and I want to see if maybe I can get in a few hours of sleep tonight."

I nodded. The feeling had returned to my leg. "Do I get my car back?" I asked the chief.

"We'll be done with it tomorrow. You can pick it up then," she answered.

"How am I supposed to get to the hotel without a car?"

"Maybe you can get your friend Puddy to steal you one," Danny sneered.

I ignored him. "And my things at the hotel?" I asked.

"Evidence, I'm afraid. Not sure when we'll be releasing them. Oh, you were right about not being welcome back at the hotel, so you probably need to find another place to stay. Let us know when you find one, just so we know where you are," she replied, gathering up the file folder and retracting the tip of her pen with an authoritative click. She turned to Gloria. "It should go without saying that we'd very much appreciate it if your client here didn't leave town before we're done with our investigation."

"Of course," Gloria answered. "And you promise you will call me if you have any intention of speaking with him further?"

"Of course," the chief replied with a slight smile and nod of the head.

How nice. So civilized, yet here I was carless and homeless, so to speak.

Gloria turned and looked at me. She didn't seem all that impressed as she held out her hand. "Gloria Stephenson," she said. "I'm your attorney on this matter."

I held out mine. We shook hands.

"Wes, Wes Byrne. Of course, you know that." I looked at her. "…um, Hoppy sent you? I don't get it."

"Mr. Byrne, I don't really ask a lot of questions. Client calls me at four-thirty—willing to pay my rates—I do what they ask and send them a bill. You'll have to take it up with Hoppy."

Disheveled in appearance as she was, tired as I knew she must be, Ms. Gloria Stephenson was professional. I liked her.

"Any ideas how I get to a motel?" I asked my new attorney, trying to appear as pitiful as possible, which of course wasn't too hard, considering the circumstances.

She let out an audible sigh. "Well, it looks like Hoppy's paying a pretty penny for a taxi service too."

CHAPTER 16

I'd become a light sleeper over the months I spent in Jan's hospital room. Most nights, I nodded off in a chair by her bed and woke at the slightest change in her breathing or the entrance into the room of the night nurse, quiet as she or he might try to be while making rounds to check on the machines monitoring Jan's condition.

The hospital made special allowances for me, or rather for Jan, since she was considered a member of their family. She'd gone there for med school, her internship, and was just a few months from completing her fellowship when the disease was found. Many of the staff had known her almost as long as I had. They let me pretty much come and go as I pleased, knowing I worked at the *Herald* and had deadlines to meet that didn't mesh well with hospital visiting hours. It was rare that I didn't arrive at some odd morning hour to find someone—a nurse, doctor, fellow student—in the room with Jan. They'd say something encouraging and then leave me alone with my wife.

She was usually heavily medicated at night, especially toward the end of her illness, and pretty much slept through the night without incidence. So I was surprised to wake up and find Jan standing in front of my chair, dressed in scrubs as if ready to go on rounds. How she had removed the tubes and sensors taped to her body and gotten out of bed without waking me, I'll never know.

"Jan, what are you doing up? Let me call the nurse.

She'll get you something if you need it," I mumbled through lips thick from sleep.

"No. It's okay, Wes. I'm fine, good to go," she answered.

She turned and walked out the door. I looked over and noticed that her bed was neatly made, as if she had never been lying in it, the poles that had held her bags of medication were empty, and the heart monitoring and other machines that stood next to her bed were turned off. I leapt up to follow her out the door.

She was already far down the hall. I began to run to catch up to her, but even though she was only walking, I couldn't seem to narrow the distance between us. She was nearing a set of doors at the end of the hallway, above which a sign was posted that read *Authorized Personnel Only*.

Jan stopped and turned to face me as she reached the doors. I was able to close the gap and had almost caught up to her. She smiled at me, that lovely smile of hers, and held up her hand.

"Stay here, Wes," she commanded and I stopped.

How beautiful she looked. I knew some men liked the way their women looked in lingerie and others might prefer a pair of tight jeans and angora sweater, but for me, it was Jan in her scrubs. Basically loose fitting pajamas, I know, but there was something in the way they hung on her body, no pretensions, just my Jan.

Before I could move again, she turned quickly and pushed her way through the double doors. A bright light flooded through the doors and Jan seemed to disappear within it before the doors swung shut after her.

I rushed forward and pushed on the doors but they wouldn't open. I couldn't see any type of latch or lock. The doors were sealed tight.

"Jan! Jan!" I screamed as I started banging on the doors as hard and loudly as I could. "Open these doors. Let me in. Please, Jan...please. Don't leave me like this. Don't leave me again." I pounded harder and harder on the doors. I'd break them down if I had to. Harder, louder I pounded.

I jerked up in bed, awake. Damn, one of my sober dreams, the kind that happened whenever I fell asleep rather than simply passed out drunk. I probably should have relished them, because Jan was always so vivid, so beautiful, so…alive. I didn't. I hated them because waking up from them only reminded me, once again, that Jan was gone. I did my best to make sure they didn't happen too often.

They were too real. I could still hear the banging on the door.

Bam! Bam! Bam! It took me a moment to realize that the sound was coming from outside my room. Someone was knocking loudly on my door.

"Wes, I know you are in there. Open the damn door!"

No mistaking that voice—Hopkins Brewster Weatherly. As if things weren't bad enough.

CHAPTER 17

O kay, okay. Hold on a moment," I yelled out.

The banging stopped as I took a look around, trying to get some bearings as my eyes adjusted to the dark surroundings. I was in a hotel room, not a very nice one, though I'd been in worse. I was in a king-sized bed, tables holding lamps on each side. Across the room, a television sat on a credenza. Off to the right was a bathroom next to a recessed area with a bar to hang clothes on. To my left was a small table with two chairs and beyond it curtains were pulled tightly shut in front of a window, doing a wonderful job of keeping any trace of light out.

I climbed out of bed and searched the floor for my pants and shirt. It took me a moment to realize I was still wearing them. A quick sniff test revealed that I could use a shower and a change of clothes. Thank goodness I didn't need to stand on ceremony for Hoppy.

I walked tentatively in the darkness across the room, slid the chain lock out of its groove, and opened the door, immediately blinded by the bright light that greeted me. The silhouette of a bulky, dark figure stood before me. I pulled the door wide open and stepped back into the comfort of the dark room.

"Doesn't anybody ever sleep in this town?" I asked as the figure stepped through the door and past me into the room. I shut the door behind it.

"Not too many do at two in the afternoon—at least not

anybody doing an honest day's work," came the answer.

I could barely make out the figure as it walked over to the curtains and, as if tearing a band aid off the skin, reached up and opened them in a quick, efficient motion. Sunlight flooded the room.

A wave of nausea swept from my toes to my hair and I gasped for breath as if someone had taken my head and dunked it into a barrel of bright, suffocating water. I stumbled forward and was able to sit down on my bed. It took a few moments but the room stopped swirling around me.

"So, were you planning on ever calling me? I have to find out you're in town over the police scanner?" Hoppy asked as he placed a bag he was carrying on the table.

I felt a little better, enough so that I could concentrate my vision on the form standing before me. It was amazing how little Hopkins Brewster Weatherly, editor of the *Daily Chronicle* and my one time mentor, had changed. He was a little heavier around the jowls and a bit of paunch hung over his belt. He didn't have as much hair as when I met him so many years ago and now what was left had turned a little grayer. He was dressed pretty much as he always was—white dress shirt, bow tie and matching gray slacks and jacket. Hoppy was old school.

When I first met him, Hoppy had scared the shit out of me. He was gruff, coarse, and had a vocabulary of curse words that would make a sailor blush. However, as I soon discovered, no one cared more about the newspaper business than he did and, if you could handle the swearing and insults he'd generously pour upon anyone he thought didn't care as much as he did, you could learn more from him than any journalism school could teach. He still appeared to be the bear of a man I remembered.

"Good to see you too. You know, I've only been in town one day," I answered.

"And quite a day it was—having your car stolen, causing a scene at a funeral, and then finding a dead woman in your bed."

"I didn't cause a scene at—how did you hear about that?"

Hoppy just smiled at me as he pulled two cups of coffee from the bag on the table.

It was a stupid question. Hoppy had eyes and ears all over Hastings County.

"So what were you doing there?" he asked.

"I was just paying my respects."

"That's all, huh?" he said, eyebrows arching ever so slightly. "It never occurred to you that your presence there might not be appreciated?" He dumped the contents of the bag—packets of sugar, small cream containers and wooden stirrers—out on the table.

"I thought people might not still be holding grudges."

Hoppy laughed. "Son, of all people, you should know that folks around here hold onto grudges tighter than a boa constrictor wrapped around a rodent." He lowered his large body onto one of the chairs, reached into one of his inside jacket breast pockets and pulled out a flask. He raised it in offering to me. "A little hair of the dog. I know it's early for you, but from what I understand that shouldn't really be a problem."

I should have been insulted. I wasn't. I nodded and watched as he took the covers off the coffee cups and poured the contents of the flask into our two cups.

"I haven't had a drink since I've been in town. You been keeping tabs on me?" I asked.

"I've been following your career—so called," he answered, ripping open two sugar packets and dumping them into my cup. "Cream?"

"No thanks."

Hoppy stuck a wooden stirrer into the cup, reached out, and handed it to me. I took it from him, gave the liquid a quick stir, tossed the stirrer onto the table, raised the cup to my lips, and took a sip. Not great, but it would do.

He added three packets of sugar and two containers of cream to his cup, stirred his drink and took a sip.

"Should have brought some Baileys, make this dishwater taste better."

"It's fine," I answered, taking another swallow. Actually, I thought it could use a little more whiskey.

"Sorry to hear about your wife," Hoppy said.

"Thanks," I answered, taking a little longer tug from my coffee cup.

A few uncomfortable moments passed as we both feigned interest in our coffee cups.

"So why didn't you call and let us know what was going on?" Hoppy finally asked.

"Nothing to talk about," I answered, averting my gaze from his penetrating eyes.

"Oh, yeah. Nothing. Your wife dies and you just go off the rails and do your best to destroy what was shaping up to be a pretty decent reputation as a newspaperman." He paused. "You know, Wes, you're not the first person to lose somebody—"

"You don't know anything about it," I snapped, not letting him finish.

I know Hoppy was only trying to help, lots of others had, but I'd learned that being brusque seemed to keep everyone at a distance and usually ended the matter. Everyone, that is except Hoppy.

"No, I probably don't. Never met the woman, don't remember you ever bringing her down here or being invited to a wedding."

Hoppy could always give as good as he got.

"Yeah, well…Jan was busy at the hospital so we just got married at town hall, didn't even invite family. We planned to have a big party after she wrapped things up with the fellowship, but—"

Damn Hoppy. He was taking me someplace I really didn't want to go—our plans, our future. I could feel the emotions rising up. I tamped them down with a big swallow of my coffee.

"Listen, I want to thank you sending along that attorney

last night," I said to change the subject. "I was getting in a little over my head with the chief. She surprised me."

Hoppy knew what I was doing, and he gave me a slight smile to let me know I wasn't fooling anybody. He took a sip of his coffee and sat back in his chair. "Yeah, Chief Roark is no fool, which is more than I can say for some other members of her department."

"You mean Danny Sullivan? How the hell did he ever become a cop?"

"It could have been worse. Some people, powerful people, wanted him to be the chief when old Frank Close retired."

"I can imagine who they are," I answered.

"Yeah, I'm sure you could. The more things change…" His voice trailed off. Small towns, big cities, there's always somebody behind the curtain pulling the levers.

We were silent for a few moments as we both looked out the window and took swigs from our coffee.

Hoppy moved forward in his chair. "I have to admit I'm surprised you didn't stop by the paper to ask some questions about what happened to Stevie Darby when you got into town. You two kinda went way back, didn't you?"

Hoppy knew damn well that Stevie and I were friends. Part of me wanted to give him the benefit of the doubt. Maybe he really did stop by to see how I was doing and maybe he did want me to open up about Jan. Chances are, though, that Hoppy was after a story. He was always after a story.

"We kinda fell out of touch, as you might imagine, considering all that happened, hadn't spoken for years. Like I said, I was passing through and just decided to pay my respects. Didn't see any need to be asking any questions. Figured it was a police matter," I answered.

"Yeah, guess so, a police matter. I see. Well, it was a shame about that woman, what's her name, the one murdered in your hotel room. Guess that's a police matter too. You're probably right to stay out of it," Hoppy said, appearing to agree with me, a little too easily for my liking.

Good old Hoppy. As frightening as he could be when he was stomping and bellowing, he was probably at his most dangerous when he turned on the charm, and Hoppy definitely could be charming when he wanted to be. You don't survive running a newspaper in a small town as long as he had without knowing when to cuddle and when to use a cudgel. And the thing I always admired about Hoppy was how he always seemed to know which was appropriate.

"Then again, it's not like you not to be a little curious about an old friend…um…two old friends. You knew the woman from high school, didn't you? Heard you had quite a crush on her back then."

Amazing, simply amazing, the shit that Hoppy could dig up. I could only smile to myself.

"That's two old friends being murdered," he continued. "Would seem only natural that you'd want to poke around a little bit, ask a few questions. 'Course that might be the old Wes I'm thinking about."

Ah, here we go, the master at work. He was right, in a way. That's what made him so damn good. He was always right—in a way.

Now, though, he wasn't dealing with the old Wes. I'd grown a bit wiser, a bit warier and a whole lot more, I don't know…tired. I was just really tired of it all. Nothing really made a difference. The bad guys always won and all I always did was seem to make matters worse—for others, for myself.

"I know what you're trying to do, Hoppy, but it won't work. You don't need me. I've been away a long time, wouldn't even know where to start—if I wanted to. You must have someone on staff that could do a much better job. Hell, you should just do it yourself. You know where every skeleton is buried in this town, what rocks to turn over."

"Yeah, well maybe I'm losing my touch. No one seems to know anything or at least no one wants to talk about it, but I know something is there, can feel it."

"Maybe you just want something to be there, ever think of that?"

"Christ, you're sounding just like Midgy. She's been after me to retire for years, you know. She thinks this is just an excuse not to."

Midgy was Hoppy's long-suffering, utterly fantastic wife. She was the only person I think Hoppy was actually afraid of.

"Well, you have made your mark."

Hoppy's neck tightened, his face flushed red. He surged forward in his chair. "You think that's what this is about? Making my mark? Those bastards the Crawfords have been stealing farm equipment for years from good people, hard-working people who depend on that equipment for their livelihood, and in the past few years it's gotten even worse. And now two people have been murdered in my town and people either don't care or are afraid to say anything. Something's going on, something…well, I don't know what…but that's not the kind of place I intend to live—or die—in." He sat back, looking out the window as he collected himself. Did I imagine it or did he seem to sag a bit? "I thought you and I shared that."

"Listen, Hoppy, if you couldn't sniff something out, there's no way I'm going to find anything of value. It'd just be a waste of both our times."

"Yeah, well," Hoppy said, pushing himself out of the chair. He approached and stood over me. I'd forgotten the way he could tower. "Seems there is a matter of, let's say seven hundred dollars and change, aww, let's call it eight hundred dollars you owe me for the lawyer. You could give me a check now or we can come to a little arrangement."

I should have been honored. He used both the cuddle and the cudgel. Bottom line? He was going to get his way—as always.

CHAPTER 18

See, the thing is," Hoppy was saying, "I'd rather not let on that you're working for the paper right now. Keep it our little secret."

Quite frankly, Hoppy Mills was full of shit.

We were sitting in a booth in the Town Crier Diner. The place was aptly named. If anyone in East Hastings wanted to keep anything a secret, the Town Crier was the very last place they would go. News traveled out into the world from the counter stools and booths of this place faster than any satellite stream could possibly compete with. Hoppy used to joke that he didn't consider radio, television, or even other newspapers in town to be his main competition for news. It was the Town Crier he had to out scoop.

So for him to sit across from me and try to sell me that load of soap about wanting to keep our situation discreet seemed insulting. By now, everyone in the diner knew that a murdered woman had been found in my hotel room the night before. Most of them probably knew that I had been questioned by the police as a "person of interest" in the murder. Most of them remembered that I worked for Hoppy at the newspaper years ago and had gone off to seek my fame and fortune.

A few of them might even remember the circumstances surrounding my brief career at the *Chronicle*. Secret? I was a human banner headline and Hoppy the newsboy standing on the street corner yelling "Extra! Extra! Read All About

It! *Chronicle* Editor Sits At Diner With Murder Suspect!"

I would have gotten up and walked out if, at that exact moment, the waitress hadn't arrived with my breakfast order. I was hungry and the smell and sight of a plate loaded with two large eggs—cooked over easy—two thick slices of scrapple, a pile of home fries, and two slices of homemade bread—toasted and sliced crosswise into four triangles— held me in my seat like epoxy.

She placed a very large slice of home-made lemon-meringue pie, the topping browned and stiff to perfection, in front of Hoppy.

"Can I get you anything else, hon? More coffee?" the waitress asked, looking at my quarter-filled cup.

"Yes, more coffee would be great," I answered.

"Me too, Dottie," Hoppy said. "And, um, no need to mention the pie to Midgy, should you see her and she asks."

Dottie was probably about sixty years old and the Crier most likely the only place she'd ever worked since the day that she graduated from high school. Her gray-brown hair was cut short with bangs swept across her forehead and she had warm, light brown eyes with slight creases around them, a small nose, and a sweet smile that showed she really loved her job.

"You know I won't say a word. If you stopped coming in here and ordering pie, they'd have to close the place down and I'd be out of work. Besides, I think all Midgy has to do is take one look at that belly of yours to know what you've been up to," she answered. She smiled at me. "Be right back with your coffee."

Hoppy laughed as Dottie turned and left us. I had the feeling they'd run through this routine with each other more than once over the years.

I watched Dottie head back toward the counter, then I took a moment to look around the place. The dark, wood-paneled walls were covered with framed photos, most of them black and white, most likely from fifty or more years ago, of customers from times past posing at the counter or smiling from the booths. It was striking how little things had changed over the years. Put the men eating here this afternoon in jackets and ties or overalls and the women in pleated skirts with hair pulled back and tied in bows, and you'd never guess it was a different century. Same napkin dispensers, ketchup bottles, and salt and pepper shakers on the counters and tables, same sign directing people to the bathroom, same worn stools and cushioned booths, same weathered linoleum floor. *It's a place like this that makes people want to hold onto the past*, I thought.

"I can't believe you are actually going to eat that stuff," Hoppy gruffed, snapping me back into the present.

I knew immediately that he was referring to my order of scrapple. It had that effect on people like Hoppy, who moved to East Hastings after graduating from college somewhere in New York. If a person wasn't born and raised in the southeastern corner of Pennsylvania, they could not conceive in any way how someone could find a dull-brown quarter-inch slab, that looks like it belongs on a mason's trowel instead of a breakfast plate, appealing.

It didn't help matters that the most common response to the question of "what's in it?" was "everything from the pig, except the squeal." But it seemed every area had a food that natives absolutely loved and outsiders found…well, disgusting. In the southern US, there were chitlins; the Scots had their haggis; in Italy, it was tripe; and French diners loved cow brains. Hell, in Wisconsin, a salad was made with Jell-O; in California, pizzas were smothered with ranch dressing; and certainly not to be overlooked, in Iowa, people wolfed down deep-fried butter on a stick.

So I thought, relatively speaking, a mix of corn meal, spices, and pork scraps formed into a loaf, sliced and browned in a pan to perfection—a crisp outer layer and warm, soft interior—was a perfectly acceptable and, I might add, tasty breakfast side order.

I ignored Hoppy, used my fork to slice off a piece of scrapple, speared the piece with my fork, dipped it in an egg yolk, and into my mouth it went. Wonderful! I'd missed scrapple.

Dottie returned with the coffee and filled our cups to the brim.

"How is everything?" she asked.

"Great," I answered, as I always do whenever a waitress asks me that question.

"Well, this slice of pie here is a bit on the small side, and it's a tad sweeter than usual," Hoppy injected, giving a Dottie a devilish grin.

"Well, if you're not happy with it, why don't I just take it away?" she answered, reaching out for his plate.

Hoppy quickly slid the plate to the side out of her reach and raised his free hand in surrender. "No, no, it's okay. I'm not complaining. It's just that you asked so I thought you ought to know."

Dottie rolled her eyes, gave out a brief "Harrumph," in mock disgust, turned, and left us.

Hoppy chuckled. "Dottie's a good old gal. I like to kid her. Now, where were we? Oh yeah, I'd rather we keep our little arrangement to ourselves, should anyone ask. Gives the paper a little bit of deniability, should any parties start asking questions or if any problems arise." He put a forkful of pie into his mouth.

"What sort of problems?" I asked.

He was a being a bit too casual, a bit too nonchalant.

"Nothing, nothing to worry about," he mumbled through his mouthful of pie.

Right. From what I remembered, Hoppy was never more dangerous than when there was nothing to worry about.

"Look, Hoppy, I appreciate you getting me out of the clutches of the police last night, and I appreciate you buying me these clothes—"

We had stopped at a local men's shop after I showered at the motel. Hoppy footed the bill for some new clothing ("I'll just add it to your tab," he'd said), since the police were still holding my "luggage" from the murder scene. I had purchased and was wearing a pair of khaki cotton pants and a blue knit polo shirt.

"—but I don't see why you need or even want me for this story. I've told you, I've been away a long time, too long to be any use to you," I said to him.

He took another forkful of pie, and raised his hand as he closed his eyes and his face took on a look of rapture. He swallowed and washed the pie down with a swig of coffee.

"Things haven't changed that much and you're the perfect person to do some poking around. Believe it or not, a lot of people still remember and appreciate what you did—"

"And a lot of people didn't," I said, to which Hoppy simply gave a shrug and continued on.

"—and I think they'll talk to you. They liked the fact that you took on some powerful interests and refused to back down, no matter how much pressure you—and of course, the paper—had to put up with."

"Even if that's so—" And I doubted very much it was. "—I don't know anything about Stevie's murder, really, just what I've heard from a few old friends. You've probably already covered all the basic facts of the story. I wouldn't even know where to start," I answered, hoping Hoppy would see how much I didn't want to do this.

"Don't worry about where to start. I have a theory I'd like you to follow up on, and you can see what you find. Look, your breakfast is getting cold. Why don't you finish while I explain what I have in mind? See, I have a feeling the Crawfords are involved in all of this, and I think these murders are tied up with them somehow."

It was amazing how the mere mention of the Crawfords, no matter how softly spoken, could cause people to stop what they were doing mid-bite and perk their ears up a bit. It was the reaction I knew Hoppy was after. Just another way to spur some interest the *Chronicle* reading population in town and the reason I was sitting with him this afternoon. I pretended not to notice their reaction.

"Sure, fine," I said, figuring it couldn't hurt to listen and besides I was hungry and hadn't had more than that first bite. I started eating while Hoppy began. He leaned forward and hushed his voice a bit.

"Okay, so what do we know? A guy is stabbed in the back in a dark, nearly empty bar around eight p.m. Let's assume that we're not dealing with some crazy person who's just running around stabbing people. Of course, we can't discount it entirely because of what happened to that girl in your motel room, but for a moment, let's just concentrate on your friend Steve Darby."

"But we could be dealing with a nutcase," I said while chewing.

"I said maybe, but I don't think so and if you let me finish, I'll tell you why." Hoppy's voice had risen a bit louder, but he caught himself, looked around, and started again. "So, we'll break this down. Why some out-of-the way dark bar, at a time when the place is practically empty? Well, according to the bartender at the Wayside, Stevie indicated he was meeting someone, so maybe whoever your friend was meeting didn't want to be noticed. So, it's very likely that some kind of deal was going down."

"Then why not meet in a parking lot or some deserted place?" I asked.

"Are you going to keep interrupting me? Maybe your old friend didn't trust the person entirely. Wanted some public place, a place he felt comfortable. Could be Steve Darby had the upper hand in the matter, that he was calling the shots, so he picks a spot and a time when he knows there'll be a few, but not a lot of people around, a place the other person won't be recognized, but it's familiar turf for him. I don't know. I haven't worked everything out, but let me get through this." He shook his head, a bit exasperated at my interruptions. "So, what kind of deal is it? Drug deal? Could be. Your friend was known to sell marijuana from time to time, but that doesn't make sense. After all, by all accounts, the killer struck and was gone, didn't take time to get any drugs off Darby. There weren't any drugs found on his body, and the police didn't find any at his place. So what's the point of killing the guy? After all, isn't the point of a drug deal to get drugs? No, something else was going down. Something to do with all those crimes being committed."

Hoppy was enjoying himself. He'd probably had this all bottled up inside himself for days.

"Now, your friend is sitting at a bar stool. The bartender turns away or gets busy taking a bottle inventory or washing the glasses at the other end of the bar, although having seen the place I don't think too much effort goes into keeping the glasses clean. Anyway, Darby's alone at the bar and this person comes along, slides a blade into his back, and then is gone. What's that tell us?"

"I don't know," I answered. "This is your theory."

Hoppy's eyes gave me a quick, angry glance. "A knife's a personal way of killing somebody. You've got to be close to the person to stick it in. So I think the killer wanted to feel the blade of the knife slide into the body, scrape across a bone, feel Stevie straighten up, hear him gasp. Maybe even give the knife a twist or pull it up a little, a little show or feeling of power. And why in the back?" he went on. "Was the killer a coward? Afraid to face Darby? Maybe. Maybe the killer didn't have the guts to look him in the eyes as he drove the knife into his body. But maybe it's something else. Maybe it's a little symbolic. Maybe the killer thought that Darby was stabbing him in the back and that it was payback for something that your friend had done or was doing to him. Do you see what I'm saying?"

"Um, not really," I answered.

Hoppy sat back, shook his head, and looked at me as if I was a grade-schooler unable to grasp the concept that two plus two equals four. He leaned forward again, took a breath, and began slowly, using the index finger of his right hand to count off the important points on the fingers of his left hand, starting with the pinky. "We have a dark, nearly empty place where two people meet for some kind of deal." Then the third finger. "We have one of the people coming up close and using a knife because it's personal." Then the middle finger. "We have a man stabbed in the back, a symbolic gesture." And finally the index finger. "And the killer moves on without taking anything off the body." Hoppy curled the fingers of his left hand into his palm and jabbed the hand forward, thumb up. "Blackmail. Your friend was blackmailing somebody and that person killed him rather than pay him off." He sat back, pleased with himself.

I sat for a moment then nodded my head slightly. "It makes sense, I guess—as much as anything else. Have you mentioned this to the police?"

His mouth fell open, then his face turned red. I had a momentary feeling that he was going to reach across the table, grab me by the throat, and squeeze real hard.

"Have I told the police? What the hell kind of fool question is that?" he bellowed.

Folks looked up from their meals at us. I wanted to slide under the table.

He took a breath, looked around at the others, gave them a sheepish smile, and shrugged. They went back to eating and talking among themselves, although I noticed that a few of them jerked their heads in our direction. Obviously, we were the topic of many of the conversations.

Hoppy lowered his voice again, but his eyes were blazing. "Are you that far gone, boy? We're in the 'sell newspapers business,' not the 'run to the police and help them do their job' business. We break the news. Hell, we make the news, if we have to. We don't just sit around and swallow the crap the police and people in power feed us. We ask questions and if we don't like the answers we get, we go out and get the truth by ourselves. I had a feeling you've lost your way, but have you forgotten *that*?"

"I'm sorry," I said, and I truly was. Maybe now, though, Hoppy could see how hopeless I really was. Maybe he'd realize I was too far gone and he was wasting his time trying to bring me back. "It's just that I don't see how you can prove any of it."

A devilish smile grew on his face. "Ah, now see, that's where you come in. If he was blackmailing somebody, and every bone in my body tells me he was, that means whatever he had on that person who killed him was probably hidden somewhere, like his house, and the police didn't look hard enough or even want to find it. Back in the day I'd of…well, I'm getting' a little too old to, so…well, you're going to break into his house and see if you can find it."

CHAPTER 19

The hell with Hoppy and his theories. I planned on putting this town in my rearview mirror as fast as I possibly could. Two murders and now it seemed my once-revered editor had lost his blooming mind. I feared if I stayed any longer, I might catch whatever was going around—either a knife through the heart or the madness which apparently could grip even the most sensible of its citizens.

"Sign this and the car is all yours," said the late-middle-aged, jowly desk sergeant, one of his pudgy hands passing me a clipboard which held a standard release form, and the other offering me a pen across a counter that separated us. I took them from him and looked over the form.

Hoppy had dropped me at the police station so I could pick up my car, which the police had finally finished going over. They apparently found nothing to identify the car's thief, only Tina's and my fingerprints, which made sense since I owned the car and Tina had driven it to the hotel the night she was murdered. They had managed to unearth a rather beat-up and most likely unplayable "Best of David Bromberg" cassette tape, a dollar and sixty-eight cents in change, and an old, very faded unpaid parking ticket from my early days in Boston, all found beneath my seat cushions during their thorough search. These items were in a sealed plastic bag that lay on the counter before me and were itemized on the release form.

"Pretty fortunate. You're getting the car back relatively unscratched. Doesn't happen very often," said the sergeant. "Either we never find them or they're pretty banged up after the kids are done joy-riding in them."

"Is that so?" I answered as I signed the release at the bottom of the page and handed him back the clipboard and pen. "I can't see anyone getting any joy out of riding in my car. I know I don't."

"Well, you may not believe this, but your car, old as it is, seems to be one of the most popular ones to steal."

"Really? You'd think thieves would want a Corvette or Camaro, something nice with some power."

"Nah," the sergeant answered. His mostly gray hair was cut short, relatively flat, and bristled on top, practically non-existent on the sides, and his large, fleshy face was closely shaved. "First of all, those cars usually have alarm systems so there's a greater chance of getting caught, whereas your car is a piece of cake to break into."

He slid the form off the clipboard, tore off the perforated strip at the top, and separated the three sheets that made up the form. "Secondly, the smart thieves aren't stealing cars to ride around in, they're taking 'em for their parts." He handed me the bottom of three copies of the release and placed the other two into a manila folder on his desk. "That's where the money is, car parts, you see," he continued, turning back to face me, "and that's what makes your car so valuable. Toyota sold a ton of those cars, not just in the US but all around the world. And they made 'em so that the parts from your car fit different models they produced over six, maybe seven years as well. Then when they moved onto newer models, they stopped making the parts for cars like yours. That's a lot of cars needing a lot of parts, especially because those cars seem to last forever."

"Appears you know a lot about this," I said.

"Yeah, my brother-in-law runs an auto parts store...claims the black market for parts cuts into his business...always bitchin' to me about it, like I can do something to stop it. See, what these crooks do—"

There was another level, lower, to the counter on the desk sergeant's side and a telephone sitting on it rang. The desk sergeant gave me a frustrated look.

"Hold on a moment."

He answered the phone with little enthusiasm.

"East Hasting Police Department, how can I help you?"

I could hear a strident, excited voice speaking very rapidly and forcefully. The officer grabbed a pen and notepad and began scribbling down some information.

I took a step forward and peered over the counter at the sergeant. His ample belly hung over his belt and strained at the buttons on his shirt that confined its bulge. On the desk surface beside the phone was a plate with two donuts, one half eaten, a large mug of cream lightened coffee, and a copy of the *Chronicle*, opened to the sports page. I looked at the computer monitor that sat to his right at an angle and could make out an in-progress game of video solitaire on the screen. A mid-back mesh office chair, its very compressed seat cushion testimony to the bulk of its constant occupant, was in front of the monitor.

"Right...sure...okay...got it...I'll send a car over immediately," he said into the phone and hung up. "Amazing I get anything done around here, what with all the interruptions," he said. I nodded in commiseration. "So, as I was saying, what these car thieves do is..." The sergeant was back on the subject of car parts. "They know what models of cars they can get the most money for parts from and they're always on the lookout for 'em—"

Something down the hall caught my attention. It was Danny Sullivan and he was with a woman. He had come into the hallway through one of the doors along the corridor.

"Thank you so much for coming in. We realize how hard this all is and we are very sorry for your loss. You can be sure we will punish the bastard who did this, trust me."

The woman he was talking to was visibly upset, using a

handkerchief to dab at her eyes. Although I couldn't see her face, something about her seemed familiar.

"I think I recognize that woman," I said to the desk sergeant.

He leaned out over the counter to take a look. "Her? We had a woman murdered last night. That's her sister. Came to identify and claim the body. Poor lady."

"Tina's body is here?" I asked.

Did that mean the whole time I was here last night and again this afternoon, Tina's body had been laying on a slab somewhere in this building? Dammit. If I had known, I could have…what? She was dead and I was going to get in my car and get on with my own sorry life. That was just the way things were, and I'd learn to accept there was no such thing as a real happy ending.

"No, the morgue is at the hospital. She just had to come here and sign a few forms. Lots of police work is nothing more than paperwork," he said. "But that's all neither here nor there and it looks like we're all finished up. You can pick your car up back in the impound lot behind the station," he said, waving me dismissively toward the front doors of the station.

"Huh? Oh, yeah, thanks," I answered.

I looked up the hallway and saw that Danny and Tina's sister were heading toward me. I got a better look at her. The resemblance to Tina was apparent, although the sister was a little taller, a little heavier, her hair cut shorter. I could see that her eyes were red and swollen from crying.

"So if you just stop by the hospital, you can make arrangements for the body there. We still need to hold onto her personal belongings until we're through with the trial." Danny was talking to her as they approached. "The desk sergeant here can help you if you have any questions and if there is anything else we can do, please call us," he said, and I was surprised by the tenderness in his voice.

He noticed me. The tenderness evaporated.

"What the hell are you doing here?" he asked bluntly

and I saw that he moved to put himself between me and Tina's sister. She looked up at me briefly from behind him, but there was no trace of recognition in her eyes, only a faraway sadness.

But now I remembered her. Terri, that was her name. She was a few years older than Tina and me, three grades ahead of us, I think. Just older enough to cast a bit of a shadow over Tina. Everyone was always comparing Tina to her "perfect" big sister. Wasn't fair, they were very different. Terri was popular, a cheerleader in high school, and, I think, a runner-up for prom queen her graduating year. Tina was always a bit of a free spirit, getting in trouble for stuff like smoking in the girls' bathrooms.

"I'm just picking up my car." I held up the folded release form to prove that everything was done by the book.

He took it out of my hand, unfolded it, and gave it a once over. "Good. The sooner this piece of junk is off our lot the better." He refolded the sheet, reached out, and rested it against my chest. "Of course, if I was you I would be careful driving it around town. We're pretty strict about cars coming to complete stops at stop signs and using blinkers to indicate turns. Awful easy to find yourself pulled over and ticketed for all kinds of violations. You'd be surprised how many there are on the books."

I took the sheet back from him, but before I could say anything to him, he turned quickly to address the desk sergeant. "Sergeant Maxwell, would you be so kind as to file these forms?" he said, handing him the file folder he was carrying. He turned to face Tina's sister, his back now to me. "Once again, you have our condolences on Tina's death. And let me just say once again that her killer will definitely pay for his crime, you can trust me on that. Now, I'll leave you with the sergeant."

"Thank you for all you've done, Officer," she said and I could see the gratitude in Terri's eyes over Danny's shoulder.

He could always lay it on when he had to, but maybe this

time there was sincerity behind those words. She walked over to the sergeant's desk.

Danny now turned to face me and, once more, I was treated to that smirk of his. He took me by the elbow and started walking me to the door. He waited until we were out of earshot of Terri and the desk sergeant before he spoke.

"Listen here, Wus. I heard about your lunch with Hoppy today. Now it's only my opinion," he began, his smirk turning to a little self-satisfied smile, "although around here my opinion does count for something—that if you really want to avoid any more trouble, it's probably best that you strongly consider just leaving town. There's absolutely nothing for you here."

Man, news does travel fast in this town, yet that made things a little more curious. Somebody had to know a lot more than they were letting on, either to the police or to Hoppy. Secrets just don't get kept around here, it's usually just knowing where to look or who to ask. Ahhh—what was I thinking? This wasn't my town anymore.

"Hey, couldn't agree with you more, but it's your chief who told me I couldn't leave," I answered.

Danny stopped and spun me so that we were face to face. He looked up at me, his eyes sharp and penetrating. He lowered his voice so that only I could hear him. "I don't think you should worry too much about what the chief says or does. She's new around here and doesn't quite know how things work, any more than you do, but it's pretty simple. We got the guy, a migrant farm worker up from Mexico to work at the mushroom farms over in Hanover Square. We got what appears to be the murder weapon and it's only a short matter of time before we get the confession—not just for Tina's murder but for Stevie Darby's too." He cast his eyes up toward the ceiling and pressed his lips together, the bottom one jutting out slightly. His eyes returned to meet mine and the smile returned. "I'm thinking a drug deal gone bad. Everybody knows these wetbacks bring drugs up with them from down there. And everybody in town knew that

Stevie loved his drugs and was always looking for the big score. See, it's not so hard to put the pieces together. Just some good old-fashioned police work and case…or should I say cases…closed. This is just all going to go away and we'll have our peaceful little town again."

He turned me and we started off again down the hallway. His hand remained on my elbow until we reached the door.

I know I should have just kept walking. Instead, I stopped and turned to face him. "So it doesn't matter if you've got the wrong guy? And Chief Roark is just going to go along with this?"

"She will if she wants to keep her job. And besides—" Again the smirk. Man, did I hate that smirk. "I happen to know deep in my heart it's going down just like I said, and nobody can do a damn thing about it. Soooo, have a nice trip."

He patted me condescendingly on the shoulder, turned, and strutted away like the cock of the walk.

I walked out through the doors of the police station, across the limestone porch, and stood on the front step. I looked up at the wisps of cirrus clouds moving slowly on the wind in an otherwise clear blue sky and felt the late afternoon sun on my face. I took a deep breath.

It was going to be good to get out of East Hastings. But first I had one thing I had to do.

CHAPTER 20

I sat in the parking lot of the Hastings County Hospital, waiting for Terri Porter to come out.

Looking at the building, I was amazed. It seemed like the quaint hospital I remembered had taken steroids. The original building remained, but growing out of it on both sides were wings that stretched for the lengths of two football fields, and then those wings had wings of their own. It was like a Lego blocked building.

Still, they had done a good job mimicking the look of the original building and the grounds were immaculate. Full, green-leafed American hornbeam trees stood guard on each side of a handicapped accessible walkway. *Hasting County Hospital* was stenciled in large gold letters in the glass over the doors.

I'd been there for about half an hour and was wondering what was taking Tina's sister so long. The waiting was giving me too much time to think about all the hours I spent in a hospital, sitting in Jan's room. Most of the time, especially toward the end, she was either sleeping or heavily anesthetized to fight the pain. Still, those moments when she was lucid just reinforced everything that made me fall in love with her in the first place. She was so strong and all she seemed to worry about was whether I was getting enough sleep and taking care of myself. I never heard her complain.

I also thought about Tina, lying on a cold, sterile table in the morgue. Was it my fault? Could I have saved her if I had gotten back sooner or not left her at all? She was so alive when I left her, with that spark in her eyes.

At last, Terri appeared through the dark sliding doors. She stopped just outside the doors and put on a pair of sunglasses, not so much to shade her eyes from the late afternoon sun, because there wasn't much on this side of the building, but, I imagined, to hide their redness from her crying.

I jumped out of my car and crossed the lot to reach her. I didn't have to hurry. She had crumpled onto one of the benches. As I reached her, she was sitting quietly, staring across the portico at the neatly landscaped flower beds that lined its edges. I don't think she noticed the neatly pruned English rose bushes with their late blooming flowers though. No, I'd seen that solemn posture, that outward gaze of hers on countless others who sat on uncomfortable chairs in waiting room areas or in pews in the chapel when I left Jan's room and roamed the hospital during her illness. Perhaps instead she was seeing shadows, memories flickering by, thinking "This is only a dream, I've had bad dreams before and when I wake up, this will not all be real." Or maybe she was creating an internal list of the tasks before her—making Tina's funeral arrangements, canceling Tina's credit cards, getting the utilities at Tina's apartment turned off—that could keep her focusing ahead, away from this here, this now.

I stopped by her bench. "Um, Ms. Porter…Terri…I want to say how sorry I am about your sister. She was a very nice, sweet person."

She looked up at me. It was striking how similar she looked to Tina—same shape of the face: the nose, the chin, the ears, and, as I noticed in the police station, the same green eyes, now hidden behind the sunglasses. There was a difference, though it was more based on how I remembered each from high school. Tina wanted to be noticed; Terri expected to be. Tina was alluring cleavage in a tight V-necked sweater accented by a long necklace with a single, sparkling pendant. Terri an elegant neck emphasized by a boatneck-collared blouse and pearl choker necklace. Tina was be-bop, Terri cool jazz.

"Yes, she was, wasn't she? Very nice, very sweet." Her gaze drifted off toward the side of the building for a moment, then she turned back to look at me. "You were in the police station, weren't you?"

"Yes, I was."

She seemed to look at me a little more closely, though I couldn't be sure because of the dark glasses.

"You look familiar. Do I know you?" she asked.

"Yes, well, you might remember me. Wes Byrne, I was in Tina's grade through school. We were sort of friends."

"Yeah," Terri answered with a short, sad, knowing laugh. "Apparently Tina had lots of sort-of friends." She took a longer look at me. "You know, I think I do remember you—kind of shy, quiet. You're the one who wrote those articles that sent the ones dumping waste into the Kithane River to jail, aren't you? Me and Tina used to go tubing down the Kithane—our parents took us canoeing in it too—seems like a long time ago," she said, her voice dropping off, her eyes drifting back to the flower bed.

"Well, I discovered what was going on but I didn't actually send—" I began to reply.

"Wouldn't figure you for one of Tina's sort-of friends," she said, turning her gaze back on me. "But I guess you never can tell. Seems my sister really got arou—" Terri caught herself and stopped. "Oh God, listen to me. Even when she's dead, I can't stop criticizing her. Some big sister I am."

Terri opened her purse, pulled out a handkerchief, and began to sob quietly into it. This is when a person who always does or says the right thing would sit down by her, put an arm around her in order to provide a bit a comfort and reassurance. I stood awkwardly where I was, silent.

After a few moments, she took a deep breath and composed herself. She folded up her handkerchief and put it back in her purse. "Well, it was nice to meet you—again. I appreciate your kindness. Now I best be getting on with things," she said, standing up.

She wasn't really noticing me. I needed to get her to pay attention to me.

"Um…didn't the police tell you it was me who found Tina's body?"

Her body stiffened. "*You* found her?"

"Yes, I did, but just so you know, there wasn't anything going on between me and Tina…well, not really. She was only in my hotel room because she'd returned my stolen car."

"*Your* hotel room?" Tina asked, turning toward me.

"Yes, didn't they tell you about me, or ask you any questions about Tina and my car?"

She was staring at me, a mix of confusion and anger welling in her eyes. "She died in your room? Where were you? Why weren't you there? You could have helped her— saved her?"

"Yes, I know I should have been there. I was down the ha—"

Terri suddenly laid a sharp, solid slap across the left side of my face with her right hand. "You bastard! You have the gall to stand there and act all nice when you're the one responsible. Get the hell out of my way and stay away from me."

She pushed me aside with a strength I wouldn't have suspected she had and began walking purposely away from me, toward the parking lot. Stunned momentarily, it only took me a few long strides to catch up to her. I've never been a very physical person, and surprised myself when I grabbed her by the elbow from behind with my left hand and turned her around to face me. "Please, stop, wait just a minute," I asked, realizing I was being a little too forceful considering the circumstances, but not wanting it to end this way.

"Let go of me," she screamed.

Her right hand came for my face again, but this time I was ready and stopped her blow with my left hand. I expected someone from the hospital to come charging out through the doors any minute. I had to make this fast.

"Listen. Yes, she was in my room. Yes, I should have seen how scared she was and never left her. Yes, I should have been there and maybe I could have saved her. But I didn't. I screwed up. I'll never forgive myself. I'm sorry."

I felt the tension in her body easing as her right hand fell to her side. She was still breathing heavy. I think we both were. She had needed to lash out at something, someone. I'd served the purpose. Now that she had, a weariness replaced her anger, and she sagged a bit under her grief, her chin falling to her chest. I let go of her hand.

"Why would someone do this to Tina? Why couldn't that son of a bitch have just taken her money, her jewelry, whatever he wanted and just left her alone, left her alive?" she asked, not to me particularly, but just out loud.

"I don't know. I've been trying to figure it out myself?" I answered.

She looked up at me, her head tilting slightly to the side. "I don't understand. The police said they have her killer."

"Well, I don't believe them or at least I have a few questions, some things that don't add up," I answered.

She straightened. I wished she wasn't wearing those damned glasses so that I could see her eyes, but I could sense them sizing me up irregardless.

"Why? What can you do? What does it matter? She's dead," she asked. 'Are you still working for the newspaper? Is this all about getting a story? That's all Tina is to you, a story."

"No, I'm not a repor—" I began.

"Why do you want to make trouble? The police caught the man who murdered Tina and that's all there is to it. Please just let it be at that? Isn't it enough that she's dead?"

"But don't you want to know the truth about what happened?" I answered.

"The truth? Oh, I know the truth—why she was in that hotel. The police know the truth. Everybody in this damn town probably knows the truth, but that doesn't mean I want it spread around in newspapers where my father will read all about how his daughter turned out or my kids will find out all about their Aunt Tina and her sort of friends."

"Terri, what exactly did the police tell you?"

She hesitated and her jaw jutted out ever so slightly. Her breathing grew rapid. "She was in your room, and you're asking me?"

"Terri, please. I told you Tina was only there because she returned my stolen car. She wanted me to take her out of town in the morning. She was afraid of something. What did Danny tell you?" I had to be careful. I might have been pushing too hard.

"Danny? Who's Danny?"

"The police officer you spoke to. What did he say about Tina?"

Terri took another moment or two. I knew she was trying to make up her mind about whether she believed me or not. Finally, when she answered there was an edge to her voice. "He was very nice about it. The officer, Danny, said Tina was a—a—prostitute. Anyway, he said she was at the hotel that night with one of her—clients—" I could feel her eyes accusing me, though I couldn't see them. "—but that didn't play any part in her murder. She was just in the wrong place at the wrong time. Said he'd do his best to keep that quiet, out of respect for Tina—our family—in spite of—" She stood facing me defiantly. "So I told you. Now you happy?"

"And you believed him, about Tina?"

"It explains a lot of things—her apartment, nice car, nice clothes. She was always vague about where she got the money."

"There could be other explanations," I said.

"Oh, yeah? Like what? Tina always had trouble holding

down a real job, said they were boring. Well, you knew Tina."

"Actually, no, I didn't. I've been away for several years. I only got into town yesterday," I answered. "Um, did Danny—the police officer—mention anyone named Puddy Salvatore? Does the name mean anything to you?"

"No, he didn't and it doesn't. Did you say you only got into town yesterday? I thought you worked for the newspaper."

"Well, no, I'm not anymore. This isn't about a story. It's just that…I'm really not sure, to tell you the truth."

So far, no one had come running out of the hospital after our little scene, but I felt a bit exposed, talking to her out in the open like this.

"Listen, I know this might be a lot to ask—" I began.

"But you're going to anyway, aren't you?" she demanded sharply.

I had to smile. Terri had been through a lot today. Finding out her sister was murdered, having the cops tell her she was a prostitute, dealing with a jerk like me. But she was tough. I liked her.

"I'd rather not talk here. What I would like to do, though, is get a look around Tina's apartment. Maybe there's something there that can help me get to the truth. You wouldn't happen to have a key to her place would you?" I asked.

"Yes, I do. I was going there to collect a few things our mother had left Tina—just to make sure nothing happens to them."

"Would you mind if I met you there?"

She again took a moment or two.

"You're not going to give up, are you? What exactly are you after? What do you think Tina was up to?"

"I really don't know. But I don't think what happened to her had anything to do with her being a…um…what Danny may have told you, although I have no proof. There's something else going on. And it might have to do with another old friend of mine. That's why I need your help."

"And what if what the police say is true, are you just going to make stuff up to get a story?"

"I told you, it's not about a story." I sensed a bit of softening, slight, but it was there. "Okay, listen, here's what I'll do," I said. "I still know someone at the *Chronicle*. I'll get him to let me do a nice story about Tina—the woman who was your sister, who grew up here, something nice for your father to read, if you let me look through her place. I'll see that they write that Tina was only at the hotel because she was visiting an old friend from out of town, which is really the truth."

"Nothing about the prostitution? You'll be kind to Tina?" she asked.

It was my turn to take a moment. "No, nothing about that. Just a woman who died way too early," I answered.

"Okay, then. You can come over," Terri said.

Hoppy wasn't going to be happy about me making a deal like this, and Hoppy going along with it probably meant I would definitely have to break into Stevie's place, but I didn't care. It was the least I could do for Tina.

CHAPTER 21

Walking into Tina's place reminded me of how different a single man's and a single woman's apartments can be, and it got me thinking about the contrasts between my own place and Jan's when we first started dating.

On one level, it was a matter of stuff. Scattered about Jan's place were what could be called collectibles—stuffed animals and dolls, porcelain statuettes, pretty containers for everything—and although there appeared to be a randomness to where everything was, each item seemed to be in the perfect place. The walls and shelves held framed pictures of family and friends, people smiling while on vacation or at special occasions, evidence of a life being lived. The furniture, while not expensive-looking, seemed to belong together, even if they hadn't been purchased as a set. Things matched—the colors in the throw cushions on her couch blended with the curtains that hung at the windows, and which, in turn, meshed coherently with area rugs. Her plants thrived.

My place more closely resembled a storage unit than an apartment. I'd purchased a few cheap, third-hand pieces of furniture at a Goodwill store and strategically placed them about to provide unobstructed viewing of the television. The centerpiece of the living room, besides the TV, was an old recliner with worn armrests and a somewhat temperamental lever on its right side that sometimes stuck and left the leg rest up and sticking out at a shin-bruising height for days. Personal belongings languished in cardboard boxes, long after I'd moved in, retrieved only when I needed them. The bookshelves, on which books were stacked, not lined up, were three-fourths-inch-by-eight-inch planks of cheap pine resting on cinderblocks. I'd inherited the dirty white aluminum window blinds when I moved in, and who-knows-how-many years of dust stubbornly clung to the slats? The grayish white walls were bare, except for the BankBoston calendar with photos of scenic New England landscapes and the current Red Sox or Bruins season schedules that were attached to the walls using multi-colored push pins. The only plant life was the mold and mildew that had conquered the bathroom years before I had arrived.

It was, therefore, no surprise that when Jan and I found a place and moved in together, the distribution of personal items that followed us to our new apartment was probably ninety-five percent Jan's and five percent mine, and every new thing we purchased as a couple seemed to replace those few items I had managed to hold onto—even, against my strongest objections, my old recliner.

"Oh, damn, I forgot about her cats. They're probably starving." Terri had said once we'd crossed the threshold into Tina's apartment, bringing my thoughts back to the present. We were greeted by three very loud, hungry, impa-tient, and demanding cats. "I hope she has cat food left or I'll have to run out and get some."

She went off to the kitchen, somehow not tripping over the cats who performed figure eights through her legs as she walked. Her absence allowed me the opportunity to take a private look around the place.

Tina, it seemed, liked purple, and all its various shades, and that color dominated her décor—lilac pillows on the sofa, lavender patterned drapes, the walls a light plum. There were a few thriving houseplants about the place and the room was dominated by frog collectibles. There were frog figurines, frog statuettes, blown-glass frogs, stuffed plush frogs, plastic frogs, frog candle holders, practically all things possibly frog one could imagine.

However, there was a very comfortable-looking, dark brown leather recliner in the living room and on one shelf of a bookcase, filled otherwise with more frogs, was a row of books on motorcycle repair and maintenance and others with titles like *Well Made in America: Lessons from Harley-Davidson on Being the Best* and *The Biker Code: Wisdom For The Road*. Maybe Tina liked to kick back in the recliner and read *The Harley-Davidson Data Book*, but I doubted it. These must have belonged to her husband and she hadn't been able to part with them.

I sat down on her sofa and noticed a stack of photo albums on the lower shelf of the coffee table. I grabbed them and put them out in front of me. The top album had a clean, white leather cover.

"That's Tina's wedding album," said Terri, who must have found something to feed to the cats and come back, alone, not trailed by the cats, into the living room. "She was so happy and Jimmy was the best thing that ever happened to her. He could handle her, you know?" She sat down on the sofa beside me and opened the album, revealing a close-up photo of a luminescent Tina in a one-tier wedding veil and a beaming Jimmy, his long hair and bushy mustache groomed for the occasion.

"Big guy but gentle. Treated her like a queen. I thought she finally had just what she wanted, what she needed," Terri said.

"What happened?" I asked.

"Jimmy drove a truck for Hunter Oil, you know, making heating oil deliveries to homes and it was around the holidays—their first Christmas being married—he was working long hours. I remember it was a cold winter. They were saving for a house." Terri's finger gently traced the outline of the couple's picture as she talked. "Maybe he was tired, or another car pulled into his lane. No one's really sure, but he lost control of the truck, crossed the median, and crashed into oncoming traffic. God, why do these things happen to people?"

"I don't know," I said, picturing Tina getting the phone call, here, perhaps a decorated Christmas tree in one of the corners, maybe a few wrapped presents already beneath it, frog dolls in red felt wearing white fur trimmed Santa hats scattered about.

"Tina was devastated. I thought—I thought she was going to crack, you know, really crack. She locked herself in here for almost a month, only came out for the funeral. Jimmy was buried the day after Christmas. She wouldn't return phone calls, open the door to anybody. Then one day she called me, asked me to pick up a bottle of tequila and margarita mix and come over. We took down the tree, packed the ornaments away, cried—lots of crying. She let me wash her hair, like I used to when we were kids. We sat here and got drunk and then went out to some bars and got even drunker. After that it was the same old Tina, only it wasn't, if you know what I mean."

One of the cats that had returned from the kitchen picked that moment to spring up from the floor and lightly thud down onto the open album. It leapt from the coffee table onto Terri's lap and began walking back and forth, rubbing first its left side, turning, and then the right side of its body against Terri. The cat's tail, sticking straight up and weaving like a cobra, caressed her face with each passing. She gently stroked the animal and it began to purr loudly.

I turned my attention back to the album, turning the pages past more photos of Tina and Jimmy posing alone together until I came to one of the wedding party, bridesmaids lined up to the left of Tina, groomsmen to the right of Jimmy. The women, Terri among them, wore rather ghastly lavender—of course—taffeta V-necked dresses with large puffy sleeves, a clinched middle and a stiff, cascading ruffled skirt that fanned out like a purple inverted open pine cone. The men wore powder-blue tuxedos with dark blue trim on the wide lapels and the outer pant seam, white ruffled shirts and powder-blue ties that matched the tuxes.

"Do you know all these people? Could anyone of them be Puddy Salvatore?" I asked, pointing to the picture.

Terri sat forward, holding the cat in place with her left hand while continuing to stroke its head with her right.

"Let's see. I know the bridesmaids. That's Monica Satsburg," she said, removing her hand from the cat's head and pointing to the girl on the far left and working her way toward Tina. "And that's Patti McGriff, and Lori Reynolds, and of course me. The guys I'm not too sure of, they were friends of Jimmy's. Who is this Puddy Salvatore? You mentioned him before."

"Just someone who knew Tina and who I'd like to talk to," I answered, still looking down at the wedding pictures. "Who's this guy? He looks a little scary."

I pointed to the man standing closest to Jimmy who was a good head taller than the other groomsmen, thin, with a long nose, small eyes, and a thin mouth. His long hair was pulled back in a pony-tail and a silver skull earring dangled from his left ear. Of all the people in the picture, he was the only one who wasn't smiling and, instead, was staring at the camera with a bit of a menacing look.

"That's Ricky, um, Ricky something…I can't remember his last name. He was best friends with Jimmy. They used to ride in the same motorcycle gang before Jimmy married Tina."

"Jimmy was in a bike gang?"

"Yeah. She made him drop out. She was afraid he'd get in trouble, end up in jail."

That explained the motorcycle books.

"Why'd she think that?"

"The usual biker shit—drugs—speed, I think—whores, fights. I know for a fact she wouldn't tolerate any drugs around the apartment, didn't like what it did to Jimmy. Wasn't too fond of Ricky either."

"And you don't remember his last name?"

"No, I just remember he was a real asshole, got real drunk at the wedding reception, made loud remarks about Jimmy being pussy-whipped, went around groping all the bridesmaids, even me, though my husband was right there. Didn't seem to care, seemed like he wanted a fight, though I had the feeling all the other guys there, all Jimmy's friends, were a little scared of him."

"How about these other guys, know any of them?"

"No, sorry. Like I said, they were all Jimmy's friends."

We went through the rest of album, but Terri wasn't really much help. Besides family, she really didn't know many of the other people at the wedding. She and Tina had lived pretty separate lives. I didn't see anyone who resembled the guy I saw Tina with at Stevie's service.

The other albums were filled with older photos, from Tina and Terri's childhood. Terri took a long time lingering over each page. Everyone seemed so happy. It took a while to go through them and they really didn't give me anything I thought I could use. The room had darkened and I got up and put on a light.

"Would you like a drink?" I asked. I had stopped at a liquor store on the way over and purchased a bottle of Powers whiskey.

"No, thank you. In fact, I have to be going. It's a bit of a drive back to Elmsville, and I promised my husband I'd be back in time for dinner. Looks like I'm going to be a little late."

"Do you mind if I stick around a little longer? I promise I won't take anything."

"Of course, do what you have to do, if you think it will help. Actually, I've got a favor to ask you."

"Well, I guess I do owe you. I know this wasn't easy. Want me to carry some boxes out to the car for you?"

"No, I was hoping you'd stay here and watch the cats."

It was probably my imagination, but I could swear the cat on her lap gave me a rather chilling Oh-this-is-going-to-be-fun look.

"Um, well, actually, I've got a motel room that I paid for through the week, and, um…that's where anyone who wants to talk to me knows where to find me."

It was a lie of course, and after all she'd done, allowing me access to Tina's things when she didn't know me from Adam, it was a pretty low one. However, the thought of being holed up with three cats, two of which I hadn't seen since we walked in and who were probably already plotting the mayhem they'd wreak the moment Terri walked out the door, sort of filled me with dread.

"Please. I'd take them with me but my youngest is allergic and I've got to figure out where I can find a home for them. I know Tina wouldn't want me to just drop them off at the SPCA."

"Terri, I'm not real good with animals—"

Terri straightened up and gave me a cold look. "Oh, I get it. I'm supposed to let you poke around into Tina's life, trust that you won't just dig up whatever dirt you can find it, and then put it all out there for the whole world to read about, but I ask you one little favor—"

"I do appreciate the offer, really, but me and cats…Isn't there someone else?"

She must have sensed that I was weakening. Her eyes warmed a bit and she leaned forward, gently laying her right hand on my left knee. "They're really very sweet and all you have to do is feed them."

I could see resistance was futile and raised my right hand in surrender. "Okay, if you show me where the food is and—"

"—and maybe clean out their litter box once or twice."

"Once or twice? How long do you think finding places for them is going to take?"

"Not long. I have some friends who love cats. I'm sure one or two of them will take them in."

"One day? Two?" I asked, optimistically.

"No more than three, for sure. But Tina's cable and all the utilities are probably paid up through the end of the month, and there are some frozen meals in the freezer that you can microwave, so it shouldn't be too bad. Besides, you can save the money you'd be paying at the motel."

Well, payback can be a bitch. I'd asked a lot of Terri. How bad could it be? She took my silence for a yes.

"Great," she said, lifting the cat and placing it on the sofa between us as she stood up. "Let me just grab a few things from Tina's room, and if you don't mind maybe you could help me carry some things to my car."

She headed off toward and through a door into what I guess was Tina's bedroom. As I watched her go, the cat walked over to me and stood on my lap.

I ran my hand across the cat's back.

"Well, it looks like we're going to be sharing a little time together," I said.

In response, the cat looked up at me, turned, and raised its ass toward my face. We were off to a great start.

CHAPTER 22

It was one thing to be alone in a woman's apartment, a new experience for me, but it was another to be going through her drawers—in both senses of the word—in her bedroom dresser and night table. The two Powers on the rocks I worked through after Terri left helped fortify my courage.

However, if Jan was anyone to go by, I knew the bedroom was where a woman's most private things would be found. After she'd died and I was cleaning out her things in our apartment before fleeing Boston, I found all sorts of items that Jan had tucked away—jewelry passed down from her mother that were not Jan's style and that she would have never worn, but kept nonetheless; a champagne cork with the date written on it from the bottle we shared to celebrate our first anniversary of dating; and silly and rather terrible poems I'd written her. There were letters from previous boyfriends, bound together with ribbon, which I did not read, out of a sense of respect for her privacy. There was her diary, which I did open and read, because, private or not, I hoped that through her words I would, in a way, hear her voice again.

I'd already searched through the living room and kitchen, opening every book and magazine, in the hopes of finding some scrap of paper that might reveal something about what she had been up to and making the search of the bedroom unnecessary. I discovered nothing in those rooms. So now I was, rummaging through T-shirts and summer shorts and panty and bras. I couldn't help feeling like a bit of a pervert rummaging through Tina's most intimate apparel and would have been horrified if someone walked in on me.

Tina had left photos of her and Jimmy on her dresser top. Maybe she intended to for us to pick them up the next morning when we came for the cats. That gave me hope that perhaps she left something incriminating behind as well, but I was running out of places to look.

A closed laptop computer sat on a dark brown laminated wood corner desk with a single drawer. Perhaps that held some secrets. I walked over and pulled out the red upholstered task chair that rolled along the hardwood floor on its casters from beneath the desk. As I went to sit down and had lowered about halfway to the seat, it became readily apparent that Tina's chair was adjusted too low for me. Gravity, and perhaps the Powers, took over before I reached the seat and I inelegantly plopped down awkwardly into the chair, sending it and me rolling back across the hardwood floor. I reached out instinctively to the desk for support, but managed only to grab the drawer pull of the center drawer. It effortlessly slid open and then out, off its runners, throwing my equilibrium completely off. I fell backward, still in the chair but with my feet shooting up into the air as I tossed contents of the drawer over my head. I landed on my back, my head smacking against the floor. Paper clips, a stapler, and assorted pens flew through the air and rained down on the floor beyond me. Then all was quiet, except for the sound of one of the chair's caster spinning slower and slower until it stopped.

It's funny how lying on one's back, still in a seated position but with ass and thighs perpendicular to the floor, lower legs draped over the end of the seat cushion, arms outstretched and gripping an empty desk drawer, in a dead girl's apartment can make a person take stock of things. What the hell was I doing? What the hell did I really hope to find? And what the hell would I do with anything I did happen to find? Most importantly, how did I let myself start believing that anything I did would make one iota of difference? Damn Stevie, damn Hoppy, and damn Tina. It was time for another Powers.

I let go of the desk drawer, rolled over to my left off the chair and onto my hands and knees. Nothing seemed too bruised, except my ego, although some aches and pains would probably show up in the morning. Surveying the wreckage of pens and paper clips on the floor, I decided to let everything lie where they had landed and stood up slowly, a little woozy at first, but that passed. Turning to leave the room, I remembered the computer and went back to pick it up, disconnecting the power cord, before leaving the room.

I was done in here. Unfortunately, it wasn't the first time I'd struck out in a women's bedroom.

CHAPTER 23

The room was dark and, in the first few seconds after I awoke, there was a little panic as I tried to remember exactly where I was. It slowly all began to come back to me—sitting in the recliner in the living room and trying to look through Tina's laptop for information—unsuccessfully because I couldn't determine any way to decrypt her passwords. Pouring another drink—or was it two? Reclining the chair in order to ponder the situation I found myself in. I couldn't remember exactly what time I turned off the light or drifted off to sleep. Now I had no idea how long I'd slept or what hour it was.

Then I heard something. It was coming from Tina's room. It couldn't be the cats. Cats didn't make noises like that. Turning my head slowly I could see, through the open bedroom door, the beam of a flashlight darting around the room. It couldn't be Terri. She wouldn't be sneaking around Tina's place in the middle of the night. Whoever it was, they were looking for something. I heard the sound of dresser drawers opening and closing. I heard quiet cursing. It was a man. Apparently, he was having no better luck than I had.

I couldn't move. Not due to fear, although I can't deny that my heart was racing a bit, but because there was no way to quietly or easily get out of the recliner. If I let the chair down, the footrest would make that "whompf" noise that footrests always make when they return to nest against the bottom of the chair. Whoever it was in the other room would be sure to hear it. I didn't know if he had a weapon, but the way my luck seemed to be running lately, I didn't want to take that risk.

I couldn't turn and roll off the recliner. On one side was the wall that separated the living room from the kitchen and on the other was a floor lamp with a built-in table that held my empty glass and the two-thirds full bottle of Powers.

I picked up the bottle by the neck and patted its body against the palm of my free hand. I hated the thought of using something so dear as weapon, but desperate times called for desperate measures. It wouldn't stand much chance against a gun, but if I used the element of surprise, and, when the intruder entered the living room, I could accurately throw it and plunk him just right in the head, then maybe I could spring from the chair, overpower, disarm, and wrestle him to the floor before he knew what hit him.

Or maybe, since it wasn't easy to throw a bottle while in a reclined position, I'd just graze or miss the intruder completely. He would put a bullet or two in my chest before I could get out of the chair and someone would find me sometime the next day dead as a doornail and being picked over by hungry cats. I needed another plan.

There couldn't be much time to come up with one, only so many places in Tina's room for the intruder to search. Soon he would be in the living room, and while I was lucky he didn't see me when he broke into the apartment, chances are a six-foot-three-inch body in a chair would be hard to overlook a second time. I needed to think. I turned the bottle upright, silently screwed off the cap, and took a deep swig. My eyes had adjusted a bit to the darkness and as I took my swallow from the bottle I saw my only chance.

It was about thirty feet from the chair to the door that opened into the hallway and the path was unimpeded. I could probably cover the distance in a few good strides, and if the door was unlocked—and what kind of intruder locks a door behind them?—be through it, and in the hallway, knocking on a neighbor's door in just a few seconds. Hell, add in the fear factor and I could probably move even faster and might run right through the damn door, open or not. It could work, and besides, I really didn't have any other options.

I screwed the cap back on the bottle and once more grabbed it by the neck. It might still prove useful. I slowly and ever so quietly began to gently rock my body forward and back as I reached down to grab the lever for the footrest. Timing was everything. I could use the motion of the recliner returning upright to gain a bit of propulsion toward the door. I counted to myself as I rocked. One. Two. *Three.*

It was an amazing display of physics at work. My left foot hit the floor just as the footrest "whompfed," and I was hurtling forward, pushing off the armrests, propelled by the back of the chair forward, and it seemed I covered half the distance to the door before my right foot landed after a long stride. I turned my head and saw the light from the flashlight spin and project through the open bedroom door. He had heard me, but there was no way the intruder could get to me before I got to the door.

What I didn't see was that one of the cats, for a reason only other cats would probably understand, chose that moment to come out from wherever it had been hiding to walk across my path to the door. The animal managed to find the perfect tripping point—its head behind my alighted right foot, its ass-end in front of my forward moving left foot— so when my feet drew parallel they became entangled with the cat's body. There was a blood-curdling screech—I think it was the cat, though it might have come from me—as I tumbled forward, arms swimming through the air, landing hard and yet somehow managing to turn my body just enough so that it was my left shoulder that took the brunt of the fall. The side of my head then slapped against the carpet and an explosion of purple, a super-brilliant deep violet flash bulb going off, fireballed behind my eyes. A momentary feeling of nausea came and went as the bright light

seemed to implode, sucking smaller into itself, until it disappeared.

I felt the furry finger of a cat's tail wipe across my face
and then all went dark.

CHAPTER 24

ho the hell are you?"

It was a man's voice, a bit on the high side with a very slight southern tinge to it that was common for some of the locals of East Hastings, a result of living so close to the Maryland border.

A flashlight beam pointed down at me. I was lying face down on the carpet and turning my head slightly I could make out a pair of old, scuffed up Timberland work boots with the bottom of pant legs bunched up on the top of each in the outer radiance light beam. They were solid boots, as I discovered when the intruder delivered a swift kick into my ribs.

"I said who the hell are you?"

If there was one thing experience had taught me, considering the way people often feel about journalists, it's that discretion is often the best course of action. Some might call it lying.

I struggled to get a breath. "I'm a friend of Terri, Tina's sister. She asked me to watch the cats. Her sister was killed. Who—who are you?"

Another swift kick. "I'll ask the questions."

He was getting better with practice. The second one hurt a lot more than the first. I sucked in as much air as I could, but it was painful.

"Right, right, none of my business. If you're here to rob the place, take anything you want. I won't say a word. Terri was probably going to give everything away to Goodwill anyway. Save her the hassle of carting it out. Hell, I'll even help you carry the big stuff to your car if you only stop kicking me."

He took a few moments and thought things over.

"All right. Roll over and sit up. But don't try anything or I'll kick your teeth in. And let go of the bottle."

I hadn't realized it was still in my hand. Was it a metaphor for my life, lying flat on my face, battered and surely bruised, and yet keeping a firm grasp on a bottle of whiskey? My head hurt enough as it was, so this was not the time for deep contemplation. Maybe later, if I got through this alive, I'd pour myself a glass of Powers and search for profound meanings. Right now, I'd just do as I was told.

I released my grip on the bottle, rolled onto my back, and, with a slight groan, pushed myself into a sitting position. He moved from my side to stand directly in front of me, keeping the flashlight trained on my face. The bright light shining directly into my eyes caused my head to throb. I still couldn't make out any of the features of the figure standing before me because of the light in my eyes, but from the height of where the beam was coming from, I could tell the intruder was not a very tall man.

"Why are you lyin' to me," he asked. "Now that I've got a look I can see who you are. You're that damned reporter whose car me and Tina stole. She pointed you out to me at Stevie's funeral. You're the reason she's dead."

So, Puddy Salvatore was the intruder. He must have been the bald guy sitting with Tina in the pew at the church.

"Listen, I had nothing to do with Tina's death. I wasn't even there when it happened."

"Yeah, well you might just as well as stuck the knife in her—stupid bitch, stealing the car back. She had to have known they'd come after her. And now they're going to come after me."

"So you didn't kill her?"

"Kill her? Why would I want to kill her? I—I loved her,

man. I would've protected her—from them—from you."

"From me? Look Puddy—and you are Puddy Salvatore, right? Well, Puddy, I had no idea what was going on. Hell, I still don't," I answered. "All I know is that Tina brought my car back and wanted me to drive her out of town in the morning. She had a bottle of vodka. I went to get something to mix with it, and when I came back, she was—she was lying dead on my bed. Next thing I know I'm in an interrogation room and the police are asking me about you.

"Asking about me? Ah, shit."

"Sure. You called her cell phone that night—at the hotel—and I answered it. They think we're in it together."

"So I called her, so what? That proves I didn't kill her. I was nowhere near that damn hotel."

I kind of remembered covering a hostage situation in Boston and the police telling me that in circumstances like that they were trained to get the hostage-taker talking, try to make a personal connection somehow. I decided to give it a try.

"You know, that's what I told them, but the police, they're always ready to jump to conclusions. Anybody who knows you would probably tell them you're not a killer."

"That's right. They can ask anybody. I mighta gotten in a fight every now and then—who doesn't?—I mean people always making fun of me cause I'm short, and I mighta had to stick a person every now and then, but only if they pulled a blade first. But I'd never really try to kill somebody, especially a girl, especially Tina."

"Yeah, sure. That's what I said—that they're looking for the wrong guy—hey, you wouldn't mind if I sat up on the couch would you and we put a light on? It's not very comfortable here on the floor and my head's screaming what with that flashlight glaring in my eyes."

"Well, I dunno…"

"Please. I promise not to try anything. I mean I know better than to mess with you."

"All right, but if you make one move I'm gonna stick

you," he answered, holding a knife—another guy with a knife—up right before my eyes so I could get a good look at it.

"Thanks," I answered, moving very, very slowly, rolling over onto my hands and knees, crawling over to and around the coffee table and then pulling myself up to sit on the couch. Not very dignified, but in the whole scheme of things I'd take being alive over dignity any day.

I held out my hands, palms up, then reached over with my left hand, and switched on the floor lamp. The room filled with light.

Puddy Salvatore stood before me. He was short, maybe five foot three or four, and chubby. I was a little surprised because I thought he'd be taller based on seeing him from behind sitting in the pew next to Tina at Stevie's service. Then again, short people do have a way of sitting tall, whereas someone tall, like me, tends to slouch a bit when they sit. His head was large and round, and seemed to just rest on his shoulders, as if its weight had gradually driven his neck down between his collarbones. He had on blue jean overalls and a red T-shirt.

"Thanks, that's better, and you know you really don't need that thing," I said, nodding toward the knife in his hand.

A slight smile creased his stubbly bearded face and he turned the weapon over in his hand. "I kinda like the way it feels, if it's all the same to you. You ever been stabbed?" he asked, his smile growing bigger so that I could see his small, yellowy teeth.

"No, can't say that I have," I answered.

Puddy didn't seem to hear my answer or even care to. He was looking at his knife. "Goes into the body like a hot knife through butter, just schhhhh—easy peasy. Person being stabbed doesn't seem to know what's hit 'em till the blade's been pulled out, and they feel their warm blood coming out of 'em."

This wasn't going quite the way I hoped. I tried to remember if the Boston police had actually saved that hostage back then. It seemed a good time to try something different.

"And you're going to let whoever did that to Tina get away with it? I thought you said you loved her."

His head snapped up from his knife and he glared at me. "What are you talking about?" he asked, taking a step closer.

"You said 'Tina should've known they'd come after her.' You know who killed her, don't you?"

"I...um...I—I'm sure as hell not going to tell you. Or anybody," Puddy answered. "Even if I did know, which I don't," he added unconvincingly. "Not that I'm afraid or give a damn about any of them. Just that I'm not a rat. You can put that in your newspaper—Puddy Salvatore is not a rat!" He punctuated his point by stabbing out with his knife, holding it menacingly about a foot from my face, the blade glinting in the light.

"Sure, right. Whatever you say, Puddy—big type, right there in the headline, right where everyone can see it. 'Puddy Salvatore is Not A Rat.'"

"You makin' fun of me?" Puddy asked, moving a step closer, the knife still held out.

"No, Puddy. No way. It's just that I'm a little wobbly here from hitting my head and I'm having trouble concentrating, but I want you to know I'm on your side. We both want the same thing, right? To see that whoever killed Tina gets caught."

"How do you know what I want? Want me to tell you what I want? I want you to shut the hell up, that's what I want. I want to get out of this town and as far away as possible alive, that's what I want."

He paused for a moment. He'd gotten himself all worked up, his breathing hard and one vein visibly pulsing on the side of his forehead. Puddy looked around the room, his eyes resting on a collection of empty boxes Terri had brought to fill up with Tina's stuff left and left behind. He sidled over to the boxes, keeping the knife raised and his eyes on me. He quickly glanced into the boxes and then back up at me. That shitty smile returned to his face.

"And you know what else I want? I want you to give me all the money you got on you. How about that?" He walked back over toward me, keeping the dining room table between us and reached out his non-knife bearing hand. "Big-time reporter like you must be loaded. Nice and easy now, give me your wallet."

"I hope you're not going to be upset if it's not as much as you think," I answered, leaning forward and lifting my butt as I reached for my wallet with my right hand. I began to slide it out of my pocket when, I guess still a bit woozy from the earlier fall, I lost my balance and started falling face first toward the table top. I reached out my left hand just in time to prevent smashing my face into the table. Puddy jumped back as I did so, and when I looked up at him I could see the slightest trace of fear in his eyes before he regained his tough guy composure. He was not a killer.

"Here, take it," I said, sitting back up and handing him my wallet. "But just tell me why, if you're getting out of here, you won't give me the name of Tina's killer so I can tell the police. It's the least you can do. I won't say where I got the information."

Puddy took my wallet and looked down at me like I was a complete idiot.

"Tell the police? They're the last people who want to find Tina's killer. You sure don't know how things work around here, do you?" He took a step back to create more space between us and, holding my wallet in his left hand and without letting go of the knife that was in his right hand, used the thumb of his right hand to open the billfold. The disappointment on his face was immediate, and I was actually embarrassed that all the money I had left in the world was such a downer for Puddy Salvatore.

"This it?" he said, pulling the bills out of my wallet and holding them up. "Shit, you're worse off than I am." He stuffed the bills into his right breast overall pocket and then looked back down at my wallet. "At least there's a couple credit cards."

"Sorry, but—um—they're pretty much maxed out," I said sheepishly.

Puddy fired the wallet at me with a flick of his wrist, and it hit me in the chest with a slap.

"I shoulda known from that cheap piece of crap you drive. Ya know, that had to be one of the shittiest cars I've ever stolen, even if the parts are worth somethin'. Man, I don't know how you drove that thing around."

"It has...well, sentimental value."

"Sentimental value? What a bunch of crap. The way Tina talked about you, she made it sound like you were some great reporter, that you were going to find us out, expose the whole operation, but you ain't nothing but a loser, a big goddamned loser." The vein on his head began to bulge and pulse again. "That car fits you perfectly...and because of you, Tina's dead and I have to leave my mother and all my friends...goddamn it..."

He reached down and grabbed the underside of one end of the coffee table with his left hand and with one violent motion lifted and threw the table from between us. He stepped closer to me, his breathing shorter and heaving. Maybe I'd misjudged him. Maybe he was a killer.

"Lie flat down on the floor on your stomach. Now!" he commanded. I dove onto my knees and then flat out in one swift motion. "Put your hands behind your back!"

I did as I was told but turned my head to watch him walk over to the empty boxes. At least I thought they were empty. He reached in to the top one and pulled out a roll of silver duct tape. Terri must have packed it to tape the boxes shut after she'd filled them.

He walked over and straddled me. I couldn't see him anymore, but I heard the sound of a strip of duct tape being pulled from the roll.

"Ya know, you're more than a loser," he began, pulling my wrists together and my arms up and away from my body. I could feel the flat edge of the knife blade against my forearm, so I knew he still had the knife in his right hand. "You're a goddamned coward. Most men would've put up some kind of struggle here, maybe tried to get the knife away from me, but not you." He jerked my arms higher and viciously began wrapping the tape around my wrists. "I bet you wouldn't have tried to stop Bones even if you were there." He tore the tape and dropped my tightly bound wrists.

"Who's Bones?" I asked.

"Shut up," he said, giving me another swift kick. "Put your feet together," he ordered and I did so. He was working quickly. Again, the sound of duct tape being stripped from the roll, then my feet being pulled up and the tape wound around them like I was a calf getting tied at a rodeo.

"What was it Tina said they called you in school? 'Wus' instead of 'Wes' because you never fought back when guys picked on you?"

He pulled my bound feet toward my head, bending my knees. Once more the zzzzzzipppppp of the duct tape and this time I could feel him wrapping it between the tape at my ankles and up through the tape at my wrists, so that my shoulders and knees rose off the floor and I balanced on my chest and stomach.

I strained to answer. "Listen, Puddy," I said. "I would have done anything possible to save Tina. If I'd known someone—Bones—was coming for her I never would have—"

That's all I got out before Puddy grabbed my hair, lifted my head, and slapped, then tightly pressed, a piece of duct tape across my mouth. Still holding my hair, he bent down to look me in the eyes. He brought his face close to mine. His breath was putrid.

"I know I'll never see you again, but if I do, you better believe I'll kill you. 'Course if you keep poking around, someone else will do it first."

He walked over and turned out the lamp. The room was

dark for a moment before he turned on his flashlight and turned to leave the room. Before he did though, he left me one parting gift—another hard kick to the ribs.

"That's for Tina," he said. Then he walked out the door.

CHAPTER 25

You're telling us you are going to break into Stevie's place, even though the police have warned you off the case, there's one, maybe two people out there who've shown they have no problem sticking a knife into someone who pisses them off, and there's a guy running around who has already given you a good beating and promised to kill you next time he sees you. You know, Wes, you're an old friend, and it's great that you have some Boy Scout kinda ideal about seeing justice done, but…well, you're fricking crazy!"

I was sitting in the kitchen of Tim's house. Denny, Bob, and Dom were there too. Seems they'd all decided a little intervention on my behalf was warranted based on the stories going around town about me. Ellen had taken the kids off to their various day camps and left us men alone, but not before shooting me a glance that made it perfectly clear where she stood in terms of my recent activities.

"I mean, look at you," Denny continued, who seemed to be leading the program. "You've got a huge bruise on your forehead and every time you shift in the chair you grimace from the pain. When Tim picked you up at the station, the desk sergeant told him what that guy…what's his name, Puddy?…did to you. You can't tell me any of this is worth…well, whatever you think it's worth."

I needed Tim to pick me up at the police station because that's where I'd been taken when the police found me at

Tina's place. An old lady neighbor discovered the cats running about in the hallway at some point in the morning. She investigated, came upon Tina's open door, saw me, and called the cops. They, in turn, apparently believed that I had broken into the place just so I could somehow bind myself in duct tape and lie on the floor to conduct some sadomasochistic exercise to determine which of the muscles in my knees, hips, lower back, and shoulders could endure the highest level of agony. They arrested me for breaking and entering and threw me in a jail cell while they tried to get hold of Terri to corroborate my story. I was actually just drifting off into the most delightful sleep on my cot in the holding cell when an officer opened the door, poked me in my bruised side, and told me I was free to go.

Go how was unclear, since my car was back at Tina's. Or where, for that matter, because upon my release I was told that her apartment was, for the time being, a crime scene and I'd called the Evergreen to cancel my room when I'd thought I'd be spending a few days at Tina's place.

So I thought of Tim. It was his phone call, after all, that got me started in this mess. I figured he owed me.

"It's not what it's worth to me that matters right now, it's what it's worth to Hoppy," I answered. "Puddy took all my money so I'm flat broke and getting him a story or two is the only way I can replenish my bankroll, meager as it was."

"If it's a matter of money, I'm sure we can help you out," Denny said.

"No thanks. I appreciate your offer but I plan to get out of this town very soon and, when I do, it's going to be a clean break. I don't want to owe anybody anything. I want to completely forget I ever came here. You know, I really don't know how you guys can stand living in a place like this."

I probably shouldn't have said that last bit, but I was sore and tired and was feeling a little ganged up on. I touched a nerve.

"You know," Tim answered, "if you didn't spend so much time behind bars at the police station, maybe you'd see that it's really not that bad a place." His voice began to rise. "Sure, it may not be the big city, but I like it here, like raising a family here. So I'll tell you what—" He got up and left the room for a moment, returning with a check book he must have pulled out of a drawer in another room. "I'll give you whatever money you need with no strings attached, nothing. And when you end up in Wonderland or Oz or wherever the hell perfect place you think you're gonna find, you can use this to buy as much whiskey as you need and forget all about Stevie and Tina and East Hastings. Go do whatever big shots like you do and leave us little people to live our lives—"

"Hey, Tim, come on," Dom broke in. "You can't blame Wes for being a little…er…cranky. You have to admit it hasn't been the best of times for him since he's been back, and…um…we're sorta responsible. We asked him to poke around."

"No, Dom, I think Tim is right." It was Bob's turn to weigh in. "In fact, I think it's for Wes's own good that he leaves town. I mean, why should he care? He hasn't lived here for years, he didn't know the Stevie or for that matter the Tina that we did."

I noticed the others looked at Bob in puzzlement when he mentioned Tina.

Bob noticed too. "Um, you know, we all heard the stories, didn't we? She wasn't exactly Snow White. At least that was the word around town. Anyway, Wes came down for Stevie's funeral. That's over. He's got a life to get back to…or a new one to start…whatever it is. It has nothing to do with East Hastings, I'm sure." Bob leaned his ample torso forward and, with a bit of a grunt, reached around and pulled his wallet out of his back pocket. He opened the fold and slid out several bills. "I say we all chip in what we can, and Wes—" He turned to me holding out his money. "You get settled. If you land on your feet, you pay me back, if not, no big deal. It was great just seeing you again."

I looked at Bob's outstretched hand, and at Tim poised with pen and checkbook in hand, then over to Denny and Dom. "I don't get it," I said. "Just the other day, you guys are telling me that you know things are corrupt in this town, how a few people might have the police and who knows who else in their back pockets. You even suggested that Stevie was killed because of something he found out about these people and they were actually covering up his death. Then I find a dead woman in my bed, get threatened by the cops, almost have my teeth bashed in, and I'm the problem here? That I should go away and things will all be better?"

"No, Wes, it's not like that all," Dom answered. "Part of it is...well, you know, it's one thing if we say the town's dirty, it's another to hear someone else tell you that. And you know, like Tim said it really ain't that bad a place. The schools are good, there ain't a lot of crime, at least there wasn't until you rolled into town." He smiled, breaking the tension in the room a bit. "And finally, well, look at you. We didn't expect all this crap to happen. We really have no right to ask you to continue doing this."

I leaned back in my chair, slowly, the pain becoming a little more bearable, though I was beginning to stiffen up a bit, adding a new dimension to my discomfort. "Okay, I'm sorry about that crack about the town. Tim, you wouldn't happen to have anything strong to drink about the place, would you. I'd prefer whiskey, but I won't be choosy."

"I'll see what we got," Tim said, laying the checkbook on the table and turning to leave the kitchen.

"Damn, Wes, it ain't even twelve yet," Bob interjected as he laid his wallet and the money on the table.

"It is somewhere in the world," I answered. "And a few dozen aspirin, if you got them," I said to Tim, then smiling at Bob before changing my request. "Actually just two would be fine."

"You know, Wes, we've been so busy telling you what

we think you should do, we haven't asked you what you want to do," Denny said.

Tim came back into the room carrying a bottle of Knob Creek Bourbon. Good whiskey, and I had to admit I was impressed. "Someone gave me this as a Christmas present once," he said, putting the bottle on the table in front of me, along with two Aleve capsules. He returned to his seat.

I looked at the bottle and the pills on the table. "Well, I know you guys think I've got a problem but it hasn't reached the point where I just drink out of the bottle," I said.

"Oh, right," Tim said sheepishly.

Dom, Denny, and Bob laughed. It seemed we'd passed the point of unease between us. Tim got up and went over to a kitchen cabinet, opened the door and pulled out an old fashioned glass and held it up for my approval. I nodded.

"Anybody else?" Tim asked, I think, out of habit because he really didn't expect anyone to join me. Dom and Bob shook their heads no.

"Why not?" Denny answered, to the apparent surprise of the others. "Bad manners to let a man drink alone, or so I've been told."

Tim took a second glass out of the cabinet, came over to the table, and sat them in front of me and Denny. "Want ice?"

I shook my head no and Denny did the same.

I opened the bottle and leaned forward to pour the whiskey into Denny's glass.

"Not too much there. It's just a social snort," he said.

I poured about a pinky finger's worth into his glass, then a good middle finger's worth, or three, into my own.

I raised the glass to Denny. "Sláinte," I toasted and we tapped glasses and each took a swallow, mine a wee bit deeper than Denny's so I could swallow the Aleve I had popped into my mouth before raising the glass to my lips.

I sat back, closed my eyes for a moment, and felt the warmth of the bourbon begin to comfort my aches and pains. It was a good start. I estimated I had taken at least a three drink beating from Puddy.

I heard Denny let out a short, quiet cough in reaction to the strength of the whiskey. I opened my eyes and saw that he was holding his glass up in front of his eyes, examining the liquid.

"That's a…well, that's very potent," he said, smiling over at me.

It was probably years since he had drunk anything stronger than a beer and even longer since he had anything to drink before the cocktail hour. He did it now just for me. He was a prince.

In fact, all four of my old friends were good guys. Besides a few bartenders, I hadn't been around anyone I could really consider a friend in a long time. It felt nice being here with them.

"So anyway," Denny started, "you haven't answered my question. What is it you really want to do?"

I took a small sip from the whiskey, put the glass on the table, and shifted slightly in my chair. The pain was definitely lessening. "You know, I haven't really thought about it too much. I did promise Tina's sister the *Chronicle* would print a nice story about Tina—if I can convince Hoppy. I owe her that, and I owe Hoppy for the attorney and other stuff, and I do need some money."

"You know, I just don't get this whole thing," Bob said, a tone of exasperation to his voice. "Sounds to me like you're just trying to stir things up, maybe settle some old scores. I mean, what happens if you find out things that shouldn't maybe be brought out into the sunlight, or what if it ends up hurting someone who is completely innocent?"

"You mean, Sue Ellen?" I asked, knowing the answer.

"Sue Ellen, Tina's sister, anybody who stands in the way of you getting your story," Bob continued. "You do remember what happened before, what happened to old man DiCarlo? There was no proof he had anything to do with that company dumping the chemicals into the river. As far as he knew they were legit. He just paid them to cart it away from the dry-cleaning business. Hell, he was barely involved with running the damned business on a day to day basis by that time. But your story comes out and there it is—front page news—and even if he wasn't he felt guilty, felt he betrayed the town, all the people who swam and canoed in and lived along the river—"

"C'mon, Bob," Denny broke in. "Wes never claimed that old man Augustino had anything to do with what was going on. His story was about the company that was dumping that crap in the river. They were the guilty ones. And it wasn't just chemicals from the dry cleaning business. They were dumping fuel oil, chemicals from the paper plant, treating the river like their own private toilet."

"Yeah, well, I'm not talking about the bad guys. I'm talking about the innocent ones. I liked the old man. He sponsored my little league team when I was a kid, gave me my first job when I was in high school. Lots of people liked him. And it wasn't five days after Wes broke that story that Mr. Augustino had his stroke, and not a month later that he was dead."

"So you're saying that Wes should have kept quiet, and we all should've kept swimming and fishing in that poison until some other innocent people, kids, got really sick or maybe even died."

"No, what I'm saying is that Wes should think deeply about the repercussions of what's going to happen. Let's be honest with ourselves here. We all know who Wes is really after—the ones he is going to piss off," he said.

"I'm not after anyone. And I'm not even going to write a damn story about anyone other than Tina. Hoppy wants me to look around Stevie's place, that's it, that's all I promised him I would do. There's no ulterior motive," I answered.

"Oh, c'mon, Wes. Don't try to kid us. It's not that I blame you, they gave you a pretty rough time growing up, but many of them now are, for better or worse, our leading citizens. Things like murders have a way of clinging to a town's reputation. People don't want to move to, bring their kids up, in a town with that kind of stigma attached to it."

"So you're saying if our 'leading citizens' are involved in murder, they shouldn't be held accountable because it's bad for the town's perception?" Denny asked. "That just sounds wrong in my estimation."

"See, see? This is what I mean," Bob said, looking at me while pointing at Denny. "A fricking drug dealer and a prostitute get murdered and right away people start assuming the worst about the best people in this town without one iota of proof. Admit it, okay, you hate Danny because he used to mess with you in school so you're going to smear the police for not catching Stevie's killer. You hate Tony and you're going to smear him because he used to sleep with Tina while he was married to Sue Ellen—"

"Wait," Tim interrupted. "Tony used to sleep with Tina? How do you know that?"

"What?" Bob answered, obviously flustered. "Why— why—why, that whore slept with everyone who had the money to pay for it. Besides, that was years ago—from what I heard," he said, trying his best to recover.

The room grew quiet. I wasn't sure if everyone was talked out or it was the break between rounds. I noticed that my glass was empty, leaned in, opened the bourbon bottle, and poured myself a second drink. I offered to pour another for Denny. He held his right hand over his glass and shook his head. I took a deep sip from my glass then took a deep breath.

"Bob, I understand what you're saying but...well, I don't see how I have a choice," I said.

"Of course you have a choice," Bob answered. "There's always a choice. You just haven't changed one bit."

"C'mon, Bob, that's not fair. He's only trying to do the right thing," Denny said.

"Right, right, sure," Bob said. He picked his money off the table and put it back in his wallet. "Well, don't say I didn't try to help." He got up and put his wallet back in his pocket. "You guys are too much, letting him do this. I thought I just heard you say how much you like this town." He looked hard at each of them. "I'm out of here," he said, turning quickly—at least quickly for Bob—through the doorway into the kitchen.

"Bob, it's not that I don't appreciate what you're trying to do," I said after him, but I don't think he heard me as he slammed the kitchen door to the outside shut behind him.

The other three sat quietly for a moment, sharing culpable looks between them. Finally, Dom looked at me reassuringly. "It's okay, Wes. I understand. You're just doing what any cracker pot reporter would do," he said.

"That's cracker jack," Denny said.

"What's being a reporter got to do with cracker jack?" Dom asked.

"Nothing," Denny said. "Never mind."

"Actually, I think Dom has it right. Cracker pot reporter sounds just about right," I answered, smiling at Dom. I stared down at my drink for a moment. "Let me ask you guys something? Do you think I'm a coward?"

My question caught them all a little off balance, and I could see the hesitation between them, the quick glances at each other, each not wanting to answer first. Denny finished his bourbon in one quick motion.

"Why…um…what brought that up?" he asked.

I sensed he was stalling. They all were.

"Something Puddy Salvatore said," I answered.

"Oh, c'mon, you're not going to let what some little thug said bother you. He was probably just taunting you…just, um, what do they call it…talking trash," Tim said.

"That's not an answer," I replied. "Tell me the truth, guys. I really want to know what you all think. It's important."

Dom stepped into the breach. "Well, um, I can't speak for the other guys, but, um, well, there were times when maybe you could have been a little more, um, insertive—" he said.

"Assertive," Denny said.

"—I mean, the way those guys used to treat you in high school," Dom continued through Denny's interruption. "Danny, Randy Smith, Glen Poppy, Tony—well, they always seemed to be ganging up on you and there wasn't much you could do—but maybe if just once—"

"I actually always thought I should have done more to help you," Tim broke in, shooting Dom a quick hard glance. "I mean, I don't know why they always picked on you, and maybe I was glad it was you and not me."

"Yeah," Denny added, "there was nothing you could have done. They were just a bunch of jerks, just had it in for you for some reason."

"Yeah, right. That's what I always told myself. But what about Tina. What would I have done if I was in the room when the killer was there. I mean, I let Puddy Salvatore wrap me up like a Christmas present and beat the shit out of me and the little pecker was only half my size."

"That little pecker had a knife," Denny said.

"Yeah, and so did Tina's killer. Would I have just lain down on the floor and let him stab her while I watched?" I asked.

"Well, truth be told, we really can't answer that question, can we?" Tim replied.

He got up, went over to the cupboard, pulled out a glass, and came back to the table. He opened the bourbon bottle and poured himself a drink, poured a little more into mine.

"I'd like to think you would have done everything in your power to stop him. And I think…well, I think regardless there's different types of bravery." He stopped and took a drink from his glass. "I heard what Bob had to say, and, in some ways, I agree with him. But if you're determined to break into Stevie's place tonight anyway—" He took another sip of his drink. "—well, I think I'm going with you."

CHAPTER 26

"Are you sure we couldn't have done this in the day-time?"

Tim was whispering. Not so much because he had to, but because something about skulking around outside the dark house of a dead man in the middle of the night just seemed to naturally make a person do it.

Dom and Denny had insisted on coming along also and, to tell the truth, I was glad they were with me.

Stevie had lived in an old fieldstone-and-wood, one-level cabin that his father built in the 1950s along the river. Stevie and Sue Ellen grew up here, and I had spent many happy hours playing with them, in and around it, as a child and into my teens. What I'd enjoyed most was jumping off the wooden dock out back and swimming in the Kithane River that ran behind the property.

The place had seemed like a plot of paradise to me back then. The house I grew up in with my mother, a trinity row-house, was wedged tightly between neighbors, fronted with an uneven brick sidewalk patrolled by pigeons and an asphalt street sentried by stunted, sad, and shadeless maple trees. Here by the river was a different world, with its open spaces and palette of common yellow throats, blue-winged warblers, orange-breasted Baltimore orioles, and other brightly colored river birds nesting, feeding, and singing their songs in the flourishing weeping willows and river birches that lined the river's banks.

Tonight, with sounds muffled by a low mist crawling up from the river and creeping out from under the raised foundation of the house, it just seemed spooky.

"The last thing I needed…" I started in a whisper before I caught myself and continued in a regular tone, "was for one of the neighbors to see me and call the police. From what I remember, they're pretty sparse around here, but they are protective of each other's property. I just figured night would be best."

We probably should have prepared a little better. Tim brought along a flashlight. However, we hadn't bothered to check the batteries, which seemed to be on their last legs because the beam was pretty weak. The light even went out a few times and needed a good shaking and pounding on the bottom of the battery casing to bring it back to life. Dom could only contribute a camping lantern to the cause, and it served little purpose beyond encircling our party in light, providing no illumination outside about a one foot radius. We had to move as a tight little group to avoid stumbling. Hopefully, we would find a better flashlight or some batteries at Stevie's for the walk back.

"Do you think we'll discover anything? I mean, the police must have already been all over the place by now," Denny said.

"Maybe, maybe not. But even if they have been here, Stevie was always real good at hiding things," I answered. "If he had something he didn't want you to find, you weren't going to find it without a little luck. Like, everyone seems to think he was selling drugs but I haven't heard that anyone actually found any. So if he was, he must have squirreled the drugs away where no one could find them. I figure the same might be true for anything that he was using to blackmail somebody, if indeed he was blackmailing someone."

"Oh, this is great. We don't know if what we're looking for actually exists and we have no idea where to look for it," said Tim, just as the beam from his flashlight went out.

"Damn, and we probably won't even be able to see what it is if we do find it," he added as he slapped the battery casing again.

Dom stopped suddenly and reached out to stop Tim's pounding.

"Shhh. Did you see that?" he asked in a hushed voice. He raised the lantern toward the house but it provided no better visibility, and, in fact, made it harder to see outside our circle.

"What?" Denny asked.

"I'm not sure but I thought I saw a flash of light inside the house—moving real quick-like," he answered.

"I didn't see anything. Did you Tim?" Denny asked.

"No, but I was fiddling with this damn flashlight. Do you hear anything?" he answered.

We stood silent, listening, but the night was quiet around us.

"Maybe it was reflection of our lights in one of the house's windows," I said.

"Maybe it was a cat. Did Stevie have a cat?" Dom asked.

"A cat with a flashlight?" Denny replied.

"Anybody there?" Tim called out.

"What are you doing? Now he knows we're here." said Dom.

"We don't even know there is a 'he' here, do we," Tim answered. "And if there is, it's better to let him know we're here than surprise him. Remember what happened to Wes?"

"Actually, he surprised me," I said, for some reason feeling the need to set the record straight.

"Whatever," Tim replied. "My point is that surprises are not good."

We had stopped about ten feet from the front porch. I had the feeling that the guys were now wondering whether this was a good idea or not. I was wondering myself, but this was my idea so I reached over and took the lantern from Dom.

"You guys wait here. I'll go check it out," I said, stepping out from the group tentatively.

"No, we're all in this together," Tim said. He began to follow me, as did the others, but I couldn't help noticing they let me stay out in front a few feet.

There were three steps that led up to the front porch. I reached the bottom one and began climbing.

"What if the door's locked?' Dom asked.

"Well, when we were growing up, there were always two little gnomes on either side of the front door, and there was usually a spare key under the one on the right," I answered as I reached the porch. I held the lantern out and saw the two gnomes standing guard at the doors. "They're still here," I said.

I waited until the others had joined me on the porch before I went forward, set the lantern down next to the gnome on the right, and tilted the figure to the side. There was no key.

"Damn, it's not here," I said.

"Then what are we going to do?" Dom asked.

"Well, we can always smash a window and one of us can crawl in and open the door from the inside," I answered.

"That's breaking in?" Dom replied. "That's against the law. We could get into trouble."

"What did you think might happen?" Denny asked him. "We are sneaking around here in the middle of the night like common burglars."

"I dunno. I thought Wes had a key or something," he answered.

"Quiet you two. I'll go around back first, maybe there's a way in back there," I said to them.

"Or maybe, the door is unlocked and we can walk right in," said Tim, who had gone to the front door and turned the knob. He pushed the door open a crack to make his point. "After you," he said to me, pointing the way with the dim beam of the flashlight.

I picked up the lantern and held it out in front of me as I

moved past Tim and slowly pushed the door open. The way I remembered the layout of the house, it was built in a variation of a shotgun house, with a large front room, a long hallway with bedrooms and a bathroom to either side, and a large kitchen in the back of the house. This was probably a result of Stevie's father familiarity with the style growing up in poor neighborhoods in and around New Orleans. It might also explain, I guess, why the house was raised a few feet off the ground, though that might just as well have had something to do with concern of the nearby river flooding over its banks.

I entered the front room and reached out to my right along the wall for the light switch, or rather the old-fashioned push buttons that were common when Stevie's dad built the house. I found the switch panel right where I remembered it would be and pushed the bottom button in. Nothing. I pushed the top button in. Again, nothing.

"Damn, I guess the power's been turned off," I said over my shoulder to the others as I moved deeper into the front room and they followed behind. I held the lantern up but could really only make out shapes of furniture to the right. Tim's flashlight provided little better vision, although it did illuminate an old desk off to the left against the wall between the windows.

"I'll check for a flashlight or batteries in the desk. Tim, why don't you and Denny go on back down the hallway and see if you can find anything in the kitchen. I think there was a fuse box back there. Hell, even some candles would be better than these things we're using."

"Sure, let's go," Tim said, and he led Denny off.

Dom stayed close behind me as I made my way over to the desk. It was an old oak roll-up desk, and I remember Stevie's mom telling me more than once that it was the only piece of furniture, a family heirloom from her father's side, that she and Stevie's father had brought up from the South when they moved to East Hastings looking for work and a place to raise a family. She was not a prideful woman, but she loved this desk. It was open and I put the lantern gently, and with a bit of respect, on the desktop.

"Must have been creepy, living out here all by himself," Dom said.

"I doubt it, I mean, he was used to it—the sound of the river rolling by, the crickets in the summer, the stillness in the winter. Besides, he had electricity so the place wasn't this dark, and he could play his music into all hours of the morning without a neighbor complaining. No, I bet Stevie loved living here."

Even in the dim light, I could see that the police had most likely been here looking for something. Envelopes and personal papers that had been in the cubby holes in the desk organizer were strewn about the desk top and the drawers were left partially open, as if someone had hurriedly rifled through them then moved on without closing them completely. One thing about Stevie was that he liked things to be in their place. He never would have left his desk like this.

I did a quick search of the drawers on my own, but found no batteries or candles or even matches. It wasn't any use trying to look through any of the stuff on the desks or in the drawers in the poor light of the lantern. Framed photographs hung on the wall above the desk. I lifted the lamp to see them better and, even in the dimness, I could tell they were pictures of the family, some which I remembered from when I used to hang about the place.

Among them was a stiffly posed wedding photograph of his parents with his mother sitting primly in a chair in her simple white wedding dress, bouquet held in her hands on her lap, and his father, in high collar and what might have been the only suit he'd ever owned, standing honorably to her side, his hand gently resting on her shoulder. I recalled thinking every time I used to look at that picture how neither one looked particularly happy, yet not particularly sad, each just having an expression that seemed to say that this is the way things are, now let's get down to business. And so they lived, no-nonsense people, but they were very kind to me.

"Eureka!" I heard Denny shout from the kitchen. "Let there be light." I looked in the direction of his voice and heard the sound of a switch being locked into position. A light filled the kitchen and floated down the hallway a bit back toward us.

"We also found a pack of C batteries to boot. That old Stevie certainly was prepared," Denny said as he approached, his flashlight on and at full light now. "Find anything?" he asked as he entered the room, turning and directing his light to where I had left the lantern on the desk. "What a mess. So where's the nearest light switch for this room?" he asked.

"Right here," said Tim, who had followed Denny into the room. He pressed the wall light button and an old floor lamp by the desk came on.

Now in fuller light, we could see that not only had the desk been rifled through, but the trash basket beside it had been dumped and crumpled paper and other debris was strewn on the floor. Books had been pulled from the bookcase that stood along the facing wall to the right of the desk and flung about injudiciously, some lying on their front or back covers, others spread-eagled and page face down, their spines upraised. It didn't seem to be the kind of mess the police would make in a search.

Dom turned to me. "Looks like we're not the only ones trying to find something here. Do you think somebody beat us to whatever we're looking for?" he asked.

"Well, we won't know until we don't find it, right Wes?" Denny injected and the sarcasm was apparent. He turned off the flashlight and went over to the desk, putting it next to the lantern. He turned that off as well.

Tim went over to the bookcase, bent down, picked up a book, and placed it back on the shelf. "What kind of a person would do this to a book?" he asked. He picked up another.

"Um…guys." It was Dom's voice, but it had a shakiness to it.

I looked over at him. He stood with his back to us and raised his hand, directing our attention to an overturned sofa on the other side of the room.

"Oh shit. Guys!" he said more forcibly. "Oh shit."

I moved next to Dom as I followed the path of his pointing finger. There, in the corner, was a body lying on the floor. The sofa blocked the upper portion of the body, but I recognized the boots. It was Puddy Salvatore.

Tim came over. "What's going on—oh my God—who—what—"

He never got to ask another question because, at that very moment, the front door flung open with a fury.

"Nobody move!"

It was Danny Sullivan. He really didn't have to worry about any of us making a run for it. We were frozen by the sight of the dead body. And, besides, in his right hand, his gun pointed at us.

CHAPTER 27

Technically, they can't arrest us for breaking and entering, can they, because all we really did was open an unlocked door and enter? That's not a crime, is it?" Dom asked.

"What about the body, Dom? There was a dead body lying in the corner, remember?" said Denny irritably. "Damn, how'd I let you guys talk me into this?"

"Hey, no one put a gun to your head," answered Tim before he caught himself. "Oh, sorry—bad choice of words—nobody forced you to come along. We all thought it would be fun."

We spoke in hushed tones. Once again we were sitting around a kitchen table. Only this time it was in Stevie's kitchen and we were being guarded by a stoic state police officer who stood off a ways in the doorway, while a crowd of police and medical-type people dressed in disposable light-blue overalls with matching hoods and boot covers and protective goggles swarmed about in the living room.

"Listen, guys, I am so sorry. I shouldn't have let you come. But you don't have to worry. No one would believe you are murderers," I said.

"Oh, is that right? Well, until tonight no one would have believed I was a burglar," Tim said tartly.

"My wife is going to kill me—oh sorry again—can't seem to help myself," Denny said. "I told her I was going bowling with Wes to help him get his mind off his problems."

"I didn't know you bowled," Dom said. "You've never invited me along."

Denny gave Dom a dumbfounded look. "I don't. It was an excuse. Damn, Dom, try to keep up, okay?"

"Sor—ry," Dom answered, a tinge of hurt in his voice. "Maybe I'm a little thrown off here because I've never seen a dead body before. I mean he is dead, right? There was a lot of blood."

"Yes, Dom. Our friend in there is definitely dead," Denny answered patiently. He turned to me. "So you're sure that was Puddy Salvatore? What do you think he was doing here?"

"I don't know, probably looking for drugs or money. I know he wanted to get out of town. I guess he thought if he could find Stevie's stash, if there was one, that it would set him up wherever he was going," I answered.

"That means he must have known Stevie would have something to stash. I guess Stevie was wrapped up with him somehow," Tim said. "Who do you think killed him? I mean, we didn't see anybody."

"The light, remember? I told you I saw a light in the cabin. That must have been the killer. We must have scared him off—or, oh, shit, do you think he was waiting for us?" asked Dom.

"C'mon Dom. Why would anyone want to kill us? And who knew we would be here? Nobody. No, I bet it was the same person who killed Tina. That would make sense," said Tim. He turned to me. "Wouldn't it?"

"What? Oh yeah. I'm sure that's it," I answered, although I hadn't really been paying full attention to them. Something I'd seen or something that had happened didn't make sense, but I couldn't put my finger on it, what with the commotion all around and my concern that I may have put my friends in harm's way.

"Yeah, sure it was," Denny said. "It had to be another

knife attack—one thing I did see was a blade lying by the body—and Puddy and Tina did have the car theft situation in common. Maybe Stevie did too. Didn't Puddy tell you as much, Wes, that the person, or persons, he was afraid of didn't like to be crossed?"

"Yeah, yeah, you're probably right," I answered a little absently. Actually, what I was thinking, and what I didn't want to share with the guys, was that if Puddy's killer was in the cabin when we arrived, and believed we could identify him or her...well, it seemed pretty obvious that killing people who might be able to point a finger at them was really not a problem. What had I gotten my friends into?

The killer must have heard us approaching. I hadn't had a chance to get too close to the body, but when Danny had rolled it over, not only did I see the knife but it looked like Puddy had not been dead too long. The pool of blood beside his body was still growing. The killer must have slipped out the back when we came in the front. We had to be careful. Puddy implied that not even the police could be trusted. I knew from my own experience in Boston how easy it was to get access to a police report if you knew the right person. The killer could find our names and addresses from the incident report. Didn't have to be a cop that let it out...could be a clerk or any other employee at the police station.

Somehow, I had to let the guys know to make sure they told the police they didn't see anyone, which of course was the truth, although in Dom's case not the complete truth. Puddy had implied no one could be trusted. Now he was dead.

Stop it! I said to myself. I was over thinking things. It had been a rough couple of days and I was only being a bit paranoid about things. Since the last thing we needed was an epidemic of paranoia, I decided to keep my thoughts to myself. No sense in alarming the guys.

"Wes, you don't think the killer thinks we saw him, do you, and that he'll come after us next?" Dom asked.

So much for not setting off any alarms. Tim and Denny's

heads snapped up the way a deer's does when it hears a twig snap in the distance while it's taking a nice sip of cool water at a pond's edge. They looked at me.

"That's crazy, right?" asked Denny. "I mean, we didn't see anything and the place was empty when we got here. That body could have been lying there for hours, for all we know."

"Yeah, right," added Tim. "and, besides, that Puddy character and Tina—sorry to say this, Wes, because I know you liked her—but they were criminals. They ran with a criminal element. It's perfectly normal for criminals to go around killing other criminals—it's all part of the business—but to go around killing perfectly honest citizens, why that's a whole other story, isn't it?"

"Shhh," I hissed sharply.

Their voices were starting to rise and the trooper guarding us, who had been more interested in the proceedings down the hall, turned to look at us.

"You wouldn't have any idea how long we are going to be kept here, do you? It's been a bit of a long night," I asked him, hoping he hadn't quite heard what we were talking about and to stop any wondering.

"No, I don't. You'll just have to wait until they're ready to talk to you," he said with the air of someone used to being obeyed. He gave us all a look that basically told us, "So sit quietly until you're wanted," and then turned his attention back down the hall.

Dom waited a beat and then leaned forward, his voice just loud enough for us to hear. "The police will protect us, right? I mean, they can put us in that witness protection program or something if they think a killer is coming after us, can't they?"

Now I leaned forward, brought my hands up, and did that patting down the air gesture that meant calm down. Looking at their faces, tense with jaws tight and eyes unblinking, I didn't think it worked.

"Listen, no one's coming after any of us. We didn't see

anything. No light in the window, right?" I whispered slow-ly, first shaking my head no then nodding yes at each of them at the word "right."

It took a moment for what I was saying to sink in, espe-cially for Dom, but they all eventually nodded yes back at me.

"Good, so let's just sit quietly until they want to ask us any questions, okay?" I said.

We became quiet. The guys were probably thinking about what they would tell their wives, families, friends, and co-workers if we did indeed get arrested. I had no such concerns. Instead, I began to try to make some sense of eve-rything.

I didn't find any sort of link between Stevie and Tina at her apartment, but she was at his funeral. Tina and Puddy were connected. Puddy was also at Stevie's funeral. He also broke into both Tina's place and Stevie's to look for money, drugs—anything to help him get away. But Stevie was killed before Tina returned my car and that's the reason Puddy gave for her death, for him running scared. If Stevie was in the theft ring with both of them, why weren't they scared when he was killed?

Maybe Stevie was acting on his own and killed because he was blackmailing someone, as Hoppy believed. But then how did Puddy or Tina fit in? They couldn't have been the targets. What could they have that Stevie would want? Money, sex? I didn't see that.

Neither Tina nor Puddy appeared to have that much money, and Stevie was charming and resourceful enough to get laid by Tina, and, unless things had changed drastically, Puddy was not his type.

Besides, Stevie always thought big. If he was going to go take all the risks involved with blackmailing someone, that person would be worth it. He'd go after a big fish. So…what if Tina and Puddy were involved with Stevie in the blackmail scheme and their killer was the person being blackmailed, and Puddy wasn't looking for money when he broke into Tina's and Stevie's places, but whatever Stevie was using for blackmail?

Well, if the answer was somewhere here in Stevie's place, I'd never get the chance to look for it now. If the police hadn't really turned the place over before, if that mess that we'd seen—the desk top, trash can dumped and bookcase stripped—was Puddy's work, then they would certainly do it now. And there was no way I'd be able to get close to this place again, not with it being a crime scene.

The kitchen door opened and in walked a crisply uniformed state trooper I hadn't seen before. The state police apparently made a concession to the summer heat by allowing troopers to wear short-sleeved cotton shirts, but they were still required to wear ties, long pants, and boots. The name ID plate on his right shirt pocket read "Winters," and the two bars pinned one inch up from each collar tip indicated that he was a captain. He was trim, obviously fit, very clean-shaven, with just the slightest tinge of gray in his almost non-existent sideburns. His uniform was completed with a dark gray campaign hat and a holster belt holding a Glock semi-automatic pistol.

He was followed into the room closely by Chief Roark. Unlike Captain Winters, she was dressed more casually, wearing a dark-blue cotton polo shirt with epaulets on each shoulder, matching dark blue knee-length shorts, and black hiking shoes over white low-cut athletic socks. Her captain's badge was pinned above her left breast and "East Hastings Police" was stenciled on the shirt over the right breast. She wore a black baseball cap with "Police" embroidered on the front and also had a Glock semi-automatic pistol in her holster belt. Casual or not, like Captain Winters, everything was clean and perfect, as if it all had never been worn before. There was not even a speck of dirt on her shoes.

Trailing them into the room came Danny. Now, he looked like I expected someone who had just discovered a bloody corpse at two o'clock on a very humid morning to look. His hair, although he must have tried to brush it back with his hand, was a bit disheveled and wet. His face was pale and sweaty and his eyes a little distant. I noticed there was some blood on his shoes and the cuffs and knees of his pants, apparently from when he knelt by Puddy's body to check for a pulse when he first arrived. He wore a crisp polyester dark blue windbreaker, with "East Hastings Police" embroidered over the right breast, that I seemed to recall him wearing when he caught us in the house.

"Have we gotten a statement from these men, Chief?" Captain Winters asked, his eyes taking stock of us. He clearly was in charge of things here.

"I've only just arrived myself," she answered. "Officer, have we gotten their statements?" she asked turning to Danny, apparently noticing his appearance for the first time in the light of the kitchen. "Are you all right?"

"Yes, sir. Just a bit of a summer cold or flu. I'll be fine. And no, no statements yet. I thought I'd keep them here for you to interview first," he answered.

The captain turned sharply to address Danny. "You mean, they've been sitting here—together—all this time? Don't you think they should have been separated so they couldn't collaborate on a story?" He leaned a bit toward Danny. "Officer, what is that smell…gasoline?"

"Yes, sir," Danny answered.

I could smell it now too. Not particularly strong, but noticeable.

"I kicked into an old can when I was searching the garage. Place was dark. It must have had gas in it. Didn't find anything there, though," Danny added.

"And that was while these suspects were sitting here?" Winters said, the tone of his voice implying a slight disregard for Danny's investigative abilities.

"Well, your trooper was here watching them—" Danny began.

"He's not my trooper—" the captain interrupted tersely.

"I was out inspecting the property, seeing if I could find

anything," Danny answered, a bit of defiance in his tone.

I don't think he enjoyed being addressed this way in front of us—in front of me.

"In this darkness?" the captain asked skeptically. "Did you find, or kick, anything else?"

"Well, yes and no," Danny answered. "I didn't find the deceased's truck anywhere nearby on the property, but there was a canoe tied up at the dock in the back. I don't think it belonged to the owner of the property because I found another canoe lying against the side of the house."

"You think the deceased was going to cart away stolen goods in a canoe?" the captain asked, and this time there was a detectable bit of sarcasm in his question.

I thought I heard a slight, restrained, mocking "humph" from the trooper standing at the door. I looked at the chief, who was staring intently at the floor and I couldn't tell if she was embarrassed for Danny or angry that one of her officers was being treated in such a condescending manner.

"Actually, sir, I don't think the deceased was after property," Danny answered, and if he had heard the trooper he didn't let on. "The owner of the property, recently murdered in a bar incident, was a suspected drug dealer and the deceased was a person of interest in the murder of a woman in a hotel room three nights ago. I think the deceased was searching for money or drugs on the property and planning to leave town."

So Danny agreed with my first thought. I was impressed. I think both the captain and the chief were too.

"Is that true, Chief? The deceased was a suspect in a recent murder?" the captain asked.

"The deceased is Puddy Salvatore and was wanted for questioning in the death of a woman, and yes, the owner of the property was murdered last week in a bar outside town," the chief replied formally.

"I think it's likely that another person, or persons—" Danny turned his gaze to the four of us at the table. "—also looking to find the property owner's stash, came upon the deceased and killed Puddy in an altercation."

"Well, you do seem to have yourself a hopping little town here, don't you?" the captain remarked, turning to address the chief. "Do any of these men have police records?"

"No, Captain. They do not, as far as I know," she answered.

"That one there—" Danny said quickly, pointing at me, "—was in the hotel room when the woman was murdered."

"Is that right?" the captain asked, giving me a closer look.

"Actually, I wasn't there when—" I started.

"Mr. Byrne discovered the woman's body in the hotel room," the chief broke in. "according to his statement at the time, which was corroborated by the hotel clerk who was with him." I noticed that she gave Danny a quick, hard glance before continuing with the captain. "He is not a town resident, only visiting for the funeral of the owner of the property, which was three days ago."

"And does he have any sort of relationship with the deceased in the other room there?" the captain asked, his gaze growing more intense.

"Last night the deceased beat him up and—" Danny began before another sharp look from the chief cut him off.

"Mr. Byrne was found bound in duct tape this morning in the apartment of the murdered woman, and he claimed he was beaten by the deceased during the course of a robbery of that apartment."

The corners of the captain's mouth curled ever so slightly upward and he tilted his head a bit to the left. "My, my, my. You certainly have been busy. I think we may have a few things to talk about, Mr…um…"

"Byrne, Wes Byrne. He's a reporter, too," Danny volunteered, again to the obvious displeasure of Chief Roark.

"Officer," she said. "Why don't you go check to see if we've received any reports of stolen canoes tonight, or if anyone has reported seeing Mr. Salvatore's truck? And get me the address of any of his relatives living in town. We'll need them to identify the body."

"But—" Danny started.

"Now, Officer," the chief said firmly.

"Yes, Chief," Danny replied, disappointed. "Captain," he said, nodding his way.

Then he turned and left through the back door, not bothering to look at us. I couldn't see his face but I know that smirk was there.

When he was out of the room, the captain turned back to the Chief. "What about these other men? What is their relationship to the deceased, or the owner of this property?"

"As I said, sir, I arrived only minutes before you did and have not had the opportunity to —" she began.

"This was all my idea, Captain," I broke in. "Stevie, er, the owner of this place, was a childhood friend of mine, of all of ours, and I wanted to get one last look at the place before I left town. I talked them into coming with me. I'm the only one who had anything to do with Puddy—the deceased—and I'd never met him before last night."

"I see," the captain answered. "So your being here has nothing to do with you being a reporter?"

"Well…um…no sir, I've been trying to tell everyone that I'm not working on any story." A little bit of a lie. I was glancing back and forth between the chief and captain, trying to get a read on either of them. I knew how the chief felt about reporters. I was pretty sure the captain's opinion wasn't much higher. "It's all like I said."

"If Wes was investigating a story, do you think he would have brought us along?" It was Tim. "I mean, look at us."

"Yeah. It's all like he said." Now it was Denny speaking up. "We were having a few drinks and got to talking about the old times, and Wes mentioned how much he'd like to see this old place, so we thought 'why not?'"

"Is that right?" the captain asked, looking directly at Dom. Tim, Denny, and I held our breaths.

"Um, yeah. Yeah, I collude with the others," he said.

"Concur," Denny whispered.

"Yeah, concur. I didn't see anything. There was no light in the window, and the door was unlocked. We just walked in," Dom answered, a bit too hurriedly, but he sounded sincere, just a little nervous.

"I see," said the captain. There was some skepticism in his voice, but I had a feeling that was a natural reaction he'd developed from years of listening to suspects' alibis. He looked us all over one more time. "I want statements from all of you—"

Tim, Denny, and I exhaled.

"—except for you, Mr...um...Byrne. I'd like you to come back to the station with me. I've got a few more questions I'd like you to answer—without your friends, here."

There was a quiet knock on the door frame at the kitchen entrance from the hallway. A hooded, petite looking woman in those light-blue overalls, goggles pulled up and resting on her forehead, stood there. It was not the same person I'd seen at the motel after Tina had been killed.

"We are all done here, Captain, and ready to take the body away. Do you want to take a look at it before we do? It's a pretty basic stabbing. Still, I know you like to be thorough."

"Yes, I would, thank you, Doctor," he answered her. He turned to the chief. "I'd like members of my team to take the statements from these men. You are welcome to sit in, of course."

"Thank you," the chief replied. "If it's all the same to you, I'd like to accompany you when you interview Mr. Byrne. He may have some information to shed light on the murdered woman based on the break in last night at her apartment."

The captain looked at me briefly. I had a feeling he really wanted to have me all to himself.

"Yes, of course, but I'll be asking all the questions," he replied, looking back at her.

"Of course," the chief answered. She couldn't have been

happy to be playing second fiddle to the captain, but nothing in her expression let on.

"Would you like to see the body, look over the crime scene?" he asked her.

"Yes, I would, thank you," she answered.

"Fine then, come along."

The captain started to leave, trailed by the chief, when he stopped to address the trooper who had been standing guard over us.

"Bellingham, once I am through in the next room, I'd like you to get Colletti, Reed, and McGuinness to take statements from these three men in separate rooms. I'd like you to escort Mr. Byrne here to my car, place him in the back, and wait for the chief and me until we get there."

"Yes, sir," the trooper responded crisply.

The captain and the chief left the room. Tim, Denny, and Dom looked up at me, and I could tell they were a little nervous.

I leaned forward to talk to them quietly. "Don't worry, guys, I don't think they're going to charge you with anything. Just tell them the truth—" I looked over and saw the trooper had turned his back on us and was talking into his mobile radio device, no doubt carrying out the captain's orders. "—and Tim, would you call Hoppy and tell him not to send a lawyer to help me out this time? I'd rather downplay the reporter thing, and I think the lawyer would send up all kinds of red flags."

"Sure, of course, but will you be okay?" he asked.

"Oh yeah," I said bravely, or at least I hope I sounded brave. "Nothing I'm not used to."

I was lying, of course. Police interrogations were something I knew I'd never get used to.

CHAPTER 28

The state police headquarters was state-of-the-art. The black-and-white-tiled floors of the hallways I was led down were polished and buffed to such a degree that I could look down and practically see my reflection. Every orderly desk in the large office space I passed through, relatively empty in the early morning hours, held large, sleek computer screens, clean white keyboards, and shiny and efficient looking telephones. Black, ergonomic desk chairs were pushed beneath the desks. Every aspect of the place screamed efficiency, organization, and professionalism—except, of course, for the interrogation room. It was almost as sparse and claustrophobic as the one in East Hastings, although the coffee I was offered tasted a little better.

I guess, much like every golfer had a unique golf swing or people brushed their teeth differently, when it came to interrogation techniques, everyone in law enforcement had their own method. Captain Winters preferred silence. For what must have been fifteen minutes, he had been sitting across a sturdy, laminated wood-topped utility table from me, leafing through a rather substantial file folder, occasionally moistening his fingertips to help him turn through the sheets of paper it contained. A few times, he paused to look at me, not moving his head, but only raising his eyes without changing his expression.

Chief Roark sat to his right, hands folded and resting on the table in front of her. She hadn't taken her eyes off me the entire time we'd sat in the room, her face expression-less. She might have been studying me for some clue in my posture, reading my body language like an opposing poker player. Or she might have been thinking about what she was going to have for breakfast. I couldn't really tell.

I was sick of the silence.

"I'd like to know why I am here," I said, "and I mean here as at the state police headquarters and not at the East Hastings PD and here as in what could I possibly tell you that I couldn't tell you at Stevie's place?"

Captain Winters did not raise his gaze from the file when he answered me flatly. "The murder happened in West Caulfield Township and the state police share jurisdiction with the East Hastings Police Department in West Caulfield Township." He closed the file folder and looked up at me. "Why were you meeting Puddy Salvatore at Steve Darby's place?"

"What?" I answered. His sudden directness took me by surprise.

The captain smiled at me. I wouldn't necessarily have called it a sinister smile, but it did nothing to put me at ease. "I just find it to be quite a coincidence that this guy beats you up one night, and then the very next night you show up at a place and find him dead."

"Listen, Captain. That guy threatened to kill me the next time he saw me. Why would I ever want to give him the chance?" I answered.

"But what if—just play along with me here—what if you had arranged to meet this Salvatore there and, considering the beating he'd given you the night before, you thought it'd be better if you snuck up on him. You even brought a little backup just in case things got rough."

"Backup? My friends? C'mon, you've met them. They couldn't back up a karaoke band," I answered. "You do re-alize the guy had left me wrapped up in duct tape last time I saw him?"

"Oh, I don't know. Maybe that was because you didn't

pay up for his part in committing a crime, say stealing your car, maybe you and this Stewart woman had double-crossed him and maybe that was just him sending a message to keep your end of the deal. Or maybe he had some information he was going to sell you, something to help with the story you're writing about the Steve Darby murder," he answered.

I looked at him, then at the chief. Now a small smile had formed on her face. Was I the only one not getting the joke?

"How many times do I have to say it? There is no story, no reason to buy information, and, besides, what was I going to use for money? I'm broke," I said, leaning back against my seat. "It's like I said, I just wanted to see Stevie's place is all, like my friends said."

The captain took a deep breath. His gaze grew stern, and he tapped his left pinky on the tabletop three times. "Mr. Byrne, please don't lie to us."

"I'm not lying. There is no story," I answered.

"You know what I've got here?" he said, holding up the file he'd been looking through. "I've got statements from your three friends, and they are all alike—too alike. How do you explain that?"

"Well, maybe it's because they're all telling the truth," I answered.

"You say you're not writing a story. That's not exactly true, is it?"

It was Chief Roark speaking up for the very first time. Winters showed a little annoyance at having his party crashed, but he let her continue.

"When we contacted Mrs. Stewart's sister after you were found in that apartment, she said she agreed to let you stay there because you were going to get an article about Mrs. Stewart into the *Chronicle*," she continued.

Damn, she was good. I had two choices. I could deny that I intended to write a story about Tina and look like a complete heel for making promises to and taking advantage of a grieving sister to get access to Tina's apartment. That would confirm to them that I was after information for some other reason, no doubt the story they seemed to believe I was writing. Or I could fess up that, yes, indeed I did make that promise to Terri and was writing a story, which I had been denying this whole time. That would indicate that I'm liar and therefore give them reason to question anything I told them, especially that I wasn't working on the story they seemed to believe I was writing. I decided to go with liar.

"Okay, yeah. I did promise Terri I would get something nice about Tina into the *Chronicle*. But that's all it was, one article. It seems one of your police officers—" I said, looking at Roark, "—implied that the reason Tina was murdered was because she was a prostitute. Terri didn't want her sister remembered that way. I agreed with her. That's all there is to it. And, for your knowledge, and Tina's sister will confirm this, the only reason I was in Tina's apartment that night was because of the cats."

"The cats? What cats?" Winter asked.

"Tina's cats. Terri couldn't take them home with her because one of her kids is allergic. I agreed to watch them until she could find them a home."

That actually made Captain Winters laugh. He turned to Roark. "Do you hear that, Chief? Not only is this guy some kinda chivalrous knight protecting the honor of a wronged woman, he's also a pet lover. Why I almost feel guilty keeping him here while he could be out saving the whales or finding a cure for cancer." He turned back to look at me and leaned forward, his smile now sardonic. "So, it's just a coincidence that everywhere you go, dead bodies appear."

I remembered what Roark had said about not liking coincidences. I imagined Winters felt the same way. It was probably a cop thing.

"Okay, Byrne, let me be straight with you here, because, frankly, I feel you're just wasting our valuable time," Winters said, leaning back into his chair. "I read the crime report on Ms. Stewart and I saw the crime scene tonight. I don't think you killed either one. What I do think is that you're wrapped up in this some way, and you know who did commit these murders. And I am going to keep you here until you tell us who it was."

I looked at Winters then Roark and then back at Winters. "This is crazy. Don't you have some sort of list of all the bad guys that you could be dragging in here and questioning about this? People who might have had an actual reason for killing Tina and Puddy—and Stevie Darby? You know, the usual suspects."

Captain Winters pursed his lips and tapped his left pinky on the table three times. "Usual suspects?" he answered, his voice rising slightly. "Do you know how many murders we've had in the past three years—and not just in East Hastings, but the entire county?" he asked.

Of course I didn't. I'd been spending the past three years flushing my career down the toilet.

"Six—only six. A couple were domestic incidents, love gone bad, that sort of thing. The others were shootings outside bars, people getting drunk and settling things with guns or knives. We caught them all. Then you show up in town and suddenly we have two murders in just three days, and you are found at each of them," he asked.

"What about Stevie Darby? What are you doing about that? Unless you think I had something to do with that too," I replied, perhaps a little to sarcastically.

"Did you?" Winters answered leaning forward, and the hardness in his eyes made me think he might have been a little serious.

"Oh, man," I said, letting out a little laugh. It wasn't appreciated.

"Something funny?" Winters asked, his jaw tightening.

"No, no. Not at all," I said, trying to ease the tension a bit. "It's just that, well, it seems like you're working awful hard trying to implicate me on all of this when, from what I understand, you've got bigger problems. Friend of mine mentioned the Crawfords, for instance—"

"Get this straight right now," Winters exploded, "You

are not to go poking around the Crawfords, you understand."

Wow, so much for easing the tension. Instead, it seemed like I stepped on a raw nerve. "Me? Poke around the Crawfords? No, no way," I said, raising my hands. "I've told you I'm not poking around anywhere, and the last thing I want—"

Winters emphatically closed the file that was lying on the table in front of him. "Okay, we're done here for now. We'll see if a few hours in a jail cell changes your mind about cooperating," he said, rising out of his chair.

"Jail cell? Oh, c'mon. You've got no reason to lock me up," I said.

"Oh really. How about breaking and entering, for starters. Then there's failure to report a crime, maybe accessory after the fact..."

"Failure to report a crime? You're kidding right? I mean we'd only seen the body for like a m—minute before Danny came b—busting in," I stammered.

"I didn't say I had to make the charges stick, I only have to come up with reasons to keep you here," he answered.

"But—but—that's not right. I haven't done a—"

Winters leaned forward and placed his palms on the table across from me. "Listen, Byrne. I know you're working on a story for Weatherly at the *Chronicle*. I know you know something that you're not telling us, and I'm going to find out what it is, and when I do I will charge you with obstructing justice and any other charge I can dream up. And I know one more thing—you're not leaving this town, not yet you're not. Oh, no. Right now I've got you dead to rights on breaking and entering. That's enough to start with, and I'm going to hold you until I get the answers I'm after, and then I'm going to either lock you up for a long time, or I'm going drive you to the county line and kick your sorry ass out of here myself," he growled.

There was a knock on the door.

"What?" Captain Winters yelled out, his eyes fixed hard on me as he straightened up.

A young trooper entered the room and hesitated at the door.

"This better be good," the captain said, turning as the trooper approached him warily.

"Sorry to interrupt you, sir, but um…" the trooper answered as he neared the captain warily. When he reached him, he leaned in and put his mouth close to the captain's ear, whispering something I couldn't make out.

"You're kidding me!" the captain snapped. "She's on the phone?"

The trooper again put his mouth close to the captain's ear and began whispering. I'd never actually seen smoke coming out of anyone's ears, but if it was ever going to happen, this was that time. Winters turned a violent red, and veins on both sides of his neck bulged out.

"Well, if that doesn't beat all," he uttered, casting a quick, mean glance my way before turning to Chief Roark. "Chief, come with me. Trooper, stay here and keep an eye on Mr. Byrne," he ordered.

The chief rose from her seat, an inquisitive look on her face as she followed the captain out of the room.

They left me in the room alone with the somber trooper for several minutes. I was just about to ask him what was going on when the door to the interrogation room opened. Captain Winters poked his head into the room, glared at me, nodded to the trooper, and then pulled his head back and closed the door.

"You're free to go," the trooper announced.

CHAPTER 29

I probably should have leapt up and scurried out of that room as fast as I could, but instead I stayed sitting in my chair and laid my head on the table. Part of the reason was relief, and part was exhaustion, but the main reason I did not rise out of my chair was because, and this was a strange thing to admit to myself, I actually felt safe in that room. Outside, things were crazy, moving too fast. I had no footing. What would it hurt if I stayed a few minutes or more? They couldn't arrest me for resisting release—could they?

"In case you didn't hear me, you're free to go, Mr. Byrne," the trooper said, more forcefully this time.

It was a bit of a struggle to lift my head up to look at him. "And where exactly, Trooper, am I to go? I have no idea where my car is, where my belongings are, where I am supposed to sleep—or eat—or—"

"There is someone waiting for you, sir," he interrupted, obviously wanting to move me along and out of his charge.

"Did you check to see if they were carrying a knife?" I asked, trying my best at sarcasm but missing miserably wide of the mark, if the stony look from the trooper was any indication.

"No, sir, only suspects are subjected to searches," he answered drily.

I pushed myself back from the table and stood up. I did so slowly, because, as before, my left leg had fallen asleep

and was just beginning to wake up. If I was going to continue spending hours in uncomfortable chairs, I should
probably start trying to find a good chiropractor.

"Would you mind telling me what time it is?" I asked the
trooper.

"Five-fifty a.m., sir," he replied.

"Ah, another night in paradise," I said, as the feeling returned fully to my leg and I was able to follow the trooper
out the door and into the hallway.

"That way out," he said, pointing down the hall to a door
at the far end. "You can collect your belongings at the front
desk. That's where your party is waiting to meet you."

"Gee, a party for me. I hope they brought balloons," I
joked—very badly, I admit, but it didn't matter because the
trooper had headed off down the hall in the opposite direction and, if he heard me, made no response.

I walked down the hall and went through the door. There
were two people standing in the room. One I recognized.
Gloria Stephenson, my attorney. The other person, a man in
his late-thirties or early forties, looked vaguely familiar, but
I knew I'd never met him before.

Gloria approached. She sized me up as before. I don't
think I impressed her any more than last time. "Mr. Byrne,
we meet once again," she said.

"Listen, it's not that I'm not grateful, but I'm also very
sorry. I asked Tim not to call Hoppy. I didn't want to get
him involved—get you involved—owe anybody anything.
See, I really don't need an attorney. The breaking and entering was just a misunderstanding. It will all be worked out.
We went out to Stevie's just for old time's sake, like I said.
And I noticed the door was open, and so—"

"You're right. It was all just a misunderstanding. There
was no breaking and entering," Gloria said. She pulled a file
out of a brief case that was resting open on a nearby chair.
She opened the file, flipped a few pages through a document held by a two-prong fastener, turned the file to me and
held out a pen.

"Please sign here," she said.

"Um, if this is a contract, you should know I don't have any money—and even if I did, don't you think I should read it over."

"It's a lease. It's all standard. Just sign it, and we're all good to go. The police can't charge you with breaking and entering into a place where you are a tenant, if you get my drift. So please sign, so I can get out of here."

I didn't understand a thing, but I signed.

"Okay," she said, taking the pen, then the lease, back. "I'll send you your copy in the morn—" She gave me an exasperated look. "—sometime this morning."

"Wait a minute."

She had turned and was closing up her briefcase at the chair.

"I really don't understand this. Hoppy rented Stevie's place out for me? Why would he—"

"I am not representing Hoppy in this matter," she said. "My client is Mrs. Augustino."

"Mrs—Sue Ellen? You're working for her? I thought you were working for Hoppy? How can you represent me for two people?"

"Here's the deal. In regard to the matter of your incident at the hotel and the murder investigation into Ms. Stewart's death, Hoppy is paying the bills. I'm not representing you. I'm representing his interests, or rather the *Chronicle's* interests."

"But I'm not workin—"

Gloria held up her hand and gave me a my-time-is-money look. "I don't care about that. I do lots of work for Hoppy. That man is always in some kind of trouble." She turned, grabbed the handle of her briefcase, and stood the case up, resting it on the seat of the chair. "It's not any of my business what you and he are after, and I don't care if you're crazy enough to get caught up in his activities. Like I said. Hoppy is paying the bills." She picked up the briefcase and turned fully to face me. "As far my being here toni—

this morning—" She looked at her watch. "—Mrs. Augustino is my client, and it is purely a real estate matter." She
took a step closer. It was probably just my imagination, but
it seemed she was holding the briefcase a little too menacingly close to my private parts. She looked up and fixed
hard eyes onto mine. "Now when it comes to Sue Ellen,
don't you dare mix her up in all of this," she said, raising
her free hand and slowly circling it in the air, index finger
extended. "You do, and I swear—" Her hand stopped circling and now the index finger was pointing up at me. "—
you do, and I will join the other side, I swear I will. I will
work, pro bono, to see you get sent out of her life. Do you
understand me?"

I probably should not have smiled. It wasn't a snide or
dismissive smile. It wasn't even that big of a smile, but it
ticked her off.

"You don't think I'm serious?" she asked, rising up on
her toes, slightly. The briefcase in her hand rose a little
higher with her.

"Yes—I mean I do," I said, taking a step back. "It's just
that…well, I'm glad that Sue Ellen has such a good friend."

That knocked her back a bit—a moment, very brief, of
confusion. She was going to say something, but instead
wheeled around. "He's all yours," she said to the man who
had witnessed the whole scene.

He smiled at her and nodded.

She reached out, patted him on the forearm, and left the
building through the front door.

The vaguely familiar stranger stepped forward and held
out his hand.

"Mr. Byrne, my name is Ronald Wesley. I've come to
pick you up. "

A Wesley. The surprises just kept coming. The Wesleys
were perhaps the oldest black family in East Hastings, or at
least one of them, here since the town was founded. They
played a key role in the development of the place, although
there was, it seems, a tacit understanding between the black

and white families that settled in East Hastings in the early years about the division of power.

There was no overt discrimination. Schools, hospitals, restaurants, bars, pool halls—nowhere was there any overt trace of segregation. Still, the black families had their own funeral home and cemetery, their own churches, took their cars to black-owned garages for repairs and shopped at the black-owned grocery stores in their neighborhood. And, although things might have changed, back in my day the chances were great that many of those establishments were run by a Wesley, if not a direct descendant then a cousin or a niece or nephew of the founding family. What was a Wesley doing here?

"Wesley—as in Larry Wesley?" I asked.

He smiled.

"A lot of people sure seem to remember my cousin Larry," he replied.

"Yeah, well, of course I remember him."

It would be impossible not to. He was probably the best athlete ever to grow up in East Hastings, a natural at any sport he chose to play. He was loud, funny, and could not help but be the center of attention. He also had a bit of a problem with authority, which unfortunately included not only teachers and school administrators, but also coaches. He was kicked off every team he played for.

"How is Larry?" I asked, making small talk while trying to figure out why this man was here waiting for me.

"He's dead, sir. Killed in a bar fight about six years ago," he replied.

"Sorry to hear that. I didn't know him well, but he always seemed like a good guy to me," I said, meaning it.

Larry had actually intervened in one of my periodic hazings from Danny Sullivan and his partners in crime. That time he had enlisted Dave Baldwin and Billy Connors. I think it had more to do with him not liking those guys very much, settling his own personal score, than it did helping a geeky, gawky white dude, but I was grateful.

I walked over to the front desk, ostensibly to pick up my belongings. I was expecting a pretty sorry lot—a cashless wallet and a set of keys for a car, which was heavens knows where. The desk trooper opened a six-inch-by-nine-inch envelope and poured out the contents. The wallet tumbled out, but no keys.

"Um…there should be a set of keys," I said to the trooper.

From behind me, Ronald cleared his throat. "Oh, I retrieved your keys and gave them to a friend of mine. He'll pick up your car and get it to Mr. Darby's."

I turned to look at Ronald, then back at the trooper. "People are allowed to do that?" I asked him. "Just get someone's property handed over like that?"

The trooper looked at me blankly. "It sounds to me like he is doing you a favor." He picked up a clipboard. It held a basic release form, similar to the one I had signed at the East Hastings Police Department. He held out a pen and nodded to the form. "He signed for it, and I'd appreciate if you would do the same for the wallet."

I did.

"You have a problem with the situation, I'd be glad to ask Captain Winters to intervene," he said.

I recognized him. He was the trooper at the door in Stevie's kitchen.

"No, no problems. Actually, I am just a little tired. I'm sure it will all be fine, thank you," I said, turning.

"Oh I was told by Captain Winters to inform you that, although you have not been charged with any crime, you are still a witness at a crime scene and not to leave town until he gives you permission."

I lowered my head and sank into my shoulders.

"I've got Mrs. A's Silverado in the lot sir, Mr. Byrne," I heard Ronald say.

I looked up. There he was, waiting.

"You know, I don't want to sound ungrateful. I mean, here you are at six o'clock in the morning to meet me, offering me a ride, but, exactly why are you here?" I asked.

"Mrs. A asked me to pick you," Ronald answered.

"You know, this is all…um…" I was too tired and confused to make any sense of anything.

Why would Sue Ellen send a car for me? I didn't talk to
her at Stevie's funeral, hadn't talked to for a very long time.
In fact, the last time we spoke, before I left for college,
years ago, she had made some not-too-subtle suggestions
about how I should conduct my sex life—alone—and told
me she never wanted to see or speak to me again, a consequence of my investigation into the chemicals being
dumped into the Kithane River. An unintended and unfore-
seen consequence. Considering the impact it had on her life,
I really didn't blame her then for the way she felt. Still
don't.

"Yes, sir. She asked me to pick you up and drive you to
Mr. Darby's place. As you know from Ms. Stephenson, arrangements have been made for you to stay there while you
are in town. I've already arranged to have your car taken
there, stocked the refrigerator, and brought over some fresh
linens and towels and such. Just brought some stuff from
Mrs. A's. I'll do some shopping later when the stores
open."

Now I was really confused. Sue Ellen wanted me to stay
at Stevie's place, recently murdered boyhood friend Stevie,
where the previous evening I had discovered a very recently
murdered body—and not just stay there, but she was setting
me up with food and bed sheets? This had to be a big joke
that I wasn't being let in on yet.

But what if Gloria was right? I pictured her circling
hand, index finger pointed up. I couldn't let Sue Ellen get
mixed up in any way with whatever was going on.

At lot of the places I went the people I met ended up
dead, someone beat me up, or someone threatened me.
Why? I had absolutely no idea, but until I figured it out, no
Sue Ellen.

"Isn't Stevie's place a crime scene? I mean I had a room

at the Evergreen Motel. I could just check in there again. It was just fine," I said.

"Well, it seems Mrs. A made a few phone calls after she was called about what happened at Mr. Darby's place," Ronald said, a brief trace of admiration in his eyes. "It belongs to her now and it seems the state police have wrapped up their investigation," he continued. "The place is no longer considered a crime scene. There was some blood, but I've cleaned that up. It needs some other work, but I'm taking care of that. It's in good enough shape to live in, though," he answered.

"She made a few phone calls?" I asked.

"Yes, sir. Mrs. A is remarkable woman, if you didn't know it, and she's got a lot of friends around this county, people she's helped out."

I imagine Ronald had taken the time to size me up while I was engaged with Gloria. If he'd formed any sort of opinion, he was not letting on.

"This way to the truck, Mr. Byrne," he said, turning to lead the way.

"It's Wes, please, and really I would be much more comfortable at the motel," I answered,

Ronald turned. "I've already picked your belongings up at the motel and everything, including your car, is at Mr. Darby's place." Then he leaned in close to me and lowered his voice so only I could hear him. "And Mrs. A, she already told the police that there was some misunderstanding and that she had invited you to stay there yesterday, so they can't charge you with breaking and entering. That's why they had to let you go," he said, stepping back and looking me squarely in the eyes. "You don't stay at Mr. Darby's, it makes it look like Mrs. A was lying."

"No, no I wouldn't want that," I said resignedly. "It will only be for a couple of days anyway. Still, I wish I knew what was going on."

"Mrs. A asked me to get you to Mr. Darby's place so you could get some sleep, and that I was to pick you up later today and take you to meet her. She said she'd explain everything to you then."

The only word I really heard was "sleep." The thought of lying down on clean sheets and drifting off to blissful sleep was too powerful to fight against.

"Okay, sure. Let's get out of here," I said.

I followed Ronald to the door, which he held open for me, and stepped out into an already humid and hazy morning. I should have been grateful for small wonders. Still, I couldn't help wondering when the trap door would spring open below me.

CHAPTER 30

The cab of the late model Silverado pickup truck was cleaner and roomier than most of the places I'd been staying at since I left Boston.

"I hope you don't mind the mess. I coulda brought Mrs. A's car, but I've gotta stop by the feed store this morning to get some food and hay for the horses, and it's just a spell from Mr. Darby's place, so—" Ronald began.

"No, no it's fine," I interrupted. Actually, it was more than fine. The cab was spotless; and it had a faint, pleasant farm-smell—of hay and horse—that had worked its way into the vinyl of the seats and the fabric of the floor mats off boots and blue jeans and saddle leather. It beat a new car scent by a mile.

We continued on in silence for a mile or two. I kind of felt I was being rude for not talking to Ronald. He must have spent a good portion of his early morning getting things ready for me at Stevie's place, besides coming out to pick me up. I decided to try my best at small talk. First, I took a moment to size the man up.

He was probably just under six feet tall, thin with taut, lean arm muscles. His hair was short and trim above his Wesley ears, and he struck me as one of those guys who probably felt scruffy if he didn't see a barber at least once a week. He was dressed casually, but outdoor work casual— black cowboy boots, blue jeans, and a polo shirt with *East Hastings Dry Cleaners* stenciled over his left breast. He seemed relaxed, very much at home in the cab of this truck, steering casually through the gentle curves of the back road we traveled along. I saw something in him that I'd seen in very few people—some reporters I'd worked with, a couple of cops, a bartender or two, and, of course, Jan—a contentment that came from doing what they loved to do.

"I take it from your shirt, that you work for Sue Ellen—er, Mrs. A—at the cleaners," I said.

"Well, technically, I guess I work for the cleaners, but I actually spend most of my time helping out Mrs. A," he answered, keeping his eyes on the road.

"Work for her long?" I asked.

"Since I got outta the navy, 'bout five or so years ago," he replied, still focused on the road before us.

"Ah, the navy. Enjoy that?" I continued.

"Wasn't a matter of enjoying—just a matter of serving my time. But, yeah, it was good for me, helped straighten me out," he answered earnestly. "I was a bit of a...well, I got in a bunch of trouble when I was a kid. Navy helped me put that all behind me."

"Sounds a little like Judge Kearney justice, if I'm not mistaken," I said.

Ronald turned to me and smiled. "You know about that?" he asked.

"Yeah, yeah, I do," I answered.

Judge Kearney was a very strict judge in East Hastings when I was growing up, and he did not suffer "hooligans," as he called them, well, especially those who seemed to always be showing up in his courtroom. His sentences could be harsh, but he always gave young people who he viewed redeemable a choice—either go to prison or join the military. Most, wisely, chose the military.

I looked out the window at the passing countryside. This was the East Hastings I remembered, with its slight rolling hills, old stone homes with fenced in horse pastures and horse barns, and overgrown woods and small creeks running alongside the road.

"Do you mind if I ask you a personal question?" I asked.

"Guess it depends on the question," he answered.

"After you got out of the navy, why'd you come back to East Hastings?"

He took a few moments and I could tell he was weighing the question carefully.

"Well, the short answer is that this is where I'm from. I saw a lot of nice places during my tour but they all just sorta felt...I just sorta felt like a stranger everywhere I went. The long answer is that, well, before I had to join up I got a girl pregnant. I was young, we both were, and I didn't want her to go through with it—" He looked over at me quickly to see if I was judging him. I wasn't.

"She insisted on keeping the baby. That's about when I got in trouble with Judge Kearney and—I'm not proud of this—I was kinda glad to get away to the navy." Ronald turned his head and looked at me. It was his turn to size me up as we reached a straight stretch of road. "You always get people to open up with you like this?" he asked.

"No—well, yes—well sometimes. I ask a lot of questions. You don't have to tell me anything you don't want to." I answered.

"No, it's okay." He turned his attention back to the road. "So anyway, I go away and think that's that. Dottie—that's the mother, my wife now—has the baby. I just send some money back at first, trying to do the right thing, and in return, Dottie sends a few pictures of my little girl. She—we—had a girl. Being at sea I had a lot of time to think. I grew up a bit and realized I wanted to help raise that child, be in her life."

"So the Judge Kearney justice worked."

"Yeah, but it weren't no piece of cake, let me tell ya. Sending me pictures was one thing, but when I came back, Dottie—she wanted nothing to do with me, though she let me spend time with my little girl. She was good about that, but, man—" He shook his head and laughed. "—woman was cold."

He slowed down as we had to move into the incoming lane to make room for a group of runners, probably on a high school or college team, running along our side of road that had no shoulder.

Once we passed them, Ronald sped the truck back up and continued his story. "I wasn't goin' to give up, though. I wanted us to be a family. Dottie had a job at the cleaners, and I started going around there—finding excuses to stop and talk to her, about baby things at first. Mrs. A—she knew what the situation was—and one day, when I was at the cleaners, she started talking to me. She wanted to know how serious I was about gettin' Dottie back. I told her I was going to do whatever it took. She tells me she's very fond of Dottie, didn't want to see her hurt, asked me my intentions. So I tell her everything, about how I know I screwed up, but that I'd changed. She listens to the whole story then says, 'Well if you're goin' to keep comin' around here, you might as well have a job.' I start out making deliveries, get to spend more time around Dottie. Mrs. A even takes up my cause after a while, telling Dottie what a great job I'm doing, that I seem serious. She gives me more responsibilities—driving her kids to riding lessons and helping out around their place. Guess Dottie figured if Mrs. A was going to give me a chance, maybe she should too. We started taking Marcella—that's my girl's name—out on weekends together, I got invited over to dinner some nights, eventually I wore Dottie down."

"Sounds like you're a lucky man."

"Sure am. I have my family, a real home, and I work for a great lady. Why would I want to be anywhere else?"

No need for an answer, so I looked out again at the countryside as we drove along. Was it really luck, though? Or did some people just deserve what they got and others, no matter how much they tried, just got the short end of every deal?

Ronald's cell phone that was nested in a cradle attached to the dashboard rang. He pushed the speaker button on the phone. "Stacey, how's it going?" he asked the caller.

"I got the car back to Stevie's. Had to wait for a tow truck, had to pay cash—"

"Yeah, yeah, don't worry. Just keep your receipts."

"Police wouldn't let me drive it off the lot. Needs an inspection and a bit of work. Man, you should see this car. What a piece of—"

Ronald had reached out and ended the call. He turned to me.

"That's Stacey. I asked him to look at your car. He's pretty handy."

"Oh, I see," I said.

He drove a little farther and pulled off the road onto the beginning of a large driveway that had a four-foot white wooden gate, part of a long white fence that surrounded the property. "He's doin' a few other things for me so I should call him back," he said. He removed the phone from the cradle, pushed the recall button, and held the phone to his ear. "Hi, yeah, Stacey, just wanted to get off the road to talk. So, what's the story?"

I couldn't hear what Stacey was saying, but I could tell the conversation was about me—and my car—from the way Ronald would look over at me while only answering Stacey with "Uh, huh, I see," and "Okay, right."

I turned to Ronald.

"Do you mind if I get out and stretch my legs?" I asked. "I've been sitting down for hours."

"No, you go right ahead." He turned his attention back to the phone. "Ho, wait, not you Stacey. Tell me exactly what you have in mind first."

I opened the door to the truck and stood up. Funny, but I hadn't realized I was still sore from Puddy's beating until I tried to get out of the cab too quickly. A sharp pain struck my right ribcage, but, with a deep breath, I pulled myself out of the truck. The pain lessened as soon as I got upright.

I walked over to the gate, rested my forearms along its top railing, and looked out on the property. All of the places

I ever lived were measured in square feet, so I was never good at estimating how large an acre actually was. This place had quite a few, though, inside the light brown paddock and estate fence that surrounded the place. There was a lovely two-story brick colonial house, with a perfectly matched addition that no doubt served as a family or dining room at back at the end of the long driveway. Off to the right of it was a converted horse barn, with three garage doors. As I stood watching, one of the garage doors opened and a red 5 Series BMW backed out of the garage. It wheeled back and turned in the ample driveway space, facing forward, and came down the long drive way toward me. I stepped back just as the gate began to open easily on tracks that were imbedded into the driveway. I turned and went back to the truck.

"Look, you just do with you have to. I'll make some calls and make sure you can charge most of what you need to Mrs. A's accounts," Ronald said into the phone as I opened the door and climbed into the car. "Right. I'll see you later." He ended the call.

"It looks like we're blocking the driveway," I said, indicating the approaching car.

"Oh, sure," he said, putting the car into drive and easing it forward to allow plenty of space for the owner's car to pull out. It did and pulled up alongside the truck. The passenger window lowered and a woman leaned across from the driver's seat. Ronald lowered the window of the Silverado. She was wearing large sunglasses and a paisley scarf over her hair.

"Hi, Ronald. Car trouble? There's tools in the garage, you know," she said.

"Hi, Betsy. No everything's fine. Just wanted to make a phone call and I prefer to do it while I'm not moving," he answered.

"Okay. How's Sue Ellen doing?" she asked and I sensed genuine concern. "I haven't spoken to her since the funeral."

"About as well as to be expected," Ronald said.

"Well, you take good care of her and remind her that Friday night, Paul and I are coming over with our special homemade chili and margaritas. You take care now."

"Will do," Ronald answered as the window in the BMW closed. He eased the truck out after the BMW had pulled away. "That's Mrs. Wilkins. Nice lady. Her daughters and Shelly and Anne, those are the Augustino girls, ride horses together."

"Seemed like she genuinely cares about Sue Ellen," I said, watching as she put some distance between us and the BMW.

"Yes, she does. Lots of people do," he answered then was quiet for a moment. He looked over at me. "So you mind answerin' a question for me?"

"Sure, guess it's only fair. Of course, it depends on the question," I said and, for a moment, we shared a smile.

"Well, I was just wonderin' 'bout the history 'tween you and Mrs. A. You know that she told me to tell you that she's not mad anymore. What'd you do to make her mad at you?" he asked.

Now it was my turn to sit and work out how much I wanted to say. Ronald was pretty honest with me. He deserved the same.

"It all has to do with the river. I was working at the *Chronicle* and I exposed a company that was dumping chemicals into the river," I said.

"That was you did that? I remember my folks talking about it. We used to swim in the river when we were kids. One summer my cousin, Celia, got real sick. They blamed it on the stuff in the river," he answered.

"Yeah, quite a few people got sick. Anyway, it turned out some of the chemicals were coming from the dry cleaners. Sue Ellen had been working there all through high school and adored old man Augustino, Tony's father. Although it was never proven that he knew anything about the dumping—they only had a contract with the company that was dumping the crap—I guess the old man felt responsible. He had a stroke shortly after the news broke and died a couple of weeks later. Sue Ellen blamed me and never talked to me again," I said.

"Do you think he knew?" Ronald asked.

"I don't know. I didn't know the man, but, by all accounts, he was a good man, gave a lot of kids their first jobs, sponsored little league teams, set up scholarships for kids that couldn't have otherwise afforded to go to college. But it turned out that the bid the cleaners accepted from the company that was guilty was way lower than all the others. If he was involved in negotiating the contract, he should have suspected something," I said.

"I don't see how Mrs. A could blame you for that," he said.

"Yeah, well she was pretty angry and really hurting, and I guess she had to take it out on someone. I wrote her a few times after I went away to school, but never heard back." I said.

"Well, I'm thinking she could use a friend, right about now," he said.

He slowed down as he made the turn onto the dirt road that led to Stevie's place. The truck took the potholes and ruts in the road pretty smoothly.

The house came into view and it looked a lot less menacing and a lot more dilapidated in the daylight than it had the night before.

I remembered seeing Puddy's dead body lying on the floor and wondered if maybe I wouldn't be a little more comfortable—and safer—if it wasn't too late to move back to the motel. He pulled to a stop in front of the house.

"I've got somebody coming around to put on some new locks for the doors and windows," Ronald said, seemingly reading my mind. "Ms. A's brother had a sorta open door policy, from what I hear. He didn't mind people just dropping by. She didn't think you'd mind a little more security."

It seemed Sue Ellen had thought of everything. I relaxed

a little. It would be nice to have my own bed and a place to sit and think things through.

"Um, Ronald. You said you heard Stevie had an open-door policy. What else did you hear about him?" I asked.

The question appeared to make him a little uncomfortable. He shifted in his seat and gripped the steering wheel a little tighter. "I don't put much trust in rumors, usually just a lota people talkin' about things they know nothing about," he answered.

"Sure, sure, I understand, but you said Sue Ellen needed a friend, and…well, best way I can help her is if I find out a little more about what happened to Stevie," I said.

He gave me a quick glance. "So it's true what they're saying? You are here to find out who killed Mrs. A's brother?"

"Who's saying that?" I asked.

He gave out a quick little laugh. "You know how it is in a town like East Hastings—people see things, people talk," he answered. "Now that you tell me how you're the one who cleaned up the river I know why."

"Ronald, that was a long time ago. Right now, I just— I'm not—" I said starting to explain for the umpteenth time that I was not writing a story. "Look, I'm just a little curious about what happened. Sue Ellen, Stevie, and I were… friends…at one time. That's all. People can think what they want."

"Well, around here people don't forget things. Remember I told you about my cousin getting stabbed? Turned out the reason the guy did it was because of something Larry did to him when they were both in third grade. Do you believe that? The man carried around hard feelings for twenty years waiting for the opportunity to stick a knife in my cousin."

"Somebody told me the reason people use knives around here is because they're more personal," I said.

"Yeah, I can agree with that," Ronald answered.

"Do you carry a knife, Ronald?" I asked.

'Oh, yeah, just for work, mind you. You want me to pick one up for you?" he said.

"No, that's okay," I said. "I'd probably just cut myself and, if there is one thing I try to avoid, it's the sight of my own blood.

CHAPTER 31

Ronald had done a remarkable job of cleaning the place up. All the papers and books in the living room were returned to their rightful place, and I gratefully noticed that there was no trace of Puddy's blood on the floor where we had found him. The work had to be a bit below Ronald's job description.

"I set you up in this bedroom," he said, leading me down the hallway to the first door on the right. "It was probably Stevie's room since it was the only one that had a bed and dresser in it. Hope you don't mind."

"Nah, it'll be fine," I answered, looking the room over. It had white painted walls that could use a little touching up. There was a double bed with its headboard against the wall to my right with a bedside table and desk lamp next to it. A simple and rather old looking dresser was to the left, with a wood-framed mirror resting atop it, and an armoire wardrobe cabinet straight ahead next to the only window in the room.

"Like I said, I took the liberty of stopping by your motel room so I could collect your things. The clerk knew me from the dry cleaners—we do their curtains and such—and she let me in. I put them in the drawers," he said, turning. "The bathroom is this way."

I remembered where the bathroom was, but silently followed him out of the bedroom down to a door on the opposite side of the hallway.

He stopped and pointed in. "You're almost out of toilet paper. I'll pick some up for you." I looked into the bathroom. It was so clean it practically sparkled and the smell of disinfectant was noticeable. There was no way Stevie had kept it like this.

Ronald continued down the hall toward the kitchen at the back of the house.

"Finally, the stores were all closed this morning so there's just the few things from Mrs. A's place—coffee, English muffins, a few eggs—so you could at least make yourself breakfast. If you want to make a list, I'll get you whatever you want before I come back."

By now I wasn't surprised at all to see that the kitchen floor and counter tops were clean as a whistle. It was hard to believe that only hours earlier a near army of police and medical personnel were traipsing mud and dirt through the room and cluttering the place with paper coffee cups. It made me think of my old Irish grandmother, a woman so devoted to cleanliness that she could polish an eight ball into a cue ball using only a rag.

"No, I think I'm good. That sounds like more than enough," I said.

"Mrs. A wanted you to be comfortable. I wrote my phone number down on that sheet of paper on the counter. You think of anything you need, you give me a call."

I walked over to a wall phone and picked the receiver up off the cradle. There was no dial tone. "This appears to be dead and I don't have a phone," I said.

He gave me quizzical look. "Really? You don't have a phone?"

"I had one from the place I used to work, but they took it back when they fired me."

"Okay, well, I'll pick you up a prepaid one and put some minutes on it."

"You really don't have to."

"No problem. I should be back in a few hours."

He turned to leave.

"Um, Ronald. When you were cleaning up, you didn't happen to find anything to drink about the place," I asked.

Ronald looked at me and I seemed to see the slightest bit of disapproval. I'd grown used to that look on people's faces.

"Isn't it a little early?" he asked.

"Well, I've been up for almost—" I glanced at the clock on the stove. It read seven a.m. "—eighteen hours. I'd say it's rather late."

"In the cabinet over there, above the sink. Think I saw a bottle of something."

I walked over, opened the cabinet door, and saw a quarter-full bottle of Jack Daniels. That would do. I took it down and then turned back to Ronald. He had started down the hallway.

"Say, Ronald," I called after him. He stopped and turned. "Thanks for all this."

He looked at the bottle in my hand, then up at me. "You're welcome. Just do right by Mrs. A." He turned and left.

❧❦❧

Having seen Ronald's handiwork, I wasn't surprised to find the ice cube trays in the freezer compartment of the refrigerator full, and, while the cubes had not yet frozen completely, I could get enough ice to fill a small glass. I poured the Jack Daniels over the ice and carried it into Stevie's bedroom. Now that I was alone, I realized that I was very tired.

I sat the drink on the bedside table, sat on the bed, and took off my shoes, then stood and undressed down to my underwear. I thought about taking a shower, but instead went over to the window and closed the curtains to keep as much of the early sun out of the room as possible.

This had been Stevie's room for as long as I'd known

him and very little had changed. The bare walls no longer held posters of sports teams and muscle cars, but the curtains and furniture were all the same. He'd spent his entire life sleeping in that bed. I opened the wardrobe and saw that there were only a few dress shirts, one suit jacket, and three pairs of slacks hanging inside it. At the bottom there was one pair of black loafers that could use a shine and a pair of Timberland boots. I slid open the bottom drawer and saw clothes that I assumed Ronald had taken out of the dresser to make room for my few things—jeans, T-shirts, underwear, and socks. There wasn't much. Of course, it was more than I had.

I walked over and picked up my drink. The ice had chilled the alcohol but the brown liquid still burned in my throat as I took a large swallow. I noticed for the first time that there were a few photographs slid into the frame of the mirror on the dresser. I went over to get a closer look.

In the top left corner was one of a smiling adult Stevie proudly holding up two bass by short fishing lines, one in each hand. On the left side a bit below that was a wallet sized headshot of Stevie from maybe the third or fourth grade, taken no doubt on the annual school photo day, right above a similar one of Sue Ellen from about the same time. There was no mistaking that they were sister and brother, their similarities so apparent. That was right about the time I met them.

Tucked into the right side of the frame was an ad with a picture, probably torn out of a boating or fishing magazine, for a Cruiser Yacht 48 Cantilus. It was a nice boat, the kind I could never afford, even if I was holding down a job, considering the asking price was $650,000. It must have been placed in the mirror rather recently because it showed no sign yellowing from the sun like the photos on the left side. Either Stevie was dreaming or he expected to come into a bit of money.

On a hunch, I slid the dresser a little bit from the wall and looked behind the mirror, just in case Stevie had hidden something there. Nothing, but I really didn't expect to find anything. Way too obvious a place for Stevie to be stashing anything. If there was anything to find, he wasn't going to make it easy for me.

After I slid the dresser back into place, I caught my reflection in the mirror. What the hell was I doing and how the hell did I end up here? I asked myself. I looked at the picture of Stevie with the bass and actually felt sympathy for those fish. They probably thought they had a great life, just swimming along, lots of other fish to eat, maybe they were the biggest fish in the lake, mating when the need arose. Next thing they knew, they had a hook in their mouth, got reeled in, and somebody with a sharp knife was all set to gut them.

I took a long drink from my glass and drained the last of the whisky. I definitely needed some sleep.

೧⊙೧

I woke up. Somebody was in the room with me. I fumbled to find the switch for the table lamp then turned it on. It was Jan. She was sitting in a chair by my bed, wearing a white lab coat over her scrubs, holding a clip board and looking over the sheets of paper that it held. She looked up as I sat up in bed.

"I was just going over your chart," she said, beautiful as ever but with obvious concern in her eyes. "This just won't do. You've got to take better care of yourself."

This was a bit odd. I didn't remember there being a chair in the room.

"What if I don't want to?" I answered.

"I'm the one who died, Wesley. You didn't."

She only called me Wesley when I had done something to disappoint her, like forgetting to take the chicken we wanted for dinner out of the freezer or neglecting to mail the electric bill payment.

"You sure about that? Maybe you should check that chart again," I said.

She stood up and there was such sweetness as she looked down at me. "I'm sorry, Wes. I didn't want this either, but you're going to have to live with it. Live, darling—for me."

With that she turned and walked to the window. I tried to get out of bed to follow but couldn't. It was if I was enveloped in a cocoon. I could only reach out my hand.

"Wait, wait—stop," I cried out.

She disappeared.

I jerked up, awake, no longer held down. There was a very large man standing at the window looking at me. He held a cordless electric drill in his right hand.

"Wadda ya mean 'stop'?" he said. "I done all the others and yours is the last one. Surprised ya didn't hear me. Ya sleep like the dead."

"Oh, Jesus—you did the others," was all I could say.

This guy was a large man, as tall as me, maybe say six feet three or four but twice as wide, with a big chest and arms thick and muscular as a body builder, which he might have been. He wore a tight white undershirt, that seemed painted onto his brawny upper body, and loose fitting jeans. The whiteness of the shirt was accentuated by the many colorful tattoos he had on his arms and neck. His eyes were a penetrating brown. His nose, obviously broken more than once over the years, was squashed flatly on his face, and he had a closely trimmed goatee. If I couldn't overpower a Puddy Salvatore, I didn't have a shot in hell getting past this guy.

My eyes fixated on the rather large drill bit locked into the portable drill. "Can't you at least use a knife, like you did on Stevie and Puddy. That's got to be much quicker— and less painful, I would imagine."

"Use a knife? This isn't a job that calls for a knife. How the hell am I supposed to put locks on these windows using a knife? And what are you talkin' about—me doin' Stevie and Puddy?" He looked at the glass on the bed table, which now held only water from the melted ice. "How much you had to drink?"

"Probably not enough. Do you mean you're not here to kill me?" I asked.

"Do ya think we'd even be having this conversation if I was here to off ya?" he answered.

"I wouldn't know—haven't been in a bedroom alone with a killer before. Not sure how it all goes down. What's your name? What are you doing here?"

"Name's Stacey. Ronald asked me ta come over ta make this place a little more secure, if possible. It's what I do—or one of the things I do—security. I'll be done in a minute, then ya can get back to sleep."

"No, that's okay. What time is it?"

"I dunno, after three."

Almost six hours sleep. That was practically a record for the last few days.

"I should be getting up anyway," I said. In truth, I feared that if I went back to sleep, I'd have another dream about Jan.

I felt more than a little self-conscious as I climbed out of bed, letting the hulking Stacey see my scrawny body as I stood up and searched for my shirt and pants. "I think Ronald said there was some coffee in the house. Can I make you a cup?" I asked Stacey.

"Already had a coupla cups, but thanks. Besides, I've still got the doors to make secure and the alarm system to install. This place ain't exactly Fort Knox."

"An alarm system? Seems like a lot of work and expense, considering I'm only staying a few days," I said.

"Wouldn't know about that. I was told ta make the place safe—cost was no matter," Stacey said, already at the window and working, his back to me.

I stretched my arms out and back as I went into the hallway and turned into the bathroom.

Odd, but there was a toiletry bag sitting on the sink counter that wasn't there when I went to bed the night before, as well as a stack of Dixie cups I didn't remember seeing.

After a very quick shower, I dried off and threw the wet towel on the floor, then brushed my teeth and applied some deodorant. I dressed in the bathroom, while Stacey finished up things in the bedroom. I left the bathroom and headed toward the kitchen. Passing what had been one of the empty rooms, through the open door I saw a military cot, next to which on the floor laid a full duffel bag. I turned and went back to my bedroom. Stacey was testing the new latch on the window.

"Um, Stacey. You wouldn't by any chance be moving in, would you?" I asked.

"Yeah, ya didn' know? Ronald asked me ta stick around for a few days—in case there's any trouble with the alarm system, see what else needs fixin' up," he answered, not turning around to look at me.

"I see. You said you were in security. That doesn't by any chance include being a bodyguard, does it?"

He turned and shrugged his massive shoulders. "Ronald said you might have pissed off some pretty tough customers—the kind a few window and door locks won't stop, and even with the best security system in the world, it would take someone a little while to get out here if it happened to go off. He thought it couldn't hurt if I hung out here for a few days—just in case, ya know."

"And how would Ronald know who I pissed off? I just met him yesterday—er, this morning."

"No idea. But even I heard things," Stacey answered.

"You heard things? Where?"

"I bounce at Kenny's place a coupla nights a week and—"

"You know Kenny? Kenny Burton?" I asked.

"Everybody knows Kenny. Anyway, some of the guys that come in there—they're not exactly angels, if ya know what I mean—some of 'em probably making money offa the stolen cars. I hear 'em saying the monies dried up, on account of the cops sniffing around after the murders. With time on their hands, they got nothin' ta do but think of ways to hurt the guy they blame for their trouble," he said.

"And that would be me. Even though I haven't done anything except get my car stolen," I said.

"Don't take much sometimes. These guys ain't exactly Einsteins—or need a good reason to bust someone up."

"Great. That's just great," I said.

I found a partially full can of ground coffee in a cabinet, opened it, and took a smell. It was fresh and robust smelling. It would do. I went over to the coffee maker that sat on the kitchen counter near an outlet. I plugged the coffee maker in.

"I'm gonna replace that outlet and the ones in the bathroom with GFCI outlets," Stacey said.

"Really," I answered while opening drawers and cabinets looking for the coffee filters.

"Yeah, tell you the truth, though. That's just a drop in the bucket to what this place needs. Did you see the light switches around here? This wiring in this place is so old— it's ancient, man—an accident waiting to happen."

"Uh huh," I mumbled, still unable to find a coffee filter anywhere. Out of sheer frustration, I opened the lid to the coffee maker and there was a filter. And into the filter, someone, I imagined it could only have been Ronald, had measured out and filled it with ground coffee. The water basin was also full. It was all ready to go. All I had to do was find a coffee cup in one of the other cupboards.

"I mean," Stacey continued, looking around the room while slightly shaking his head, "I'm gonna get quite a few smoke alarms, but as quick as this place would probably go up, they wouldn't do much good, all the old wood in this place."

"What?" I said, forgetting the cup, even the coffee, and turning to look at Stacey. "What are you saying wouldn't do any—what's that about the wiring—go up quick?"

"Ah, man, I'm just saying this place needs a lot of work,

going to be keeping me busy," he answered.

"Right," I said, not quite satisfied with the answer but deciding to pursue it a bit more after my cup of coffee.

I finally opened the right cabinet and saw three ceramic cups to choose from. Each was a little chipped or had a slight crack in the glazing. I picked the largest one.

There was a loud knock on the front door. I looked at Stacey.

"So how's this work—you handling security and all? You going to answer the door?"

"Oh, sure, you're safe. Any of these guys—they'll recognize my truck out front, and they won't want ta mess with me."

"Right." I headed off for the door, secure in the knowledge that, if there happened to be a killer on the other side, it wouldn't be anyone who knew Stacey.

CHAPTER 32

It was Ronald. His arms were full with three grocery bags and he held a fourth, a reusable red and blue striped shopping bag, in his right hand.

"Good afternoon," he said, moving past me to the kitchen. "I see Stacey's here. Good. I've come to take you over to visit Mrs. A, soon as I put the cold stuff away. The rest can wait," he said over his shoulder.

I looked out through the still open door and saw my weary-looking car parked alongside a sparkling maroon Ram quad cab pickup that I assumed was Stacey's. There was also a blue Honda Pilot with *East Hastings Animal Hospital* in a logo with a dog and cat on each side of the lettering painted on the front passenger door. I couldn't make out the driver.

Stacey came up beside me. "Where did you drive that car from to get here?" he asked.

"Rhode Island. I was working in Providence," I answered.

"I can't believe you made it. That thing needs a tune up real bad. I could tell that just by turning the ignition and listening to it while I waited for the tow truck. When's the last time you had a mechanic look at it?"

"Hard to say. I did a lot of walking in Providence—"

"Don't they have car inspections in that state?"

"Well, I knew a guy who knew a guy—" I began to answer sheepishly.

"Well, that car is not safe to drive, no matter if some guy slapped an inspection sticker on it," Stacey said. "I'll start working on it once I've finished with the security system."

"You fix cars too?"

"There ain't much Stacey can't do," Ronald answered as he joined us at the door.

"Except answer doors," I muttered.

"What?" Ronald asked.

"Nothing. But speaking of Stacey, whose idea was it to hire me a bodyguard, anyway?"

"Well, he's not exactly a bodyguard, more like a...a..."

"Babysitter," I said.

"Well, Mrs. A and Mr. Weatherly thought it might be a good idea if—" Ronald answered.

"Mr. Weatherly? Hoppy? How the hell—"

"Mrs. A called him this morning."

"Wait a minute," I said. "Mrs. A—er—Sue Ellen called Hoppy about me?"

"Yeah, the dry cleaners is a big advertiser with the *Chronicle* and she wanted to make sure the paper wasn't going to let the story about her brother fade away. I don't think she trusts the police will stay on it."

"So Hoppy suggested she hire Stacey so I won't be afraid to poke around?" I said.

"I don't know what Mr. Weatherly said. I only heard Mrs. A's side of the conversation. I only know that, when she hung up, she asked me to give Stacey a call," he answered.

"And you know Stacey how?" I asked.

"We go a little ways back. He did the security out at the Augustino place, and he's got what you might call a unique skill set."

"Yeah, it seems so," I answered. "Okay, well, I haven't had my coffee or any breakfast yet. I'm not much good before I've had my first cup."

"We talking coffee or—"

"Coffee," I answered, skipping over his implication.

"Actually, I stopped at the WaWa in town and picked up a cup for you," Ronald said. "It's waiting in the doc's car. I wasn't sure how you liked it, so I just took some sugar and creams and figured you could make it how you like it."

"Black's fine. I haven't had my breakfast though." I asked.

"Well, it's a little late for breakfast, but Mrs. A had me set out some food before I left," he answered.

"She seems to have thought of everything."

"She usually does," Ronald answered. "Hope you don't mind, but it was taking a little longer running errands than I expected, so I left the truck in town with one of the other guys who work for Mrs. A to finish up, so I called up Doc Andrews. She was coming out to the place to look at Mrs. A's horses anyway, so we could hitch a ride with her. I'll bring you back in Mrs. A's car."

"Seems like you think of everything also," I said.

Ronald smiled at the compliment. "I try."

"Okay, hold on a second—and hold onto this for a moment, please," I said, handing him the coffee back. I went back into the bedroom where Stacey was just finishing up securing the window. I took my wallet off the dresser where I'd left it the night before. "I'm going out. Thought you should know," I said to Stacey.

"Well, you'll probably need these when you get back," he said, handing me a set of keys. "They're for the front door and back doors, which I'll have finished by the time you get back. Small one's for the doors, larger one for the deadbolts. I'll wait to program the security system until you get back and I can show you how it works."

I put the keys in my pocket. "Thanks."

I walked with Ronald out to the vet's vehicle.

"I'll ride in the back," Ronald said, opening the rear passenger door. I climbed into the front. The vehicle smelled of animals. Sitting in the driver's seat was an attractive woman, probably in her early thirties, with brown hair cut in a long bob that framed her face. She had blue eyes with specks of brown and a small, petite nose. She was dressed in dark jeans and light blue denim shirt that had the same logo as on the side of the SUV sewn over the left breast pocket.

"Wes, this is Doctor Andrews. Doctor Andrews, this is Wes Byrne," Ronald said from the back seat.

"Call me Jackie, please," she said, holding out her right hand and smiling warmly. "Only my patients call me doctor."

"Nice to meet you," I said reaching out, turning toward her to shake her hand. I had a sudden twinge pain in my side from the motion and lurched a bit—the gift from Puddy that just kept giving. My left hand, which I hoped to place on the console between us for support, went a little long and it slid off the other side of the thing, so that I fell awkwardly toward her. She quickly raised her right hand from an offer of a handshake to a defensive, palm-up position and caught me firmly above my left breast. I was suspended over the console for a moment, my face very close to hers and rather than that familiar look of terror that I seemed to inspire in women when alarming them with my complete lack of co-ordination, I saw an amused sparkle in her eyes. She kept her hand on my breast as I regained my balance and sat upright in my seat. It might have been my imagination but she seemed to keep it there for a brief moment before pulling it away.

"Do you fall for every woman this way?" she asked, smiling.

"Actually, no," I answered, feeling the heat of embarrassment on my neck and knowing that my face was a bright red. "Usually, there is also the spilling some type of liquid involved as well. I'm very sorry."

"Guess it's a good thing I didn't hand you your coffee yet," Ronald piped up from the back seat. "Should I risk giving it to you now?"

Jackie pulled up one of the doors on the console, revealing two cup holders.

"Here, why don't you hand it to me?" she said, turning to Ronald. She took the cup from him and placed it in the cup holder nearest to my side. Then she turned to me. "And why don't you buckle in before we get started, just in case?"

Again she gave me a disarming smile. I think she was actually enjoying this.

I did as told. She started the SUV and we were off.

Jackie and I made small talk during the drive, and I was pleasantly surprised at how easy it was. I tried to include Ronald in our conversation, but he kept himself busy texting on his smart phone in the back seat.

It seems Jackie got her undergraduate degree at the University of Delaware and went to the University of Pennsylvania's School of Veterinary Medicine. Then she started working with old Doc McClaren, here in East Hastings after graduation.

I remembered him because there was a stretch, early grade school maybe, where I had an assortment of small pets—hamsters, guinea pigs, parakeets—that never seemed to do too well, and I took them to the doc for healing. Wasn't much he could really do, and now as an adult, I realize he had more important things to do, but he was always kind and always patient. He was a nice man.

When he retired a few years ago, she took over his practice, which was basically geared to family pets, and grew it to include a lot of work on horses and other livestock, as in the case of Sue Ellen's horses.

Jackie asked me about my college experience and what it was like in Boston, about how I knew Sue Ellen. It wasn't until we reached Sue Ellen's place that I realized she was the first person who didn't ask me about Stevie or mention anything about my old story that exposed the dumping of waste in the river.

We had been driving along property bordered by a three-foot-high stone wall for a little while when we came to a wide driveway with tall stone pillars on each side that matched the wall and had bronze pillar lights mounted on top. We turned in through the pillars. In the distance, I could see the house, as well as a horse barn with a small, horse-fenced paddock. As we neared them, I saw Sue Ellen standing at the fence, one foot resting on the bottom rail as she watched a young girl, presumably her daughter, leading a horse around the paddock.

Sue Ellen turned and walked over to meet us once we parked. Her dark hair was pulled back in a ponytail, and although she was as beautiful as ever, her face showed a strain. She wore an untucked white baseball undershirt with yellow sleeves and an *East Hastings Cleaners* logo on the front, blue jeans, and green Mudrucker mid boots.

"Hi, Jackie," Sue Ellen said, giving Jackie a hug as she climbed out of the driver's side. "Thanks for coming out. Cherokee seems to be favoring his left front leg a bit— won't seem to put any pressure on it. I haven't noticed any swelling, but thought I'd let you look at as soon as possible. You know how Anne is about that horse."

Jackie smiled at her and answered her in that calm, reassuring manner common among medical people who work to manage the uncertainty as much as the ailment. "It's probably just an abscess. Nothing to worry about. I'll take a look."

She went to the back of the Suburban and pulled out her own pair of Mudruckers, only these were taller than the pair Sue Ellen wore. As Jackie slipped them on, I noticed the way they contoured to and accentuated the shape of her calf. She grabbed a medical bag from the back as well and headed off toward the paddock.

"Nice to have met you," she called over her shoulder.

"Yeah, me too," I said, but I don't think she heard me. She was now all business.

Ronald had headed into the house after taking a carry bag out of the back of the Suburban as soon as we arrived, leaving me and Sue Ellen alone. We both stood there looking awkwardly at each other for a moment or two.

"Um…I…um…I really appreciate you coming back to town for Stevie's funeral. It was nice of you," she said, breaking the silence, tapping her left hand on her left thigh and taking a few tentative steps toward me.

I took a few tentative steps forward of my own.

"Well, I wanted to pay my respects. Stevie—and you—were such good friends—once. I'm so sorry for your loss."

"Oh, Wes," she answered, rushing to me, tears welling in her eyes. "I miss him—and I've missed you so much."

She put her arms around me and her head against my chest. I could feel her gentle sobbing and the warm tears through my shirt. I was never good in situations like this, and I slowly and tentatively put my arms around her.

"It's okay, Sue Ellen, it's okay," I said.

I looked up and noticed that Jackie was watching from the paddock. She was smiling. When she saw me looking at her she quickly went back to tending the horse's leg.

"No," Sue Ellen said into my chest. "I've been such a jerk—to Stevie—and to you. I've never felt so alone. I just don't know what happened." Sue Ellen took two deep breaths and pulled herself up and away from my chest. She rubbed her eyes with the sleeve of her shirt then rubbed her cheeks dry with her hands. She looked up at me with a sad smile. "That's the first time I cried since I first got the news about Stevie. But enough of that," she said. She hooked her arm under mine and led me toward the house. "Ronald is laying out a real East Hastings spread for us, and we can talk while we eat."

We walked through the door Ronald had entered moments before. After pausing in a mud room while Sue Ellen swapped her Mudruckers for blue canvas boat shoes, we walked through a large clean kitchen, down a hallway, and into a large den.

The room was bright, a result of two rows of large windows, stacked and separated by a panel of wall, that looked out over the property and down to the road we had traveled on to arrive. Along the far wall was a fireplace with a white mantle and, above that, a recessed cove within which was mounted a landscape painting of an idyllic Hasting County farmhouse and property. In the center of the room hung a magnificent bronze ribbon chandelier.

A large silver tray topped with a plate holding two halves of a roast beef hoagie sat on a large coffee table that was between two leather couches. Also on the table were small bowls of sweet peppers, hot peppers, and lemon slices beside the plate holding the hoagie. Two empty plates, silverware, and napkins were beside the tray. There was also a glass pitcher with iced tea and two tall glasses and several coasters sitting on a smaller wood tray.

"I thought we'd eat in here," Sue Ellen said, indicating that I should sit down on one of the couches. "The hoagie is from Jerry's."

My mouth watered at the sound of the name—Jerry's— the best sandwich shop in town, possibly the world. My friends and I had spent countless chow downs on Jerry's hoagies, debating how he could take the same rolls, meat, and cheeses found in every deli in East Hastings and create the most unbelievable hoagies and cheesesteaks known to man. I realized that the only thing I'd lacked more than sleep since arriving in town was food, but it was all worth it for one bite of a Jerry's hoagie.

"Wow, this is really nice, Sue Ellen," I said, moving toward the couch that faced the window.

"Yeah, almost as big as the entire house by the river." She pointed to the table. Her voice still had a little of the Tennessee coal mine twang, a remnant of her childhood before she moved to East Hastings. "Help yourself. I've already had my lunch."

"This is very kind of you," I said. As hungry as I was, and as much as that sandwich was calling out to me, my long-ago instilled manners dictated that I wait for Sue Ellen to sit down. She remained standing.

"It's the least I can do," she said.

No, I thought. *The least you could do is sit down so I can devour this hoagie*. Rude, but I felt like one of those dogs that have a treat balanced on their nose and have to wait for their master to give the command to flip it into the air so they could eat it.

"How about some iced tea?" she asked, reaching for the pitcher and filling a glass. "There's lemon and I can get you some sugar if you'd like."

"Thanks, this is okay," I said.

I noticed her hands were shaking slightly as she poured the tea, and, after she put the glass down she began rubbing them together nervously. The treat would have to stay balanced a little longer.

"Sue Ellen, what's going on?" I asked.

"Um…Wes…Oh, God, this is so hard and I don't know how to start…um…I…um…I want to apologize for the things I said and the way I treated you…before."

"Listen, it's okay," I answered. "I understood. I pissed a lot of people off—and I hurt some people you cared about. I didn't want to, but—"

"No, it's not okay. You only did what you thought was right, and you were. I see that now. I blamed you for everything and it wasn't your fault. I—I found out—the truth," she replied, looking down and avoiding my eyes.

"What truth? What are you talking about?"

She moved quickly, sitting down on the couch opposite me and leaning forward. The words came flooding out. "It was Tony. I've seen the contracts. He hired the company that dumped the waste in the river. He took the low bid for the job. It wasn't Dad Augustino, it was Tony, and he knew what the company was doing but he didn't care. He just wanted to save money and show Dad Augustino that he could run the business, but of course he couldn't—"

The words were just flowing out. She had been staring off a bit, over and above where I sat. She turned her eyes on me.

"—and when you uncovered what was happening, he let Dad Augustino take the blame. He says Dad Augustino insisted, but Tony was just being a coward. He didn't want everyone to know what a cheap conniving bastard he is, how he didn't have what it took, how he was—is—nothing like his dad. I blamed you for everything, and it was Tony."

She was breathing heavy. This must have been pent up for quite some time.

"One night, he was drinking a lot because the television station was failing, and he had sunk everything we had, even the dry cleaners, as collateral for the loan to start it. Of course, he didn't seem to care that everything would be gone. Oh, no, not Tony. He only cared about what people would think. He was feeling sorry for himself, and he started talking about what a failure he was—had always been—and he talked about what happened to Dad Augustino, and…well, he didn't quite come right out and admit what he'd done but he said enough that I knew what he was talking about."

She looked me hard in the eyes. "I hate him, Wes. Hate him as much as one person can hate another. And I hate myself for being so goddamned blind."

I stood up to go around and comfort her, but of course, being the clumsy oaf I am, I banged my knee hard on the coffee table as I rose. The pain was excruciating, and instead of being chivalrous, I gave out a high-pitched yelp. If nothing else, it seemed to trigger a change in Sue Ellen and her eyes went from angry to caring.

"Oh my God, Wes, are you okay?" she asked. She walked over and gently pushed me back to the couch. "Sit down." She smiled as I did as I was told. She sat down on the sofa cushion next to mine. "You always were a little bit…um…"

"Ungraceful," I said.

"Yeah, ungraceful," she said, and her smile widened. "Do you remember that time we—you, me, and Stevie— were doing flips off the dock behind the house into the river, and you just couldn't seem to get it right. You kept crashing into the water flat on the back of your head. I thought you were going to break your neck."

"Yeah, you and Stevie were having no problems. You were naturals. I think that's when I realized I'd never be an acrobat."

The bright moment of that shared memory was brief, however. She grew serious and looked at me with such sad eyes. "Wes, what am I going to do? I can't leave him. It would be terrible for the children. And he'd get the dry cleaners—and that's my life. I kept it going after Dad and Mom Augustino passed. Tony wanted nothing to do with it."

"I really don't know what to say, Sue Ellen. I…um…guess you could talk to an attorney," I answered weakly.

She sat up straighter. "I'm so sorry, Wes. Here I haven't seen you in so long, and all I can do is unload all the crap in my life on you. I'm responsible for all this. It's not your concern. As Momma used to say, 'You make your bed, you lie in it.'" She pulled at her ponytail to straighten her hair a bit and messaged her checks below her eyes gently. "Besides, I must look a mess—all this crying and such."

I smiled warmly. "Sue Ellen, you look great," I said, and I really meant it.

"Yeah, well here I am chattering away like a jaybird, and you haven't touched your hoagie. I remembered you liked roast beef. Jerry's son took over the business. Of course, the debate rages in town over whether his sandwiches are as good as his father's. I think they are, but you be the judge," she said, sliding the bowl holding the peppers closer to my plate.

"Well, it certainly looks fantastic," I said, opening the roll and using a spoon to lavish some of the hot peppers on top of the lettuce and tomatoes that covered the plentiful meat.

Sue Ellen must have seen something out of the corner of her eye. Her head jerked to look out the windows.

"Shit," she said.

I turned to follow her gaze and, through the window, saw that a recent model salsa red F-Type Jaguar convertible had driven through the gates and was approaching the house. Sue Ellen stood, walked over to the window, and nervously stroked the window curtain.

Ronald gently knocked on the door frame and came into the room. "Mrs. A, I think you should know that—" he began.

"I see him, Ronald. Thank you," she said, turning back to the room.

Ronald gave her a brief, concerned look and left the room.

"Wes, I was hoping we'd have more time to talk. See, there was something else, besides apologizing to—" Sue Ellen began.

"It's about Stevie, right?" I said, getting up off the couch and walking over to her. "Listen, I appreciate all you've done for me, with the police and a place to stay for a few days. And I understand you've been talking to Hoppy, but I'm not a reporter any more. Those days are over," I said.

"Wes, I've just got to know the truth, what really happened to him. No one else will give me any answers and...well, I know you will, no matter what the truth is, even if it hurts."

"Sue Ellen, I'd like to help but —"

She took my hands in hers and held them tightly. "Please, Wes. I know I probably don't have the right to ask you after everything, but not knowing—that's the hardest part."

"Sue Ellen, just because of something I wrote about years ago...well, I'm not the same person."

"Please? Talk to Kenny, that's all I ask. He knows something but he wouldn't tell me. I think he thinks it's too dangerous for me to know."

"Kenny? How's he wrapped up in this?" I asked.

That's the second time this morning someone mentioned Kenny Burton. Back in the day, he was sort of the unofficial mayor of East Hastings, probably still was. He knew everybody, and I mean everybody. Politician, biker, police officer, college professor, black, white, Hispanic, rich man, poor man. He also knew everything that went down in East Hastings. A lot of the knowledge came from the bar he owned, the favored watering hole of the old money, new money, and dirty money. He was a lot of people's father-confessor, someone everyone trusted for his discretion and advice. He'd also been my main source back when I uncovered the waste dumping scandal, sort of my Deep Throat, tossing out breadcrumbs and leaving it up to me to follow them.

"Just talk to him, that's all I'm asking. If he tells you there's nothing there—that it's just what the police are saying, just some random crime—then I won't ask you to do any more."

What the hell was I supposed to say? She needed me, although I didn't like the "too dangerous" part.

"Okay, I'll talk to Kenny and see what he has to say. If there's something, I'll follow up. If not, we drop it, okay?"

"Oh, Wes, thank you."

She put her arms around me and kissed me on the cheek.

"Wus Byrne, what the hell are you doing here? I thought I made it clear I didn't want you anywhere near my house—or my wife."

It was Tony, standing in the doorway.

Sue Ellen stepped back from me quickly and moved toward him and between us. "It's my house too. I wanted to see him," she said.

He pushed past her. I took a step back. It seemed instinctive.

"Don't you dare touch him, Tony. If you do, so help me—" Sue Ellen said from behind him.

Tony turned to look at her then looked back at me with a furious sneer. "So this is what it's come to, eh, Wus? Having a woman do your fighting for you? Shouldn't surprise me. You never had the guts to fight back," he said.

"Listen, Tony, we're not kids anymore. This is stupid," I said. "You want me to go, I'll go. I know you told me not to come here, but I wanted to pay my respects to Sue Ellen, and I've done that."

I took a step forward to move past him, and he reached out his left arm and pushed me hard in the chest.

"Oh, yeah, I saw you 'paying your respects.' I know you always had a thing for her. That's why you did that whole story about the river, to impress her and get back at me because you couldn't handle it that she was going out with me. You don't make a play for my wife and just walk out of here."

"Oh, please, Tony," Sue Ellen said with a trace of weariness in her voice. "You know Wes and I are old friends—and don't give me any of that wronged husband crap."

"Was I talking to you?" Tony answered her, turning his head slightly and talking over his shoulder before turning back to stare hard at me.

"Get back at you?" I said to him. "I had no idea you were involved with that waste being dumped—"

"Who said I was involved?" Tony said. He swiveled his head quickly to look at Sue Ellen.

"Isn't that what you just implied?" I answered, drawing Tony's attention back to me. "I mean, how was I getting back at you? I don't remember pointing a finger at you—or even at the dry cleaners and your father. I exposed the crime and the people doing the dumping. They were the only people I wanted to get back at."

"You're putting words in my mouth. That's what you do, isn't it, big time reporter? You just make stuff up. I understand you're writing a story about that whore Tina Sanders. I'm sure that will be jam packed with the truth. She was just a stupid whore, and you're probably going to make her out to be some kind of damaged angel."

"How do you know she was a whore?" Sue Ellen said from behind.

He turned his head to look at her again. "Everybody

knew. I could name a dozen guys who banged her."

"Really," I said. "You think any of them would want to kill her—and how did you know I was writing a story?"

Tony turned back to look at me. The two-front attack was keeping him off balance.

"What? You think I'm going to point a finger—I've had enough of you," he said, pushing me hard in the chest again, driving me back a step.

"Tony, I told you to leave him alone," Sue Ellen said, loudly and with a bit of menace.

We both looked at her. She was holding a poker that she must have picked up from the fireplace in her right hand. I don't know about Tony, but I had little doubt she was prepared to use it.

"Mrs. A." It was Ronald. He was standing in the doorway, looking entirely nonplussed. "Dr. Andrews is finished treating Mr. Twaddle. She'd like to speak with you about what to do next."

Sue Ellen lowered the poker, but her eyes still burned at Tony. "Tell her I'll be right there," she answered.

Tony stepped back from me.

"Wes," she said, "let me walk you to the door."

I moved past Tony, who stood motionless, his back to us as we left the room. Sue Ellen handed the poker to Ronald as we passed him in the doorway.

"Thank you, Ronald. I won't be needing this. I think the fire is out—for now."

CHAPTER 33

The ride back to Stevie's place with Ronald was quiet. So many things from the old days came rushing back to me—the teasing and taunting, the bullying and the occasional beating. Now, here I was a grown man, and I let it all happen again. I just stood there and let Tony do what he'd done to me all through school. I was going to let him hit me without putting up any fight. I didn't want to even know what Ronald must have been thinking about me.

We pulled up to Stevie's place and there was my car, tires removed, raised on four jack stands. The front hood leaned against the driver's side door and the engine was suspended about a foot above the front end of the vehicle on an engine hoist. Stacey, dressed in work bib overalls with no shirt, was wiping his hands with a towel and watching us pull in. Ronald barely pulled to a stop before I jumped out of the car.

"What's going on? Ronald told me you were going to have a look at the car, not perform major surgery." I said excitedly as I approached my poor, dismembered vehicle.

"Yeah, well, I gotta tell ya the car's in pretty bad shape. Once I started poking around, it was obvious it weren't goin' be no matter of just changing out sparkplugs. You really didn't take too gooda care of it, did ya? Just goes to show how well the Japs built these damn things that they could be treated like this and still keep on going."

"But—but—I need my car," I sputtered. "How am I going to get around without it? I can't be stranded out here."

"Don't worry, I'll have it up and running like new in a couple of days. Finding parts was the toughest part. I can see why those thieves stole your car. This thing's worth way more chopped up than it is whole, even as bad as you treated it. I hadda to order all the way from some dealership in New Mexico to get parts for the front end and motor block—"

"Ordered parts? But how am I supposed to pay for them, or for your labor—" I began to ask.

The front door to Stevie's swung open and Hoppy stepped out onto the front porch. I was so preoccupied with the state of my car that I failed to see his dark blue Lincoln Town Car parked on the property. He had a can of Pabst Blue Ribbon in his right hand.

"I guess I'll just have to add it to your tab, although I must confess I'm certainly not getting much in return for my largess. At the rate you're going, it'll probably seem like indentured servitude by the time you pay it off."

Although I'd only been up a few hours, it already seemed like it had been a long day. Now I had Hoppy to contend with, but it was just as well. I had a few things I wanted to get off my chest about our arrangement. I walked up the steps to the porch.

"We have to talk," I said as I passed Hoppy to enter the house. Before I did, I turned back to Ronald, who was standing beside Sue Ellen's car.

"Thanks for the ride," I called out to him, "and everything."

"No problem. And oh, wait. I got you this," he said, pulling a cell phone out of his pocket. "It's on a pay as you go plan, but I put five hundred minutes on it so you should be good." He jogged over and up the steps and handed me the phone, as well as a business card. "There's Mrs. A's number and I wrote my number on the back. Anything else you need, you let me know."

"Thanks, Ronald. Five hundred minutes should be more than enough."

"Right then. Mr. Weatherly, nice to see you," he said, nodding toward Hoppy and, if I wasn't mistaken, giving him a slight, sort of knowing smile.

"Ronald. Always a pleasure to see you," Hoppy answered.

Ronald then turned and walked down the steps back toward the car. "Stacey, take it easy. I'll check in with you later," he called out.

"Sounds good. I'll see ya," Stacey answered, waving a grease-covered hand that held a socket wrench. He then turned his attention back to the engine.

I went into the house and headed back to the kitchen. Hoppy followed. I walked to the cabinet that held the bourbon, pulled open the door, and grabbed the bottle and a glass. Then I took a few ice cubes out of the freezer compartment of the refrigerator and tossed them into the glass.

"I don't suppose you'd like a little?" I asked over my shoulder.

"No, thank you. Although there may be exceptions, like the other day at your motel room, as a rule I don't drink any liquor that's brown until the sun goes down," Hoppy answered.

"Oh?" I said. "The sun hasn't gone down yet? Then why do I feel like I'm in the dark here?" I said, the slightest trace of sarcasm in my voice.

"What do you mean, son?"

I sat down at the table, poured a few fingers worth of bourbon into the glass, and took a good swallow. A blast of searing warmth exploded in my empty stomach and mushroomed up through my chest, then my throat, and finally escaped out my mouth.

It rocked me a bit. I needed a second or two before I could answer Hoppy, but, when I did, I looked him squarely in the eyes. "Hoppy, why the hell did you bring me here? And don't try to tell me you didn't. Remember, I'm a reporter—or used to be," I said. "I can tell when people are bullshitting me."

"Who told you I did, and why would I want to bullshit you?" he answered.

"No," I said, taking another swallow of my drink. This one didn't burn near as much. "That's not how it works—you answering my questions with questions. You don't think if I ask Tim why he called me after all these years—how he even knew where I was working—that he won't admit you put him up to it? He's not a good liar, Hoppy. And I already know that since I came into town, you and Sue Ellen have been conspiring to get me to try to dig up some information about Stevie's death. I can understand why she would do it, now that I've talked to her. She's angry, she's been lied to, and she's reached a point that a pathetic, cowardly drunk is the only person she can turn to. I get that. Yet, I think she's just asking me because I'm here. I don't think she ever expected to see me again, to tell you the truth. But you—you knew, didn't you? You knew I was in Providence working at the *Chronicle*. You mentioned following my career—so-called—and you knew the only reason I'd ever come back here was if something…something was wrong…something…I don't know if I'm getting this right or not, but if there was some way I could make things up to someone I once cared about, and hurt, then I'd come back."

"You seem to be giving me an awful lot of credit," Hoppy answered, taking a sip of his Pabst, his eyes not leaving mine.

I had to laugh. Humility was not one of Hoppy's strong suits.

"I don't think so. But I just can't figure out why. I mean, knowing you the way I do—or did—was it all just an amazing stroke of luck that my car got stolen, that I got beaten and wrapped in duct tape, that Tina and Puddy were murdered—"

"Now wait a minute here, son. You're giving me way

too much credit," Hoppy interrupted. "I may have passed your number along to Tim, but to think I had anything to do with your car, or you getting beaten, that's just crazy, and you must know I'd never want to see anyone murdered. I can see you're upset but you're going just a bit far of field here."

He was right about the murder part. That was low.

"Okay I apologize for accusing you of murder. But the other stuff—it's all just drawn me in more and more, and even if you're not behind it all, I bet you've been loving it. Hell, you wanted me to look around Stevie's place for some kind of evidence of something you don't even know exists, and here I am—installed and stranded—with nothing better to do than tear the place apart. Everything just seems to be working out perfect for you. And I just can't figure out why. Why do you want me here? You know this town better than anybody. You can get people to talk when no one else can. You could turn over every rock and expose every insect to the harsh light of day. I don't get it—unless you're afraid of something?"

Hoppy's eyes flashed. "Afraid? Me afraid?" he growled.

"Sure, why not? I am. I mean, we've got three dead bodies. We've got powerful people who seem to want everything to go away, and who knows what else?—police corruption, drug dealers, car thieves, the Crawfords—"

"I ain't afraid, you stupid son of a bitch," Hoppy roared. He looked to his left and right, taking a moment before looking me right in the eyes. "I'm old."

"Oh come on," I answered. "You can do better than that. Men like you don't grow old, their teeth just fall out, and they just lose their bite," I answered, "and you look like you still got all your teeth to me."

"Is that right, you've got it all figured out. Well, let me tell you, if I was a younger man, I'd..." He stopped and appeared to grow a bit wistful for the briefest of moments. "...well, I really don't know what I'd do, probably never get in the newspaper business if the first place—if you can call it that anymore. Paper's pretty much a thing of the past and what passes for news these days…well, it's just people taking sides and making the facts fit their point of view. I'm not long for this game. Hell, practically everything I loved about it is gone."

He took a long poke from the Pabst can, crushed it in his hand, and angrily tossed it into a kitchen trash can that was in the corner. He got up, went to the fridge, and pulled out another can. He must have brought the six-pack with him because I didn't remember seeing it there earlier. He pulled the tab and opened it, took a swig, and then leaned back against the counter.

"You should see how empty the newsroom is. I don't have reporters anymore, I have bloggers—can you believe people actually call themselves that?—and most them don't have the first idea about how to report a story. They just give opinions on what someone else has already given an opinion on. It's so quiet now. The place used to be almost like a symphony hall—filled with music, something Mozart would compose—the typewriters clacking out notes like a piano, the phones trilling like flutes, the loud voices shouting over the noise like bassoons, and underneath it all the steady bass of the printing press. God, I loved the way the earth used to shake with the vibration of the printing press. It was as if our stories, what we were doing, gave the world its pulse. I used to believe we made a difference."

His eyes had drifted off me and out, away somewhere, over and beyond. He paused, took a deep breath, then a long swallow of his beer before returning his gaze to me. The fire had returned in those eyes. "But I'm not going out without a fight, and I wanted you to help me. That's why I got you here. There's something big that's just waiting for us to pull the cover off. I can feel it, practically smell it. And you could too if you weren't so busy feeling sorry for yourself and numbing your senses with that whiskey. I can't do it alone—if I could, I would."

"So why didn't you just ask me?" I said.

"Would you have come if I did?" he answered, giving a look that said he knew the answer.

"Okay, probably not. But honestly, Hoppy, do you expect me to believe all this 'I can feel it, I can smell it' crap? What would you say if I came to you with that kind of a reason to do a story? Come on, tell me the truth. It's about time somebody did."

"Okay," he said. "You're right. It's like this. About a week back, I got a phone call. Caller wouldn't identify himself. Said he had some information that would blow the roof off this town—something about someone who he called a 'leading citizen' and connections to the Crawfords."

"Okay, so this guy says he has information. What do you do?" I asked.

"Well, he says he wants fifteen thousand dollars to give me everything he's got, says he needs it to get out of town once the story broke—fifteen thousand dollars do you believe that? Who did this guy think he was talking to? I told him there's no way we had that kind of money and that we don't pay for information anyway. Told him that if his information was credible, I could see that he got police protection."

"What did he say?"

"He laughed. Said that once the story got out, even the FBI couldn't protect him. Said thanks but no thanks, just thought he'd try to do the right thing before exploring other options. I tried to talk him into coming into the office, or meeting someplace discreet. He hung up on me."

"And…" I asked.

Hoppy took a long drink from his can and looked me in the eyes.

"And two days later your friend Stevie is found stabbed in the back."

Now it was my turn to take a long swallow of my bourbon.

"You think there's a connection?"

"Yeah, I do. Nothing substantial, just that…"

"I know, you can 'smell it, feel it.'"

"Yeah, and I can't help wondering that maybe I should have strung the guy on the phone out a little longer, maybe made a few promises just to see what he had."

"But you're not even sure it was Stevie. It could have been anyone. Maybe Puddy."

"Of course, I know that, but I don't know…and here's the kicker—the police don't seem all that interested in who killed him. It all seems to just get swept under the rug. Brother-in-law of one of the wealthiest guys in town and there's nothing."

"And this guy, he didn't say anything at all about who this 'leading citizen' is or what kind of information he had?" I asked.

"No, just what I told you."

I got up and went to the kitchen window, looked out at the view of the river running by. I turned back to Hoppy. "Do you think—whatever it was—had anything to do with Tina or Puddy's death?"

"To tell you the truth, I really don't know, Wes, but three murders in less than a week. Maybe that caller kicked up a hornet's nest."

"And you want me to walk into that swarm?"

"You afraid of that?" he asked.

"I'm afraid of everything, And if you didn't know it, a single hornet can sting more than once."

CHAPTER 34

The sound of clacking billiard balls resonated throughout the bar from a back room. I stood just inside the doorway to the place, letting my eyes adjust in the lowly lit interior. The Last Chance, Kenny's bar, was where people came to drink and, more to the point, drink and not be seen. It was the place in town where moneymen passed along orders and plain white envelopes to local politicians in the cozy booths along the wall, judges and lawyers waived ethics and discussed cases, bosses worked late with their secretaries, husbands brought their mistresses and wives brought their lovers. Discretion was the word at The Last Chance and long before it became the motto for Las Vegas, what happened at The Last Chance stayed at The Last Chance.

Earlier in the day, I had attended Tina's funeral. It was a small one, just a few of her friends, no one I knew but only recognized from her wedding album. Terri was there, of course, with her family and her father. She introduced me to some people who knew Tina. I interviewed them and, riding with Stacey afterward, I worked out the story I planned to write. He dropped me at the *Chronicle* and I wrote and filed the story with Hoppy. I even gave Hoppy a few photos of Tina from happier times that Terri had lent me. I'd kept my bargain with Terri. Now, I was keeping my promise to Sue Ellen.

Across the darkness of the room was the bar itself, an

oasis of vibrant glowing bottle shapes and sizes displayed with cool white back lighting beckoning the parched and weary. Finally I could see well enough to start moving further inside without worrying about crashing into tables or chairs.

Stacey was sitting in a counter stool at the corner of the bar. I could make out his large silhouette, if not yet his features. He'd driven me over here and we'd agreed that he'd go in first, give the place the once over, and watch to see what kind of reaction I stirred up from the patrons or staff. A few heads turned, a few people looked up from their drinks, but I put that down to idle curiosity, just checking out the new guy in the place.

There were a few empty swivel barstools with backs and armrests stationed along the bar. I liked barstools with backs and armrests. Always felt secure, safe, sitting in one. It had never happened to me, but I'd seen more than one guy, sitting on a regular old barstool, who tilted back to down that one last shot and kept right on going, crashing to the floor, landing on his back, and bouncing his head on the floor, his feet perched on the stool cushion where he'd sat only moments before. I swiveled the seat my way, sat down and rotated to belly up to the copper topped bar.

"Hi," I said to the bartender when she came over. "Kenny around?"

She was attractive and blonde, hair in a classic bob shape and tucked behind her ears, probably in her late-twenties. She was wearing a tight light blue denim long-sleeved shirt with the sleeves rolled up to her elbows. The shirt, with "Last Chance" stitched on the breast pocket, was pulled up and tied at the bottom, revealing a svelte midriff with an emerald stud piercing her navel. The tightness of the shirt accentuated her ample breasts, and she had the top four buttons of the shirt undone to display the upper edges of a black lace bra and her cavernous cleavage. She had on tight white shorts. Chances were great she made a very healthy living off tips.

"I think he's in the back." She turned her head and called out in a jarringly loud voice to a guy sitting on a stool outside a closed door toward the back of the bar, "Billy, tell Kenny's there's someone to see him." She turned back to me and in a softer, sweeter voice asked, "What's your name, darling?"

"Byrne, Wes Byrne," I answered.

She turned her head back to guy in the chair and again with that jarring voice called out, "Says his name is Wes Byrne."

The guy in the chair got up and went through the door.

She turned back to me and, in that sweet voice, asked, "Can I get you something while you're waiting?"

"Sure can. Double Powers, a couple cubes of ice, with water back," I said.

"Coming right up," she answered and turned to walk over to where the Powers sat on an upper shelf of the bottle display behind the bar, looking as good leaving as she did coming. She came back with the bottle, grabbed two rocks glasses from underneath the bar, and laid them on the counter. She dropped a few ice cubes and poured a very healthy amount of Powers into one of the glasses and filled the other about a quarter way with water from a soda dispenser.

"Do you want to pay now or run a tab?" she asked.

"I'll run a tab, I guess—and put that guy over there's next drink on it as well," I said.

"Who—Stacey? You know Stacey? Better put a limit on it, if you want my advice," she said, half-jokingly. "I haven't seen you in here before. I'm Audra. Are you new in town or just visiting?" she asked, leaning over the bar a bit, and I could see a small, multi-colored tattoo of a butterfly on the inside of her left tit. I tried hard not to stare, casting my eyes down at the bar counter.

"Um, just visiting, used to live here, back to see old friends," I answered as I took a very quick swallow of my drink—a little too quick, a little too big of a swallow. The whiskey stalled about half way down my throat for a moment or two, thought about coming back up, the continued on its intended journey. I couldn't help letting out a few choking coughs. Audra stood up straighter and stepped back, a mixture of concern and fear on her face.

"You okay? Maybe you should have a drink of water," she said. "I can pour you some more."

I nodded through a few last coughs and reached out for the rocks glass with the water in it.

"Here," she said, pulling up the soda dispenser and pushing the water button on it just as I lifted the glass to take a sip. The water shot out from the dispenser, hitting the copper topped bar right where my glass had just been, bouncing off, up, and soaking the front of my shirt.

"Oh my God. I'm so sorry," she said, reaching for a bar towel. "Here, let me dry you off."

I heard Stacey stifling a laugh from his perch at the bar.

"N—No, that's o—okay," I stammered, as she reached across the counter to pat me off, dabbing me gently once or twice. Now I could see a small daisy tattooed on her right tit, and it became obvious that butterfly on her left one was fluttering in the direction of the flower. This time she caught me looking and gave me a knowing sort of smile. I felt heat rising on my face and neck.

Luckily, at that moment, the large guy from Kenny's door approached. He looked at the scene dubiously.

"Um, Kenny said he'll see you. Come with me."

"Thanks," I said, getting quickly off my bar stool. "Um…I'll be back to settle my tab," I said to Audra, grabbing my Powers, but leaving the water. I figured if I need a chaser, I'd just suck my shirt.

"I'll be here, and…um, the next one's on me," she said with a laugh, using the towel to wipe the counter dry.

I followed the big guy past Stacey, his head lowered to avoid eye contact and body shaking to control his laughter, and back to the door the large guy had been tending.

He knocked three times, turned the doorknob, opened the door inward, and stepped aside so I could pass into the office. He reached in as I passed, grabbed the doorknob, and pulled the door closed behind me.

CHAPTER 35

Kenny rose from behind his desk to meet me as I entered his office. The room was, in contrast to the dark bar, bright and warm, thanks in part to a large barred window, curtains pulled to the sides, that looked out over the parking lot. The large desk, with only an open Apple Macbook Pro laptop computer and mobile phone sitting on it, faced away from the window and dominated the room. A small bookcase, atop which a small printer sat, held some reams of paper and other office supplies on its shelves. A fold out table along one wall held some colorful, logoed, unused beer taps, folded T-shirts with the Last Chance logo showing, and other tools of the bar trade. There were two comfortable looking, cushioned lounge chairs in front of the desk.

Kenny was much as I remembered him—short and wiry, although his unkempt hair had grayed a bit and his once dark beard had grown more salted than peppered.

"Well, well, if it ain't the prodigal son. I been following your exploits and wondering when you'd get around to seeing ole Kenny," he said.

He wore a comfortably fitting black T-shirt tucked into a pair of bootcut blue jeans, a black bridle leather belt with a brass plaque buckle, and brown square-toed steel-tipped cowboy boots.

He extended his hand and, when I took his in mine, pulled me into a hug. He was stronger than he looked, but

I'd learned long ago that nothing about Kenny was as it seemed.

He stepped back and held his eyes firmly on mine. "Sorry to hear about your wife. She must have been one terrific gal to have corralled and put up with you."

"How did you hear—" I began to say.

"Son—" Only Kenny and Hoppy called me son. "—you gotta know that when you're from someplace you never quite break free of the tentacles that follow you, no matter where you go. Not if people care."

"Well, thanks," I said. "She was…terrific."

"Wish I'd met her. 'Course you did sorta cut bait when you left, but you had things you hadda do, I guess."

Kenny always had such an air of mystery about him. He was not originally from East Hastings but there were stories of his life before settling here and setting up shop. Lots of them, and it was often hard to tell the fact from the fiction. Take the name of the bar, for instance. One telling had it that Kenny was from a pretty wealthy family, the black sheep who insisted on doing things his way. When he went to his family for money to start the bar, his father, apparently fed up with Kenny's rebellious ways, told him he'd give him what he needed but it was his last chance. Another story had it that after years of running with biker gangs and unsavory sorts, Kenny had an epiphany and realized that if he was going to live long enough to see his kids grow up, then going legit and opening the bar was his last chance.

Another mythology grew around Kenny's military record. One story had it that he enlisted in the army, served as a Green Beret and retired from the service as a decorated hero. The flip side to that story was that, much like Ronald, he joined the army to avoid being sent to jail and was eventually dishonorably discharged for striking a superior officer.

Kenny never owned up to any of these stories, nor completely disavowed them either. He seemed to like keeping people guessing.

He patted at the front of his shirt, which had absorbed some of the wetness from mine during the hug.

"Damn, don't you know you're supposed to swallow our drinks, not bathe in them?"

"Just a little accident. Only water, not the good stuff," I answered.

"Well, long as you pay for it I don't care what you do," he said, turning and walking to sit behind the large desk. He motioned for me to sit in one of the chairs across from him. I sat.

Here's what I did know about Kenny. He ran a clean place, despite its clandestine nature—no drugs, no prostitution. He had people's respect. A few years before I left town, there was one occasion where the practical rapport between the races in East Hastings threatened to turn ugly. A young black man was killed, many witnesses say murdered, by a police officer. The blacks wanted justice, the offending police officer got off with a warning. An organized march turned violent, some looting ensued, a curfew was announced. Neither side trusted the other, and there was no telling where things would go. The two sides agreed on a mediator—Kenny, of all people. There was talk for years about this slim white man fearlessly striding past angry blacks with baseball bats and broomsticks right into the Duke of Earl Bar, the watering hole for the black power base, and coming out with an agreement that put an end to all the troubles. People trusted him, and so did I.

"So, what can I do for you?" he asked, putting his feet up on his desk, a knowing smile on his face.

"Actually, Kenny. I have no idea. I know Hoppy wants to sell papers—and Sue Ellen wants to know who killed Stevie—but where you come into this, I really have no idea."

"You know," he said, "I wasn't too surprised to hear you lost your job at the *Sentinel*. Seemed like you kinda lost your way."

"You've been reading my columns?" I said.

"Sure, we do have a thing called the Internet here, you know," he said, indicating the laptop.

"Yeah, well I guess I did. That's why I'm putting all that behind me. It's time for a change."

"And yet, here you are working for Hoppy," he said.

"I'm not working for Hoppy. I'm just paying off a debt," I said.

"You could do—or rather have done—worse. And Sue Ellen, what about her?"

"I guess you could say I owe her as well," I answered.

"You didn't mention Tina. Feel like you owe her too?" he asked.

I took a sip of my drink. "Yeah, maybe. How well did you know her?" I asked.

"Who said I did?" Kenny answered.

I gave him my best don't-kid-a-kidder look. Kenny reached into a drawer, pulled a drink coaster out of it, and flicked it across his desk toward me. I set my drink on it.

"Okay. All in all she was a good kid. A little on the wild side, especially after her husband died, but she seemed to be settling down a bit. I didn't see much of her the last year or two."

"You know, the police insinuated to her sister that she might have been…um…well, a prostitute?" I said. "You know anything about that?"

Kenny smiled. "Still a bit of a boy scout at heart, huh? I don't know as I would call her a…um…well, a prostitute," he said, gently mocking me. "Every once in a while she stepped out with some of the big shots in town—behind their wives' backs of course—maybe some money changed hands. Basically, I think she just needed to let off steam, have a good time. Like I said, she was a little wild after her husband's accident, and she was still quite a looker."

"Yeah, she certainly was," I said, remembering those green eyes. "She was afraid when she came to my hotel room. Do you think it was Puddy Salvatore she was afraid of? Because she brought my car back? And don't act like you don't know anything about him or who's behind the car thefts."

"I don't think anybody was afraid of Puddy Salvatore…well, almost anybody," he said, giving me another quick, knowing smile. "'sides, he wouldn't hurt her. He was completely ga-ga over her. She ever threw him a crumb, he'd think it was a banquet, but from what I heard she never did. That stuff they pulled off—the arrangement was all strictly business from what I heard, and that's all I'll say about the car ring. Now, can I ask you a question, Mr. Reporter?"

"Sure, go ahead," I answered, picking up my drink and taking another swallow.

"What exactly are you after?" he said. His eyes stayed direct on mine.

"What do you mean what am I after?" I answered.

"I mean, why are you here?" he said.

"I told you, because Hoppy and Sue Ellen seem to think there's more to Stevie Darby's death than the police are letting on, and each, for their own reasons, want me to poke around. Sue Ellen seems to think you might have a thing or two to share that could help me figure where to look, without, of course, betraying any confidences. So here I am," I said, believing I'd satisfactorily summed things up.

"But you haven't asked me a thing about Steve Darby, only Tina," Kenny pushed on.

"Just making conversation," I said.

This time he gave me the don't-kid-a-kidder look.

"Okay, maybe I am interested in finding out who killed her as well."

"My, my, aren't you a regular Sherlock Holmes…or is it Sam Spade?" he answered.

"No. It's not like that. I don't expect to really find anything out, but I mean, if I had been there…I don't know…maybe I could have stopped whoever it was, maybe we wouldn't have even opened the door. I let her down."

"Oh, so you were gonna stop the killer? Listen, son, she

may have only been working with Puddy, but she was deal-ing with a pretty rough crowd. No offense, but I think you both would've ended up dead."

"Maybe that would have been better. At least then…"

"Then what? You wouldn't have to deal with the shit hand life's dealt you?" he said, his voice raising. "Damn, son, grow a pair. You think you're the only one crap has ever happened to." He paused for a moment, then a smile returned to his face. "I'm sorry, that was out of hand. You still haven't answered my question, though. Why are you here?"

"I told you, Hoppy wants to sell newspapers to the few people left in town who still read them, Sue Ellen wants answers, and…okay, I guess I want a few of my own. There's your answer."

"Not really, but it seems as close to one as I'm gonna get right now. So you had questions about Steve Darby." He leaned back in his chair. "Go ahead, shoot."

I took the last swallow from my glass.

"Okay, I'll start with the obvious. Did Stevie have any enemies that you knew of?"

"Nah, I highly doubt it. He was pretty well liked, a good time guy, bought drinks when he was flush, never caused any trouble—at least not here."

"Was he selling drugs?" I asked.

"Again, not here—you know my policy—but probably a little grass once in a while, probably just to get a skim. He wasn't a big-time dealer by any account."

"Anything between him and Tina?"

"Nah, maybe way back in the day before Tina got mar-ried, but, no, that's all ancient history."

"So he wasn't he involved in the car thefts with Tina and Puddy?"

"I said I wasn't gonna talk about that anymore," he an-swered.

"You don't have to tell me anything about it, just wheth-er Stevie was involved in it," I said.

"No, I'm pretty sure he wasn't. It's kinda of an exclusive club, if you get my drift. And the operation is run like a business—a regular Pep Boys of stolen parts. People need hard-to-find parts, the gang goes and get them. Stevie was a bit too much of an entrepreneur, didn't handle structure well."

"So you don't think Stevie had anything to do with the Crawfords?"

Kenny leaned back a little more in his chair, looked at the ceiling for a moment, then lowered his head, and leaned forward across his desk. "That's a name you should be very careful how you toss around," he said, his eyes fixing on mine.

"Well, Hoppy seems to think—"

"I don't give a shit what Hoppy thinks. I'm talking to you. That family is trouble. And they are evil, everyone of 'em, right down to the bone. Stay the hell away from them. Focus your attention elsewhere."

"But if they are responsible for—"

"They ain't. You'll have to take my word for it, but they ain't. First of all—" He held up an index finger. "—those stolen cars are way too small-fry for them, though they probably gave permission for it to go on, but that's about the extent of their involvement. Secondly—" His middle finger joined the index finger. "—you've got what? Police found three bodies? Well, if the Crawfords want someone dead, there's never a body to be found. Anywhere. People just sorta disappear, gone without a trace. And third—" His ring finger joined the others. "—if they get just a whiff of you poking around their affairs—involved or not, and I'm telling you they are not—they won't hesitate to send you to your maker, and probably not in one piece."

I sat quietly for a few moments and let what Kenny had said sink in. The part about disappearing didn't rattle me. I didn't think I'd really be missed. But the thought of being chopped up into little pieces…well, that was a whole 'nother story.

"Okay," I said. "No need to drag the Crawfords into this if you say they had nothing to do with it."

Kenny smiled. "Good to see you still have some sense left."

"Besides, I've got enough on my plate with Stevie and Tina," I said.

"And Puddy," Kenny answered, his smile growing slyer.

"Puddy? I never said anything about Puddy."

"Isn't he the only one that sort of links Tina and Stevie?"

"Well, yeah, but not directly. I haven't found anything that—do you know something you're holding back?" I asked.

"I know lots of things I'm holding back. That's what I do. That's how I stay in business."

"Well, c'mon, give me something."

Kenny tapped his fingers on his desk. "Kinda feel like I'm doing your job for you."

"Want to share my by-line?" I asked sarcastically.

"No, you can get all the glory—if it ever comes to that."

"Then what is it you can tell me?"

"I'm not going to tell you anything, but I will ask you one question. Have you explored the fact that Stevie and Puddy worked together on the night shift at TSN warehouse?"

"They did? Why didn't Sue Ellen tell me that?"

"She didn't know."

"But Puddy knew?" I asked.

"Story is Puddy helped him get the job."

"Wait a minute. Wait a minute. You're telling me Stevie and Puddy were friends?"

"I don't know about friends, but they partied together once in a while, used to come in here for a beer now and then."

"Why didn't anyone tell me this before?"

"I don't know. Maybe you didn't ask the right people— or the right questions."

"Do you think Puddy had anything to do with Stevie's murder?" I asked.

"Don't know and, besides, that's your job to find out."

"Right. Any big ideas on how to do that?"

"You could always ask Puddy's mother. He was, by all accounts, a bit of a momma's boy."

"Right, I'm supposed to just walk up to her, introduce myself as the man Puddy beat and who later found his dead body, and she's going to open up. I mean, how would I even get to her?"

"Well, Puddy's funeral is tomorrow. You could always talk to her there."

I looked at Kenny like he had just suggested I walk into a lion's cage wearing a meat suit.

"His funeral? Me? With not only his mother, who probably hates me, there but also a few people that he might have been stealing cars with—people who may have killed Stevie, may have killed Tina, may have even killed Puddy, and, in all probability, wouldn't mind seeing me dead as well. Jeez, I was getting the feeling you didn't want to see me hurt."

Kenny took his feet off his desk and leaned forward in his chair. "Actually, what I'd like to see you do is just drop the whole thing," he said, his eyes deadly serious. "Like I said, these are dangerous people. But if you feel like you got obligations to pay, I want you to see exactly the type of people you are messing with." He leaned back in his chair. "Besides, no one would do anything to you at his funeral, they're not that stupid. You show his mother you have good intentions, who knows? She probably wants to know who killed Puddy. Maybe you'll make a few friends."

"Friends? You've got to be—" I started to blurt out. Then I saw that Kenny had a mischievous smile on his face.

"Look," he said. "You came here looking for answers. Unfortunately, I don't have much for you—"

I looked at him skeptically.

"—really I don't. These guys run a tight operation. I'm

just saying that if you really want to get some of the answers you are looking for…well, this is the way I'd suggest. Besides, I'll go with you if you want. It's only right that I pay my respects—part of doing business with the people I do business with."

I rubbed my temples hard with my right hand. "Ah, what the hell," I said. "Another day, another funeral."

Of course, chances were I was setting the stage for my own.

CHAPTER 36

aybe they'll just dig a hole right next to Puddy's and throw your dead body into it."

It was Tim, filling me with confidence, as we sat at Stevie's place that evening over a dinner of rice, beans, and sausage prepared by Stacey, who continued to surprise with his multiple talents. The meal was really good.

"I mean, you can't seriously be considering going to that funeral. Don't you think that maybe one or more of those people might think that Tina, or Puddy for that matter, told you things that could put them in jail?"

"Kenny said they wouldn't try anything—at least not at the funeral," I answered.

In addition to Tim and Stacey, Ronald had also stopped by for dinner. He said his wife was out with friends, but I had the feeling he wanted to stop by and check up on the work Stacey had been doing. We were sitting in the kitchen around the table. I'd introduced Tim to the guys, and it had taken no time for them to get comfortable with each other, making small talk until I dropped the news about going to the funeral.

"Ah, famous last words as some guy is running a knife into you, 'Kenny said you wouldn't try anything,'" Tim replied.

"Look," I said, taking a forkful of the food on my plate. I was talking with my mouth full but I really didn't care. This was the first real meal I'd eaten in weeks. "I'm not exactly thrilled to be going, but Kenny's right. Sometimes the soil is richest where it's the rockiest."

"Oh, Jesus. That is one of the stupidest metaphors I've ever heard, and I don't even think it's true. Richest where it's rockiest…"

He was right. That stunk, but it was the best I could come up with. I changed the subject. "So did any of you know that Stevie was working at TSN warehouse?" I asked.

"I didn't, and I don't think Mrs. A did either, but it makes sense that no one knew," Ronald said. "Stevie and Tony didn't get along too well. No secret there. Last thing Stevie would probably want people to know is that he was actually working for him."

"Is that right? Any reason in particular why they didn't get along? I mean, besides the fact that Tony is a major league asshole?" I asked, taking a sip from my ice-cold bottle of Dos Equus.

Beer just seemed to go better with Mexican food than whiskey. It was also a little too hot and humid for Powers, despite the window fan that basically just moved sticky air about the room.

No one answered at first. Stacey was no doubt silent because he didn't have a clue. Ronald didn't say anything, perhaps because of loyalty to Sue Ellen, just one of what I suspected were his many admirable traits. Tim…well, Tim avoided eye contact and pushed some of the rice on his plate into a tidy little pile.

"Tim, do you know something?" I asked.

He looked up. "All I have is rumors, gossip, nothing I can really attest to…just, you know, Town Crier blather."

"Are you kidding me?" I asked. "At this point I'd take information from an old gypsy in a wagon with a crystal ball. What have you heard?"

"Okay, word is that Tony started fooling around on Sue Ellen practically as soon as they were married, and that when Stevie heard the rumors he got pretty hot. I heard, but again this all just talk, that he even threatened to kill Tony, although no one really believed he would. You knew Stevie…"

"Yeah, he'd definitely stick up for his sister. One of the step outs by Tony, could that have been Tina?" I asked.

"No, word is Tony likes 'em younger, just out of college," Tim answered.

Stacey spoke up for the first time. "So, maybe Stevie threatened to tell Sue Ellen. Maybe he was blackmailing Tony, and rather than pay out, Tony offs Stevie."

"Could be. A knife in the back would be just Tony's style," I said.

"She knew."

It was Ronald.

"What?" I asked.

"Mrs. A knew about Tony's…dealings. She told me once—I guess she had to talk to somebody—said she didn't leave him because of the kids." He looked at each of us in turn. "I'm only telling you guys because Mrs. A said to tell you whatever you needed to know, but everything I say—" he said, pointing his index finger down and moving it in a circular motion around the table, "—doesn't leave this room."

"Well, so much for a motive for Tony," Tim said.

"Yeah, too bad. That was the first theory that made any sense," I said, stuffing my mouth with another forkful, "at least as far as Stevie's death."

"You think maybe Puddy told Stevie about the car ring and Stevie was blackmailing someone involved in that? And whoever it was decided to take care of both Stevie and Puddy?" Stacey asked. He seemed to be enjoying working up blackmail scenarios.

"I don't know. I don't think Stevie would be stupid enough to take on the kind of guys who are stealing and chopping the cars and, from what Kenny told me, it was a rather small-time operation. They wouldn't have the kind of money at any one time that would make it worth it for Stevie to take on the risk. He'd want to make a big score—big enough to buy a forty-thousand-dollar boat and probably get out of Dodge."

There was a knock at the front screen door. The outer door was open so some air could get into the place. Feeling very full and a little too lazy to get up and answer, I yelled out for the person to enter. Stacey got up and moved to the inside of the kitchen doorway, out of sight and ready to stop any undesirable visitor. He needn't have bothered. It was Dom.

"Hi, Dom. Join the party," I said as he came out of the hallway and into the kitchen.

"What are you celebrating? Your first night not spending time in jail?" he said.

"Very funny. I'm surprised to see you here. Didn't think your wife would let you hang around with me after what happened. Beer's in the fridge," I said.

"Yeah, me either, but she kinda liked the article you wrote on Tina. She read it online. They were friends once it seems—back in high school—so she said it was okay. She made me promise not to break any laws, though," he said, crossing over to the fridge, opening it, and taking out a beer. "Anyone else?" he asked. We all raised our hands. He reached in and grabbed three more. As he laid them on the table, he sniffed over our plates. "Smells good. Any left?"

"Help yourself. Plates are in that cabinet over there," I said, indicating with my fork. "Silverware's in the drawer."

"So—" Dom asked as he opened a couple cabinets before he found the one holding the plates and then did the same with the drawers until he found the one with the forks, knives, and spoons, "—you guys figure everything out yet?"

"Not even close," Tim said. "We were waiting for you to show up to solve it all."

"You kidding?" Dom said as he put his plate on the table and sat down next to me. "I'm still seeing that dead body with the knife sticking out of it and all that blood."

He piled a heap of the rice meal onto his plate. Didn't

seem like the image of Puddy lying on the living room floor affected his appetite.

"Yeah, that was the first dead body I ever saw," said Tim. "Did the police say how long he'd been lying there?"

"They weren't exactly sharing information with me," I answered.

"What about the knife?" Dom asked, coming up for air. "Can't they check for fingerprints or run some kind of…what do you call it…ballistics on it?"

"Ballistics is for bullets, Dom," Tim said.

"One thing the police did say was that the handle of the knife was wiped clean, when I was proclaiming my innocence and denied ever touching it," I answered.

"Well, they must have some way to tell if that knife was the same one that killed Stevie or Tina—size of blade or something like that," Ronald said. He turned to Stacey. "You wouldn't happen to have a knife on you, do you?"

"Sure," Stacey answered, reaching down and pulling a blade out of his right boot.

I shook my head. "Of course, he does. This is East Hastings, after all."

"Well, mine's in the truck, but I can tell just by looking at Stacey's that his blade is thicker and wider than mine."

"Probably longer too," Stacey said with a smile.

"I wouldn't go that far," Ronald said, returning a smile of his own. "But it would surely make a different entry wound in a body than mine."

"Sure, probably. That makes sense, but like I said, the police aren't sharing that kind of information with me," I said.

"You are an investigative reporter, aren't you? There must be some way for you to investigate and find out," said Tim.

"Well, something like that is probably in the coroner's report, but I don't see—" I started to say.

"You know," Ronald interrupted, "I think the coroner has a daughter who rides a horse. I've seen him at a couple of horse shows when I've gone with Mrs. A to watch her daughters ride."

"Yeah, so?" I asked.

"Well, maybe Doc Andrews knows him. She takes care of most of the horses in Hastings County. Maybe she could—"

I stopped him right there. "No, I'm not getting her involved in this, and I don't see why she'd help anyway," I said, looking down and poking at the remaining grains of rice on my plate.

"I don't know," Ronald answered. "I kinda got the feeling she liked you a little."

I looked around the table. Stacey, Tim, and Dom all had an amused look on their faces.

"Well, what do you know?" said Tim. "Looks like it's time for our boy Wes here to turn on the charm."

"Forget it," I said. "It would be real stupid to count on my charm getting me anywhere."

What was even more stupid was the flutter I felt when Ronald said Jackie kinda liked me.

CHAPTER 37

Seeing Puddy's mother sitting beside the gravesite, it was apparent where Puddy got his looks. She was a milk jug of a woman, with a large head covered by a black lace mourning scarf, and an elongated chin beneath a toothless mouth. She sat on a metal fold-out chair and, beside her, holding an umbrella above her that shielded her from the sun, stood a man I recognized from Tina's wedding album. It was the guy with the scary, intense eyes. He leveled them at me as Kenny and I approached the small gathering at the grave.

Puddy was being buried in what must have been a private graveyard on his family's property. Kenny and I entered a square plot of land enclosed, except for a small entrance, by a two-foot-high decorative wrought iron face. There were several gravestones inside it, some very weather-worn, which I assumed marked the resting places of earlier generations of Salvatores. There wasn't much room left, probably just enough for Puddy and his mother, when she followed. It was just as well, since Puddy was the end of the Salvatore line.

The property was in Crankerville, a very small borough in Hastings County. It was only a few miles outside of East Hastings, but it might as well have been another world. I'd never been here before, but when we turned off Route 182 onto the road that led to the place and drove down a twisty road that eventually led past wooden clapboard houses with dilapidated front porches, I was shocked at its resemblance to photos I had seen of "hollers" in West Virginia. Suspicious eyes followed us as we drove past people idly gathered on the front porches. Even the young, barefooted children playing in the hard dirt front yards watched us with a hand-me-down wariness.

There were only a handful of people at the funeral, a mixture of older and younger women and men. The women wore simple black dresses. Some of the men wore what must have been their Sunday best suits, white shirts, and ties, obviously uncomfortable with the tight collars in the heat and humidity. A few others wore black leather jackets with identical biker patches, a deep red, fire-breathing silhouette of a devil's horned head sewn on the back, black t-shirts, black jeans and biker boots. Puddy's simple, pine coffin sat on a raised platform beside the grave. Two guys wearing overalls and no shirts leaned on shovels a little ways off to the side.

Kenny and I stayed back from the gathering. Kenny was wearing a black suit, white shirt, bola tie and his cowboy boots. Ronald had managed to get the dark suit I had brought with me for Stevie's funeral pressed at the dry cleaners, and I wore it with a white shirt opened at the collar.

"Those guys belong to the Demons. You should be careful around them," Kenny whispered to me, nodding in the direction of the bikers.

"Yeah, I kind of assumed that on my own. How about the umbrella-holder? Is he one of them too?" I whispered back.

"Yeah, Ricky Tiffin. They call him Bones. He's a road captain," Kenny answered.

I looked at Kenny blankly.

"I'll explain later," he said.

The service was down to earth, so to speak. A priest, wearing a simple white vestment over a black robe and a white stole with a bar of gold fabric at each end, said a few words over the grave about Puddy being a loving son and loyal friend and then read the Twenty-Third Psalm. When he was finished, several of the bikers came forward, lifted the coffin with straps that were lying under it, carried it over to the grave, and lowered it down, tossing the straps into the grave. Ricky Tiffin then led Mrs. Salvatore over to the grave, scooped up a handful of dirt, and handed it to her. She took the dirt in her right hand and lifted her veil with her left. Her eyes were moist but she wasn't crying. She stood quietly for a moment, looking down into the grave. She crossed herself and then threw the handful of dirt onto the coffin. Tiffin then scooped up another handful of dirt and this he threw onto the coffin.

They stood beside the grave for a few more moments and then he whispered something to Mrs. Salvatore. She nodded. With Tiffin holding the umbrella above her, they both turned and walked past Kenny and me out of the iron fencing, neither making eye contact with us or even appearing to know we were there, and off toward a two-story house that sat a short distance away. The other mourners formed a line by the grave and each in turn scooped up dirt and tossed it into the grave before filing past Kenny and me out toward the house. These guys made eye contact with me, and it wasn't hard to sense what they were thinking. They then looked at Kenny, letting him know they weren't too pleased with the company he was keeping. He merely nodded and said hello to each by name as they passed.

"C'mon," Kenny said once they had moved past us, heading toward the grave. "Let's go pay our respects."

"You sure I should? Won't it piss some of these guys off?"

Kenny laughed. "Well, you aren't exactly the guest of honor, but it's the right thing to do."

We walked over to the grave just as the two guys in overalls came over with their shovels. Kenny raised his right hand, palm out, and they stopped. He bent down, grabbed a handful of dirt, and tossed it onto the coffin. I did likewise, but there must have been a stone in my handful, because there was a loud clunk when I tossed it in. The two guys looked at each other and shook their heads, frowning.

We turned and looked at the house.

"Ready?" Kenny asked.

"No," I answered. "I still think this is a bad idea."

He stopped and looked at me.

"Did your balls stop growing when you left East Hastings? I told you nothing is going to happen."

"Did you see the way those guys looked at me? I know they all have knives—I mean, it is Hastings County so they must—and I felt like they were sizing me up like one of those diagrams you see at the butcher shop that shows all the different cuts of meat, just a matter of who got the choicer cuts."

"You worry too much," Kenny said, taking me by the elbow and guiding me out of the gravesite. "You may not believe this, but a lot of these guys actually appreciate what you did to clean up the river. Not all of them, of course— okay, maybe only a few—but that river means a lot to quite a few people.

"You mean I've got a fan club," I said.

"Well, I wouldn't go that far. One step at a time. These guys can smell fear so just try to relax. Breathe."

"Sure, take a breath. I mean, I may not have that many left so I might as well use them before I lose them." I inhaled deeply and walked with Kenny toward the house.

Several of the mourners had gathered on the front steps and porch. They let Kenny through, but as I followed they inched closer together to block my entrance.

"Guys," Kenny said, turning back to them. "The man came out here to pay his respect. Let him say his piece, and he'll be gone."

The sea parted, and I walked up the steps and onto the porch toward the door, although I got a few not too subtle bumps from shoulders and elbows along the way.

We entered the house through a two-paneled wooden

screen door with a rusty spring that squeaked loudly as we opened it. The door closed with a loud bang behind us once we passed through it, and I jumped at bit. I hoped no one noticed.

It was a large, bright room thanks to large, open-curtained windows and filled with scents from flowers arrangements—lilies, carnations, and lavender—sent by people who could not attend but wanted to show their sympathies.

The furniture in the room was simple, old but well cared for. A large sofa sat in the center of the room, covered with a brightly squared quilt. There were a few chairs, all with doilies on the arm rests, a couple of floor lamps and small end tables at either side of the sofa, also topped with doilies. The only modern looking component of the room was a large flat screen television that took up most of the wall directly across from the sofa. The other walls were a light brown paneling and on them hung a few family photos and hand-embroidered artwork in wooden frames. A slowly revolving ceiling fan kept the room cool.

Mrs. Salvatore sat at the far end of the room in a rocking chair to the left of a stone fireplace at the back wall. On the mantel of the fireplace sat a photo of Puddy in happy times, posing next to a Harley Davidson Ultra Glide motorcycle. The frame was draped with black crepe and a single rose sat before it. Hovering next to her was Ricky Tiffin. A small circle of older women were gathered around her. She looked up as Kenny and I approached. The women took notice and moved off, looking over their shoulders to give me a once over and whispering to themselves. Tiffin remained right where he was. Kenny stepped forward.

"Mrs. Salvatore, I am very sorry for your loss. I know Puddy was a good son and never caused a bit of trouble at my place. People liked him. He'll be missed."

She looked at him with rather dark, penetrating eyes and nodded. "Thank you."

Kenny brought me forward. "This is Wes Byrne," he said.

I stepped up. I noticed Tiffin's body stiffened a bit and his black eyes burned at me as he sized me up. Mrs. Salvatore showed nothing, just sat there looking at me, her toothless mouth moving in a slow circular motion as if chewing on something. "Mrs. Salvatore, I'm—" I started.

"I know who you are," she said curtly. There was a slight twang in her voice that was not unfamiliar in East Hastings, owing to a migration of families over the years from points south.

"Well, um, I just want to say how sorry I am. My wife— died about a couple of years ago—and it was terrible. But I can't imagine the sorrow of losing a child—"

"You wrote that article about that whore Tina, made her out to be some kind of saint. She weren't no saint," she replied, moving forward in her rocking chair.

Well it was good to see that some people still did read the *Chronicle*.

"I—I—just wanted to give her family some peace."

She sat quietly, rocking a bit. She looked up at Tiffin slowly. Their eyes met and held for a few moments. Then she looked back at me. "Yeah, I can understand them wanting that," she said.

Kenny was standing behind me and I felt him give me a very quick, discreet poke in the back.

"Well, maybe I could...um do the same for you and Puddy," I answered. "Perhaps I could come sometime, sit, and talk with you."

"Can I trust you? You're not going to make him look stupid, or like a bad man?" she said.

"No, that would not be my intention. Just a story about a good son."

"Can I read it before you print it, give my final say so?" she asked.

"Yes, of course. Of course, you can."

Again she looked up at Tiffin and I saw the faint trace of

smile appear briefly on her thin lips. Her jaw grinded her toothless gums. "Okay, I don't see no harm. Long as I get to see it first. You got a card."

I reached into my inside jacket pocket, pulled out a small notepad, wrote my cell number on it, and handed it to her. "You can call me and let me know a time that's good for you."

"I will—and Mr. Byrne," she began, taking the slip of paper from me.

"Yes, Mrs. Salvatore?"

"I am sorry for the loss of your wife." She paused and looked at me squarely with her black eyes. Her lips curled into the semblance of a smile. "We should all remember that life is short."

"I will. Thank you," I answered.

I turned and Kenny and I walked out through the door. I held onto it as I closed it to prevent any banging. We went down the steps. This time the men let me through without a hassle. We continued off toward his car. Except for the poke, he had been quiet throughout my exchange with Mrs. Salvatore.

"That went better than expected," I said, feeling the dread I'd been carrying lift off my shoulders.

"Yeah, maybe," he answered. "Seemed a little too easy."

"Aw c'mon. This was your idea and it worked out great."

"What was that she said to you at the end?" Kenny asked.

"That she was sorry for my loss. A nice thing to say, considering the circumstances," I answered.

"No, after that," he said.

"Um…to remember life is short," I answered.

We had reached Kenny's car. We stood on opposite sides, looking at each other over the roof. Kenny used his key fob to unlock the car doors.

"Exactly. Lots of ways a person can take that," Kenny said, opening his door and getting into the car.

I opened my door but stood for a moment looking back at the house and the men on the porch still watching us. "Life is short," I said softly to myself, "No, come on." I leaned down and looked at Kenny through my open door. "You don't think she was threatening?"

Kenny had an amused smile on his face. "She may not have any teeth, don't mean she might not bite."

CHAPTER 38

I had to admit this was a first—contemplating the ways a dwarfish, old toothless woman could do me harm should we face off.

I was pretty sure I could overpower her if she made a direct attack with any sort of weapon. She could, of course, use the element of surprise, so I determined to stay vigilant. There was poison. I remembered reading or hearing somewhere that poison was a preferred method for women who wanted to kill someone, so I made a note to politely turn down any drink or food she offered, social conformities be damned. Did she have the know-how to rig a booby trap, maybe a bomb wired to a front porch step that would explode when I tripped the device? I'd have to remember to look for wires.

There was no trace of a large dog that she could sic on me, but I hadn't really been on the lookout for one. It could have been tied up somewhere out back. She might deny it food, just to make it especially hungry and aggressive. Not sure how I'd handle that. Maybe take along some bacon treats or a meat bone I could toss to the hungry mongrel that might buy me some time to make a getaway. Electrocution? Gas? An arrow in the back from a crossbow as I walked to my car? The list seemed endless. I mentally prepared appropriate countermeasures to each possibility that arose.

Kenny initially tried to make small talk during the drive, but eventually left me to my thoughts, popped a Willie Nelson CD into his car's player, and sang along to Willie's crooning.

When we pulled into Stevie's driveway, I could see I had company. Sue Ellen's Silverado was parked near my Camry, and I could see the back ends of Ronald and Stacey leaning under the hood on opposite sides of my car. Behind the Silverado was Jackie's SUV, though she was nowhere in sight.

I was surprised to see Sue Ellen come out of the house at the sound of Kenny's car approaching. She was wearing a green floral romper, white-strapped slide sandals, and a white canvas sun hat. A large, excited, barking Golden Retriever pushed past her through the open door and came bounding up alongside the car as we pulled up, seemingly intent to take a bite out of Kenny's right front tire. Jackie came out of the house behind Sue Ellen. They were both laughing at the dog's antics.

When we came to a stop, the dog stood up on its hind legs, its front paws resting against my door. It continued to bark and I could see its sharp teeth. Thank goodness the window was closed.

Jackie came up and stood by the dog. She had on beige canvas jumpstart shorts that showed off a pair of tan, shapely legs and a maroon Swiss dot pullover, its sleeves rolled up to just below her elbows. She wore black cross training sneakers with black laces. Her hair was pulled back and held with a simple beige scrunchie. She was enjoying the show.

"Don't worry, she won't hurt you, she's a sweetheart," I heard her shout through the closed window.

Obviously from the look on my face she could tell I was more than a little skeptical. She took the dog by its collar and pulled it back away from the car. The dog strained forward, but Jackie held on tight and said something to the dog that I couldn't hear. It sat down obediently at her side, although it didn't take its eyes off me.

"You can come out now," she hollered.

I did so tentatively.

"This is Ginger," Jackie said. She knelt down next to the dog and began stroking its head and neck. "Ginger's a good girl, isn't she?" she said to the dog.

The dog's mouth opened and its tongue flopped out. It was breathing heavily.

"Is she yours?" I asked.

"Um, not exactly," Jackie answered, and she turned to look at Sue Ellen, who came forward past Jackie and the dog and gave me quick peck on the cheek.

"How was the funeral?" she asked.

"Oh, pretty typical, though I think I've just about had my fill of them," I answered.

"He was the hit of the party," Kenny said, a big smile on his face, as he got out of the car. "I wouldn't be surprised if he made some new friends."

"Hi, Kenny," Sue Ellen said as he came around the car. She gave him a hug and a quick peck. "Do you know Dr. Jackie Andrews?"

"Haven't had the pleasure, but I've heard good things. How do you do?" he said, giving her a polite nod.

"Nice to meet you too," Jackie said, still kneeling by the dog and petting it.

"Beautiful dog," he said and he walked over, bent down, and began scratching the dog behind the ears. "I had a Retriever once, until we found out one of my daughters was allergic. Found it a good home, though I still miss him."

While Kenny and Jackie lavished attention on Ginger, Sue Ellen walked over to and slipped her arm through mine.

"Can we talk—out back?" she asked.

"Sure," I said.

We walked quietly together around the house, across the back yard, and out onto the small, worn, wooden dock that jutted out over the river. We stopped about halfway across it and I waited for Sue Ellen to talk. Instead, she stood looking out at the river and the people floating and frolicking past in canoes and on inner tubes.

"Ronald told me he told you about me and Tony," she began, still watching the activity on the river.

"Yeah…well, no one will say anything," I said.

"Hah," she replied sharply, "you think I don't know that practically everyone in town already knows? I don't think Tony has been particularly discreet."

I didn't really know what to say so I just stood there, looking down at her.

She turned her head and looked up, her eyes sad under the brim of her hat. "I really did love him. I know people said I only married him for his money, but that's not true. He was fun. He treated me so good, at first. I knew he wasn't perfect, but I thought—well, I know how stupid it sounds, but I thought I could change him. I thought he might become more like his dad."

"It doesn't sound stupid," I said, thinking about Jan and how she made my life into something I'd never imagined could happen.

"Well," she said with a brittle laugh, "obviously I didn't, and you must think I'm so weak and pathetic to put up with everything. But I'm sticking it out for my children. They're the most important thing in the world to me, and I'm not going to let anything destroy the world I've created for them. I'm an adult. I made my choices. They are not going to pay for my mistakes."

Her eyes had started to well up with tears and she turned her head quickly to look back out over the river. A mother and father with two children were splashing each other with paddles as they floated past in their canoe.

"What happened, Wes?" she asked. "How was it all so easy when we were kids?" If my parents were alive today, they wouldn't recognize the woman I've become."

"They probably had their problems too, only they didn't let on. Life is hard, but look at what you do have. Friends, beautiful kids, Ronald, and his wife. So it's not perfect, but I bet if you added up all the hours in a day, you'd find that most of them are pretty good."

She looked back at me with a sweet smile and dabbed her eyes dry. "I've missed you, Wes. I'm so glad you came back."

"Yeah…well…um," I stammered. Fortunately at that moment we were interrupted by the sound of Jackie's voice.

"Ginger, come back here. Ginger."

We turned and saw Ginger racing toward us in an all-out sprint, Jackie trailing behind.

The dog raced past us and leapt off the end of the dock into the river, landing with a large splash that sent water cascading back, washing over Sue Ellen's and my legs. Jackie continued chasing until she joined Sue Ellen and me on the dock.

"I took my eyes off Ginger for one second and she was off," she said, trying to catch her breath. "I think she really missed this river."

Ginger had swum out to about the center of the river where she retrieved a floating tree branch and then turned and started paddling back our way.

"C'mon, Ginger. C'mon out," Jackie yelled.

Sue Ellen started doing likewise, the two of them patting their thighs and urging the dog back. Ginger reached the shore and seemed to know the perfect spot where she could climb out onto dry land. She shook and water sprayed off her body.

"Did you say she missed the river," I asked. "Have you brought her out here before?"

Jackie and Sue Ellen shared a conspiring look.

"Well…um…Ginger was Stevie's dog. I've had her out at the house since…" Sue Ellen's voice trailed off and she took a moment to continue. "She's a good dog, only she's been scaring the horses, chasing them around the paddock, and Tony's been complaining about her barking all night, and I'm afraid he'll do something rash, so…um…well Jackie and I thought…" She looked at Jackie for support.

"She's probably missing Stevie, and her home. That's why she's barking so much. So we thought it shouldn't be too hard to find her a good home, only—" Jackie began and then stopped.

They were both looking at me and I got a queer feeling that I knew where this was going. "Wait a minute," I said. "If you're suggesting what I think you're suggesting, there's no way. No way at all. I can barely take care of myself. I don't know the first thing about dogs and this one looks like a handful." I looked over at Ginger and she was lying on the ground where she'd come out of the water, gnawing on and making splinters of the large tree branch that she'd taken from the river. "I mean, look at that. Is she supposed to do that?" I asked.

Ginger paused for a moment to stop chewing on the branch, looked at me, and gave out a large bark as if to say, "You think you can take this away from me?" She went back to chewing.

"No, no, she isn't," Jackie said. "Ginger, leave it and come over here. Right now," she hollered firmly at the dog.

Ginger took a moment to think it over then slowly got up, left the branch lying on the ground, and began to slowly and sulkily walk over to us.

"See, you just have to be firm with her," Jackie said. "I'll bring out some meat bones and chew toys for her. She's over two years old, but in many ways, she's still a puppy," she said to me.

"Really, it's too much, taking care of a dog. I'm pretty busy and don't dogs need lots of attention—feeding and walks and things like that, don't they? I wouldn't know the first thing to do with it."

"Oh, come on," Sue Ellen said admonishingly. "It's not too hard and, besides, Stacey's here and you can always call Jackie if you have any questions."

Ginger had finally made her way over to us. She walked over to me and began sniffing me, starting with my feet and working her way up my legs toward my crotch. I put my hand on her head to stop her progress. Her tail was wagging.

"See, she likes you," Jackie said, smiling at me. I noticed the slight flecks of green in her brown eyes. "Just pet her. She's really very affectionate."

I bent over slowly and stroked her dry head like it was an eggshell. Sue Ellen and Jackie both laughed.

"She's not going to break. Give her a good hard scratch behind her ears," Sue Ellen said.

I rubbed the tips of my fingers more firmly into her scalp. She began to move her head to maximize the effect and help me get exactly the area she wanted scratched. It was pretty cool, I have to admit.

"Well maybe I could watch her for a few days," I said.

"Great," Sue Ellen said. She smiled and it was nice to see her do so.

"And I'll tell you what. I'll do you a favor as a reward," Jackie said. "Ronald told me you wanted to talk to Doc Livingston."

"Who?" I asked. I was engrossed in scratching Ginger, who had managed to move so that now I was rubbing her back end above her tail. Her fur was wet but I didn't mind. One of her legs began to thump up and down on the dock. She turned her head and looked up at me with bright, happy eyes.

"The medical examiner for East Hastings. Ronald said you wanted to see him. I can set it up," she continued.

I stopped scratching Ginger, who took her act over to Sue Ellen.

"You don't have to do that," I answered her. "I really don't want to get you involved in this."

"Nonsense," she said. "Doc Livingston is a pretty good friend. It's no big deal. Let me go get my phone in my car and call him. It might take a little convincing, but I think I can get him to agree."

Before I could say another word, she turned and headed off across the back yard toward her car in the front. She bent over and picked up a stick that was lying on the ground.

"C'mon, Ginger," she called back to the dog, who, see-ing Jackie now waving the stick, went charging off after her. Jackie threw the stick ahead of her and Ginger went chasing happily after it.

"She is so great with animals," Sue Ellen said, watching her. "People too," she added, turning to give me a not too subtle nudge with her elbow.

"A dog, a woman—what's next? You going to start dropping orphans off at the door?" I asked.

"One of us should be happy," she answered.

"Who said I'm not?"

"Oh, please. Like my daddy used to say," she said, look-ing at me squarely. "Don't piss on my back..."

CHAPTER 39

This was definitely the stuff of nightmares.

Two sheet-covered bodies were lying on two of the three stainless steel tables in the sterile, cool, brightly lit morgue in the bowels of the East Hastings hospital. They were on their backs and the outline of their feet, toes pointing to the ceiling, legs, upper body, and head shaped the sheets. While Jackie and Doc Livingston made small talk—about what I'm not sure because I wasn't really paying attention—I couldn't take my eyes off the covered bodies, and I swear that every once in a while I saw a slight movement.

Doc Livingston caught me staring. He was a paunchy man, probably in his early sixties, with a few wisps of gray hair on an otherwise bald head and vague, gray eyes that looked out over half-rimmed glasses that rested halfway down his nose. He wore a white lab coat over a white shirt, a bow tie, and black slacks. "Car accident this morning—pretty grisly or I'd let you have a look," he said, apparently oblivious to my pale shade and the cold sweat forming on my forehead.

"Um, that's okay. Maybe we could go somewhere else to talk," I suggested meekly.

"First time in a morgue, eh? It's not really that big a deal. In most cases, they just look like they're sleeping, although perhaps a little grayer than usual. Of course, sometimes, if they've been fished out of the river or if they've been dead for a while before the body was found and the maggots have got at it—well, then they're a little more decomposed and not a pretty sight at all."

I began to teeter back and forth a bit. Jackie took notice and moved quickly to my side. "Maybe we better get him to a chair," she said.

"Oh my, he does look a little peaked," Doc Livingston said, aware of my condition for the first time. "Perhaps he should lie down here for a moment?" he said, pointing to the remaining empty stainless-steel table.

"No!" I said, perhaps a little too emphatically. Doc Livingston actually looked hurt.

"How about over there," Jackie said, as she took hold of my arm above my elbow, indicating a chair by a neatly kept desk in a far corner of the room.

"My chair. Yes, that's a good idea. The files are over there anyway," he answered.

Jackie escorted me to a leather office chair with coasters and padded armrests and guided me down onto the seat. I took a deep breath.

Doc Livingston pulled two adjustable stools, also on coasters, from under one of the occupied tables and rolled them over to the desk alongside me. He turned on a large computer monitor that sat toward the back of the desk and while it came on sorted through a stack of files piled on the right side of the desk. He pulled three out. "Let's see," he said, sitting down at my right on one of the stools. "You're interested in the three recent stabbing deaths. I'm really not supposed to share this information with anyone, but Jackie here is a member of the fraternity, so to speak, even if she deals with four legged creatures. The way I see it, we all tend to God's children."

"We appreciate it, Brian. Wes just wanted to get a little background on the article he's writing for the *Chronicle* about the murders."

I started to correct her about writing any article, but I decided to let her run this show.

"So you said on the phone," he said to Jackie. He turned to me. "To tell you the truth, I'm glad to help you. You know, I've fished the Kithane for most of my life—always catch and release. Just as well because who knows what kind of poison I might have been putting into my body before you cleaned things up. That was good what you did. Thought I'd heard you went away."

Jackie looked at me quizzically.

"I'll tell you later," I said to her. I turned back to Doc Livingston. "I really wasn't responsible—" I began. He wasn't really listening to me.

"Glad you're poking around these murders as well," he said. "Maybe you'll get HPD off their collective asses so they start doing some police work. I haven't seen them lift a finger to find who did these things, just had me send everything off to the staties, passing the buck, if you ask me. Still, I kept a copy of everything for my own files." He used the mouse to click on a few file icons once the screen came on. An image of a bare back with a horizontal red strip on it appeared.

"This is Steven Darby's blunt force stab wound," Doc Living began. "As you can see, it appears to be a hilt mark injury. The wound is clean and continuous along the margins, approximately three inches in length, a quarter inch in width, entering the body about two feet from the top of the head, between the T-seven and T-eight vertebrae, travelling back to front, entering the heart and severing the superior vena cava. Blood loss was minimal due to an air embolism, making death fairly instantaneous. I have photos of the heart if you'd like to see them."

I looked at Jackie for clarification.

"A hilt mark injury means that the entire length of the knife entered the body. It was a fairly big knife, like a hunting knife I imagine, held sideways, not up and down. The knife entered the back right about on the level of the heart and severed a major vein. An air embolism occurs when a severed vessel continues pumping and sucks in air, which stops the heart's beating and blood flow."

"Thanks," I said to her. I turned back to the doc. "Any way you can identify the weapon?"

"If I had it in front of me, sure, but without the weapon, no, other than the fact that it was a pretty big knife, as Jackie said. There were no specific tool mark impressions on the vertebrae to distinguish the knife."

That I understood on my own. "Can you tell anything about the murderer, like height, anything like that?"

"Well, the wound was administered on an upward angle."

"So that would mean the killer was short, like Puddy Salvatore," I said.

"That's a natural assumption, but—" Doc Livingston opened a file folder on his desk. He noticed me taking notice. "I still like to have printed copies of my reports, old-fashioned I suppose." He flipped through a few pages in the file then clicked on an icon on the screen labeled *Salvatore*. "My records show that the deceased was sitting on a bar stool, approximately two and half feet tall, and there's a likelihood he was leaning forward, onto the bar, as people often do, rather than sitting erect. That would impact the direction of the entry wound. Then there's this." He clicked on a photo file and pulled up a shot of a knife labeled *Exhibit A*. "This was the knife found at the scene of Mr. Salvatore's death. Presumably, it was his knife, since there is an engraving on the knife handle with the initials *DAS*. His middle name was Angelo. As you can see, the blade on Mr. Salvatore's knife is thinner than the one that killed Mr. Darby."

"So Stevie was killed by a different knife, and the killer was probably taller than Puddy, roughly—"

"Between five foot ten and six foot, I'd imagine, though you'd have to measure the bar stool to get a better idea," the doc said.

"Was either knife used to kill Tina?" I asked.

"Ah, Ms. Sanders," he said, reducing both the photo of

Puddy's knife and Stevie's wound. He clicked on a file icon labeled *Sanders* and pulled a manila file folder from the three he'd pulled out earlier and opened it. The image of a stomach with a long red wound appeared.

"Here you can see the margins of the wound are much longer, the stab wound vertical. I suspect, based on damage to internal organs, that the killer in this case penetrated the body just below the rib cage and pulled the knife upward to inflict maximum damage. Once again, it was a hilt mark injury, so there was minimal blood loss until the knife was removed. Although this knife is similar to the one used to kill Mr. Darby, it doesn't appear to be the same one because the blade is thinner and shorter. Close but not quite the same."

He flipped a page in his manila folder.

"There was also bruising around Ms. Sanders's mouth, which indicated that the killer applied pressure there, most likely with his or her hand, to prevent Ms. Sanders from crying out. Unfortunately, we were not able to extract any DNA from her mouth or around the wound. Would you like to see a photo of that?"

"No," I said quickly. The scene at the hotel, Tina's dead body on the bed, was enough to haunt me. No need to see more. "So we're talking about three different knives," I said, changing the subject, "if not three different killers. How about the height of the person who stabbed Tina?"

"Tall, most definitely over six feet and fairly strong, able to tear up through the body with the knife the way he or she did, although I'd guess it was a male. And it definitely was not Puddy's knife or the same knife that killed Puddy?"

Doc Livingston again turned pages in the manila file with Puddy's records.

"No, the knife found at the scene was definitely the one that killed Mr. Salvatore, although if the knife hadn't been found, with his blood on it, it would have been much tougher to determine any characteristics about it. His wounds were more gaping than slitlike like the others. He was apparently stabbed during a struggle and there was considerably more blood loss. The killer no doubt got some of Mr. Salvadore's blood on his or her clothes."

I sat up straight in the chair. I guess I knew a little bit more, but I wasn't sure how it would help me. "Thanks, Doc. I hope you're not going to get into trouble for this," I said.

"Tell you the truth, I don't really care—and here," he said, handing me a flash drive that was lying on his desk. "This has the photos and notes on the three deaths, in case you want to review it later."

I took it from him. Wasn't my idea of bedtime reading but something in the files might prove helpful.

"Thanks, Brian," Jackie said, standing up, walking over to him, and giving him a peck on the cheek.

"Really no problem—and thank you for this," he said, indicating a brown paper bag containing the bottle of Powers that we'd picked up, at Jackie's suggestion, on the way over to the morgue. I'd almost forgotten about it.

Something in the way I looked at it must have given Doc Livingston the idea that I could probably use a good stiff drink right about now. He stood up and went over to a steel cabinet along the wall, opened it, and pulled out three empty polyethylene specimen holders. He brought them back to his desk, pulled the bottle from the bag, and opened it.

"Just a small one for me. I'm driving," Jackie said.

He poured about a quarter inch of Powers into one of the glasses. He looked at me over the rims of his glasses.

"I'm not," I said.

He smiled and poured a few inches of the whiskey into another of the holders and then matched that amount in the remaining one. He raised his cup. "You did pretty well for your first time in the morgue. I've seen third-year medical students turn the most amazing shades of green the first time they came in to watch an autopsy. Next time, it'll be a piece of cake."

The three of us tapped our cups.

"To the next time," he toasted.

Over my dead body, I thought as I took a good long swallow of my drink.

CHAPTER 40

She hogged the bed. The occasional whimpers, that were cute at first, grew tiresome, and she kicked me awake several times throughout the night. Sharing a bed with Ginger was going to take some getting used to.

Early in the morning, at least to me, she woke me up by shoving her wet nose under my chin and pushing my head up. Even though I had little experience caring for animals, I realized she probably needed to go out and take care of business. I wasn't really sleeping anyway. I kept picturing Doc Livingston pulling back the sheet on one of the bodies lying on the morgue tables to reveal Tina, eyes open and staring past me as when I found her on the bed.

Ginger and I went out back. The ground was still damp with morning dew, which I felt under my bare feet. When I was a kid I used to run over this entire place on feet with soles so tough that not even a piece of glass could pierce them. Now, every little pebble and stick on the ground felt like daggers stabbing my tender feet. I followed Ginger until she squatted and then picked up her pile with one of the neat little baggies Jackie had left for me. I threw it in one of the trash cans sitting alongside the back of the house.

Ginger romped around the yard, uncovering the smells of animals that might have trespassed onto her realm during the night. She found a stick and brought it to me. I had to wrestle with her to get it out of her mouth and, once I did, she kept her eyes on it with an unwavering intensity. I tossed it as far as I could and off she went on the chase. In no time, she was back in front of me, gripping the stick so that most of it was in her mouth and I had only a small end to grab onto to loosen it. We repeated this over and over until my arm felt like it might fall off and my throws went shorter and shorter. She must have sensed my fatigue because she eventually lay down a distance from me and made short work of turning the stick into toothpicks.

I went and sat on the end of the dock, dangling my feet into the water. It was cool and soothing and the scene so peaceful and quiet, the water flowing by slowly. Hard to believe three people could be murdered in a place that could provide such tranquility. But they had been and, for some reason, I still couldn't fathom, it had seemed to fall onto me to expose the people behind it. Of course I wanted to do right by everyone who was once important to me, but they were really overestimating what I could possibly accomplish. I knew deep down I was going to let them down. Sitting there and looking at the river roll by I wondered if it all wouldn't be simpler if I just slid my entire body off the dock and into the water, letting the current just carry me away downstream.

Ginger came to edge of the dock, stood beside me, and barked twice loudly, bringing me back to the here and now. I took her barks to mean it was time to feed her. Guess I wasn't going to be too tough a human to train.

We went back into the house. I read the feeding directions Jackie had provided for me, measured out the appropriate amounts of dry and canned food into Ginger's bowl and laid in on the kitchen floor. She attacked it ferociously and, in no time, was pushing the empty bowl around the floor, intent on getting every last molecule of food out of it.

As I was waiting for my coffee to brew, Stacey came into the kitchen. He was barefoot and wearing a pair of deep blue lounge pants and no shirt, revealing a set of six-pack abs and chiseled chest. I instinctively sucked in my stomach, even though it was not visible beneath my T-shirt.

"Can I get you some coffee?" I asked him as I opened a cabinet and grabbed a coffee cup.

"No thanks," he said, walking past me, grabbing the tea-kettle off the stove, and going to the sink to fill it. "Never touch the stuff. I'm a tea man."

He reached over, grabbed a cup of his own out of the cabinet, and threw a tea bag that he had taken from a box on the counter into it. "Got some good news for you. Finished working on your car last night. It's about as good as it will ever be, although I think it's time for you consider looking for a new ride," he said.

"Well, I don't see that happening anytime soon," I answered. "Besides, I have a sentimental attachment to my Camry."

"Your call," he said, opening the refrigerator and pulling out a jar of strawberry preserves and a package of Thomas's English muffins. He opened the package and pulled out one, split it, and put it in the toaster. "I even filled your gas tank with a gas can I found in the garage," he said.

"Thanks. That must have been the old gas can Danny tripped over the night Puddy was killed," I said. "Do you mind putting one of those in the toaster for me?"

He did and pushed the toaster levers down for each pair of slots.

"Old? No man, this can was brand new, and I can't believe Stevie kept it in that garage, seeing as it's full of nothing but old boxes of stuff. Don't think that guy ever threw anything out. Bit of a fire hazard if you ask me," he said.

The muffins popped up. Stacey took two plates from one of the cabinets, tossed the hot muffins onto them, and crossed to the table. Ginger watched the plates intently. Stacey grabbed a butter knife out of a drawer and placed it and the preserves on the table near the muffins. We sat down at the table.

"Um...I want to thank you for working on my car and...well, everything you've done around here for me," I said.

"No problem," he answered while slathering some pre-serves on his muffin.

"Can I give you anything? I don't have much—" I start-ed.

"No, man. It's cool. Ronald will take of me," he said, of-fering me the knife. I took it and covered my muffin in pre-serves.

"You two good friends?" I asked.

"Yeah, me and Ronald go way back. I used to be a bit of a bully back in the day, 'cause I was always bigger than the other kids. Ronald was the only one who wouldn't take my crap. I'd beat him up but he'd just keep getting up until he wore me out. He was one tough mother-fucker."

"And you stayed in touch all this time?"

"When he got back from the navy, he looked me up, started giving me little jobs to do around the Augustino's, hooked me up with Kenny…well, him and Mrs. A."

"But where'd you learn to do all this stuff—fixing cars, security systems, cooking?"

"I like to keep busy. Always been good with my hands. My mom was a car mechanic, I learned that from her," he answered.

"Really? Your mom was a mechanic?" I replied.

Stacey broke out in a wide grin. "No, man, I'm messing with you. Both my parents worked for the school district. My dad was a custodian and my mom worked in cafeterias at a couple of schools. Man, I thought you were some big-time reporter, falling for that," he said, laughing.

I laughed too, couldn't help it. Stacey had an infectious personality.

"Yeah, well, I'm a little rusty. But really, if there's any-thing I can do—" I started.

"You just do right by Mrs. A," he said.

"I'll do my best," I answered.

"Listen," he said, finishing off his muffin and tea. "I've got to run over to Boyersford to pick up some things for the house, can't get them in East Hastings. Be gone most of the day. You be all right without me?"

"Sure," I said. "Matter of fact, this is going to be the first uneventful day I've had since I got here. I was going to start looking through Stevie's things for Sue Ellen. Might as well start with the garage, and Hoppy gave me a little walking around money so now that I've got a car, I think maybe I'll just run into town and shop for some new clothes."

"Yeah, you could definitely do with some new threads. Tell you what. You talk to Antonio at Williams Clothing for Men. He'll set you up. Always does right by me. 'Course I look good in everything," Stacey said, again with a smile.

"Will do, thanks," I said, thinking that old Antonio would have to be a miracle worker to make me look as good as Stacey.

He got up and put his dishes in the sink. "Well, I'm gonna grab a shower and hit the road. You sure you'll be okay?" he said.

"Sure, of course. Like I said, my first non-eventful day. It'll be a nice change," I answered.

∽∾∽

I spent the better part of the morning carrying boxes from the garage into the living room and sorting through them. Stacey was right, in that Stevie didn't throw anything out. There were boxes full of broken toys from when he was a kid, tattered baseball gloves and spikes, old report cards and homework assignments, birthday cards and decade-old bank statements. Most of it was clearly of no use, and that stuff I stuffed into large trash bags and carried out back. Anything I was unsure about I set aside, boxed and put back in the garage. I made a pretty good dent in the number of boxes by mid-day.

When I first started clearing out the garage, I had noticed the gas can sitting outside next to the garage, where Stacey must have put it. It was new, so new in fact that the price sticker from Kegler's Hardware was still on the can. It struck me as a bit odd that Stevie would have any need for a gas can. It's not like he had grass to mow, since the lawn, if you could call it that, was mostly dirt because the abundance of shady trees on the property prevented grass from growing. And besides he didn't even own a lawnmower. The can was empty now. I guess Stacey had poured the gas into my gas tank. It didn't seem to pose any threat where it was, so I left it next to the garage.

It seemed like a good time for a nap. I hadn't done any kind of physical labor in a long time, and the mere act of carrying boxes back and forth from the garage had tired me out a bit. Instead, I decided to take my repaired Camry out for a drive.

Not only had Stacey performed major surgery on the engine and replaced worn shocks, struts and other components of the car's undercarriage, he had done a remarkable job cleaning the inside of the car as well. The dashboard glistened, as much as a sixteen-year-old car's dashboard could glisten, there were new floor mats, and he'd somehow managed to dispel the accumulated smells. In many ways, it was like I had a new vehicle. One thing was still the same, however. The way my body fit so perfectly in the driver's seat that had taken years to sculpt to my contours. It was still my car.

It handled like a champ and it actually took me a while to stop overcorrecting the steering as I'd grown accustomed to doing over the years. It felt so good, in fact, that I decided to test it out on the winding, long-forgotten back roads I'd driven on so often as a teenager. I actually got lost a few times. I didn't mind. I just turned around and retraced my journey until I came to a road I remembered. It really was a beautiful area, the musky smell of fallen tree limbs rotting in the thick growth running along small streams and the quaint stone houses tucked behind neatly painted wood fences. I could have driven for hours.

Instead, I ended up at the *Chronicle*. Maybe that had been my intention the whole time. Seeing as how Hoppy had bankrolled the repairs to my car, I did owe him an article, after all.

It took me a couple of hours to write about the fact that evidence suggested there were actually three murderers, not one as initially claimed by the police. I tried my best to avert any suspicion from Doc Livingston being my source, even though he said he really didn't care. The powers that be would probably figure it out, but some room for deniability couldn't hurt. Besides, maybe they'd be too busy trying to explain themselves and the lack of progress on any of the murders to worry about retribution in the near term. Or maybe they'd just be more pissed at me for writing the story. I saved the article and sent it along to Hoppy's inbox for his review.

I had to admit it felt good to write something that was newsworthy again. It seemed like a long time. The piece on Tina was nice, hopefully giving a little comfort to her family and maybe setting a few things right, but it wasn't the same as digging my teeth into a story.

I leaned back in my chair and looked around the near-empty newsroom. Something had been nagging me since we left the morgue—about what Doc Livingston said about the blood probably getting on Puddy's killer and something that I saw at the crime scene that night at Stevie's, but I couldn't put the two things together yet. It wasn't much, a fleeting image.

I had been tired that night, maybe a little drunk, and a little shook up after discovering Puddy's body, naturally, but I knew it would come to me if I just sat back, relaxed, and let it reveal itself. Or at least I hoped so.

It was not to be. My ringing cell phone snapped me out of my thoughts. I looked at the number displayed on the screen, but didn't recognize the caller's number.

"Hello, Wes Byrne," I said, pressing the number to activate the call.

"Mr. Byrne, this here's Ada Salvatore—Puddy's mother."

She really didn't have to identify herself as the old woman I'd met the day before. The twangy, high-pitched voice reminded me of one of those old prospectors you hear in classic western movies. I could practically hear her gums smacking.

"Yes, Mrs. Salvatore, what can I do for you?" I asked.

"Can ya really write a nice article 'bout my son sos people don't think he was a bad boy?" she answered.

I tried to hide the surprise in my voice. "Yes, yes, of course."

"Had some time ta think it over. I apologize for being a little rude to ya yesterday. I was a bit shook up, ya see, watching my boy put in the ground like that. Ya won't pull nothin' will ya, make him look stupid?"

I pictured the Puddy Salvatore that stood in front of me, waving a knife in my face, those yellow teeth. I guess almost everybody had some redeeming character. I might have to be creative, but I'd do my best. "No, ma'am, I won't," I answered.

"Okay, well come right over before I change ma mind and let's get this done," she ordered and then the call ended abruptly.

"Mrs. Salvatore…hello?"

She was gone. I looked at my watch. It was a little after four in the afternoon. I debated giving Stacey a call and having him meet me to drive over to the Salvatore place. Frankly, I felt a little embarrassed thinking I needed his help. Mrs. Salvatore was barely five-foot-tall and had to be in her late sixties. I had a good foot and a half and fifty pounds on her. If I couldn't face her alone, what kind of man was I?

Then I remembered the thoughts I had of the old lady doing me harm when Kenny and I were driving back from the funeral. I'd be on guard, but there was always that possibility of her slipping something into my drink. I decided to stop at the liquor store on the way over to her place and pick up a bottle of Powers. If I was going to be poisoned, it would be on my own terms.

CHAPTER 41

A sap—a flat, black, beaver-tailed leather weapon approximately eight inches long, also known as a black-jack—sat on the table beside the rocking chair in which Puddy's mother rocked to and fro slowly, a menacing, satisfied smile on her face. Another sap, me, stood before her, a gift-wrapped bottle of Powers in a bright silver bag tied with a purple string in my hands, staring at her with must have been one the dumbest looks she'd ever seen on anyone's face. And that said a lot considering she'd raised Puddy.

"I, um, I hope you just use that thing to open walnuts," I said, nodding in the direction of the sap.

She picked it up in her right hand and admired it.

"Beautiful, ain't it? It was ma grandadda's. Took it offa a police who tried ta subdue 'im." She cackled. "I used ta use it on Puddy when he was a young'un, when he started actin' up. Didn't do much good. Us Salvatores got hard heads."

"You know, I don't think now's a good time for us to have our chat. Perhaps I should come back some other time," I said, slowly backing my way toward the front door.

"Actually, now's probably the perfect time."

The voice came from my left, from the doorway to the kitchen. I turned and saw Bones coming out of that room, where he must have been lurking. There was a long, slender-bladed knife in his right hand. He was also smiling and his eyes were two slits just opened wide enough for some of the evil in them to leak through. I turned my head to look back at Puddy's mother. She was patting the palm of her left hand with the sap.

"Can't believe ya was actually stupid enough to think I'da wanna sit down with ya and talk to ya about ma dear, departed Puddy. You, who as good as put the knife inna his belly."

"Mrs. Salvatore." I stopped to gulp. "I had nothing to do with Puddy's death. Someone else killed him before we found his body." My voice was a little shaky and I could feel the perspiration forming in my armpits. It wasn't from the humidity.

Her black eyes hardened. "Ya know, ma people goes back a long way in this county—a long way. And one thing that could always be said about us is we take care of our own. An eye for an eye, like the Bible says. Ain't that right, Ricky?"

"That's right, ma'am," Bones answered. I turned my head slowly and saw him moving farther into the room to stand behind me. It was really hard for me to imagine this very threatening person could be a "Ricky."

"Now I don't know who stuck that knife in ma boy. He shouldna run—we coulda worked something out with the powers that be—but his runnin' made people nervous. He set his self on that path. But I do know that if you and that bitch Tina—" She turned her head and spat on the floor as she said her name "—hadna started messin' with 'im, he'd still be alive today."

"But I didn't even know him, only met him that one time, and he left me hogtied with duct tape." I turned to look at Bones standing behind me. "He didn't tell me any-thing, just took my money and left." I looked back at Mrs. Salvatore. She seemed unmoved. "I—I even offered to help him carry stuff to his truck."

"Well, that was mighty kind of ya," she said, rising slowly with a bit of effort from her chair. "But what's gotta be done has gotta be done. It's a matter of Salvatore pride. I couldn't face him or his Pappy in heaven if I didn't do some settlin' up. Now turn around and get on your knees."

"But—please listen to me—" I pleaded.

"You heard the lady, turn around and face me and get on your knees," Bones said from behind in a voice that wasn't the sort one quarreled with.

I turned and faced him. He had a mean grin on his face and was rolling the handle of his knife around in his hand.

I kneeled slowly, first onto the right knee then the left. I still held the neck of bottle of Powers I'd brought with me in my right hand. I gripped the barrel of the bottle with my left hand, tightly. It seemed to help keep me from shaking. I stared at the twirling knife in Bones's hand.

Then I heard Mrs. Salvatore scuffling toward me from behind.

"You summabitch," she said.

I heard a dull thump and it took a moment to realize it was the sound of the sap crashing into the back of my head, then another moment for a searing pain to begin where the sap had hit its mark. Next thing I saw was the floor rushing up to meet my face. Then nothing.

◌∽◌∽◌

It hurt at first to open my eyes. I did so one at a time. My head was lowered, chin on my chest, and I was staring down at a concrete floor with a few uneven splotches of oil stains here and there. I raised my head slowly. I was some-place that wasn't particularly well lit, but what light there was brought on a feeling of nausea as it flooded into my eyes. I took a large gulp of air. It seemed to help.

I was inside a large empty garage, sitting in a wooden chair with my hands tied to the stiles. Actually, the garage wasn't empty. Bones and Puddy's mother were standing in front of me, about three feet away. In a corner was a Harley

Davidson Superlow motorcycle. I guessed it belonged to Bones. I hadn't seen a motorcycle when I arrived earlier, so he must have parked it here, out of sight.

"Well, boy. You certainly don't have a Salvatore noggin', that's fer sure. Thought maybe I hit ya a might too hard, way ya crumbled like a sack of taters—sure was one heckuva load for Ricky to drag out here," Puddy's mother said when she saw I had regained consciousness.

"Where's here?" I asked.

"Why this here's ma garage. Know it don't look like much right now, but back when bizness was good, we were turning over pretty much a car a day. Ain't that right, Ricky?"

"That's right, ma'am. Things were good," Ricky—er—Bones replied.

She turned to look at Bones and there was a trace of anger in her voice.

"Yeah, until ya let ma boy get that damned bitch involved. Told ya she was bad news right from the beginnin'."

"Aw, you know Puddy had a thing for her. I just thought…well, he thought…that she might be impressed if she saw how things were, change the way she looked at him. I didn't see the harm," Bones said sheepishly.

She turned fully to face him, her body tense.

"No, ya didn't see the harm. Well, ya also didn't see that way she wrapped him around her fingers, how he was spendin' good money to buy her 'spensive things."

"But Puddy was right. His plan actually worked out pretty good," replied Bones, pleading his case. "He'd spot a model of a car we wanted, follow it, and, if it parked downtown, he'd send Tina in to keep the owner busy while he boosted the car. Worked like a charm. I mean, she was pretty good at it, and we got us some real fine vehicles right in broad daylight."

Puddy's mother took a step toward Bones, her hands clenching. For a little lady, she could give off a powerful sense of terror. Bones actually took a step back.

"I tol' that boy—I tol' you—that bitch was not to be trusted," she growled. "Ya shoulda seen her, the way she come runnin' in here after they stole this here 'uns car—all hysterical that we'd stolen some hot shot reporter's car and that he'd find out all about us, send us all to jail, and demandin' we give the car back. I woulda killed her right there, swear to God I shoulda, but Puddy said he could talk some sense to her. I blame myself for leavin' them alone. He warn't no match for her and her female wiles."

She seemed to soften a bit at the memory of her son. Her hands relaxed, her head dropped a little and she shook it slightly left to right.

I sensed an opportunity to get a little information. Not that it was going to do me any good most likely. I just the longer I kept them talking the longer I might live.

"But how did you find us, how'd you know we'd be at the hotel?" I asked.

Puddy's mother turned and looked at me like I was a three-year old.

"Oh that warn't hard. Bitch said she heard ya tell the police were ya was stayin', knew she'd go runnin' to ya. I called Ricky here and tol' him where to go—knew Puddy warn't capable of doin' what had to be done—but Ricky—" She turned her head and looked at him admiringly. "—he's a good boy, knows how to take care of bizness."

I looked at Bones. He seemed genuinely touched by Mrs. Salvatore's compliment.

"So you killed Tina?" I said to him.

He just smiled at me.

"Why didn't you kill me too?" I asked.

"Why, killin' that bitch was within our rights. She worked for us, but ya—we didn't have permission to kill no stranger and there's rules that have to be followed, what ya'd call protocols." She seemed pleased to be able to use such a big word.

"Whose rules? Somebody else is calling the shots?"

Puddy's mother walked over to me, a gentle look on her face.

"Oh, sweetie," she said. She pulled her right hand back and then came forward with it, slapping me hard across the face. Then she wagged at finger at me. "That ain't for ya to know. But if it's important to ya, ya should know we're making an exemption for ya, 'cause like I said, this is personal and sometimes rules just don't apply."

She walked over to where my gift of Powers sat on a work bench that ran along a wall of the garage. She picked it up, untied the ribbon, and slid the gift bag off, her back to me.

"'Course, we gotta make this look like an accident...can't just come right out and kill ya. 'Cause there are consequences for breakin' the rules. We're takin' a mighty big risk."

She tried to unscrew the top off the bottle but wasn't able to. She held out the bottle to Bones.

"Here, ya do it. My arthritis is actin' up a bit."

Bones handed his knife to her and took the bottle from her. He easily screwed off the top.

"Nice of ya to bring your own likker...that way I don't have to waste none of mine," Puddy's mother said.

Bones approached me.

"What are you going to do? People know I came out here," I lied. I'd told no one. "They'll suspect you right away."

"And I'll just tell them the truth. Ya came out here, we had a nice chat about ma boy—just like lots of witnesses heard you ask for at ma son's funeral, only ya was drinking a bit heavy and even tho' I tol' ya not go driving off, ya insisted. What could I do to stop ya? I'm just a little ol' lady." She chuckled. "So when they find your car where it run off the road and inna the river, it'll look like ya were drunk and missed a turn. Why, what else coulda it been but a tragic accident?"

"Bottoms up," Bones said as he grabbed the back of my head by my hair.

I tried to protest but he forced the bottle into my mouth. The whiskey began flowing freely. I had no choice but to swallow a good quantity of it, although some of it spilled out of my mouth, down my chin and over the front of my shirt. Oddly enough, considering the situation, all I could think at the moment was *Slow down, you're wasting some of it*. I started gagging. I felt like I was drowning. Bones paused for a moment, smiled at me with a sick grin, then pushed the bottle back into my mouth.

Suddenly, a door next to the larger garage door at the far end of garage burst open and sunlight flooded into the room.

"Stop right there. Put the bottle down and step away from the chair."

Bones pulled the bottle from my mouth. I looked around his body to see three state troopers, each standing with their feet shoulder width apart, each holding a Glock 22 with both hands, pointing it at Bones. They all wore bullet proof vests and appeared to mean business.

Bones turned slowly to face them. "Or what? You going to shoot me. I'm unarmed," he said.

"Just step away from the chair, put the bottle down, and get down on your knees. I'm not going to tell you again," the trooper in the middle answered, his voice firm and in control.

"Big man with that gun in your hand. Why don't you put it down and we settle this man to man?" Bones said, taking a slow step forward.

The trooper raised the gun slightly. He jaw tightened. "I will shoot you if you don't stop right there," he said.

The scene was tense, but out of the corner of my eye I saw a movement to my left. I turned my head to see Puddy's mother, about twenty feet away, holding Bones's knife, and beginning to move in my direction. There was a crazed look in her eyes.

I looked back at the troopers but their attention was focused on Bones.

"Hey," I yelled out to them.

I looked over and saw that Puddy's mother was shuffling my way a little faster. They didn't seem to take notice. I rocked forward a little bit and straightened my legs. I was able to stand up. Probably not the best idea, because although I was ambulatory, I was still tied to the chair and was bent over at a angle, my face now just about at the level with the approaching knife Mrs. Salvatore held out in front of her. I was also feeling the effects of the Powers and was unsteady on my feet, staggering forward, even closer to Puddy's mother.

"You summabitch!" she screamed as she shuffled toward me at a faster pace, swinging the knife wildly back and forth.

"Hey, help!" I screamed as I began backpedaling as fast as could, bent over as I was.

Puddy's mother continued to come at me, closing the ground between us, and the knife passed within inches of my face. I had no idea where I was going, but just kept moving back and away from her attack.

I glanced over quickly at the troopers. They were just standing there, mouths agape in disbelief, watching the scene. Bones, who had turned around, had the same look on his face. No one moved as she chased me around the room.

"Do something!" I screamed as the knife made another pass close to my face.

I knew I had to be running out of room and she was going to get me. I pivoted on my left leg, bringing the chair around like a tail. Its legs crashed into Puddy's mother, knocking her off-balance and the knife out of her hand.

The move seemed to wake the troopers out of their stupors. Two rushed forward and tackled Bones from behind, sending him crashing down onto the garage's concrete floor. He struggled with them but they were able to cuff him. The third came to my rescue, kicking the knife out of her reach and wrapping his arms around Puddy's mother from behind. He lifted her up off the ground. She struggled to get out of his grasp, but he had a good hold of her.

"You summabitch. This ain't over. I'll get you someday. A Salvatore never forgets. You'll see," she screamed at me, spit flying from between her gums.

One of the other troopers came over and helped put cuffs on her. He led her away and followed the trooper with the shackled Bones toward the door.

"He killed ma boy, that summabitch killed ma boy," she hollered at the trooper as they went out of the garage.

The trooper who had come to my rescue went over and picked up the knife and came to stand before me. I could only see as far up as his chest in my bent over condition. He twirled the knife much as Bones had.

"Captain Winters wants to see you—and he's a not happy man," he said.

CHAPTER 42

I should have let them kill you," Captain Winters voice boomed.

I was back in the not-so-friendly confines of the state police interrogation room. I hadn't been brought in on any charges. Apparently, Captain Winters just wanted to get some things off his chest, and I guess this was the least conspicuous place to do so. He was standing across the table from me and, just as in my previous visit, Chief Roark sat in a chair to his right. She didn't look too happy to see me, but in comparison to the raging state trooper, she seemed rather composed.

"Didn't I tell you to lay off? Do you have any idea what you've done?" he asked, his face a scary shade of red and his bulging neck veins thick as drinking straws.

I was used to taking my whiskey in swallows, not gulps, so despite two cups of very strong, terrible-tasting coffee I was still a little drunk. My head hurt, my jaw ached, and I just wanted to be in bed awaiting the mother of all hangovers. So I was a little irritable and not sure why I was even here.

"Yeah," I said. "I helped you catch the guy who killed Tina Sanders and who also was behind the car theft ring. You have a funny way of showing your appreciation."

"Appreciation!" he spat out. "I ought to throw you in jail for interfering with a police investigation. Hundreds of man hours have just been flushed down the drain and the best chance we've had in years of putting the Crawfords behind bars is gone—shot—because of you and your meddling."

If I was sober, I probably would have just let Captain Winters blow off steam and then gotten the hell out there. But downing half a bottle of whiskey does funny things to a man's judgment. Besides, I had no idea what he was talking about. "My meddling? If it wasn't for me, you wouldn't have a murderer and a pretty vicious old lady who was in on it behind bars."

Captain Winters jaw tensed and his eyes flashed. "So we have a murderer, do we?"

"Yes. Bones killed Tina," I answered.

"He told you that?"

"Well…" I began, thinking back through my alcohol haze. "…maybe not in so many words, but he sort of nodded when I asked him."

"Sort of nodded. Oh that will certainly stand up in court," he said.

Damn it he had a point. Neither Bones nor Puddy's mother had come right out and said they'd killed Tina.

"Well, you've got his knife," I said. "It will match Tina's wound and must have some trace of her blood on it. Blood's hard to clean away. That should prove it."

"Oh, sure, there might be some trace of her blood on the weapon, but how are we going to prove it's his knife? My men said when they entered the garage the old lady was holding it and she was the one trying to slice you. Her fingerprints are going to be all over it. His lawyer can claim it was hers."

"But he had it first, she just took it when he started pouring the whiskey down my throat." I looked from Captain Winters to Chief Roark for support. She shook her head no. "C'mon," I said loudly. "I know he did it…and she told him to."

"You knowing it is not enough," Captain Winters said sarcastically. "On the other hand, we've been staking out the Salvatore garage for months, building a case against them for the car thefts, hoping we might even pin the girl's murder on Bones, who we've suspected from the start. That's how my trooper saw you getting dragged into the garage."

"If you suspected him, why didn't you arrest him?"

"Because we were after the bigger fish—The Crawfords. See, we know they're behind it all, but we need a little thing you might have heard of called proof. We were hoping Bones would lead us to them. Now there is no way that is going to happen. They wouldn't let him get within ten miles of them."

"And the fact that he killed Tina really wasn't that important. You just let a killer walk around free," I said accusingly.

"Of course, her death was important, and I wanted to put him away," Chief Roark said, speaking up for the first time. "I don't like people being killed in my town. But there is no statute of limitations on murder, and we could continue to build the case against him while we also went after the Crawfords. They are bad people and responsible for more than just the murder of one girl. That's why I cooperated with the state police. Bones was under surveillance. He wasn't going anywhere."

I sat forward, put my elbow on the table, lowered my head into my right hand, and began rubbing my forehead. What had all seemed so solid just minutes before was crumbling all around me. I hadn't helped Tina. I'd probably made things worse.

"Well, what about me?" I asked, raising my head to look at the two of them. "You can get them for attempted murder. I mean, they were going to kill me."

Captain Winters shook his head. "That's only your word against theirs. Most we can probably be sure of getting them on is kidnapping and assault, although even that's a reach since you drove out there on your own and it was your whiskey. Not exactly the result we were after. Face it, Byrne. You screwed up."

There was a knock on the door.

"Come in," Captain Winters ordered.

A trooper opened the door and entered the room. He handed Captain Winters a folded note, gave me an angry look, then left the room.

Captain Winters opened the note and read it quickly. "Son of a bitch," he said loudly. He had been calming down a bit, like a hurricane downgraded to category three from a four, but his fury jumped to five in an instant. He crumpled the note and threw it at me, hitting me square in the face. Lucky for me it was paper. Anything of substance would have broken some bones. He appeared to reach at his hip, as if for his weapon, almost reflexively. Lucky for me he wasn't armed. "Get him out of here before I do something I'll really regret," he said to Chief Roark, his breathing short and furious. "I've got to go see about my men."

He turned and stormed out, slamming the interrogation room door behind him as he left. Chief Roark reached across the table, picked up the note from where it landed after bouncing off my face and uncrumpled it. She read it and glared at me.

"Bones is dead," she said. "The van taking him to prison was run off the road by a tractor trailer. The two troopers escorting him were injured in the accident. The attackers took Bones. He was found dead in the middle of the road a few miles away from the ambush. His throat was slashed and his tongue cut out."

"Oh my God, are the troopers okay?"

"You better hope so," she said, laying the paper on the table between us. "You sure are making enemies fast. Bones's friends are going to put his death on you and if, or maybe I should say when, they come after you and if these troopers are hurt bad…well, let's just say you shouldn't expect law enforcement to come running to your rescue." She stood up and pushed her chair in. "Okay, I guess that's it then. You're free to go."

"Can I have a minute?" I asked. A lot had happened in

the few minutes I had been in the room. I needed a moment to myself.

"Sure, I guess it's all right, but I wouldn't stay too long in here alone. This might not be the safest place for you, if you know what I mean." She walked over and out the door, closing it behind her.

I reached over, pulled the paper across the table, and gave it a quick read. It basically said just what Chief Roark had told me. It was short on details. It didn't even have the names of the troopers involved. I folded the paper, stood up, and put it in my pocket.

I walked out of the interrogation room and through the squad room. The room grew quiet and the troopers at their desks paused at whatever they were to doing to watch me. If looks could kill, I wouldn't have made it more than a few feet.

I reached the lobby and there was Hoppy. It was good to see a friendly face.

"What the hell do you think you were doing?" he screamed as he rushed toward me, "Going out there on your own, not telling anybody. Why do you think I hired Stacey? So you could go off and play intrepid reporter all by yourself? I thought you had more brains than that."

"She was just an old lady and I really didn't think—" I started to answer.

Yeah, you didn't think. Son, you take it from an old man like me, old women are some of the most dangerous creatures on the planet. Well, come on, you've got a story to file."

No "how you doing" or "are you hurt." The paper came first. Pure Hoppy.

He crinkled his nose and took a step back. "Damn. You smell like a distillery. You know, you really should cut back on your drinking. It's gonna catch up to you someday."

CHAPTER 43

I f a guy can't write a story when he's a little drunk, he
don't deserve to call himself a reporter."
Hoppy was pacing behind me, occasionally looking
over my left shoulder as I worked to string together an account of what happened at Puddy's mother's house and the
subsequent events. He critiqued as I wrote. It was like old
times, when I first started out and Hoppy led me through the
construction of a good news article. Now, however, it was
more than a little annoying, what with my years of experience. Also because his suggestions were actually making
the piece stronger. I wasn't that drunk, but I was rusty.

After we'd left the state police barracks, Hoppy drove
Stacey, who had been waiting in the reception area, and me
over to the Salvatore house to fetch up my car. It was eerily
quiet. I kept expecting the gnomish Mrs. Salvatore to leap
out at me from behind every tree and bush.

After Stacey left with my car, on account of the fact that
I was still not in the best shape to get behind a wheel, Hoppy and I were alone on the property. We took the opportunity to do a little snooping, even though we knew the police
must have done a pretty thorough search of their own after
taking Puddy's mother and Bones into custody.

As expected, there wasn't much to find in the living and
dining rooms, just old family keepsakes. It really did appear
that the Salvatores had lived in Hastings County for a very
long time, as Puddy's mother had said, judging from the

old, sepia-tinted photographs we came across. One in particular showed five men dressed in Union Civil War uni-
forms, a bit disheveled and worn, lounging outside a tent. I
presumed the shortest, least attractive of the group was
Puddy's ancestor.

Another looked like it had been taken in the 1920s or so.
It was black and white and showed a couple, maybe Puddy's grandparents. They posed in front of an old Model T.
Knowing what I did about the Salvatores, I couldn't help
wondering if the car had been stolen.

Hoppy took Mrs. Salvatore's room, and I searched Puddy's. There wasn't much to his room, yet it was pretty obvious he'd slept in it his entire life. There were a few faded
Phillies and Eagles pennants tacked to the walls, each with
what might now be called vintage team logos that indicated
how far back in time they went. There was a wall-mounted
thirty-two-inch flat-screen television and an Xbox console
on the floor below it. The game's controller sat on a table
beside Puddy's bed.

Over by his bed, a half-filled olive-green duffel bag was
laying on the floor beside a pair of Timberland boots I remembered all too well from the night at Tina's. I picked up
the bag and emptied the contents onto the bed. This must
have been what he'd packed when he decided to make a run
for it. In addition to some folded underwear, jeans, and
shirts, a few cans of Bumblebee tuna fish, Underwood
chicken spread, and a couple of Hershey chocolate bars,
tumbled out. The police must have returned it after they'd
found his body and Puddy's mother hadn't bothered to put
his things away. After all, what was the purpose in doing
that?

Digging through the clothes, I also found a picture of Tina which I recognized as the wedding photo I'd seen at her
apartment and which Puddy had taken with him the night
we had gotten acquainted. It had been torn in half, from top
to bottom, so that her husband was no longer part of the
scene. There was only Tina, at her most beautiful, dressed

in her wedding gown, holding her bouquet of flowers, and smiling as if only wonderful things lay ahead for her. It was the only personal item Puddy had packed. Guess he really did love her.

Hoppy came to the bedroom door.

"Nothing in the mother's room to speak of. Any luck in here?" he said.

"No, nothing," I said, hiding Tina's picture from him.

"People like these, they probably got a million places on their property to hide things. I did find a couple photos we can choose from to run with the story, so it wasn't a total bust."

He turned and walked away. I took one last look at the smiling Tina and dropped the picture on the bed with Puddy's things, then followed Hoppy.

Next we went to the garage at Hoppy's insistence. I had no desire to see the place again. It smelled of oil and stale whiskey. The chair remained where I last sat in it, the rope still knotted onto the posts. Hoppy walked around, appraising the place as if he was considering buying it.

"So this was where they chopped up the cars. Quite an operation they had going," he said. He looked at me, and I swear I could detect a flash of admiration in his eyes. "You know, Wes, all-in-all you've done real good, better than I really imagined. I think this story will make the national news wires." He walked over to the chair and pulled up one of the ropes by the end severed to cut me free and inspected it for a moment. "Of course, you put some people out of business and I don't think they'll be too happy about it. I mean, you already had one close brush with death and I'd hate to see you come to any harm on account of this story. I realize I've asked a lot of you."

What do you know? I thought. *Hoppy does care and we're going to drop this whole thing before anyone gets hurt any worse.* Of course, by anyone, I meant me. A wave of relief swept from my head to my toes. Hoppy looked up at me, he was nodding. I smiled at him.

"But now we really gotta turn up the pressure, bring these insects out from under their rocks. That's what the *Chronicle's* readers want. They're looking to us to make some sense out of all this crime and murdering going on in their county."

My jaw dropped. It wasn't enough that I had stupidly stumbled into a trap and almost ended up dead, Hoppy wanted me to be a tethered goat to draw out even more killers, all in the name of increased circulation.

"But we've got Tina's killer, and we've effectively shut down the car theft ring. Your readers should be plenty happy about that," I replied, detecting the slightest bit of a whine in my voice.

"Sure, sure. People will eat this up. But I'm still convinced there's more going on. I told you, I can feel it in my bones that Steve Darby's murder is part of a bigger picture. Now that you're no longer preoccupied with finding that girl's murderer—and I don't blame you for that, I know you felt somehow responsible, but you took your eye off the ball—we can really get somewhere. Now's the time to make some people really sweat."

That wasn't going to be a problem. Perspiration was already beading up on the back of my neck and my armpits were growing damp.

"But—but—" I stammered, trying to come up with a good reason why the crazy man standing in front of me should reconsider and just let me write articles about garden shows and local sports teams and whatever other safe things were going on in East Hastings until my debt was paid. "There's nothing there, your creaky bones to the contrary," was all I could come up with.

Hoppy gave me a sly, rather condescending, smile. "Son, I'm not going to ask you to do anything you're not comfortable with."

I waited. I knew more was coming.

"But can you tell me you've really spent any time looking into that Darby fellow's murder? Have you searched the house—given it a thorough going over? Have you asked the sister where he might've hidden something he could use to blackmail somebody or that would make someone want to kill him? Have you gone out to look over the joint where he was killed or talked to the bartender working that night or even sniffed around at that place where he worked nights with that Salvatore boy?" he continued. "You think I'm wrong, well okay then, I'll tell you what. Why don't you prove that, convince me there's nothing to what years of experience and, yes I'll say it again, something deep in my bones tells me is out there? You do that and we are done. You can walk away, not owe me a thing. We're finished."

I cocked my head a bit and tried to size Hoppy up. Was he serious this time or was it just another ruse to string me along. He was right to point out that I really hadn't worked on how Stevie spent his last days—who he might have talked to, where he went—and I did have the fact that Puddy had helped Stevie get a job on the night shift at TSN. That could be a coincidence, the place was one of the largest employers in East Hastings, but I couldn't say for sure.

Then there was Sue Ellen. I had sort of promised her to ride this all out.

So against my better judgment—again—I gave in to Hoppy. I'd poke around about Stevie. But first, I had an article to file on Bones's death and the arrest of Puddy's mother.

❧❀❧

Once we got over to the *Chronicle*, Hoppy worked the phones while I started the article. He called someone he knew at the hospital and found out that the state troopers were going to be fine, just some minor scrapes and bruises and tests for concussions, and got their names. He followed up on an earlier call to a photographer that he'd dispatched to both the scene of the ambush and where Bones's body was found. The body had been removed by the time the photographer got there, but the state police van was still there, laying on its side. Pictures were on their way. Finally he was unsuccessful in his attempt to get crime scene photos or much information from anyone at the police station or from Doc Livingston at the morgue. We had enough, though, and I finished the story.

Then I called Terri to give her the news before she read about it in the paper. She asked me if I was sure. I pictured Bones's nod and that evil smirk. It may not have been enough to convince a jury, but I knew he'd done it. I told her yes. Tina's killer was dead. She thanked me and said she'd invite me for the laying of Tina's gravestone. I said if I was still in town I would definitely be there.

When it was all done, all I wanted was a nice hot shower and a long, long sleep. It had been quite a day. The body count had gone up in East Hastings, but fortunately it didn't include me—yet.

CHAPTER 44

Iawoke to the smell of coffee brewing and bacon cooking, the sound of dishes clattering, and the murmur of muffled voices.

It was all coming from the kitchen. I must have slept for about sixteen hours. I got out of bed, slipped on a pair of sweat pants and a Hastings University T-shirt, and headed in my bare feet for the kitchen.

The gang was all there—Tim, Denny, Dom, Bob, who I hadn't seen since before Tim and Denny and I were caught in Stevie's place, and the ever-present Stacey. They were gathered around the kitchen table eating, except for Stacey who was at the kitchen range cooking up the eggs and bacon.

"Hey, it's Wes Byrne, crime stopper," Tim said as I entered the kitchen. The others all greeted me warmly.

"Hi, guys," I said, still wiping the sleep from my eyes. "Don't you have jobs?" I asked.

Tim and Dom were all dressed casually, in khaki pants and polo shirts. Bob was wearing a pair of dress slacks, collared shirt, and tie. Stacey was in a sleeveless muscle shirt and cut off sweat pants.

"School's still out," Tim answered.

"I pretty much set my own hours," Bob said. "I've got an appointment later today, but I thought I'd swing by here first."

"I'm on vacation. The family's still at the shore, but I

had to come back for this," Denny said, getting up and offering me his seat, which I took.

Tim reached over with that morning's edition of the *Chronicle* folded so that my article was prominently displayed with the front-page headline *Killer Murdered After Daring Escape* and a picture of the overturned state trooper van.

"Man, Wes, you did it. You got Tina's killer. You must feel awful good," said Dom.

Stacey came over and placed a cup of steaming coffee in front of me.

"Well, actually, I didn't exactly—" I started.

"Did you really think he was going to kill you?" Tim interrupted. "He looks like one scary dude, judging from his picture on page two."

"And how about that mother?" Dom added. "Damn, she's sounds like a regular Ma Parker."

"Barker," said Denny.

"What?" asked Dom.

"It's not Parker, it's Barker," Denny answered.

"Barker? She sure is. Did you see her picture? AOOOOO, ruff ruff," Dom howled.

We all groaned good-naturedly at Dom's bad joke. The mood was light. I think they were really concerned about what almost happened and glad nothing too bad had, though none of them would come out and say it.

"Hello! Where is everybody?" It came from the front door and sounded like Sue Ellen.

"We're back here," I called out.

Sue Ellen came through the hallway and into the kitchen. She was wearing beige shorts that fit her rather nicely with a brown belt, a faded blue chambray shirt with the sleeves rolled halfway up her forearms and thin-soled wedge sandals.

She had a thick collection of those color strips you find in paint departments at hardware stores in one hand and some swathes of fabric draped over her other arm. When she saw me, the relief was apparent in her eyes and bright smile.

"Oh, Wes I am so glad you're all right. I read the paper this morning. It must have been terrible," she said.

I know that the only thing keeping her from hurrying over and giving a big kindhearted hug was the presence of the guys.

"Terrible?" Denny asked. There was a trace of facetiousness in his voice. "He was tied up in a chair and someone poured whiskey down his throat. If the person doing it was named Bambi and not Bones, he would have been in heaven."

"Very funny," I said to Denny. "What have you got there?" I asked Sue Ellen.

"Well, I decided to fix this place up a bit and Stacey agreed to help me pick out some colors for the walls and fabric for curtains."

I turned to Stacey. "You're an interior designer too?" I asked.

He shrugged his massive shoulders. "I'm good with colors, what can I say?" he answered.

"Um, Sue Ellen—" I started, rising and moving over toward her. I took her by the elbow and led out of the kitchen and earshot of the guys, down the hallway. "I hope you're not doing this on my account. You know I haven't said anything about staying and—"

We'd reached the living room. She turned to face me, tilted her head, and gave me a slightly disapproving look. "You know, Wes, not everything is about you. I've been wanting to get in here and brighten this place up for quite a while, but Stevie wouldn't hear of it—said he liked it just the way it was, the way Momma had it." She turned and scanned the walls, the pictures, the furniture. "Besides, I— I—really should collect his things up and decide what to do with it all. Probably just throw most of it out, just junk, most of it."

She looked up at me, just the smallest trace of tears

forming in her eyes. She still had trouble talking about him, though it seemed to be getting a little easier. I knew it would never be too easy. She dabbed at her eyes as if brushing a stray eyelash away.

"She was a prostitute. You do know that, right?" Sue Ellen said, as much a matter-of-fact statement as a question.

"What?" I asked, knocked a bit off balance by Sue Ellen's abrupt shift in tone.

"Tina Sanders. She really did sleep with men for money—rich men, granted. She wasn't the type to proposition men in their cars, but she was a whore, nonetheless."

I could only smile. There was no beating around the bush with Sue Ellen, and it could never be said that a person didn't know exactly where they stood with her. "Um, I think I'd prefer to think of her as a 'good time girl,'" I answered. "But yeah, I did figure that out."

Sue Ellen snorted softly. "'Good time girl?' Wes, that's you in a nutshell, such a sweet romantic," she said, patting me on my forearm. "But good, I'm glad you know. She had an effect on men...and...well, after that article you wrote about her, I just hope you haven't forgotten about Stevie while being her knight in shining armor."

"No, of course not," I said, hoping I sounded convincing.

"Good. What you did was a good thing. You gave her family a little comfort...closure." She looked me straight in the eyes. "That's what I want. That's what you promised me."

"Sue Ellen, I said I'd try," I answered.

"You're gonna try as hard as you did for that whore?" she responded sharply.

She turned her head away from me and began absently looking at the pictures on the wall. I know people change, but this didn't seem like Sue Ellen.

"Um, this might be a personal question, but Tony wouldn't happen to be one of those 'rich men' you referring to?"

She turned to look back at me. There was just the faintest flash of anger in her eyes. "I couldn't say for absolutely sure. I told you I knew about the other women, but yeah, I think he was on her dance card once or twice." Her eyes softened. "But I don't—didn't—hate her. She wasn't the first or the last, I'm sure. I told you things weren't great between me and Tony, but this isn't about that. It's about my brother and some bastard who stuck a knife in his back."

I really didn't know what to say. There was no way I could tell her what I really believed, that there was about as much chance of me finding Stevie's killer as me flying to the moon. I could see she still needed some hope to hang onto, and I guess, while I was working to prove Hoppy wrong, there was no point in taking that away from her.

"Listen," I finally said. "I haven't given up." It was a bit of a white lie, but not completely false. "In fact, I've been meaning to really go over this place to see if Stevie might have hid anything away around here—something that, you know, might make somebody…you know…want to…" I let that thought trail off before coming to my point. "I've already started in the garage and you wanting the place cleared out gives me a great opportunity to really do it right. Let me pack up his things, empty the place out, sort everything out for you in boxes, while I search every nook of this place."

"Wes, I can't ask you to do that. It's something family should do," she answered, but I could see relief on her face.

"No, really, I insist. In fact, I've also been meaning to ask you, do you have any idea if Stevie had a favorite hiding place, maybe from when you were growing up here, an old standby that he trusted no one could find, someplace I should start?" I asked.

She let out a small laugh. "You kidding me? Ever since we were kids, if Stevie wanted something hid, even a bloodhound wasn't going to sniff it out. He was like a packrat that way. I remember when we were in our teens when Stevie first started smoking dope. Mama would say she knew he had it in the house, and she turned the place upside down but never found nothing. Drove her crazy. Stevie would just smile that smile of his and tell her it was no use, there was nothing to find. Make her even madder."

"Well, it's a long shot anyway," I said. "Just a theory Hoppy and I thought we'd pursue."

Damn, the lies just kept coming.

"I wish I could help, but in a lot of ways it seems like Stevie and I had become strangers. I know it was my fault—mostly—between Tony and raising the girls, still…"

"Sue Ellen, sometimes life takes funny turns and we always think there'll be plenty of time—" I began.

"Hey," a call came from the kitchen, interrupting us. It was Denny. "Are you going to come in here and give us all the hairy details or not. I didn't drive all the way back from the shore to watch Dom get egg yolk all over the front of his shirt."

"It's not my fault. Stacey made the eggs too runny," Dom answered.

"My eggs ain't too runny. You just eat too fast," Stacey said.

"Actually, Stacey," I heard Bob chip in, "you could have made the bacon a little more crispy—at least that's the way I like mine."

"This ain't no restaurant I'm running here. You guys don't like the way I cook, nobody said you had to eat it."

Sue Ellen smiled at me. "I guess we better get in there before the dishes start flying."

"Guess so. I might have been safer at Puddy's."

CHAPTER 45

There was, no doubt, more light in the deepest caves in Europe than in the Wayside Tavern, the bar where Stevie had been stabbed, and in which I now sat. It was so dark that I could only hope that the liquid in the shot glass in front of me really was Powers. I didn't see it poured, couldn't actually really see who did the pouring. The only way I knew my drink had arrived was the sound of the shot glass being plunked down on the bar counter and a voice demanding five dollars.

Kenny's bar was dark, but not like this. The weak bulbs in the few pendant lights that hung intermittingly over the bar didn't throw enough light to actually reach the counter top. The brightest source of illumination in the place came from the beer cooler containing six-packs for sale that radiated an eerie cold white glow in the far back of the bar. A small television screen was mounted high over the bar at the other end, casting a little more light into the place. It showed a feed from an area racecourse. The colors of the jockeys' silks and the horses' saddle pads burst forth in high definition splendor.

I could understand why no one was able to give any sort of a description of the person who put the knife in Stevie's back. The place was so black that, if I hadn't had years of practice, I would have had trouble just finding my mouth with the whiskey glass. I took a sip. Miraculously, the bartender had found the right bottle. It was Powers.

I saw, or rather, sensed the return of the bartender with my change. He placed it on the bar.

"Say, isn't this the place that guy was stabbed in a few weeks ago," I said, hoping he was still there and I was not just speaking out loud to myself.

"Yeah," came an answer. "He was sitting right where you are."

My eyes were slowly adjusting to the darkness, but I could still only make out the shape of a rather large, bulk of a man standing in front of me.

"Really? Wow, that's a little spooky. Maybe I ought to move," I said.

"Nah, you're okay. We usually don't have that kind of trouble around here," the bulk answered.

I really wasn't that worried. After all, Stacey had entered the bar ahead of me and was a few bar stools down from me, his largeness defined by the back light from the cooler. Still, it was a little eerie that I would choose the very bar stool where it happened to Stevie.

What were you doing here? I asked Stevie in my thoughts. *Were you meeting someone? Why did that person want to kill you?*

My eyes were adjusting to the place and I looked around quickly. There were so many directions the killer could have come at Stevie from without anyone noticing what was going on.

"Were you working that night?" I asked.

"I work every night. This is my place," came the reply.

"Nice. Just driving past and I saw your sign hanging out, realized I was a bit thirsty." I emptied my glass. "Speaking of which, I'll have another."

The owner retrieved the bottle from somewhere behind him and poured the Powers into my glass.

"Did you know the guy?"

"Sure, everybody knew Stevie," he answered. "Nice guy. That night he was buying drinks for the house—not that there were that many customers. It was early," he answered.

I reached for my glass but waited for a moment. "Say, can I buy you one?"

Down the bar I heard Stacey clear his dry throat.

"You know, actually, how about a round for the bar—if you think it's safe." I tried my best sincere, one of the guys, chuckle. "After all, it didn't seem to do that guy much good."

"Me neither," came the reply.

My eyes continued to adjust. The trick was not to be drawn to look at the television screen but instead focus on the darkness. I could now make out the bar counter and the shapes of bottles behind the bar. Even the large shape before became a little more recognizable as a member of the human race—ears, chin, nose, jowly face, white teeth. The only thing I couldn't really see was his eyes. The figure turned and stepped back a bit into the darkness but quickly reappeared holding an empty shot glass. He placed the glass on the table, opened the bottle, and poured himself a drink. He picked it up and leaned forward, raising his glass out ahead. I raised my glass.

"Sláinte," I said.

"To The King—that's Elvis," he said with a sure nod.

We tapped our glasses together and downed our shots. He leaned forward, both elbows on the bar. I got the impression the shot I bought him was not his first of the night. I wasn't going to complain if it made him talkative.

"I was just coming back to have him pay up for the second round he bought when I found his body. What he had on the bar didn't cover it, and I couldn't exactly go through his pockets—him being dead and all. I mean, if he had just passed out, okay no problem. But a dead guy? No thanks. So the difference was about thirty dollars I was out for the round, then the police close me down for the night—a Friday night, my best night. I took a beating."

"Yeah, I guess you couldn't exactly ask everyone to give their drinks back," I said, pulling out the cash to pay for the round. Hoppy was a little hesitant to lay out more money, just so I could spend it in a bar, but information cost money, and it was his idea that I visit the Wayside. "So I guess your new policy is customers pay before you pour the round?" I said with a laugh.

"Wha—no, ah—ha ha ha—that's funny—before I pour—ha ha—no you don't havta."

"No, it's okay. I have it right here. How much do I owe you?"

The bartender did a headcount from behind the bar, pointing into dark spaces that could have hid a tank. Then he counted down from the far end of the bar. I could make out Stacey and maybe one person beyond him silhouetted in the glow of cooler. "Make it sixty dollars," he answered.

Of course, I did not doubt his word, but I couldn't believe there were more than four or five people out there. Still, I was here to make friends, and it was Hoppy's money. "Great, keep it," I said, handing him eighty dollars. "Wow, closing you down. Did they, you know, 'take you downtown and go through mug books' like on TV?" I hoped my voice conveyed the right level of enthusiasm. I was approaching that point where it often dawns on a person that I seem to be asking a lot of questions.

The longer I could just seem like a normal guy, with a slightly morbid interest in a murder that took place right where I am sitting, the better.

"Nah. It was mostly the usual crowd that night. And the only other guy in here—I didn't get a good look at him. He sat back at a table, had a cap pulled low, and kinda sat scrunched forward, his head down. So looking at a bunch of pictures wasn't goin' to do no good."

"What was he drinking?" I asked.

"Who? Stevie?" the bartender answered.

"No, the stranger. What was he having?" I said, hoping to sound casual.

"Makers Mark and Coke. Why you askin'?" the bartender asked, the beginning of suspiciousness creeping into his voice.

"Oh, no reason. I was just thinking of something a friend who tended bar used to say. He could never remember a customer's name, but what they were drinking he never forgot."

"Yeah." The bartender laughed. "That and who's a big tipper and who ain't."

"Well, the police must have talked to him anyway. Like you said, only a few of you here when it happened," I said nonchalantly.

"Oh no, the guy was gone. Couldn't say when exactly. Don't blame him for not sticking around—bunch of cops askin' questions…"

"Did he leave a good tip?" I asked, just to keep things going, though I couldn't see where I was heading.

"Not a cent. Didn't touch his drink, either, from the round Stevie bought. I know he was there when I brought it to him."

"That must not happen much. I mean, who leaves a drink to waste, especially a free one?"

"Oh, it didn't go to waste," the owner said with a sly smile. "It just didn't seem right—the glass untouched, just sitting there. I didn't figure him coming back for it and I was being closed down anyway…" He pushed with his arms off the bar and stood up. "Better go pour that round or they'll be at me like wolves," he said.

"Sure, and when you're done, I'll have a…um…what bottled beer do you have?"

"Bud, Rolling Rock, Yuengling…"

"I'll have the Yuengling."

"Right," he said and off he went to spread cheer and good will into the darkness.

After the owner had poured Stacey a drink and moved on down the bar to the other customers, Stacey got up and came over. He stopped beside my bar stool.

"Thanks for drink," he said loud enough to be heard. Then he leaned forward so only I could hear him, "So is there a plan? You learning anything? What's next?"

"Well, it seems there was one guy here who wasn't a regular and had left by the time the police came. Could have been the killer." I was beginning to see things a little better and looked around to make sure no one was near us. "How high to you think these bar stools are?" I asked Stacey.

"I don't know…maybe thirty inches or so," he said.

"Yeah, that's what I thought. Okay, do me a favor. Stand behind me and act like you're sticking a knife into my back," I said.

These stools were the type that had a round seat and no back.

"Really?" Stacey asked.

"Yeah, I'm trying to determine how tall Stevie's murderer might be. Doc Livingston said the knife entered between the T-seven and T-eight vertebrae—that's roughly just below the shoulder blades."

"Okay," Stacey said, moving to stand behind me. "Ready? Here goes."

I felt the pressure of his hand on my lower back.

"No, that's too low. The doc said it went in at a slightly upward angle. Try it now," I said as I leaned forward and rested my forearms on the bar.

Again I felt the pressure as Stacey mimicked the stabbing. Higher up this time, but still not high enough, although the angle was right.

"Wait a minute. Stevie was shorter than me, maybe three inches, right?" I said.

"Yeah, probably just under six feet," Stacey answered.

"How tall are you?" I asked.

"Just over six feet," he answered.

I got off the bar stool and stood next to it. Then I crouched down a bit and tried to approximate Stevie's sitting height. I leaned forward.

"Okay, try it now. Stick it in," I said.

That was it. Same entry point and pretty close to the same angle.

"Perfect," I said. "It would go in just like that."

I looked up and saw that owner was standing a little bit to the left of us down the bar and was watching us. I don't know how long he'd been there.

"Listen, you two," he said. "I got no qualms about how people live their lives, but I don't run that kind of bar. I suggest you take your act elsewhere."

I looked up at him, realized I was still crouching, and quickly stood up.

"What? Um…no, it's not what you think. My name's Wes Byrne. I'm a reporter, doing a little work for the *Chronicle*."

"A reporter? Jayzus," the owner replied.

"Yeah. I'm just doing a piece about your old customer Steve Darby for the *Chronicle*. Thought I'd come out and see where it all happened, soak up a little of the atmosphere."

"I already told the police everything I know. I don't want any reporters sniffing around. Bad for business, run my customers off," he said.

Whatever camaraderie I had established had evaporated with the mention of the *Chronicle*. *What the hell?* I thought. Might as well go all in and follow up on Hoppy's theory. "None of those customers work for the Crawfords, by any chance?" I asked.

I guess I went a little too far. The owner pulled an axe handle out from under the bar and laid it out in front of me. "I've asked you nicely. I run a decent place, and I don't need nobody coming in and stirring up trouble. So, why don't you and your buddy here hit the road before the atmosphere crashes in your head?"

I took a step back as coolly as I could, considering I couldn't take my eyes of the axe, and rose my hands out in front of me to show I'd gotten the message.

Stacey had moved beside me. "Take it easy, old man," he said.

"Look, last thing we want is trouble. But if you should think of something—" I began as I backed away from the bar, "—just call the *Chronicle* and leave a message."

He lifted the axe handle by one end off the bar with one hand and pointed it at me. "I said get the hell out!"

I turned and headed toward the door. I looked over my shoulder and saw that Stacey was backing away slowly, keeping his eyes on the owner. I cursed myself for not sitting closer to the door, which still seemed a long ways away, fighting the urge to break out in a dash to get out of the place.

There was still about ten feet to go, when the front door swung open and one large and one small man blocked my exit. I turned to look for Stacey. The little guy I could probably handle. The big one was definitely Stacey's assignment. I balled my hands into fists.

"Hey, sorry man," the small guy said when he saw me. "Grinder, let the man pass."

The big guy laughed and stepped aside. "Sorry, dude. Couldn't see you in the dark."

I needn't have worried. They were just a couple of kids in their early twenties out for a good time.

"You're not leaving already, man? The night is young," the smaller one said, his voice rising to emphasize the last part.

"Yeah, we're here to get smashed," Grinder added, matching his mate in volume.

I turned and saw that the owner was still holding the ax handle in one hand, tapping the top of it into the palm of his other hand.

"Well, guys," I said as I passed them on the way out. "You may have come to the right place."

CHAPTER 46

Y ou know, I could've taken that old guy. I've been threatened with worse," Stacey said as we drove off from the Wayside Tavern.

He was having a pretty good time at my expense as we drove out of the parking lot. I had to listen to him rib me all the way to our next destination—the TSN facility on the other side of town. If Hoppy wanted me to check out where Stevie died and where he worked, I was going to do it all in one night and get it over with. There was no sense dragging things out, and the sooner I could tell him there was nothing to find, and that maybe he should get an MRI scan for those bones of his, the sooner I could move on and find a place where I didn't need a sarcastic bodyguard trailing along with me.

The TSN parking lot was pretty empty when we pulled in. The only cars and trucks there probably belonged to the night production staff and late-shift workers. Just the way I wanted it. The fewer people around the better, the easier to snoop and get questions answered.

I had to admit that as much as I disliked Tony, it certainly appeared as if he had created a world-class operation. Even at this late hour, and it was about eleven p.m., a row of exterior security flood lights brightly displayed a clean glass, concrete and orange brick, two-story main building, probably for executive offices, attached to a larger structure at its rear that most likely housed the studio and warehouse facilities. The white, manicured walkways, lined with small shrubbery and domed pathway lighting were immaculate. Three huge satellite dishes sat off to the far left of the building, applying the amazing advances of science that conquered space to beam images of rhinestone jewelry, superabsorbent microfiber cleaning products, and tsotchkes of every kind into the homes of impulse buyers, insomniacs, and agoraphobics twenty-four hours a day, seven days a week.

I'd done my research and knew the mythology behind the TSN or Television Shopping Network Empire that Tony had built. How late one night he was transfixed by an infomercial for a set of stainless-steel knives that never dulled and could chop wood and cut through nails, tin cans, and even rubber hoses without losing their sharpness. How he couldn't resist the hard-sell, direct marketing pitch that made every knife he'd ever owned seem obsolete and the way the advertiser's spiel managed to overcome every impulse to change the channel. It was impossible to defy the call to "order now."

He saw the future and it was around-the-clock product marketing using the techniques so successfully applied to sell those knives. This was just as cable television was in its infancy and air space was relatively cheap, so with a small investment he was able to grow his vision into a multibillion-dollar business.

We drove around the back of the large warehouse, where tractor trailers were backed up to a series of loading docks. A few beefy guys stood off to the side smoking cigarettes. I asked Stacey to let me proceed on my own, got out, and approached the men.

"Hi, I was wondering if the supervisor was around," I said as neared them.

They were all wearing overalls with the *TSN* logo on a patch attached over their left breast. I got the once over from each of them before the oldest looking of the group answered me.

"Dingo? Sure, he's probably in there somewhere. Only one not wearing overalls," he said.

"Dingo?" I asked.

"It's because he's all bite and no bark," said the tallest one.

The others all laughed.

"Right, thanks," I said as I walked over to and up a set of metal stairs the led to an open door. I could hear the sound of forklifts purring and loud music blaring from inside.

It was louder once I was inside. The place was a hive of activity. Men in those same overalls and yellow hardhats carted boxes of all sizes on hand trucks and pallet jacks. Platform stackers pulled merchandise of all sizes off steel shelve racks that towered to the ceiling. Forklifts carrying pallets laden with boxes held in place with stretched plastic wrap scooted across the floor like go-carts.

Across the way, I saw a tall, pot-bellied man wearing brown khaki pants, a white polo shirt, and a white hard hat. He was chewing on an unlit cigar while monitoring the activity with an iPad tablet. That had to be Dingo. I dodged my way across the floor to where he was standing. When I was a few feet from him, he looked up and his eyes flared.

"Who the hell are you and where the hell is your hard hat? You trying to get us busted by OSHA?" he snarled.

If that was no bark, I really didn't want to experience his bite.

"Um, no, not at all. Should I get one?" I answered.

"Damn right. Something falls on your head, we'll have lawsuits up the wahoo," he answered.

"Where are they?" I asked.

He shook his head, let out an exasperated sigh, then looked across at a petite woman in overalls who was standing around talking to two other men in similar attire.

"Hey, Carlisle, if you ain't too busy shooting the goddamn breeze, grab this guy a hat and bring it over," he yelled to her.

"Right, boss," she yelled back over her shoulder. Then

she made a remark to the two men, who both laughed and watched her walk away with looks I wouldn't quite call wholesome. She disappeared behind a long row of shelve racks.

"And, you two, ain't you got some work to do?" he yelled to the men.

"Yeah, sure, boss," one of them answered, jumping up into the seat of a nearby forklift.

He said something to the other guy, who looked at Dingo and chuckled. The guy in the forklift drove off, and the other one grabbed a pallet jack and headed in the other direction.

The woman came back into view, carrying a yellow hard hat. She walked over and gave me a flirtatious smile as she reached out to hand me the hat. She was cute, with deep blue eyes and dimples at the corners of her mouth. She had a lovely neck and her the front of her overalls were zipped open down to the point where it was possible to just make out the upper edges of a pink sports bra. She was probably a little young for me, in her early twenties, but I was flustered nonetheless.

I fumbled with the hard hat and dropped it onto the concrete floor. It bounced a few times before coming to rest between us at our feet. We both bent over to pick it up at the same time. She was a little quicker to get to it and when she straightened up, I was still bending over. The top of her hard hat cracked into my nose.

"Ow!" I yelled out, not too loudly I hoped.

"Oh, I'm so sorry. Did I hurt you?" she said, holding out the retrieved hat cautiously.

My eyes were a bit watery from the blow to my nose, but it didn't look like she was sorry. There was just the trace of a smile on her face. I took the hat from her without any further incident.

"No, no, I'm okay. Thanks," I said.

"You're welcome. I don't see any blood," she said, studying my face. "Maybe I should get some ice."

"Maybe you should just get back to work," Dingo said sternly.

"Yes, boss," she said, putting an emphasis on "boss" before she turned and sauntered away. I wasn't sure, but it looked like she was laughing to herself.

"She has that effect on all the men around here, but what can I do? She's my daughter," he said as we both watched her walk off.

"Well, she seems very sweet," I said.

"Yeah, you could say that," he answered with a very intimidating look. His message couldn't have been clearer if he had an uncocked double barrel shotgun draped over his forearm—"Look, but don't even think of touching."

I quickly put the hard hat on. The plastic headband on the inside was too small, so the hat wobbled precariously on my head. Best to get right to the point.

"Um, I'm here because I'm a friend of Mrs. Augustino, Tony Augustino's wife. Seems she just found out her brother, Steve Darby, used to work here, and she asked me to come by and see if he had left anything that belonged to him in a locker or anywhere."

I handed him an envelope with a signed note that I had gotten from Sue Ellen earlier in the day giving me authorization. Dingo took it from me, opened the envelope, and read the note.

"Darby—he was the boss's brother-in-law? Had no idea," he answered, handing me back the note.

"Well, I don't think he wanted anyone to know, probably didn't want any special treatment," I said.

We were interrupted when a forklift with a loaded pallet pulled up. Dingo shifted the cigar to the other side of his mouth without using his hands. He looked at the large, barcoded label glued onto the plastic wrapping and scanned it with his iPad tablet. The screen displayed information on a digital form that he scrolled down with his finger.

"Okay, that goes on the truck at bay four," he said to the driver, who drove off toward one of the waiting trucks.

Dingo touched the screen and the form disappeared.

"Wow, you guys really are state of the art," I said. "I'm surprised there are so many trucks here, though. Would have thought everything was sent out by UPS or DHL."

"The day shift uses them for domestic. At night, we pack up all the stuff going overseas and we truck that to the docks ourselves," he answered.

"Overseas? Really? I had no idea the station was that popular," I said.

"Oh, yeah. Very big in Europe, especially Eastern Europe. You name it, they're buying it," he answered.

Another fork lift drove up. Dingo shifted the cigar back to the other side of his mouth and repeated the scanning process. This time, I watched a little more intently. There was a digitalized official looking form with a Department of Homeland Security seal in the upper left corner and *US Customs and Border Protection* in typeface across the top. Information gleaned from Dingo's scan of the packing label filled in the fields of the form in seconds. He scrolled down and approved the information by touching an empty signature block at the bottom of the form. That form disappeared from view and a new blank one appeared in its place.

"Bay two," he said to the forklift driver, before turning his attention back to me. "So anyway, about Darby's stuff—I'm afraid you're too late. One of his friends that worked here asked me if it was okay for him to take it, said he'd give it to the family."

I could only think of one person who might be interested in Stevie's stuff.

"Was that friend Puddy Salvatore?" I asked.

"Yeah, then he goes and gets himself killed. I tell you, it's been quite a month, first Darby, then Salvatore, and then Tiffin. Of course, they say deaths happen in threes."

"Tiffin. Do you mean Bones—um, I mean Ricky Tiffin?"

"Yeah, it was in the news. He was one of our truck drivers. State police arrested him for something and somebody ambushed them right in broad daylight."

"'Bo—er, Ricky worked here too, as a driver?"

Dingo gave me a quizzical look. "Yeah, had the route to Baltimore. You know him too?" he asked.

At last I'd found something that linked Stevie, Puddy, and Bones. They all worked together here at TSN. Unfortunately, it was all I had.

"Well, not that well. Bumped into him a few times, just surprised to hear he worked here is all," I answered as nonchalantly as possible. "Like you said, a little weird that three people who worked here died so suddenly."

"Yeah, well, I guess it happens, but speaking of work, since there's nothing of Darby's to collect, guess we're done here?" he said. It was more of a statement than question.

"Sure, sure. I'll tell Stevie's sister. Probably nothing too valuable anyway," I said. "Do you want this now, or do I have to wear it until I get to the door," I asked, indicating my hard hat.

"Rules say hard hats to be worn inside at all times so keep it on and put it on that table over there by the door just as you're leaving," he answered, just as another forklift carrying a pallet pulled up. Once again he scanned the packing label and ran through the process like before. I waited for him to finish.

"I want to thank you for your time. You've been very helpful," I said.

Actually, what I'd found out tonight only muddled things up. Sure, while working together, Puddy might have let it slip out about the car theft ring to Stevie, who in turn blackmailed Bones. Stevie underestimated whom he was dealing with and Bones killed him rather than pay out, and, after killing Tina for returning my car, Bones then murdered Puddy for telling Stevie in the first place. But what about the different knives? What about Bones, if he could be trusted, denying killing Puddy? What about the fact that Stevie's killer was a good three inches shorter than Bones?

Instead of getting answers, I was only coming up with more questions. It looked like getting out of East Hastings was going to be harder than I thought.

CHAPTER 47

There is no way that Bones was the one who stuck a knife in Steve Darby."

The next morning, I was in the morgue with Dr. Livingston and we were standing around one of those life-sized skeleton models that you sometimes see hanging from a pole in doctors' offices. The skeleton, sitting on the rigged stool, was playing the part of Stevie. The doc had used tape to approximate the angle of Stevie's knife wound passing through the skeleton's back.

This time, I played the part of Stevie's killer, plunging the knife in from behind as the murderer would have done it from behind Stevie. I did it with the skeleton sitting erect and the skeleton leaning forward, resting its bony arms on the counter. I did it left handed and right handed, palm up and palm down.

"See?" Doc Livingston continued. "No matter how you do it, the trajectory of the blade through the skeleton only makes sense if the killer was like you determined—probably between five foot ten and six foot?"

"Well, I'm about the same size as Bones. How about if he did this?" I said, taking the knife from him. I squatted down as Bones might have and put the knife through the skeleton so it lined up with the tape.

Unfortunately, Newton's Third Law of Physics—namely, that for every action there is an equal and opposite reaction—came into play and the stabbing forward motion caused me to rock onto my heels and then fall backward onto my ass.

Doc Livingston looked down at me skeptically. "Um...why would he do that? It seems a bit...um...awkward," he said.

"Maybe he wanted to duck down so he wouldn't be seen," I answered, looking sheepishly up at him.

"Well—and this is just my opinion—I believe there's a greater likelihood that someone who just stabbed a fella is gonna be noticed a bit more if he's sitting on his rear end holding a knife behind a bleeding body than if he'd just stayed upright and headed on out the door after sticking a guy."

"But it's got to be Bones," I said, sitting there and knowing that Doc Livingston was right, but just not wanting to let it go. "I mean, it all makes so much sense—except for the fact that he didn't do it. I mean, there were the three of them, all working together at the warehouse. I worked out a motive for him to do it—the blackmail. Bones definitely had the means. He owned a knife and as good as admitted to me that he stabbed Tina, so why not Stevie? And he had the opportunity, in that he could have done it unnoticed in that dark bar."

"Kinda frustrating when the facts don't back up the story, heh?" he replied.

I tried to ignore the sarcasm and got up onto my knees. Now I was about Puddy's height.

"It couldn't have been Puddy. He might have wanted to kill Stevie for taking advantage of what he told him about the car theft ring, but he was too short. See?" I said, pushing the knife into the skeleton palm up from an angle that Puddy would take. The trajectory of the angle was too sharp upward. I raised my arm and plunged the knife in overhand, but that resulted in a downward angle for a wound.

I stood up and put the knife on the counter. "The only one left who could possibly be a suspect is Tina, and I just don't see that. I mean she might be about the right height, maybe a little short, but dark or not, I can't see a woman not being noticed in that bar. Besides, what motive did she have? There's nothing connecting her and Stevie."

"Well, if it's any consolation, it seems the police share your theory about Bones. They've pretty much closed the case on Steve Darby's murder."

"I suppose Bones is here," I said, indicating a wall of doors behind which bodies were kept on sliding platforms for examination. "Anything interesting you can tell me about him?"

"No, nothing more than what the police already released. His tongue was cut out, probably while he was still alive, and he was beaten pretty severely before his throat was slashed. Terrible way to go," he answered.

"Yeah, well, it's hard for me to draw up much sympathy," I said, as I picked the skeleton up off the stool, carried it across the room, and hung it back up on its stand in a corner. I couldn't help thinking that I was never going to find out the truth here, and Hoppy would have me covering flower shows and boring borough meetings the rest of my life. My cell phone rang. I recognized the number. It was Sue Ellen.

Damn, I was so sure I would be calling her with good news this morning, and now I was back at square one with nothing.

"Hi, Sue Ellen," I said.

Doc Livingston shrugged his shoulders and began putting the books and magazines back where they had come from.

"Hi, Wes. Where are you?" she asked.

"Um, I'm with Doc Livingston at the morgue, just pursuing a few theories," I answered.

"Listen, I want to apologize for yesterday," she began.

"What do you mean?" I answered. "You didn't do anything."

"I was, well, very rude. I know you're doing your best and probably right on the verge of some big breakthrough, and it doesn't help to have my laying any kind of guilt trip on you," she said.

"Hey, I understand. I wish I did have more," I answered, looking over at the skeleton, the piece of tape still showing the wound trajectory. "I…um…just don't want you to get your hopes up too high, is all."

"Hey, I believe in you. And to make up for yesterday, I made a reservation at Chez Maurice for tonight, seven o'clock."

"Sue Ellen, you don't have to do that," I answered. "It's enough giving me a place to stay and sending around Ronald to help with keeping an eye on things."

"No. I insist. So let me give you Jackie's number, and you can tell her what time you'll be picking her up."

"Jackie? You made a date for me with Jackie?" I asked.

"Of course. I'm a married woman. How would it look if I was seen out having a romantic dinner with an attractive man?" she answered.

I felt the heat around my neck and ears and knew I was probably blushing a bit.

I looked over and noticed that Doc Livingston was absently shuffling papers and looking at files in an attempt to do his best to not let me see that he was listening to my end of the conversation.

"This sounds like a nice restaurant and I don't have anything to wear," I said, digging around for any excuse I could find.

"I know, that's why I wanted to find out where you were. I'm buying you a suit and I've asked Ronald to meet up with you. There's a Big and Tall Men's Shop in the mall and he has a real nice sense of style. There's no way I'd leave it up to you," she answered.

"Sue Ellen, I can't let you do that," I said.

"You really don't have a choice. I can't have you showing up to one of the nicest restaurants in East Hastings wearing khakis and a polo shirt."

"Yeah, but—"

"You don't like Jackie? Is that it?" Sue Ellen said, more of an accusation than a question.

"Well, no—of course I do, what's not to like? But—"

"Then what's the big deal? You're a grown, unattached man with a car that finally is safe and clean enough to drive someone around in, and you've been spending way too much time just hanging out with Stacey and the other guys. A night out with a smart, pretty woman will do you good."

"It's just that—"

"Look, I know you're still missing your wife," she said, seriously. "All I'm doing is giving you a night away from everything." She waited a few beats. "It's not like I'm expecting you to sleep with her or even kiss her good night. Just be your charming self," she said with a sweet laugh to lighten the mood.

I laughed. The woman was formidable. "Are you sure she wants to go out with me?" I asked.

"What is this, eighth grade? She's asked me about you and I said the best way to get answers is to ask him yourself. Relax. It will be fun," Sue Ellen answered.

"You're sure?"

"Call her." It was a demand.

"Okay, but I'm paying you back for the dinner and the suit—when I have the money," I said.

"Fine, whatever. Just go out and have a good time. Ronald will meet you at the mall in one hour. And Wes?"

"Yes?"

"Just breathe. It'll be okay." She hung up.

I looked over and noticed that Doc Livingston had dropped all pretense of not eavesdropping and was looking at me with a bemused smile on his face.

"What?" I said.

"Nothing. It's just that, well, since I've met you you've seemed a little...um..."

"Scared?" I said, finishing the sentence. "Well, considering I've found two dead bodies, been threatened by the police, received several death threats, and actually been bound and almost killed, I think I have the right to a little fear."

"Sure, sure, of course, you do, but it seems the prospect of a date with a very lovely lady has you more shook up then all that other stuff."

"Yeah, well, it's been a while. Damn Sue Ellen and her matchmaking."

Doc Livingston closed the book, that he wasn't reading anyway, and wheeled around on his stool to face me. "Son, you have any idea why you're here?" he asked, very directly.

"Here?" I said, looking around the morgue. "Yeah, I was hoping to solve Stevie's murder so I can get on my merry little way."

"Well, yeah, here and in East Hastings, it's all the same thing," he answered. "I'll tell you why—and you better not repeat a single word of this. It's because Sue Ellen wants you here. She needs you. You think Hoppy couldn't find another reporter? You think I let anyone in my morgue? You think Jackie would even consider having dinner with you if she'd just met you on the street, if Sue Ellen hadn't told her all kinds of nice things about you?"

"Well, she wants me to find Stevie's killer," I said.

"It's more than that. Let me tell you a story. Sue Ellen— well, the dry cleaners—sponsored my youngest grandson's baseball team. That boy has a lot of great qualities, but being a ball player isn't one of them. Still, his older brothers and all his friends played, so he insisted on playing too. So the season starts, and Micah, that's my grandson, he's not playing much, can't hit or catch worth a lick. After a few games, when he didn't get to play at all, I think he was about to give it all up. Sue Ellen notices how sad he is, not playing and all, so she starts staying late after games and practices and plays catch with him and shows him how to hold the bat just so and stand at the plate. She actually gets on the mound and throws pitch after pitch to him, always encouraging him."

"Yeah, well she was a bit of a tomboy growing up," I said.

"So this goes on all through the season, and we all saw the improvement Micah was making—not so much that he was going to set the league on fire, even play that much more—but it was his confidence. He carried himself like a ballplayer. And you're probably not going to believe this, but the last game of the season, Micah not only got a hit but he drove in the winning run. I've never seen a boy so happy. And it was all because of Sue Ellen."

"Nice story, but what's it got to do with me?" I said.

"Wes, I think Sue Ellen just wants you to not give up and for you to get yourself back in the game, and, son, let me tell you—that woman's going to keep pitching until her arm falls off."

CHAPTER 48

We'd made it through the appetizers and, much to my surprise, I hadn't spilled a drink or knocked a plate off the table. Things were going much better than expected. It had to be the new clothes.

I've never been what you would call a "clothes hound." At my size, I was always fortunate to find a shirt with sleeves that didn't end halfway down my forearms and pants that didn't ride high above my ankles. It didn't matter much, because I found out that, as a reporter, it was always better to look as casual as possible, like a regular person, because people tended to be overly suspicious and withdrawn, as it was when I started asking questions. Look too sharply dressed, and I'd create an even greater distance between us. Basically, I'd shopped at used clothing shops and only made out if some guy of my approximate size had died recently and his family had decided to clear out his closet.

Of course, things changed a bit when I met Jan. Women have that way of looking at every piece of clothing a man holds dearest like it carries a plague. Whenever we went clothes shopping, I often felt like one of those cardboard cut-outs dolls of a man who has an assortment of paper outfits that can be attached and removed at will. I just stood there while Jan held shirts, pants, and jackets, still in their wrapping or on their hangers, up against me while she decided what I would buy. I had no say in the matter. Well, actually, I did in that if I thought something looked good it would immediately go back on the rack, and we'd move on to the next selection.

I'd only splurged once on a really nice suit and that was when Jan insisted I buy one for our wedding ceremony so that I'd look good in the photos in our wedding album. I wore it only on that day and the day she was buried. It was so painful to see it hanging in my closet that a week after her funeral I burned it in a barrel in our back yard.

Shopping for a suit with Ronald was a lot like shopping with Jan. He looked at me, whenever I pointed to a jacket or tie that I liked, with the disappointed expression of an art teacher with a student who insisted on drawing rainbows but was color blind. I really had no choice but to give in to his style choices, but, as usual, I had to admit that Sue Ellen was right. The man did know how to pick out an outfit. We, and I use that word very loosely, ended up with a tan, herringbone tropical blend linen/silk two button sport coat, navy blue Clarendon twill trousers, white cotton shirt and maroon basket weave tie. The only real point of contention was the yellow and gray stacked argyle socks he selected. I thought they were a bit too flashy, but he insisted socks were the one item a man could wear to make a bit of a fashion statement. I gave in. We finished things off with a pair of black moc-toe tassel slip-on loafers. I looked good and felt poised and confident, in spite of my initial nervousness.

Of course, Sue Ellen was also right about getting out. It was really nice to share an evening with a smart, attractive woman like Jackie to get my mind off things. She looked wonderful, but if she noticed, as I did, the admiring glances she was getting from the other restaurant patrons, she didn't let on. Her hair was swept into a loose updo, tear drop chandelier earrings with lapis stones dangled from her ears, a simple lapis-beaded cylindrical necklace encircled her neck, and a sleeveless white/black floral print sheath dress provided just the right touch of elegance without being overly formal.

Over appetizers, we had talked mostly about Sue Ellen.

Each of us knew her in different aspects of her life and, at least for me, it was interesting to hear what the adult Sue Ellen had accomplished, about her children, and the contributions she had made to the community. Jackie laughed at my stories of the tom-boy Sue Ellen, beating up boys and protecting both Stevie and me against bullies.

When the waiter took away our plates, we both grew quiet, each a bit unsure about where to go next.

This was the part I dreaded. I played around with my napkin for a couple seconds, smiled awkwardly at her, took a drink of my wine, smiled awkwardly at her again. She smiled back.

"So," she stated, filling the quiet. "Other than the arrests, deaths, beatings, and threats, are you glad you came back to East Hastings?"

I laughed. She laughed back.

"You know, I never really thought I would come back, but now that I have, well, it has changed a lot, but it has its charms and…I don't know…maybe there is something to that sense of place where the rhythm of life just seems a part of a person. What about you? Do you like living here?"

"Oh, yeah, very much. It is really so beautiful, so different from where I grew up," she answered.

"That was somewhere in Delaware, I think Sue Ellen told me," I said.

"Yeah, Middletown. It was nice—don't get me wrong—but it was kinda flat and there weren't a lot of trees or streams or old farms like there are around here. Plus I've made some very nice friends."

"Well, people say very nice things about you. Doc Livingston, for one. I felt he was sizing me up as if I was taking his daughter out for a date when he heard we were going to have dinner."

"He is sweet. He took me under his wing when I took over from Doc McClaren. He seemed to know it wasn't going to be easy for a female vet—introduced me to the right people, encouraged me to get out."

"Was it that tough, being a female vet?" I asked.

"Not really. The toughest part was getting into vet school. The competition is fierce and there aren't a lot of them around," she answered.

"So what made you decide to become a vet?"

"Well, when I was a little girl, like a lot of little girls, I wanted a horse. We couldn't afford one, so as soon I was old enough, I volunteered to work at a local horse farm in exchange for the chance to ride—clearing out stalls, feeding and brushing the horses, things like that. I loved it."

Our waiter came over. He was wearing black pants, a crisply pressed white shirt, and a clip-on black tie. His attire suited the place perfectly. The restaurant was unpretentious, with clean white tablecloths and just a few prints of works by French artists hanging on the wall and medium light provided by several French Empire crystal chandeliers that hung from the ceiling. It was the kind of place that let its food do the talking, and, based on the appetizers, I liked what it had to say.

"Your meal should be out any minute," he said. "Would you like another glass of wine?" he asked me. Jackie's wine glass was still half full.

Actually, I could have killed for a Powers with two ice cubes, but both Doc Livingston and Ronald made me promise to be on my best behavior. "I think I'll wait and order more when the meal comes," I said. They both would have been proud of me. The waiter left and I turned my attention back to Jackie. "Still," it's a long way from mucking out stalls to becoming a vet," I said to her.

"Mucking out stalls? So you know something about horses? I'm impressed," she said with a smile.

"It's hard to grow up in East Hastings and not learn a little of the horsey lingo," I answered, surprisingly happy that I could impress her.

"Do you ride?" she asked.

"Um, no," I said emphatically. "I've only been on a horse once in my life, and I spent the entire time ducking down to avoid the low tree branches the animal seemed intent on taking me under. I actually think it was disappointed I managed to stay on for the entire ride."

Jackie laughed. "Well, most of them do have a mind of their own. The horse was probably just testing you."

"Yeah? Well, I flunked miserably—but back to you and your journey to vet-dom."

"Well, I hadn't really planned on becoming a vet, but one day one of my favorite horses developed a bow tendon." She must have noticed my puzzled look. "It's an inflammation of the flexor tendon, on the back of the lower part of the horse's leg, sort of where we have the Achilles tendon and lower calf."

"Oh, okay. Is that serious?"

"Can be quite serious, and costly. In this case, the horse's owner was considering putting it down. I couldn't stand the thought of that and volunteered to care for the horse. The owner was reluctant at first but I guess I was pretty convincing. I moved into the barn and stayed with the horse around the clock. The most important factor is care— applying lotions, short exercise regimens, making sure the horse didn't do anything to reinjure the tendon. The horse improved, completely healed, and I loved caring for that animal so much, right then and there I made up my mind that's what I was going to do with my life."

There was no doubt she had made the right decision, the way she seemed to glow as she told me the story. Once again, I was struck by the way a person who finds the right calling seems so at peace with themselves. Was I ever like that with my newspaper work? If I was, it was in another lifetime.

CHAPTER 49

The waiter brought our meals. Jackie was a vegetarian, which I did not, in any way, hold against her, and had ordered Portobello mushrooms that were stuffed with homemade roasted eggplant puree, Parmesan cheese, roasted garlic, and served with grilled baguette slices. I, not being a vegetarian, which Jackie did not seem to hold against me, had ordered a pan-seared rib-eye steak with Béarnaise sauce that came with a side of creamy mashed potatoes. I was amazed that I'd actually gotten what I ordered, having murdered the pronunciation of the order in French.

We each took a bite of our meals and ooohed at the delicious flavors that filled our mouths. Sue Ellen certainly knew her restaurants. Not bad for a poor girl from the wrong side of the tracks.

For a few moments, it was as if we'd each forgotten the other was there as we dove into our meals. When we came up for air, it was apparently my turn to tell the story of my life.

"So, I've heard people talking about how you were responsible for cleaning up the Kithane River with a series of stories you wrote a few years ago, but I haven't heard any of the details." Jackie asked. "Will you tell me about it?"

"Sure," I said, putting a forkful of steak into my mouth. "There's really not that much to it and people tend to exaggerate my role in the cleanup." I took a sip of wine to wash the steak down. "See, the river had been pretty polluted for years," I began. "Everybody griped about it, but they just seemed to accept it. They blamed the paper mill in Briartown up the river for dumping crap into the river and, well, the paper mill had a lot of friends in high places, employed a lot of people, and going after them seemed a pretty fruitless endeavor. But I was young and idealistic and believed the power of the press could take on anything. So I went out, got samples of water from the river, and took it to a lab at the University of Pennsylvania to have it tested. Turned out, although the paper mill was polluting the river, there was something else that was a lot more dangerous, chemicals that were traced to stuff used in dry cleaning fluids primarily."

"Dry cleaning chemicals—like they use in the cleaners that Sue Ellen runs?" Jackie asked.

"Yeah, although at that time she just worked there. She wasn't even dating Tony then, and to tell you the truth, it was pretty hard to envision his family had anything to do with it. Tony's parents were great people—really involved in the community, sponsored little league teams, helped build a community center," I answered.

"So what did you do?"

"Well, I figured the best way to find out who was doing it was to find out where it was being done. So I had water tested at various points in the river. If there were no chemicals at one point and chemicals below that, I could narrow down the dump site."

"And did you?" she asked.

"Yes, and for several weeks I staked out the places that made the most sense. One night, I saw a truck dumping fluids out of a long hose into the river—just flushing the chemicals into the river like it was a toilet."

"Then what did you do?"

"I took a few photos using a night lens, got the name of the company off the truck, a few shots of the guys doing the dumping."

"And then you wrote the story and exposed the crime?" Jackie asked.

I noticed she was making great progress on her meal and wondered if she had got me talking just so she could eat while my meal sat ignored. A despicable thought, I know, but all the while I was talking my wonderful meal sat untouched.

"No. To tell you the truth, I didn't know what to do. So I went to Hoppy. I wasn't technically an employee of the paper—had mostly been stringing stories, covering borough meetings, a few sporting events, pretty boring stuff. I was taking a few classes at East Hastings University, working part-time in a pharmacy, just looking to earn a few bucks—kinda without direction. In fact, I undertook the investigation on my own and it cost a lot for all that testing. Had to cover a lot more of those boring meetings to pay for things. No one at the paper knew what I was up to."

"Seems surprising Hoppy let you keep the story then. He must have had other, more experienced reporters to give it to."

"Yeah, but I think Hoppy saw something in me—don't ask me what. The biggest surprise was that he actually let me pursue the story at all. Small town like this, pressure can come from all sides. The *Herald* got its paper from the paper mill, so any unwanted publicity on their part could affect the prices they paid."

"But you said the paper mill wasn't responsible," Jackie said.

"No, I said they weren't the worst offender. Any light shown on the pollution had to involve them. Then there was the dry cleaner. Tony's family owned three stores, a shopping complex, advertised heavily in the paper, and, like I said, had a lot of friends in the community. If they were responsible, and I really had no idea if they were, but if word got out that I was poking around…well, it might not have been too good for the *Chronicle*. In fact, Hoppy may have let me pursue the story just so he could claim deniability if things went south—just some wanna-be Woodward and Bernstein going off on his own."

"Do you really believe that?" Jackie asked, skeptically.

"I wouldn't put anything past Hoppy. He's always thinking a few steps ahead. But he worked hard with me; showed me how the build a story; double, triple check all the facts; develop sources. We started with the disposal company, wanted to find out who owned it, who their customers were. For all we knew, it could have just been the work of some lazy employees who couldn't be bothered doing things right."

"But that wasn't the case?" she asked.

"No, I finagled my way into getting the company's records—don't ask how, it wasn't all quite legal and I don't want you to think I'm some sort of criminal. Turned out, the company had been dumping the chemicals for about a year, and the dry cleaners was one of their clients. After a few months and a lot of digging around, I had enough for a series of articles. Hoppy helped me write them. He was tough, I'll tell you, but I learned so much. When the story broke, people were shocked and angry. The owners of the disposal company were arrested and sent to jail and even the paper mill cleaned up their act, though they weren't charged with anything. A movement started to clean up the river for good. I covered it all—the trials, the efforts to rid the river of pollution."

"And became a local hero," Jackie said, raising her glass to me.

"Well, in some people's eyes—to some I did more damage than good," I said.

"Like Sue Ellen?" Jackie said, a knowing look in her eyes.

"You know about that?" I asked.

"Small town, and I've gotten to know Sue Ellen," she answered.

"Yeah. See when the news broke about the dry cleaner's involvement, there was some backlash from the town. Hurt their business for a while, even though I never found proof the dry cleaners had any knowledge. They were just contracting a waste disposal company. Still, Tony's father took it hard, felt responsible, even though he wasn't the one who signed the contract with the company. And Sue Ellen adored him, lots of people did. He had a stroke about a month after the story came out—bad one—died a few weeks later. Sue Ellen blamed me."

"You said old man Augustino didn't sign the contract. Who did?" she asked.

I paused a moment to take a quick bite off my steak. "Tony did," I said without looking up.

"Did you suspect him?"

"Let's just say I didn't have any proof, and after what happened to his father, I...well...I...saw that he and Sue Ellen were getting close and I'd done enough damage," I said.

"You have nothing to be sorry about. You exposed a crime, maybe even saved people's lives," Jackie said, reaching out and placing her hand atop mine.

"Well, I learned that sometimes the right thing can hurt the wrong people," I said. I turned my hand over, palm up and took Jackie's hand in mine, squeezing it gently. There was a deep understanding in her eyes. I was happy to be with her.

Our young waiter came over. He seemed a bit nervous.

"Um, sir, the manager would like to speak with you—in the back," he said.

Must be a problem with the bill, I thought. Maybe we'd gone over the limit Sue Ellen had provided for. Since I was broke, the evening might end with me having to ask Jackie to cover the difference. Not the way I envisioned things going.

"I'll just be a minute," I said, releasing her hand and standing up. My half-eaten meal languished on the plate. If we had spent more than provided for, maybe I could get a refund for the portion I hadn't eaten.

I followed our waiter to the back of the restaurant. He stepped aside and pointed me down a small hallway with a women's and men's bathroom on the left-hand side and a door with an exit sign over it at the far end. I took a few steps forward, but didn't see any sort of office door and looked back.

The waiter was gone. I turned and started back to the main room of the restaurant just as two very large men quickly came out of the men's room.

"What the—" I started to say as they spun me around, grabbed me by the elbows, and rushed me down the hallway toward the door at the rear. The door had one of those crash bars that opened the door when pushed in. They slammed me against the door, my face hitting it square on. I felt my nose crack. My midsection provided the pressure on the crash bar to open the door.

I was outside, in a poorly lit alley that ran behind the restaurant. Still holding me, the men came single file through the door behind me and, when again on either side of me, threw me down onto my hands and knees forcefully. I felt my new pants tear at the knees as small pieces of stone or glass embedded themselves into my knees. My hands scraped across the paved surface and I could feel my skin tearing.

On my hands and knees, both beginning to burn, I lifted my head slightly. I could taste blood, no doubt flowing from my nose. My vision was blurry, water-hazed, from the blow to my face. I could barely make out a dark Escalade with tinted windows. The passenger door, which faced me, opened and the first thing I saw was a pair of large tan cowboy boots stepping out and onto the pavement. I had to lift my head higher to take in the full scale of the man who wore them as he got out of the car. He must have been about six foot four and was broad and powerful looking. "Well, Mr. Byrne. You being a hot-shot reporter, you must have some idea of who I am," said the man in a slight, calm voice, the accent having just a tinge of southern to it.

"Off the top of my head, I'd guess you're a Crawford," I muttered, my eyes clearing a bit.

He was wearing blue jeans, a large square belt buckle, and tucked in yellow polo shirt. He was heavy, but it was a thick, firm heavy. He was clean shaven, with short cropped, what probably was graying hair, though it wasn't possible to tell for sure in the dimly lit alley.

"Very good," he said, "Ferdie Crawford. You might call me the family patriarch. I hear you been sticking your nose into business that don't concern you, asking questions about my family."

I could still feel blood trickling from my nose and sniffed hard to stop it. A deep pain exploded right between my eyes, as if someone had hit me above the bridge of my nose with a ball peen hammer. "Ferdie?" I asked, just to say something to let the pain pass.

"Yeah, short for Ferdinand—named after a king. I always thought it was fitting," he answered as he leaned back against the Escalade. I had the feeling he was used to talking down to people on their hands and knees.

"Listen," I said. "I was just asking a few innocent questions, didn't get any answers, never really figured you were involved in any of the murders."

"That so?" he said. He spit of spray of tobacco juice onto the ground about a foot in front of me. I looked closer and could see a slight protrusion in his lower lip…probably a large pinch of Copenhagen chewing tobacco. "Not even Bones?" he asked.

"You know, I really don't care who killed Bones. That's for the state police to investigate. None of my business."

He seemed to find that funny. He let out a short, sneering sort of laugh and then let loose with another shot of tobacco juice that landed in approximately the same place as the previous one. "So exactly what is your business?'

"An old friend of mine, Steve Darby, was murdered. The East Hastings police didn't seem to care—"

"And you think my family had something to do with it?"

"No, not at all. I already said that," I answered.

I didn't like the whiny nature to my voice, but I also didn't like the idea of one of those big old cowboys smashing into my ribs.

"I see. Well, I tell you what. I'm going to do you a favor here tonight—just on account of wanting to set the record straight. Then I'm gonna ask you to do one for me. Does that sound fair?" he said. The menacing tone in his voice suggested I really didn't have a choice in the matter.

"Sure," I said. "Whatever you say."

"Okay, I'm gonna let you ask me one question—only one—so go ahead, ask away."

Of course the most important question I wanted to ask was if he was going to kill me, but I figured I'd find that out soon enough. Instead, I decided to ask the one question I had a feeling he wanted from me.

"Did you kill or have Steve Darby killed and if not, do you know who did?" I looked as deeply as I could at him in the dim light of the alley.

He gave that sneering laugh again and again spit tobacco juice in my direction, this time a little closer. "That's two questions, Mr. Byrne. You think a man like me doesn't know how to count? Still, I don't see the harm. First off, no, I did not have anything to do directly with the death of Steve Darby. Secondly, yes I do have an idea about who killed him but I prefer to monitor that situation myself. So how's that, satisfied."

"Not directly?" I said.

"Now, now Mr. Byrne. I think I fulfilled my end of the bargain. You had your questions. Now let's get to the favor I want from you."

"Sure, what do you want?"

"I want you to leave town immediately and never look back. In a way, it's me who's doing you the favor—because I could just have you killed. However, I don't think it's good business to kill members of the press. You know how when you kill a bee, the dead bee sends off an aroma…called phera' something."

"Pheromones," I said, immediately angry at myself for doing so. No need to look like a smarty pants.

"That's right, pheromones. Very good. Yeah, well they let off those pheromones and it sort of sets the other bees off, and they all come aswarming to the location of the smell. That's the way it is with the press. Kill one and it just brings more attention."

"Okay, sure, I wasn't planning on sticking around any," I said, even though this evening with Jackie had made me think hard about delaying my departure.

"Good, very good," Ferdie said. "'Cause like I said, I really don't want to kill you. On the other hand, a veterinarian—a lady veterinarian, for instance—should something happen to her, maybe when she was out driving alone to an appointment…well, I don't think that would stir things up quite as much. If you understand me. 'Course it could really be anyone of your friends, I ain't real particular."

I stared hard at him. I don't think I'd ever hated anyone as much as I hated him at that very moment. "I understand," I said.

"Good, very good. Well, Mr. Byrne it was certainly a pleasure to meet you and so glad we could come to our understanding." He let loose with one last gob of tobacco juice, this one landing between my hands on the pavement. "You have a good night now."

He turned and climbed into the back of the Escalade. The two men who were behind me passed by. I steadied for a quick kick of departure, but they only walked to the car, one going around to the driver's side, the other climbing into the passenger side.

The doors closed, the car started up and it drove off down the alley. I remained on my hands and knees.

The restaurant door flung open and in a moment Jackie was at my side, crouching down to look me over.

"My God, Wes. What happened?" she asked, her voice full of concern. "Are you hurt?"

"No, no, I'm fine but if you don't mind, I think I'd like to skip dessert and get the hell out of here."

CHAPTER 50

Whoa, looks like someone got a little too fresh for a first date. Remind me not to mess with that vet," Stacey said over the exited barking of Ginger as I walked through the front door of Stevie's place.

Ginger jumped up, front paws on my stomach, and it was a little painful to push her away because of the skin loss on each of my palms. I should have been grateful that she even wanted to greet me. I was probably quite a sight to behold.

Jackie had insisted on taking me to her office and treating my wounds, so there were large band aids on each of my palms and larger cotton gauze pads taped onto each of my knees, which were visible through the bloody torn fabric of each pant leg. She had stuffed two small wads of cotton up my nostrils to stop the bleeding from my nose. I couldn't tell, but I had a feeling dark bruising was developing under my eyes.

Besides cleaning and treating the torn skin on my hands and knees, Jackie had also, as delicately as possible, straightened my broken nose back into place. I had undelicately screamed like a two-year old when she did so. Afterward, I had asked her how many broken noses she had treated in her career. She told me broken noses were really not a common injury in the animal world, so I was her first. As a matter of fact, she informed me that I was the first two legged animal she had ever treated, not counting a few parrots and parakeets. If I wasn't so embarrassed and in so much pain, I would have been honored.

"Actually, the date was going very well—until a certain Ferdinand Crawford wanted to have a word with me," I began saying in a very nasal voice due to the cotton in my nostrils. Ginger again raised up and placed her paws against my stomach. "Down, girl, c'mon please." I pushed her gently and Ginger obeyed and returned her front paws to the floor.

"Crawford? He did that to you at the restaurant?" Stacey asked.

"Out back," I continued, pulling the cotton from my nose because I couldn't stand the sound of my voice. The cotton was bloodied but the bleeding appeared to have stopped. "He lured me into the alley behind the place and— AHHHHHH."

Ginger had now firmly pressed her cold nose against the gauze covering my right skinned knee and was inhaling in short but powerful bursts like a bloodhound tracking an escaped convict. The pain was excruciating. I tried to back up but she switched her attention to my left knee and pressed in harder. I couldn't shake her.

"Help, pull her off," I called out to Stacey.

He put down the blue masking tape he had been using to prepare the walls in the living room for the paint job, came over, and dragged Ginger back off my knee by the collar. "It's the blood. Drives dogs crazy," he explained to me. "C'mon, Ginger," he said to the dog, "go to your bed."

She strained but eventually relented, gave my knees one last longing look, and then turned and went to lie down on the dog pillow that sat in the corner of the room. Stacey took a good long look at me.

"So, tell me what happened," Stacey said.

"Not much really. A couple of his guys threw me on the ground out back of the place where Ferdie was waiting. He told me to get out of town, and that was pretty much it," I answered.

I left out the part about him threatening to hurt people if I didn't. I wasn't going to tell anyone about that, except maybe Hoppy. There was no need to spread any unnecessary fear. "I need a drink," I said, passed Stacey, and headed down the hall toward the kitchen.

He followed. "I'm sorry, man. I probably should have been there. Damn, this shit only seems to happen when I'm not around. Some bodyguard," he said.

I reached the kitchen, opened a cabinet door, and pulled out two glasses and the bottle of Powers.

"It's not your fault. I really didn't want you chaperoning my night out and didn't think I had anything to worry about at a nice place like Chez Maurice."

I poured some whiskey into the two glasses and handed one of them to Stacey.

"Yeah, well, from now on I don't leave your side, man. These guys are beginning to really tick me off," he said.

I reached out and we clinked our glasses together. "I appreciate that but I don't think it's going to be necessary," I said, "unless you want to escort me all the way down to Florida." I emptied my glass in one long swallow.

"Florida? What do ya mean, Florida?" Stacey asked, not bothering to take a sip of his whiskey. "You're gonna let them run you off?"

I poured another couple of fingers worth of whiskey into my glass. "I most certainly am," I answered, draining about half my drink this time.

"You're gonna to let them get away with this?" he said, pointing at my body from bloodied knees to blackened eyes. "What about the story? You must finally be on to something to draw Ferdie Crawford out in person. This ain't the time to run," he said, putting his untouched drink on the counter. His eyes were piercing.

"Oh please," I said, "I've got nothing, absolutely nothing. I've given it my best shot. I never intended to stay here. I mean, I only came here for the damn funeral, but everybody just kept—" I finished my drink.

"Really?" His eyes were damning. "You're serious? That's it? Just like that? Now I know you ain't no hot-shot reporter."

"Never said I was," I answered. "I've gotta pack," I said.

I poured another two fingers worth of Powers into my glass and moved past him into the hallway.

"You're not even going to say goodbye to Sue Ellen or Hoppy or Ronald or any of your other friends? Just pack it all up and drive off in the middle of the night?" he said, following me.

I turned. "You just don't understand. Everybody will be a lot better off if I leave. I'm just getting people's hopes up. It's time to just drop it."

"Oh, I understand. I see it now. You're afraid. You've been afraid the whole time, just looking for an excuse to run away, and now Crawford's gone and done given you one," Stacey answered, an edge to his voice.

I hadn't known him long, but Stacey was not a difficult person to read. He came at things straight on, said what was on his mind, and didn't give a damn about hurt feelings or ruffling feathers. I admired him for that—quite a bit. Maybe he was right. Hell, I knew he was right. I had been scared, but I fought it, best I could. I'd actually begun to think that this time maybe I could set everything right.

What an idiot. In Boston, I fought and lost a career. Before that, I'd fought and, well, hurt some dear friends. Now I was older, I'd like to think wiser, and I saw that my actions had ramifications. This time was different. It wasn't about a job or a few bruised feelings. It was about real pain, real loss, for innocent people, and I wasn't going to be the cause of it this time. "Look, I appreciate everything you've done for me—" I started to say to him.

He let out a loud, derisive snort. "Sure, man. Sure," he said as he gave a disgusted wave and turned to head back to the living room.

I should have let him go and just gone to my room, packed, and hit the road. Instead, I followed him. He was the only one I was going to say good-bye to, and I hoped I could make him understand, just a little. I'd probably call Hoppy in the morning from the road. I owed him that, but I didn't want it to end quite this way with Stacey.

Once in the living room, he walked over to the large, empty bookcase along wall. All the furniture in the room was pushed to the center of the room except for the bookcase and the desk. Both were empty and we'd cleared everything else out of the room as part of my fruitless search of the place for something Stevie might have squirreled away. I'd gone over the entire house. If nothing else, it was the one good deed I felt I did for Sue Ellen—going through Stevie's stuff and boxing it up. I remembered how hard it was to pack Jan's things. The way the memories flooded back and finality of it all. It was her scent on things that affected me the most—her lingering fragrance on clothing, hair brushes, even some of her text books that she must have rested her head on like a pillow after hours of studying.

It was the most painful part, or at least another very painful part, of losing her—the finality of losing her smell. I had spared Sue Ellen that.

Stacey grabbed one side of the bookcase. He tried to move it, but even as strong as he was, and as much as he seemed to want to channel his anger at me onto that piece of furniture, he could only manage to inch it a little way from the wall. It was obviously pretty heavy.

"Listen," I said. "You don't have to do that. It can wait. I'm not moving in here so there's no need to kill yourself moving furniture tonight. Maybe Ronald can help you in the morning."

He gave me a hard look. "*I* finish what I start," he said and turned his attention back to the bookcase. He crouched down a bit to get more leverage, grabbed a shelf with his right hand, and lifted with his legs while pushing the bookcase from behind with his left hand. He let out a loud grunt. The bookcase moved slightly. "Damn," he said, frustrated.

I shook my head in resignation. "Okay," I said. "Let me help."

"No, man, I got this. You go pack and get on your way," Stacey said.

I ignored him and walked over by his side. There was probably no way for me to do this without pain, but maybe I deserved it.

"I'll lift from the bottom, you push up from a top shelf. I think we can angle it away from the wall enough for you to get behind it," I said.

"I told you, you don't—" he began.

"Let's just get this done, okay? On three," I answered.

I bent my knees a little and crouched down. It hurt immediately and the tape holding the gauze stretched and pulled away a little from my skin. I turned my left hand palm up and tried to grab the low shelf primarily with my just my fingers, but it was quickly obvious I'd have to use my entire hand, skinned palms or not. I was hoping we'd make quick work of moving the bookcase, at least. I counted to three.

No way. The bookcase was solid oak, thick and heavy, built to last, and I understood why Stevie had never bothered to move it. It was a bear of a piece of furniture, and there was no easy way to get leverage to lift it. It could only be shifted away from the wall in small increments of exertion. By the time Stacey and I had managed to slide the entire thing away from the wall enough for him to get behind and eventually tape the wall and paint it, we were both sweating and the bandages and gauze were hanging uselessly from my wounds.

I looked over at the old desk. It was another solid piece of furniture, but not near as daunting as the bookcase. I turned to look at Stacey, and he met my gaze.

"Let's do it," he said, wiping a little sweat off his brow and back over his hair.

We walked over to the desk and each took our place at the far ends. Once again, we both crouched and prepared for the strain. This time it was Stacey who began to count.

"One…two…three," he said.

We put our backs into it and had to hold onto the desk for dear life as it unexpectedly and easily rolled away from the wall and into the center of the room. It must have been on caster rollers, not visible but positioned beneath the four corners of the desk, so that it could be moved by the slightest effort.

"I didn't see that coming," Stacey said, laughing, when the desk had come to rest.

"Me neither," I said. "You know, for a second, I felt really strong." I joined him in laughter.

After a moment or two, we walked over to the wall where the desk had sat. It was obvious right away that the floorboards that had been under the desk were loose.

"Son of a bitch," Stacey said, "You don't think?"

"I don't know," I answered.

I was so excited seeing about what might lie beneath those loose floorboards that I forgot all about my skinned knees, now exposed because of the slackened gauze, and knelt down on my left one to get at those planks. The pain was instantly severe—so much so that, for a moment, I couldn't move or even scream, though my mouth was wide open. My eyes filled with tears. I managed to fall to the side, onto my left thigh and buttock, but in doing so I leaned out and onto the palm of my left hand, no longer protected by the Band-Aid, for support. More pain, a different pain.

"Holy mother of—ahhh," I managed to spit out through clenched teeth as I rocked to my right and squarely on my ass. My left hand had formed into a spasming claw. I rocked forward and squeezed my knees to my chest, careful to keep my palms up and to grip my legs at the shins, below each knee, feet flat on the floor. Clenching seemed to help focus the pain away.

"Whoa, man. Take it easy there. That's gotta hurt," Stacey said.

"You think?" I hissed at him.

After a few deep breaths, I rotated on my butt so that I sat parallel to the floorboards, my legs spread out straight. There were three boards, each about a foot and a half long and a foot wide, which had been sawed and fitted back in place above the floor joists.

"Here," Stacey said, handing me his Swiss Army Knife. I pulled out the largest blade from its nesting place on the knife and used it to pry each board up, handing them to Stacey, one after the other. Fitting snugly into the space no longer covered by the boards sat three large rectangular, covered, Tupperware containers.

"Whaddaya think's in them?" Stacey asked.

"Only one way to find out," I said, reaching down and pulling one of the containers up and placing it on my lap. The container was opaque, so it was not easy to see what it held, but there was something heavy inside. I pushed up on the tab of the green lid that hung over one corner. It opened easily.

"Oh, baby," Stacey said when I removed the cover.

Inside the Tupperware container was three thick rolls of bills, what denomination wasn't clear, each held tight by a thick rubber bands. There was a Glock 19 handgun and four boxes of nine-millimeter cartridges for the weapon. There were also two bags of pot, maybe each containing about an ounce, a couple packs of rolling papers, and two unlabeled brown pill vials.

Stacey bent over, took the container off my lap, stood up, and carried it over to the desk. The flat back of the desk faced us so he put the container on the top ledge. He pulled out the Glock and slid the clip out. It was empty. He pulled back on the slide. It held no ammo. He slid the clip back into the grip, balanced the weapon in his hand, sighted down the barrel, and pulled the trigger, which clicked sharply. He smiled at me. "Nice gun. Can't tell if it's ever been fired. Judging from the unopened boxes of cartridges, I'd say no," he said. Then he put the gun back into the container. "Looks like Stevie wanted a little protection."

Next he pulled out one of the rolls of bills. He bounced it in his hand, as if they could tell him something, then peeled the rubber band off the wad and let the bills unfurl. It ended up being about a half inch thick, maybe a little more. He stood the bills in his left hand, length-wise, and thumbed through the wad like a deck of cards with his right thumb. "Mostly twenties and fifties. If the other two are the same, I'd say there was a couple of thousand here."

He placed the bills into the container without bothering to roll them back up and tossed the rubber band on top of them. Then he lifted one of the bags of pot out, opened the bag, stuck his nose into it, and inhaled. A smile formed immediately as he pulled his nose out of the bag. "Very nice. I heard Stevie always had the best," he said. He tossed the bag onto the ledge next to the container, pulled one of the packs of rolling paper out of the Tupperware, and put that next to the bag of pot on the ledge. "'Course, I won't know for sure until I try some," he said, still smiling.

Finally, he took out one of the brown pill vials, applied downward pressure on the white lid, and unscrewed it. He poured a few white pills into his hand. "Oxy," he said. He put the pills back into the pill bottle, closed it, and dropped it back into the container. He looked down at me, nodded toward the pills. "Be good for your pain, but the way you've been drinking, I wouldn't recommend it. What's in the other boxes?"

I pulled out a second Tupperware container. It was opaque like the other, but much lighter. I opened it. Stacey came over and looked down.

"I like the first one better," he said.

As far as initially being interesting, he had a point. This container held a small spiral bound notebook and sheets of eight-and-one-half-inch-by-eleven-inch paper folded in half and stuffed into a large, clear, zipper-sealed freezer storage bag. I slid open the slider seal and pulled out the sheets of paper and unfolded them. They appeared to be shipping manifests. Across the top of every page was the logo for

TSN. Below that was a section that had spaces for information labeled Date, Manifest No., Vehicle ID, Driver ID, Carrier ID, and Destination. Farther down below that were columns with headings for serial number, product, and weight. They were all filled in with information. Not exactly sexy stuff. I put the container aside on the floor beside me.

I pulled up the final opaque Tupperware container. It had a little heft to it, although not as much as the first one. I placed it on my lap, and, as before, Stacey stood over me and waited like a kid at Christmas to see what the container held, watching me pull off the cover.

"I think our man Stevie might have been a spy," Stacey said and he wasn't probably too far off. This container held a thirty-five-millimeter digital SLR Canon camera, battery charger, wide strap, and an EF-S ultra-wide zoom lens. "Ya know, between that gun, this camera and shit, and those rolls of bills, he was pulling in some serious coin from somewhere."

"Yeah," I said. "I doubt very seriously it was from working the nightshift at TSN."

I pulled the camera out of the container and pressed the power button. Nothing happened. I checked and found a memory card in the camera.

"Wonder if he got around to using this? If so, I'd love to see what he was shooting with it," I said.

"Really? I thought you were out of here? Don't see why you'd give a crap what he was doing. Maybe I should just give everything to Sue Ellen or Hoppy, maybe even the police, and let them follow up on it," Stacey said, reaching out to take the camera out of my hands.

I shifted so that he couldn't get the camera and popped out the battery pack. Then I reached into the container and pulled out the charger.

"Oh, I'm still going. There's no way I'm sticking around this town. Only it's probably not a good idea for me to go driving anywhere right now...you know...the drinking, and

I am still in a little bit of pain. Don't see why I can't wait until morning," I said a little sheepishly. I slipped the battery into the charger. "I mean, after all this, I've got to find out what everything might have been about."

"Sure, sure. I was thinking the same thing. You're in no shape to drive," Stacey said with a slight laugh. He took the charger out of my hand, walked over to the nearest wall socket, bent over, and plugged the unit in. A red light came on. "That'll probably take a coupla hours to juice up," he said, straightening up. He walked over to the desk and picked up the bag of pot in his right hand. "In the meantime, the oxy's out but why don't we see if a little smoke can do something about your pain?"

CHAPTER 51

Y ou know, Wus, you really missed your calling. Instead of working for newspapers all this time, you should have been writing fiction."

Tony's office was large, spacious, and clean. So clean, in fact, that it was difficult to believe anyone actually spent much time in the room. He sat in a brown leather high-back chair behind a mahogany executive desk that had shaped top edgings and carved base moldings. Only a bronze-finish piano desk lamp sat on the desk. The desktop was polished to a bright sheen and I imagined if I ran my finger across the surface it would produce a screech.

The only other pieces of furniture in Tony's office were a mahogany credenza—on which sat three beveled crystal orbital decanters holding brown spirits of some type and a round stainless-steel tray containing a half dozen crystal highball glasses—and two brown leather lounge chairs, a shade or two lighter than the desk which they faced. I sat in one of the lounge chairs.

By my side on the floor sat a raggedy old cloth back pack I'd brought with me.

There were no frames holding family pictures on the desk, or, as a matter of fact, mounted on any walls in the office. There were, however, six high-definition television monitors on one wall in a tic-tac-toe pattern, no doubt for viewing and overseeing TSN broadcasts, and on the wall behind him, displayed prominently and obviously holding a place of honor, six Ginsu steak knives were mounted in a fan-like pattern, points toward the ceiling.

"Well, they say the best fiction should always have a tinge of the truth. My story must have had enough to make you want to meet me here tonight," I answered. "And by the way, it's Wes."

He smiled at me, and it was a condescending, smarmy smile. He was wearing a black micro pin-striped long sleeve walking suit with a collared shirt and pleated pants. He leaned back in his chair and clasped his hands together in front of him, index fingers and thumbs extended. He rested his chin on his thumbs and tapped his nose with his index fingers, studying me for a moment.

"Why did you come back…Wes?" he asked.

"For Stevie's funeral," I said.

He leaned forward and rested his hands on the desk. "Oh, come on, don't bullshit me. That's not the real reason. When was the last time you saw Stevie? Talked to him? Did you even think about him once while you were living the life of a big-shot reporter in Boston? Of course not, because he was a loser. He couldn't hold a job. Hell, he couldn't even cut it as a drug dealer, and who can't make a living selling drugs? There's no overhead and your customers are hooked on your product."

Tony leaned back in his chair and began swiveling back and forth, working his right hand as if it held one of those soft rubber stress-reduction balls. "He thought the world owed him—always coming to Sue Ellen for handouts— thought I owed him." He stopped swiveling and stared hard at me. "Stevie was a major league fuckup and everyone, including you, knew how it was going to end for him, so don't tell me you came back because of him. Just admit it, you weren't satisfied with what you did to my family the last time. You came back to finish us—me—off."

I hadn't really thought about Tony too much in all the years since I left East Hastings, but when I did, I often wondered if there was some jealousy behind the way I felt about him. After all, he was popular in school, his family was rich, and he always seemed to get what he wanted. He drove the coolest cars and went out with most desirable girls. Everything just came to him naturally. He never had to work for anything. Did I feel the way I did because he had everything that maybe, deep down, I wanted? When I heard he'd married Sue Ellen, it was if someone had kicked me in the gut. Before Jan, she was the most important person in my life, and he'd gotten her too.

Now, sitting across from him, here in his office, seeing that smile, listening to him, and knowing what I did about him I realized it wasn't jealousy. It wasn't even the humiliation I endured at the abuse by him and the other members of the Fearsome Foursome. No, it was simply because Tony was an asshole, and that was the reason I'd always despised everything about him.

"You can think what you like, but that's the truth. If my car hadn't been stolen, if Tina hadn't been murdered in my room, I'd be long gone—probably be sitting in some tiki bar on a beach in Florida, darn near broke." Now it was my turn to smile at him. "Funny how things work out," I said, lifting the old backpack off the floor, resting it on my lap, and giving it a few gentle, loving pats.

Tony stared hard at it.

"You've got nothing that can hurt me. Stevie's dead, Bones is dead. Hell, even that moron Puddy is dead…if he knew anything."

"Well, that's sort of true," I said. This was enjoyable. I thought I noticed just the slightest bit of sweat appear on his upper lip. "I agree that there may not be anything here—" I patted the backpack again. "—that can necessarily put you behind bars or even that old Hoppy could print in the *Chronicle* without fear of a libel suit, but there is enough to maybe get people looking in certain directions, or maybe worry some people who may not like loose ends hanging about. People you know very well."

"And how do I know I can trust that you won't take this

to police or the newspapers anyway, that you haven't got copies of everything?" he asked.

"Like I said, much as I'd like to write a story based on what I got and get a little glory, there isn't a paper around that would print it. And as far as the police go…well, my even being here, proposing what I am, is probably a little illegal and the way they feel about me after what happened to those state troopers—why I think I'd be the one they'd put away. Besides, it's sort of in my best interest to get out of East Hastings as soon as possible and leave this all behind."

"So the great Wes Byrne—defender of truth and justice—is no more than a common blackmailer, just like that bastard Stevie," Tony sneered.

"I prefer to see it as just taking advantage of a business opportunity. I thought you, of all people, builder of this great empire, might appreciate that. A little entrepreneurial spirit. I mean, why should I be broke in a tiki bar when, with a little capital to invest, I could have a tiki bar of my own?"

"You blood-sucking bastard," Tony said.

He got up, crossed over to the credenza, and opened one of its front door panels, revealing a small refrigerator. He opened that, pulled down a top door that housed a freezer section, and removed a small plastic ice tray. He flexed the tray, popping a few cubes up out of their seating, and dropped a few of them into one of the highball glasses. He opened a decanter and poured a healthy amount of brown liquor into his glass, then closed the decanter. He opened the refrigerator again and pulled out a can of cold soda. He opened the can and filled his glass to the top with the soda.

"Let me guess," I said, "Makers Mark and Coke."

"Yeah, aren't you perceptive? What gave it away, the words 'Coca-Cola' on the can?" he answered sarcastically.

"Well, that and another thing," I answered. My jaw tensed for a moment. I didn't want that. I wanted to be relaxed through all of this. "You know, I'm not much of a bourbon drinker, but I'll take mine straight with three cubes—about half a glass should do."

He put down his drink and plopped three ice cubes into a glass. He picked up the bourbon decanter, turned, and stared at me. I could tell that what he really wanted to do was bust me over the head with it, but instead he turned back to pouring my drink. When he finished, he walked over and roughly put down my drink on his desk, far enough out of my reach that I had to sit forward and lean out to pick it up. He sat back down.

"So what's this going to cost me?" he asked, after taking a long pull from his drink glass.

"We'll get to that, but first things first. See, deep at heart I still am a reporter and there are a few details I'd like to have fleshed out, even if I'll never write a word of it. There are some gaps that need filling in—things that might keep me up at night. I just need a little peace of mind."

"Why should I tell you anything? I don't give a shit about your peace of mind," Tony answered.

I took a good long pull from my drink. It tasted of oak and burned a little going down. I really would have preferred the sweet smoothness of Powers. "Because it's part of the deal, that's why. I don't get everything I want, you don't either. So how did it all start? You need a little extra money getting this business off the ground? Things didn't work out as planned at first? What?" I said.

I knew from experience that the key was to get a person talking, just get them started on the journey. Once they did, the words usually just kept coming.

We sat in silence for about a minute. Tony stared at his drink, shook his glass gently so that the ice cubes swirled around. He looked at me, then around the room, then back at me. His eyes were vacant, off somewhere else.

"Yeah, I needed money. There were overruns all over the place—the cost of building this place, dealing with unions, guaranteeing inventory, insurance, all kinds of little things that ate up my capital. Then the economy tanked and people didn't do much shopping and the big box discount stores started opening up everywhere. I was overextended with the banks—"

"So you turned to the Crawfords," I said.

"Yeah. We'd done a little business before," Tony continued.

"Right. When you hired that company to dispose of the dry cleaner chemicals. It was run by a Crawford, or one of their relatives," I interjected.

Tony was back from wherever his thoughts had taken him and he stared hard at me. "Yeah, that was me that hired them," he said.

"And you knew exactly what they were doing."

"Yeah," he screamed. "I knew. What was the big fucking deal anyway? The damn river was already polluted by the paper mill. What? People thought they could swim in it and not get sick? I mean, how stupid were they? We weren't the only ones, you know. I mean, c'mon, what difference was a little more crap in the river going to make?"

"Kids were getting sick, Tony, real sick. Some of them almost died," I said.

"And that was my fault? What kind of parent lets a kid swim in a polluted river? Join a swim club, for chrissake."

I thought back to my days swimming in that river with Sue Ellen and Stevie as a kid, swinging out on a rope hung on a tree branch and letting go, flying through the air, then—splash down. Hot summer days when there was no school and there were no rules, when the river was the only place to go to beat the heat.

"So you went to the Crawfords…" I said, getting him back his story.

He calmed down. His eyes cooled off. He nearly finished his drink with a long swallow. We were just two people talking. "Yeah, and we made a deal. I got through the tough times and the business took off. Only the Crawfords…well, they aren't the kind of people you can stop doing business with if they don't want to stop."

I opened the backpack that was still on my lap and pulled out the sheets of paper Stacey and I had found in the hiding place at Stevie's and tossed them onto Tony's desk. Then I reached into the backpack and pulled out a dozen eight-inch-by-ten-inch glossy photos that I'd had developed earlier in the day, photos from the camera we'd found. I tossed them on top of the papers. "And this was your deal?"

Tony picked up the material off his desk and leafed through each page and photograph. The manifests were for containers holding inventory from the TSN warehouse that was loaded onto TSN trucks and intended to be shipped overseas out of a terminal at the Port of Baltimore. Only a stop was made along the way, at an out of the way warehouse on the Pennsylvania/Maryland border. The photos showed the containers on the trucks being loaded at TSN and then being unloaded at the clandestine warehouse and replaced with identical looking and labeled containers, containers that no doubt held tractor and auto parts stolen by the Crawfords and their cronies. Bones was in many of the photos, supervising the activities.

"It was a brilliant idea, really—shipping stolen goods out of the country using the bona fides of an established, respected company. I assume the whole thing was the Crawfords' idea. It all seems a little bit beyond you. I'm sure they have the ability to reach out and bribe port personnel to look the other way once a week. You had the bar-coded labels on your computer and could send them along to the other warehouse, repackage everything, match the weights of the goods that left your warehouse with the weights of the stolen parts that were being shipped on, so it wouldn't draw suspicion. Hell, Homeland Security and everyone else is probably more worried about what's coming into the country, than what's being shipped out. Long as the paper work matched, why bother to check?"

Tony tossed the material back across the desk toward me, trying hard to feign nonchalance. "Like, I said," he said, "just fiction. These documents don't prove a thing.

They could easily be created and printed off any computer. And the photos? A bunch of guys loading a couple of my trucks somewhere in the middle of the night. Who knows what's in the containers? There's nothing there that ties me into anything. Maybe I've got a few corrupt employees. I can't be held responsible for everybody who works here. And after what happened to Bones, even if any of them know anything, or are involved with the Crawfords, it's probably safe to assume they won't cooperate with the cops, just do the time, and live to see another day."

"Sure, but do you really want to take that chance?" I asked, collecting up the sheets of paper and photographs and putting them back into the backpack. "Stevie apparently didn't think so. He figured everything out—not sure how. Probably one night he was partying with Puddy and Puddy, like you said, being a bit of a moron and a small man who wanted to look bigger in peoples' eyes, let something slip about the car theft ring and the TSN connection. So Stevie got the job here. You had no idea he was working here, did you? Like you said you don't know what your employees are up to, especially on the night shift. He sees Bones working here once a week and knew his connection with the Crawfords, realized moronic little Puddy was telling the truth. It must have been a magic moment for Stevie. He saw a way to make his dreams come true and screw you at the same time. You know he never liked you much, don't you?"

"Didn't stop him from coming to me for money whenever he needed it, did it? I finally had enough, cut him off. And then he does this. He was nothing but an ungrateful piece of trailer trash."

"Yeah, well for a piece of trailer trash, he was pretty damn thorough. Guess you also know about these," I said, removing a few photos I'd held back when I showed him the previous batch. I also pulled out the spiral notebook that we'd found with the papers. I slid the photos across the desk to Tony and leafed through the notebook until I came to a page I'd earmarked by bending the top corner over. "Now,

I'm not sure these photos match up with the entries in this notebook, but it's enough to give you an idea of what Stevie had," I said as Tony picked up the photos. "Okay, so let's just say they do. That top one, showing you with a large man. The lighting's not great, but I am real damn sure it's Ferdinand Crawford, and he's handing you an envelope that appears to be stuffed pretty full with something. Well, here Stevie has written…" I glanced down at the notebook. "'April, twenty-fourth, seven forty-eight p.m., Old Casper Golf Course parking lot. Tony meets with Ferdie Crawford, receives envelope…'"

I looked up at Tony. His face had lost a little of its color. "I was right. It is Ferdinand Crawford, how about that? Now the next photo…"

Tony shuffled the top photo to the bottom of the pile.

"Why, I believe that is you and Ferdie once again. Let's see what Stevie has written here…'May eleventh, eight-oh-five p.m., Doylesburg Acme parking lot. Tony meets with Ferdie Crawford, receives envelope…' Do I need to go on?" I held out my hand and motioned for him to return the photos to me.

"No," Tony said, sliding the photos back across the desk to me. His shoulders were slumped and he was staring down at the top of his desk.

"So, we're clear here. Stevie knew about your operation with the Crawfords, he knew you were letting the Crawfords use TSN trucks to smuggle stolen automotive parts out of the country."

"Yeah," he said, not looking up.

"So what was Stevie's play? He might have had enough to take to the police, although like you said, a lot of it is circumstantial. No telling what was in the containers or, for that matter, what was in the envelopes. Besides, if he did that, it would create a scandal—end up hurting his sister as much as it did you. And, for all his faults—and I know he had more than his share—he loved his sister. No, he must have had another plan."

"You know perfectly well what he planned. Same thing you're threatening to do," Tony said before finishing his drink.

"Yeah, give it to Ferdie Crawford. You'd be dead in a heartbeat if he knew Stevie—or I—had this information on you. Of course it's risky, for Stevie, for me. Ferdie would probably want us dead as well when he found out. Like I said, the man doesn't like loose ends. But Stevie had—and I have—something going for us. There is no way you'd let it get that far. You know Ferdie wouldn't just kill you. He'd take it slow and make it painful, just to spread the message that no one—ever—screws with the Crawfords."

"You know so much, why are we even bothering talking? Just tell me how much you want. You give me the material and you go off and get your damn tiki bar," Tony said.

I was a bit surprised to see that there didn't seem to be much fight left in him.

"There's just one last thing. That night—did you go to the Wayside Tavern intending to kill Stevie?" I said.

Tony looked at me and the look in his eyes wasn't so much defeat as it was relief.

"No, no, I didn't. I mean, he was bleeding me, but he said this time was really the last time. That, after that night we'd be through. So I got there early. What a dive. It was so dark. No one even noticed me when I went in. I got a table and waited."

Tony went to take another drink from his glass and noticed that all the bourbon and coke was gone. He put his glass back down. "Stevie got there, sat at the bar. He was in a great mood. I couldn't so much see him as hear him, joking with bartender, saying what a big night it was for him. All at my expense. And then—then the bastard buys a round of drinks for the house, with my money, with money he was bleeding from me. And he was spending it on those low-lifes at that shitty dive.

"I mean, I figured he was using my money to buy drugs, pissing it away, but to see it—that money that I took so many risks for. So I waited until the bartender brought my drink, watched him go somewhere toward the back of the bar. I had the knife with me. Brought it for protection. I was carrying a lot of money and who knew what kind of people hung at that bar? I got up and moved toward where Stevie was sitting.

"He was watching the TV. Nobody noticed me. I came up behind him, and I drove that knife as hard and as deep as I could into his back. He straightened up for a moment. Let out a little groan, but no one could hear it over the TV. He turned his head, trying to see who it was doing this to him. I put my hand on his left shoulder, leaned forward, and whispered in his ear, 'This is the last thing you'll get from me,' then thrust the knife in deeper. He slumped forward. I pulled out the knife and walked out. That was it. It was that simple. My problem was solved." He stopped and his eyes stared off into the distance. "I need another drink," he said, got up, and slowly walked over to the credenza. He fixed himself another Makers Mark and Coke. He didn't bother asking me if I wanted mine topped off. Just as well. I didn't want more anyway. I'd gotten what I'm come for.

Tony came back and sank slowly into his chair, swiveled to face me, place his drink on the desk. "Will you take a check? I don't keep any cash in the office." he asked, sliding open a top desk drawer.

"Um…sure," I answered. I hadn't really planned this far ahead. It was the confession I really wanted, not the money. "I guess I can trust you."

Tony gave me an odd little smile and nodded his head slightly. Maybe I had him wrong, I thought. Maybe carrying around the knowledge of what he did really was eating away at him. Maybe, yeah, he was a creep and maybe he had very little in the way of a conscience for the consequences of his actions in the past, but murder was such a different animal than polluting a river. Perhaps he wasn't all bad, maybe there was one tiny iota of decency left.

I was an idiot. Tony pulled his hand out of the drawer. In it was a black Colt 1911 .45 caliber pistol. He pointed it at me.

CHAPTER 52

Y ou really didn't think I was going to let another son of a bitch blackmail me, did you? I learned my lesson with Stevie. It never stops. You'd just keep coming back. No, this time, I shut it down before it even gets started."

We were in my Camry. I was driving and Tony sat in the passenger seat, the 1911 automatic trained on me. He'd directed me out of the TSN headquarters at gun point, making sure I brought the backpack and the incriminating evidence with us. His and mine were the only two cars in the parking lot. He made me throw the backpack into his trunk and then waved me over to my car. He had me open the passenger side first, then go around and unlock the driver's door.

"Now get in real slow, and put both hands on the steering wheel," he had said. I did so. He slid into the seat beside me. "Start it up and pull out of the lot, then turn right. I'll tell you where to go. I'll think you'll like it," he then said, and in the glow of the dashboard lights, I could see he was smiling.

We drove in silence for about ten minutes. "Turn here," he said. "I think it'd be better if we stuck to back roads. There's really no hurry."

"Listen, Tony, you shouldn't do anything too rash. What do you say we just forget about the whole thing?" I pleaded. "I mean, I don't really need the money. I'll find a job somewhere. I'll just leave town, not say a word to anyone."

"You think you're getting out of this? After sticking your nose into my business—again? Come on, you should know better than that. This goes way back, and it's way too personal for me to let you just leave town again."

"But what about Ferdie Crawford? How do you know I don't have an envelope all ready to go out to him if anything happened to me tonight? We both know what he's going to do when he gets it. He's going to kill you, that's what," I said.

Tony laughed. "First of all, you are a terrible liar, Wus—and I will call you Wus. I don't think there is any envelope waiting to be mailed. Second of all, so what? You call yourself a reporter? It is so goddamn funny how much of this you got wrong. If anybody was to receive the stuff that Stevie dug up, I'd prefer it was old Ferdie."

"You're telling me you are not afraid of Ferdie Crawford," I said.

"See now, right there, you got my relationship with the Crawfords all ass-backward. Sure, Ferdie can be a bit of an ornery old cuss, and I did go to the Crawfords looking for money. But not with my hand out. I went with a plan. Using TSN to ship stolen parts to Europe. I knew about his theft ring, and we had done business before, so that was my idea. Bribing port inspectors. That was me. Connections overseas, again me. Those redneck farm boys could never think this big. They were taking all those risks to steal those parts just to make pennies. I showed them how to make millions. Turn left up ahead."

I did as he directed. We were driving along typical East Hastings back roads—no shoulders to speak off, winding, lined with trees, boulders, or occasional small creeks. The thought did cross my mind that maybe I could accelerate and swerve into a tree or off the road and have a chance to escape.

Of course, Tony would probably be able to get three or four shots off before we even left the road and, seeing how he was so close, I doubted if any of them would miss. If anyone would walk away, it would most likely be Tony. I just kept driving.

"You know what the problem is, Wus? You know why you got so much wrong? You're lazy. Pure and simple. You got it into your head that Ferdie Crawford and his family are some big crime syndicate—ruthless, violent, always one step ahead of the law. It just all fell into place that I would be shivering in my boots at the thought of them doing me harm. You know, I should probably be hurt, you underestimating me the way you did. Take a right at the T."

Again, I did as directed.

"So, you know what you should have been asking yourself once you found out that Stevie had the goods on me? Who could really hurt me? Who did I have to fear the most?" he continued after I turned.

He was right. I did just jump to conclusions. But it was only natural, once I saw the pictures and the smuggling operation came into focus, to assume that Stevie was using the Crawfords to threaten Tony. He really didn't have enough to go to the police, there was nothing to gain monetarily by doing so, and I did remember that Stevie did nothing if it wouldn't result in money or getting a woman into bed. He must have been the one who called Hoppy—the day before he was killed—but the money wasn't there. Who else could it have been?

"I imagine from your silence that you're trying to work it out. Well, let me give you another little clue. Not only were you underestimating me, you were overestimating your old friend Stevie-boy. You had no idea what a real low-life scum he was. I mean, you actually said to me that despite all his faults, he loved his sister."

I weighed what he was saying. It didn't make sense.

"Sue Ellen?" I said slowly, working it all out. "Stevie was using the threat of Sue Ellen finding out to blackmail you?"

"Bingo. See, he knew that, although Sue Ellen had found it in herself to overlook some of my shortcomings as a husband—and I do admit to occasionally straying from my vows—the one thing she would not accept is my being part of a criminal enterprise and putting our children at risk. He knew that if she found out that she would divorce me in a heartbeat and then…well, let's just say things could get complicated for me. She'd get half of everything, which would seriously impact my operations at TSN. And, then, I really would have something to fear from Ferdie."

"I don't believe it. Stevie had to know what would happen to Sue Ellen if the police ever found out. She'd lose everything," I said.

Tony laughed. "Are you kidding me? He didn't give a shit about her. Take a left up ahead then about a hundred yards and we're there. Things looking familiar?" he asked.

The half moon had slipped behind some clouds, making everything I looked at little more than shapes, but yes, I recognized where I was.

"Stop the car right here," Tony demanded.

We had come to the river and were about twenty feet away from the bank's edge. For many nights, years ago, I had sat in bushes across the water, watching and taking photos, as men in overalls attached hoses to nozzles of tanker trucks and emptied the poisons out of the tanks and into the river. We had come to the dump site.

"See? Like I said, poetic justice. I just love it. Here's where you became such a big man, and here's where it's all going to end for you. Here's where I lost so much and now this is where I'm going to get everything back to the way it should be. And look at that, you've got an old friend here to see you off."

Parked off to the side was a dark blue late model Honda Accord. I hadn't seen it before, but as the headlights of my Camry reached the car, I wasn't really surprised to see Danny leaning against the back end of it. He stood up as I pulled to a stop.

"Get out of the car," Tony said. "We're going to take a little walk."

"Come on, Tony. I get it. You won, okay. You won. But if you kill me, you only create more trouble. Ferdie understands that. It's why he let me live the other night. Told me to leave town, which I will. I promise. Police find a journalist with a bullet in his head, on top of everything else that's been happening, that's just going to make things hotter—" I began.

"Oh I'm not going to kill you. You're going to commit suicide, or at least no one will be able to prove otherwise. I said get out of the car," Tony said, waving the gun.

And what if I don't get out, I thought. *Then you'll have to shoot me, won't you? So much for your staged suicide plans, Mr. Big Shot. No, instead then you'll probably have to set the car on fire to destroy any evidence, with me in it, either already dead or, even worse, just severely wounded but alive, so that I feel my skin burning and my lungs filling with thick black smoke until I do die.* I unbuckled my seat belt and opened my car door.

Danny came over to my car and opened the door fully.

"Hey, Wus. So glad to see you could make it," he said.

With the interior light now on, I could see Tony clearly. He had a self-satisfied glint in his eyes and that smarmy I-get-everything-I-want smile on his face. The gun in his right hand appeared to have grown a little larger. "Again, just take it nice and slow. We've come so far, I'd hate to see anything go wrong now," he said as he reached across his body with his left hand, undid his seat belt, and opened his door. "When you get out, put your hands flat on the roof of the car."

Again, I did as I was told. I stretched my arms out onto the roof of the car and inhaled deeply. The smell of honeysuckle filled the air, and, as usual, it was cooler, the air not as heavy, down here by the river. I could hear the water gently rushing over rocks. I looked up to see a few stars visible in the patches of sky not filled with clouds. The moon peeked back out for a moment.

Danny roughly shoved my head down on the top of my

car. I was just able to turn my head to avoid having my still-tender nose smash into it.

"You know," he said. "Even if Tony didn't need me to drive him back to TSN, I would have begged him to let me watch this. You should have never come back. You should have known this wasn't gonna end nicely."

Tony got out of the car and walked around to my side. He handed Danny the gun and spun me around roughly.

"You know, I don't want you to think I'm rubbing it in, but I'll tell you even more about how wrong you were about everything, especially Stevie. See, I knew he was working at TSN. I hired him because he said if I didn't give him a job, he'd tell Sue Ellen all about my extra-marital activities, make things even worse at home than they were."

"Let me guess. He found out about you and Tina," I said.

Tony laughed. "Oh, man, you can't get nothing right. Tina was something, back in her day, but her day was a long time ago, at least as far as I was concerned. No, I get bored quickly, see. Funny thing is Sue Ellen already knew about my habits. We had an arrangement. She didn't do nothing, she kept the kids."

"Sorry if I'm letting you down," I said.

"Hear that, Danny? Same old Wus. He's apologizing to me like he always did—when I'm about to kill him," Tony said to Danny.

"Yeah, I was always amazed how he was even able to stand up straight, seeing as he never had a spine," Danny said, laughing.

"No, no. It's all good," Tony continued. "You're just confirming what I've always known. Stevie, well, he didn't know about my arrangement with Sue Ellen, so he started following me around. Guess I could have been more discreet. But see, here's what I'm telling you. Even a job that he didn't even have to show up for wasn't enough for him. He wanted to squeeze me for more. That boy was a piece of work. Okay, let's start walking, down to the river."

Danny poked the barrel of the gun sharply into the middle of my back to start me moving.

"I'm gonna stay right here, but don't try anything. I couldn't miss you at this distance," he said. "Wish I could come along, but it will be just as much fun to watch."

I started off. Guess I was moving a bit too slow for Tony's liking. He kept pushing every few steps.

"Like I said, he was nothing but a rotten piece of trailer trash. And after all I did for his sister. I don't know what I was thinking getting involved with those damn hillbillies. Worse thing that ever happened to me, even if she was the sweetest tail in this town when I met her. You know that bitch wouldn't give it up while we were dating? With her reputation? Just kept teasing me and teasing me until I was about mad and I begged her to marry me just to get in her pants. Do you believe that? Me, taken in by a woman, who growing up, well, indoor plumbing was a luxury."

"I guess you could say she took you to the cleaners," I said over my shoulder.

It was weak, real weak, and I hated to think that they may be my last words, but I wanted to shut him up. If these were my last minutes, I didn't want to think about Stevie, or Sue Ellen, or indoor plumbing. I wanted to think about Jan—about how my time with her may have been too short but it was so very good, how for one brief moment, I was the luckiest man on earth. No matter how it ended, that bastard behind me couldn't take that away. We reached the edge of the river.

"Okay now, we're going wade on out into the river. Not too far. I'm going to tell you when to stop, and when I do I want you to get down on your knees."

The river was really not that deep in many places, and, even as a kid, it was possible here and there to actually wade across it completely. Even after a good rain, it might not be higher than the armpits. It hadn't rained for a while, so the level was low and the current slow. I walked out until the water was just above my knees.

"Stop there. It's going to seem like old times, Wus. Remember back in school, a few of us would get you in the bathroom, give you a swirlie, holding your head down in the toilet, flushing it, make you feel like you were drowning. Now it's time for the real thing. Okay, now get down."

I had my hands up, the way I'd always seen in movies when a guy is walking at gun point, and began to crouch down, sliding my right leg back, and slowly touching my right knee down. Still very tender, it hurt—a lot—as my knee came into contact with the muddy but rock-and-gravel-strewn river bed. I winced and gritted my teeth tightly. I was damned if I was going to let Tony know I was in pain. Oh yeah, I had my pride.

"Come on. Hurry up," Tony demanded as I bounced my knee around a bit, trying to find the cushiest spot, or at least the one with the least objects digging into my knee.

I finally did, not a perfect spot, but one that would have to do. Funny in a way that it even mattered, since I had a feeling things would all be over quickly. I moved my left leg back and lowered slowly, a little unsteady. More pain, more trying to find the least agonizing place. Finally, I was on both my knees and the water was at my hips, below my waist.

"Now, on your hands," he commanded.

I bent forward and reached my hands into the water and down onto to river bed. This didn't hurt as much because I was able to feel around with my fingers before placing my sore palms down. My face was about two inches from the water's surface.

"Come on, Tony. No one is going to believe this, me coming all the way out here to kill myself," I said.

"Are you kidding me? They're going to wonder what took you so long. Your wife dies. Yeah, I know about that. You lose your job, actually quite a few jobs. You come back here and you're a suspect in several murders. You got squat for a future. Why wouldn't you end it all here? It's—"

"Poetic justice," I said, interrupting him.

"Nah, more like the circle of life," he answered as he came up quickly on my right, stepped forward with his left leg, grabbed my hair on the back of my head with his left hand, and violently pushed my face down into the water.

I was unprepared and my mouth was open as I went under. Water rushed into my mouth and I swallowed some into my lungs. My arms groped about on the river's floor and I tried to push my head up but it seemed like Tony had his full weight pushing down on me through his left arm. I was coughing water out and swallowing more in at the same time.

He pulled my head up out of the water. I coughed out water and gasped for air. He still had me by the hair and leaned down, bringing his mouth close to my ear. I could feel his hot breath on my face. "Just like school, still such a wus," he said and then he pushed my head under again.

He was right. I was—am—a wus, and maybe it was just as well that this is where everything should end. There was nothing for me. I closed my eyes, just let go.

Then I heard it—a voice, faint, *'Live.'*

I shook my head, or rather tried to. Tony had a tight grip on my hair and was pushing down hard. I heard the voice again, louder. *'Live.'*

Jan? No, it was my voice, clear and commanding. *'Live.'*

I opened my eyes. I couldn't see a thing in the murky river water. I felt around with my left hand. I found a rock about the size of my palm. It was stuck in the muddy bottom. I twisted it, and it came loose. I went down onto my forearms and I could tell that I had brought Tony, still pressing down and clinging tightly to my hair, forward, a little off-balance as I did so. I reached around with my right arm and hooked it around his left calf then pulled it forward as I pushed up from the river bottom with my left hand. My head came out of the water and I could tell Tony was falling backward.

I continued up, was upright on both knees, and raised my right arm as high as I could, still keeping a tight grip of Tony's lower leg in the crook of my elbow. I felt Tony tumbling behind me, saw his left leg point up to the sky, heard him begin to curse, "Son of a—" and then there was a splash.

I spun and landed on top of him, my right elbow crashing hard into his chest, pushing his shoulders and head under the water, the weight of my entire body upon him. I pushed up and away from him with my right forearm, straddling him at his thighs as I rose up. Glancing quickly at the river bank, I saw Danny raising the gun. He couldn't shoot though, because he might hit Tony if he did.

I got a handful of Tony's shirt with my right hand and pulled his head up out of the water as I crashed down at his face with the rock I still held in my left hand.

The water lessened the impact of my blow, but it still landed solidly against the right side of his face. I heard him grunt. I pulled his head up higher and struck again. This time, I could feel a crunch beneath my blow—a cheek bone, maybe his nose. His head flopped back. I pulled him up higher out of the river, raised my left hand up as high as I could, and—

Someone grabbed my left arm, was pulling me away from Tony, off of him. Then someone else grabbed me at the right shoulder, under my armpit, and pulled me back. I let go of Tony. He flopped back into the river.

"That's enough. We need him alive," I heard from my left. A woman's voice. I recognized it. It was Chief Roark. I was pulled upright, out of the water. I heard splashing as a few more individuals rushed through the water to pull Tony up—police officers, two of them, though I couldn't tell if they were state or East Hastings.

"Damn, Byrne. You were going to kill him, weren't you?"

The voice came from my right. I turned my head to identify the speaker. It was Captain Winters.

"Maybe," I said weakly. I was breathing hard.

"Well, you can drop the rock, now," Chief Roark said.

I did so and heard it splash as it landed back in the river. She and Captain Winters placed my arms around each of their necks and led me out to the river bank and up onto the shore.

I saw that two other police officers were standing, holding Danny. Roark and Winters led me past him, spun me around, and leaned me against the front hood of my car, each now holding an arm. As they let go, someone came and wrapped a blanket around my shoulder.

Chief Roark lifted the front of my polo shirt up to my neck, revealing a small recording device that was taped to my body.

"Damn, this thing's all shot to shit," she said as she tore the wire off my chest, "but we got what we needed."

"Yeah, well, you sure took your time coming to help me," I said.

"We wanted to make sure he actually was going to kill you," Winters said, "make our case even stronger."

I didn't care if he was telling the truth or not. I let the blanket fall from my shoulders and walked over to Danny. He had a confused, scared look on his face. I reared back and punched him squarely in the face. His knees buckled.

Damn, it hurt, but, in truth, nothing ever hurt so good.

CHAPTER 53

Winters, Chief Roark, and I were standing in a small room next to the state police interrogation room. Through a one-way mirror, I could see Danny sitting in one of the chairs I had sat in myself only a few days before. He didn't look happy.

It had been three days since my run-in with Tony and Danny, a very busy three days. My stories on his crime organization had led to increased sales of the *Chronicle* as well as an unbelievable increase of hits on its website. People in East Hastings couldn't seem to get enough of this story about a local boy gone bad, and it was the main topic of conversation at the Town Crier, as was to be expected, but also at the Bean Me Up, Kenny's bar, every hair and nail salon and country club in the county and even, so I was told, at the Wayside Tavern. Within twelve hours of my first article, the story was picked up nationally and within twenty-four hours The *Chronicle* was fielding calls from reporters throughout the world. Stevie's death had barely rated a mention on page four of the *Chronicle*, but once people found out his killer was the wealthy founder of TSN, they couldn't get enough of the story.

In addition to the straight news stories that filled the front pages of the paper and website, Hoppy made sure I was creating items on every imaginable aspect of Tony's operation. The Business Section had articles about the economic impact of TSN being shut down—if only during the crime investigation—on Hastings County, a retrospective on how TSN revolutionized shoppers' buying habits, and even a piece on what the future held for the television shopping networks versus the increased popularity of the Internet for consumers. For the Sunday Automotive Section, I wrote an article about the most popular stolen cars in America. For the Society Page, I developed a story about the effect closer scrutiny on the TSN operation might have on non-profit organizations and charitable events in Hastings County that over the years had enjoyed tremendous financial support from the company, like the annual People For Paws Dinner Dance that raised money for animal welfare. I even did a piece in the Sports Section about a pee-wee football team that was sponsored by TSN and nicknamed "Tony's Tigers," and the predicament of coming up with a new sponsor and team name in time for the upcoming fall season. My story generated an outpouring of support and the season was saved when a new sponsor came forward and the team got a new name--Dom's Dynamos.

Over every word I wrote, however, hung the ominous threat from Ferdie Crawford to get out of East Hastings, and, although I had no plans set in stone for my future, staying alive was a very high priority. Even if Ferdie himself, whom I had personally seen taken into custody—resulting in a front-page account of his arrest—could not perform the deed, I was sure any one of his family members would gladly do it for him.

However, more important matters were at hand, and amazingly enough, Captain Winters and I were on the same team, at least as far as Danny was concerned.

"Well, we're ready for you to talk to Sullivan. You know I'm against this. You screw up and we might lose whatever leverage we have in this case against Tony—and Ferd Crawford," Winters said.

"Thanks for the show of support," I answered.

"Captain, I agree with Wes's suggestion," Roark said, talking to Winters as if I wasn't in the room. "We've been

talking to Danny for several days, and he won't give us anything. Maybe we can use the way he feels about Wes to get
him off guard, get him to finally open up."

"Yeah, take advantage of the fact that he hates me so
much," I added.

"Okay, Okay. I just want my reservations on record.
Let's go," he replied. He turned and led Roark and me out
of the room, into the hallway and through the door into the
interrogation room.

Danny looked up as we entered. He looked at Winters
and Roark blankly, but, when he saw me, that damn sneer
appeared. Man, I hated that sneer.

"What's he doing here?" he asked the two officers as
they sat at the table across from him, ignoring me completely.

"Wes? He's just following up on a few things for an article he's writing. We thought as much help as he's been, we
couldn't say no," Winters answered.

"Well, I ain't going to talk to him. Take me back to my
cell," Danny said.

I really didn't think he'd want to cooperate, at least not
without a little prodding.

"How's the jaw, Danny?" I asked. "You know, all these
years, I thought you were so tough, but you crumpled like a
dry brick."

Danny eyes flashed. "Go to hell—" he said.

"Of course, of course, you don't have to talk to him,"
Captain Winters interrupted in a calm tone, "and if you do, I
suggest you have an attorney present. I mean, after all he's
done to put you here—the way he's outsmarted you—I
wouldn't want to talk to him either. Would you, Chief?"

"No, no. Not me. I'd know when I was beaten, take my
lumps, and stay as far away from Mr. Byrne as possible,"
Roark answered. "For once, it appears you're doing the
right thing, Danny."

"I ain't afraid of him, and I don't need no attorney. This
is all some kind of conspiracy. You've got nothing on me

that'll stand up in court," Danny answered.

Winters, Roark, and I had discussed the best way to approach Danny to get him to talk. Basically, it came down to good cops, bad reporter, using the way Danny felt about me to get him to waive his rights and let me poke and prod until he burst.

"Well, that's not exactly right, is it?" Winters replied, opening the file folder he had carried with him into the room. "We have you for kidnapping, aiding and abetting in a murder attempt—oh, and we found some traces of Puddy's blood on that jacket you were wearing the night of his murder, found some on your shoes and trousers, as well."

If Danny was worried, he did a good job of hiding it. "Of course, I had some of his blood on me. I must have gotten it when I was checking his vitals when I found him on the floor," he answered.

"Sure, that makes sense. But how did it get on the inside of your jacket?" Winters asked.

Danny was caught off-guard. "Well, um, you see..." he began to answer.

"Checking for the blood inside the jacket was my idea," I said, still standing. "I thought it was kind of odd how disheveled you looked that night. You were always so neat, every hair in place, shoes shined. And then, there you are—hair all messed up, wearing a jacket in that humidity. It just didn't look right."

"I told you, I had the flu," Danny answered, glaring at me. "Guys going to look a little messed up when he's been sick all day."

"That doesn't explain the blood, Danny," Chief Roark said.

"You know what I think, Danny?" I said. "I think you got Puddy's blood on your shirt when you stabbed him. Then you put the jacket on to cover it up. You've probably gotten rid of the shirt by now, but you didn't consider that some of the blood would get on the inside of the jacket."

That was one of the other things we discussed, the way

we'd take turns going at him, keep him looking from one of us to the other, keep him off balance, dealing with different levels of authority and trust, and in my case, hate.

"It was self-defense," he countered quickly. "Puddy came at me with a knife. I didn't try to cover anything up. I really had the flu. That's why I had the jacket on."

Roark looked at Winters and nodded.

"That makes sense. After all, Mr. Salvatore did attack Mr. Byrne only the night before, and Mr. Byrne said that Puddy was scared, afraid someone was after him."

Winters made a notation on the top sheet in the file. Danny looked at him with a look of satisfaction.

"Of course, what I can't understand is why you were even there in the first place," I said.

Danny ignored me and addressed Captain Winters.

"See, I had a feeling Wes was going to go out there, the way he was poking around, figured it was just a matter of time before he went out to Darby's place. Figured I catch him in the act—breaking and entering."

Winters made another notation, nodding.

"So you sat out there all by yourself, just on a hunch? What if I hadn't shown up? Wouldn't it have been smarter to just follow me?" I said.

"What do you know about police work?" Danny said, looking at me with that sneer again on his face before looking back at the two officers for confirmation.

"And yet Puddy still got into the house without you seeing him. Then he got the drop on you, little old Puddy Salvatore got the drop on you when you entered the house. Sounds like real good police work to me," I said, not even trying to hide my derision.

Danny looked like he wanted to leap across the table and wrap his hands around my neck. He turned back to the officers. "He came in the back way. I found the canoe he used to row up to the house. He was quiet," Danny said to Chief Roark.

Again, she looked at Winters and nodded, giving her

shoulders a slight shrug. He nodded back and closed the file.

"I think we've got all the answers we need—" Winters began.

"What about the gas, Danny? When you came into the kitchen we could all smell gasoline on you," I said, interrupting him. We'd set this up too.

"Huh? What? Um, I told you, I kicked a gas can over in Darby's garage, must have spilled some on my clothes, so what?" Danny said to me quickly.

"Actually, what you said was you kicked over an old gas can. Thing is, the only gas can I found in the garage was brand new," I said.

"New can…old can…what's the difference? Gas spilled on my clothes. That's the way it happened," Danny answered.

"And the cap was screwed on tight," I answered, realizing that Stacey had used the can to fill my car's tank and closed the can. Of course, Danny didn't know that.

"Yeah? So what?" Danny answered indignantly.

"It's just that I can't see how any gas spilled out of it, it being closed up tight and all," I answered.

For the first time, Danny looked a little flustered. He looked at Roark and Winters, as if looking for a little help.

Winters opened the file folder again and turned over the top sheet, pulling the one below it out of the file. "Well, Danny, it seems like the can was so new it still had the price sticker from Kelger's Hardware on it. We sent an officer around there to check on it. Seems you bought the can the day Puddy was killed."

"So I bought a gas can, so what?" Danny answered, and I sensed just the slightest bit of panic in his voice.

"It was a five gallon can—" Winters continued, again consulting his file and pulling out another sheet. "—and we also found a receipt in your wallet for a gas purchase later that day, just a few hours before you must have gone out to

Darby's place, for five gallons of gas. You used your credit card to buy it."

"Actually, well, let's see…" I said, following up quickly on the information Winters had just hit Danny with, "I've never been real good at math, but the gas cost two dollars and thirty-five cents a gallon, so you should have paid eleven dollars and seventy-five cents or less to fill the can. The receipt is for twelve dollars and fifteen cents. That means there's a good chance the can overflowed. Easy thing to do. And some of the gas got on your pants and shoes when it did. You went out to Stevie's to burn the place down, didn't you? Who told you to do that? Tony? He did, right? He knew Stevie had something to blackmail him with and knew that Stevie probably had it at his house. Burn the house, destroy the evidence. That's what happened, isn't it?" I said, my voice rising as I took a confrontational step closer to my side of the table.

Danny's eyes bulged and, for the first time ever, I saw actual terror on his face.

"I don't want to talk to him," he said, pointing at me. "I told you that when you came into the room."

"Danny," Chief Roark said quietly, confidingly, "it's really better for you if you tell us everything now. We—" She looked at Captain Winters, conspicuously leaving me out, "—know you wouldn't do something like that on your own. Tony put you up to it, didn't he?"

Danny turned to her. He had the look of a cornered animal on his face.

"Actually," I said rather calmly from behind the officers, "there's more to it than that, isn't there? You were waiting for me, weren't you? You were going to kill me and let my body burn in the fire, weren't you? You could blame it all on Puddy Salvatore. He'd already threatened me. That's what Tony wanted you to do, isn't it? You saw the light from Puddy's flashlight and thought it was me. Must have been a surprise to find him and not me. You fought, killed him, and realized your whole plan was shot to pieces. Then you heard us coming up to the house. We made enough noise. It was your flashlight Dom saw in the window."

"What flashlight in the window?" Roark asked.

"Um, I'll explain later," I said to her, realizing I may have drawn Dom into things. I turned back to Danny. "You heard us, realized you didn't have time to get rid of the body or burn the place down, so you slipped out the back door while we came in the front. Probably cleaned the blood off your hands at the dock and then went to your car and put on the jacket. When you saw the light come on in the house, you realized we'd find the body and that's when you came bursting in—to shift all suspicion to us. Only thing I don't know is who told you I would be there?"

I had gone off script and both Roark and Winters turned to look at me. Neither seemed too happy with the direction I'd taken the interrogation. In fact, I'd only thought of it that minute.

Danny sat silent but he was breathing hard and sweat was beginning to appear on his forehead. I'd hit a nerve. I pressed on. "C'mon, admit it. You'd never killed a man before, had you? That's why you were so pale and clammy in the kitchen that night. C'mon, tell me, who told you I would be there."

I thought I'd seen hate in Danny's eyes before, but nothing compared to the way he looked at me now. Then the slightest of smiles appeared on his face. "It was Bob, your good friend Bob. He's the one who told us," he said.

I'd had my suspicions once Danny said he was waiting for me. Bob knew I was going out there. He was at Tim's when I said I was. Of course, he left before the others decided to come along, so he didn't know they'd be with me. Still, actually hearing it was a bit of a shock.

"Bob was a part of all this? He was working with you and Tony and the Crawfords?" I said.

"What? No. Tony wouldn't trust that fat tub of lard as far as he could throw him. Tony knew Keith was worried that if you started writing articles about the murders, it would look bad for the town. He was worried about some new housing development him and Tony were working on, thought it would frighten people away. We convinced him I would just threaten to arrest you for breaking and entering unless you agreed to leave town. He just wanted you gone."

Roark and Winters had turned their heads to look at me again. There was just the slightest, and almost imperceptible, trace of admiration in Roark's eyes. Winters mouth was agape.

"But I'll never admit any of this in court. I know my rights. I've been coerced," Danny said.

Winters regained his composure and turned back to Danny. "Actually, you waived your right to an attorney, but if you won't testify, that's not really that important. We'll take what you told us to Augustino, get his side of the story," Winters said.

"Danny," I said, and again Winters turned to look at me. I had a feeling that he thought I'd said enough, but I wasn't through yet. "You know Tony as well as anyone. What do you think he's going to do? You think he's going to stand by you? You know that's not the way he operates. He's going to trade whatever he can to get a better deal, even if that means hanging you out to dry. If I was you, I'd be the one making the deal."

Danny looked from Roark to Winters. Each nodded their heads in agreement. Danny lowered his head. "Okay," he said, almost so quietly it was hard to hear him.

"Trooper," Captain Winters called out. The stoic officer who had stood guard over Tim, Denny, Dom, and me at Stevie's place the night of Puddy's murder entered the room. Winters and Roark both stood up. Winters left the file on the table. "I want you to take this man's statement. Make sure he signs it."

"Yes, Captain," the trooper answered. He sat down across from Danny, gave him a pen, pulled an empty sheet of paper from the file, and turned it to him.

I began to follow Roark and Winters out of the room.

"Wus," Danny called out. "I won't forget this."

"Neither will I," I answered. "And it's Wes."

I left the room, but before I did, I couldn't resist giving Danny a little smirk of my own.

CHAPTER 54

I followed Chief Roark and Captain Winters into Winter's office. I was surprised to see Hoppy sitting in a chair, waiting for us. Winters sat behind his desk. I sat next to Hoppy. Roark remained standing off to the side.

"Listen, I never really thought I'd hear myself saying this, but I would appreciate it if you stayed around East Hastings a few more days while we line up everything we can in our investigation of Tony and Officer Sullivan. We could use your testimony at the preliminary trial."

"Don't you think this young man has done enough?" Hoppy said. "I mean, he put his life at risk, wearing that wire and going in with that killer Tony Augustino. Why, he almost died when you let that man take him to the river right out from under your noses."

"I admit what Wes did was extremely helpful in our investigation—" Captain Winters began.

"*Your investigation?*" Hoppy roared. "Why this entire thing is the result of the indefatigable and fearless pursuit of the truth by the *Chronicle*. If we had left it up to law enforcement to track down the perpetrators of these heinous murders—and subsequently revealed criminal activities, why you'd still be chasing your tails around in circles."

"Hoppy, you know that both the East Hastings police force and, I'm sure, the state police, appreciate everything the *Chronicle* has done. It's just that we—" Chief Roark began.

"Do you? Do you really appreciate what this fine reporter has done? I have heard no words of apology for the harassment he received at your hands, for the sleepless nights he spent under your relentless inquisition, for the trampling of his rights. Nor have I heard any words of thanks or praise for his efforts, as a member of the press, to seek justice wherever and whenever it is in jeopardy."

I had to hand it to Hoppy. When he got on one of his rolls, it was truly a beautiful thing to behold. He was doing so well, his eloquence so mesmerizing, his compassion and concern for my well-being so overwhelming, in fact, that it was almost hard to remember that, just a few days earlier, he was more than willing to cover me in blood and drop me in a tank of sharks in order to increase the circulation of his newspaper.

Still, it was a great show. It was comforting to know, that really deep down, Hoppy cared. How could I have questioned that he did not always have my best interests at heart?

I stood up and walked over to a credenza along the wall in Winters's office and poured some coffee into a cup from a carafe that sat beside it on top of the credenza. There was also a box of donuts, and I selected a chocolate covered donut from the assortment it held. I was going to miss Hoppy. Any day now, I expected some inquiries to come in from leading news organizations who had seen my articles and were looking for a good investigative journalist to join their staff. I'd be moving on. So, I guess, if at the Captain's behest, I had to lay low at Stevie's place for a few days with Stacey, so be it.

"Furthermore," Hoppy continued, "you make this request when I have it on good authority, and from impeccable sources, that not only is Ferdie Crawford not in custody and, therefore, a direct threat to Wes's safety, but that the criminal, and I'm talking about Augustino, the criminal at the very heart of your investigation, while in custody, does not sit in a jail cell, but instead enjoys all the comforts and pleasures of a free man while living in his own home."

I stopped mid-bite into my donut. Ferdie was free? I looked at Captain Winters. "You let Crawford go free?" I asked. Then I looked at Hoppy. "And you knew?" I said.

Captain Winters spoke first, selecting his words carefully. "Truth be told, we really didn't have much to hold Crawford on, at least nothing that a judge could deny him bail for. To make something really stick we need Augustino's testimony in court to establish a direct correlation between the documents and photos and criminal activity, and we're still negotiating a plea bargain with him in return for that. Furthermore, we still have no direct evidence any of the Crawfords were involved in Bones's killing."

"But you had him in handcuffs. I wrote an article stating he was b—b—being ch—ch—charged—" I stammered out as best I could.

"That was largely for show. We were hoping someone in his organization would panic and turn on him. It didn't happen. He made bail on the charges we could come up with in hours, so yeah he's free—for now," Captain Winters continued.

"We have men watching his every move, and, besides, we really don't think you have anything to worry about. His bigger concern at the moment is Tony Augustino. He's the key in all this. We desperately need him to cooperate," Chief Roark added.

"Tony, who—" I said immediately, "—if I heard correctly, is sitting in his large, comfortable house, on his large comfortable furniture, drinking Makers Mark and Cokes, and watching hi-definition television, while I will now be looking over my shoulder everywhere I go."

"It was part of his initial plea agreement, and it's only until the final agreement is all fleshed out, and then we'll stash him in a safe house until the trial. That all takes a little time. Besides, we determined that he is actually safer at his place than he would be in jail. We have guards stationed all over his property for his protection, whereas behind bars it would be much easier for one of Crawford's men to get him," Captain Winters explained, who seemed to assume that even the most rational explanation for giving a rat's ass about the welfare of a confessed murderer, a man who tried to kill me, would make the slightest bit of sense at this moment.

I turned again to look at Hoppy.

He shrugged and gave me his best mea culpa look. "Son, I just found out myself. Of course, I was going to tell you, make sure Stacey stayed tight by you. Besides, I'm sure they wouldn't put you at risk like this without giving you something in return, like—" He turned at looked at Chief Roark. "—maybe an exclusive about the arrest of the killer of Puddy Salvatore."

My head was on a swivel—from Hoppy, to Chief Roark, back to Hoppy and stopping on Chief Roark. "What is he talking about?" I asked her.

Her face turned crimson, her eyes grew fiery, and if her jaw got any tighter her teeth would have shattered. She was breathing hard. "Goddamn you, Hoppy," she said through those clenched jaws. "I swear I'll find out where you get your information."

I looked at Captain Winters. His mouth was open slightly and he seemed as surprised as me. I turned back to look at Chief Roark. She had regained most of her composure. Her face had returned to its normal color, her jaw was much less tense, her eyes calmer. She straightened up a bit and delivered her report on the situation as if this was a press conference.

Hoppy slid back in his seat a bit, crossed his right ankle over his left knee, and clasped his hands on his lap. There was just the slightest trace of smugness in his demeanor. Captain Winters leaned forward, put his hands on the table, and focused his eyes on Chief Roark. I just sat there, waiting.

"You know," I said, shaking my head in disbelief at what I'd just heard, "people ask me why I stayed away."

Hoppy leaned over and slapped me on my knee. I winced. It was still tender.

"Oh, come on, son. That's what sells papers. This is all manna from heaven. No one in this room wants to admit it, but these are exciting times. This is what it is all about, not arresting speeders—" he said, tilting his head Captain Winters's way, "—or giving out parking tickets." Now he nodded at Chief Roark. "Or covering school board meetings. You're a newsman. This is what makes your blood flow. You can't tell me you haven't felt more alive than you have for years these past few days."

"The only reason I feel alive is because three days ago I was almost dead." My fist was clenched and I had a thought that I could very easily get used to hitting people. "All that crap about the fearless pursuit of the truth and my rights being trampled—that was nothing but you gaining leverage to get a story that would sell newspapers, pure and simple. That's all you care about. That's all you ever cared about and that's all you will ever care about. Well, let me tell you, Hoppy, you can take your story and—"

The phone on Captain Winters's desk rang.

Funny thing about a phone ring. Sometimes that's all it is, just an ordinary sort of sound we've all become accustomed to, a sound that announces that someone wishes to communicate with us, like the next-door neighbor tapping on the door and asking, "Hello, anyone home?" Sometimes it can be annoying, like someone continually poking at us, demanding attention, "Answer me, I know you're there, answer me." And other times, like the tone of the ringing phone on Captain Winters's desk, it can carry an urgency, a sense of distress, "Trouble, something's wrong, trouble."

We all sensed it. Captain Winters moved quickly to answer his phone. I don't know if I've ever seen a person turn paler quicker. The receiver was barely to his ear when the color began to drain from his face. Everything about him seemed to sag as he heard whatever news was being relayed over the phone line.

"When?…How?…Anyone else?" He mostly stood and listened. The call was over in less than a minute, though it felt much longer to us waiting to hear what had happened. He stood for a moment, frozen in place, the phone to his ear. Then he exploded, slamming the receiver down hard. The phone's console stood no chance against his volcanic eruption. There was a short, brief burst of sound from base unit's ringer, like the whelp of a wounded dog, and then pieces of shattered plastic scattered across his desk. He was no longer pale. He was seething. He turned to Chief Roark.

"Augustino. He's dead, the bastard's dead," he said, spitting the words out.

We all started shouting at him at the same time, repeating the same questions we had heard him ask only moments before. "When? How?"

He only looked at us.

"Was it Crawford? Did he get to him? What about Sue Ellen, is she okay?" I asked urgently.

He ignored me. "We'll take my car," he said to Chief Roark. They headed to the door.

"I'm coming with you," I said, following right on their heels.

He turned, looked at me hard, and brought his right hand up forcefully, index finger extended. If he hadn't stopped his hand where he did, inches from my face, I honestly believed he could have driven his finger through my skull.

"No. Enough of this shit. It's over. Get it? Over," he said, struggling to contain his fury.

"You owe me, dammit," I said, refusing to back down.

"Captain, Brian—the wife is his friend—he's helped us," Chief Roark said calmly.

He turned his head to look at her, then at Hoppy, then back at me. "Okay, only you. And stay the hell out of my way."

CHAPTER 55

Things were oddly calm. For all the anxiety and stress that Captain Winters, Chief Roark, and I were feeling on the drive over to the Augustino estate, we arrived and entered the house to find a scene that was subdued and quiet, with EMT and law enforcement personnel all going about their business in an efficient, seen-it-all before fashion.

We were met by the same trooper who had arrived in the nick of time and rescued me from the clutches of Bones and Puddy's mother. He stood at the door to the study where I had sat with Sue Ellen only days earlier. His countenance was of a man bravely facing execution. His eyes looked unwaveringly and directly into those of Captain Winters. He didn't even acknowledge my presence.

"What the hell happened here?" Captain Winters demanded without any greeting.

"Mr. Augustino was found in his study this morning, about half an hour ago, by his cook. She was bringing him his coffee and breakfast," the trooper answered.

"In his study?" Winters asked.

"Yes, sir. He was taking all his meals there, spending his nights there too. A bed had been moved into the room. It has its own bathroom, shower, and all," the trooper answered.

"No one heard or saw anything at all in the night?"

"No, sir. Trooper Covell was on duty outside the study

door. Troopers McNeill and Logan were posted outside the windows. The curtains in the room had been drawn earlier in the evening before. All reported that there was no activity last night and that things were quiet."

"What were his movements? Who was the last person to see him alive?" Winters asked next.

Trooper Covell pulled a top spiral, three-inch-by-five-inch notebook out of his top left breast pocket and leafed through a few pages before coming to the one he wanted. "It appears that Mr. Augustino had been spending the majority of his time holed up in his study. Throughout the entire day, he had only left the room three times, for twenty-minute-or-so walks around his property. The rest of his time was apparently spent working on his computer and watching television, primarily his own network and movies."

"He had access to a computer?" Winters asked. He didn't seem happy to hear that.

"Only for word processing, sir. The Internet connection had been disabled to deny access to email or any on-line accounts. We'd also taken away his mobile phone, and there is no landline phone in his study. He had no contact with the outside world from his study—not even his attorney, who had to call and arrange visits with the trooper on duty."

That all seemed to take the captain a step down in his aggravation level. "Go on," he said.

Trooper Covell again consulted his notes. "The last person to see him alive was Mrs. Augustino. They had eaten a late dinner together in the study—that was about seven thirty—and were together about an hour. She left and came back about an hour later and then left Mr. Augustino alone for the night about an hour after that, about ten thirty."

"And where is she now?"

"She is in the stables. She hasn't given a statement. Thought it would be best to wait for you."

"Right. Anything else?" Winters asked.

"Yes, sir…um…" the trooper began, again looking over

his notes, "…the only other person to see him last night, after his last walk, was a Mr. Ronald Wesley. He brought Mr. and Mrs. Augustino their dinner, left, and then returned when Mrs. Augustino did and removed the dinner dishes shortly thereafter, at approximately nine forty-five p.m."

"Okay, let's go look at the body," Captain Winters said, slipping on a pair of latex gloves that were handed to him. He put on a pair of white sanitary booties over his shoes and strode briskly into the room. I started to follow him but was stopped by Trooper Covell.

"I'm sorry, law enforcement personnel only," he said, putting his hand up, nearly but not quite touching my chest.

"You can let him in, Trooper," Chief Roark, said as she moved past me and toward the door.

Trooper Covell moved to block her way. "Sorry, ma'am, but this is state police jurisdiction. Neither of you are permitted—" he began.

Chief Roark stiffened a bit, obviously quite unhappy to be treated like a second-rate citizen.

"It's okay, you can let both of them in," Captain Winters said from inside the room, "but make sure he doesn't touch anything." He emphasized the *he*, meaning, of course, me.

Chief Roark gave the trooper a quick glance from his shoe tops to his hat, straightened her back, and strode past him. I followed, smiling, and nodded to the trooper as I passed. We were both handed a pair of latex gloves and booties by another state trooper. Chief Roark put hers on quickly and expertly. I had a bit of difficulty with the gloves because they were a little small for my hands. I managed to get most of my hand in, but not all the way through to the fingertips of the gloves, so the end of my fingers resembled the nipple of a baby bottle top. The booties slid on easier.

There, hanging from one of the horizontal beams in the exposed ceiling truss, was Tony. He was a sickly gray, his eyes closed and his head cocked to the right. The right side of his face was puffy and bruised, and probably as a result from when I had hit him days earlier. His lips were blue, and his tongue, dark and swollen, protruded slightly from his mouth. He was wearing red silk satin pajamas and was barefoot, his feet darker than the rest of his exposed body. A foot stool lay on its side below his feet, which were about a foot above the floor. There was a slight, sickly smell in the room but it was not particularly strong, owing, I imagine, to the open windows that let a warm breeze waft through the space. I wasn't at all upset that this might be the way I'd always remember him.

Captain Winters looked around the room. "Has anything been touched?" he asked.

A trooper who was already in the room and appeared to have been overseeing things came forward. He held out a clear plastic evidence bag that contained a single eight-and-a-half-inch-by-eleven-inch sheet of paper.

"This was on the coffee table. It's a suicide note, written to the wife and apparently signed by the deceased. There is an electronic copy of the letter on the computer as well."

Captain Winters took the note and without removing it from the evidence bag scanned it quickly. "Damn," he said and handed it to Chief Roark. I sidled over to get a look at it over her shoulder.

Dear Sue Ellen, it read. '*I have tried to tell you how sorry I am and don't blame you for refusing to accept my apologies. What I have done is reprehensible, and I realize that my actions have put our family, our children, at risk. That is the very last thing in the world I intended. By ending it all now, I hope that it will be easier for you and our children to begin moving forward with your lives. I also hope that someday you will understand that everything I did, I did for all of you, and the bitterness and anger you feel toward me will lessen.*' It was signed *Tony*.

"Okay," Captain Winters said. "You can get him down now. Let the ME examine him. Any idea where he got the rope?"

"Well, sir," the trooper in charge of things said, "there are lots of ropes in the stables. He may have brought it in with him after one of this walks. He did stop in to see his daughters when they were with their horses earlier today. It seems one of their horses got loose."

"And no one was watching him?" Winters said.

"I'm still investigating that, sir, but it seems our troopers joined in to help corral the horse," the trooper answered.

"What are we? A bunch of cowhands?" Winters asked incredulously, his aggravation level ratcheting back up. "I want the name of the troopers who was guarding him—or supposed to be guarding him. Corralling a horse," said a clearly agitated Winters.

All the troopers in the room were suddenly studying the tops of their shoes, avoiding any eye contact with him.

While Captain Winters was putting the fear of God into his men, the EMT people, clad in those white sterile overalls and white booties over their feet that seemed to be standard EMT wear, had come into the room with a step ladder and set it up next to where Tony was hanging. One of them climbed up and untied the slip knot that was around the exposed beam while two others held the body as it was released. It appeared to be rather stiff. They carried it over and laid it atop a tarp that had been spread out on the study floor.

I stepped forward to look at the body. The rope was still around his neck when they laid him down. It was a one-inch nylon cord, about six feet in total length. The rope had been fashioned into a hangman's noose with six turns in the knot, which was below his left ear, and had slipped tightly around his neck.

Doc Livingston, who I had not noticed up until then, came forward carrying a medical bag. He was also wearing one of those EMT suits and, pudgy as he was, I couldn't help thinking that all he needed was a white chef's hat and he'd look just like the Pillsbury Dough Boy. I stepped back and allowed him to pass. He kneeled beside the body, opened the bag, removed a pair of latex gloves, and easily put them on, snapping each at the wrist. Next, he pulled out a small black notebook, opened it to a blank page, and then scrounged around in his bag for a few moments until he found a pen. He made some notes on the page as he studied the body, probably about the rope and type of knot. He then loosened the noose and slid it up and over Tony's head, placing it on the tarp beside the body. He examined the yellow-brown area around the narrow groove in Tony's neck where the noose had made its imprint and scribbled a few more notes in his book. He opened each of Tony's eyelids and examined the eyes. Finally he picked up and studied first Tony's left, then his right, hand, looking closely at the knuckles and examining the finger nails. He gently placed both hands on the front of Tony's body, at about his thighs, palms down. He jotted a few last notes into his book then, with a slight bit of difficulty and a mild groan, rose from his kneeling position.

"Well?" asked Captain Winters.

"It appears to be suicide. There are no signs of struggle on the body. The rope around his neck appears to be the one that killed him. He may have taken some kind of drug. His eyes are a little glazed, but I won't know until I perform the autopsy."

"How long do you think it took him to die?" Captain Winters asked.

"He appears to weigh about, I'd say, two hundred pounds—probably took between five and eight minutes. May I remove the body?"

"Not yet," Captain Winters said. He came forward and kneeled next to the body. He essentially repeated all the things Doc Livingston had done only moments before, although he took a little longer examining Tony's eyes. "What do you estimate was the time of death?" he asked without looking up.

"Well, a preliminary guess—it was a hot night so the air conditioning was probably running—judging from the degree of rigor mortis that has set in, I'd say between nine and twelve hours ago. I'll be able to give you a more accurate time once I've got him back at the morgue."

Captain Winters looked up at Doc Livingston. "That would make it…" He looked at his watch. "…between ten and one o'clock last night," he said.

"Yeah, well, it would have to be later than ten-thirty. That's when Sue Ellen left him," I interjected, drawing disapproving stares from everyone in the room, except Doc Livingston, who gave me a little smile.

Captain Winters got up and walked over to inspect a table that Tony appeared to have used as a desk and computer that sat on it. I stepped forward to get a better look at the noose, bending over and reaching out to see just how tightly the turns in the knot had been wound.

"Hey, the captain said you weren't to touch anything," Trooper Covell called out, stepping between me and the body.

"Oh, yeah, right, sorry," I said, straightening up, though I did manage to note from my brief inspection of the noose that it appeared the knot had been tied expertly.

"You said the wife…Mrs. Augustino…is in the stables?" Captain Winters asked the reporting trooper from across the room.

"Yes, sir. She's with her daughters. Mr. Wesley and a friend, the vet, Dr. Cox, are also with her," he said.

"Right. I'm going to go talk to her. Have this place thoroughly dusted for prints, though I doubt we'll find anything unusual. Check the computer for anything besides the suicide note. Also check the bathroom, the medicine cabinet, under the sink—anywhere—for any drugs."

"Yes, sir," the trooper answered.

Captain Winters turned and left the room, Chief Roark and me trailing behind. We all removed our gloves and booties before leaving the house. We crossed the yard to the stables and entered to find Sue Ellen sitting on one of a few bales of hay, her daughters on either side of her. Each had an arm looped inside Sue Ellen's arm that was on their side and their heads resting on her shoulders. Jackie was at one of the stalls, stroking their chestnut horse's neck, looking concerned at the group on the hay bale. The other horse, a golden Palomino with a black mane, was poking its head out of its stall, seeming to share Jackie's concern. Ronald stood protectively just off to the side of the family.

"Mrs. Augustino," Captain Winters said as we approached. "I'm sorry for your loss."

"Yes, very sorry," added Chief Roark.

I remained silent, feeling like any words I could say would be inadequate.

Sue Ellen was wearing a light blue, long-sleeved denim shirt with the sleeves rolled up to about her elbows, blue jeans, and her green muck boots. As before, her hair was pulled back into a ponytail. She looked up at Winters and Roark, her eyes strong and clear, yet seeming a bit tired. She took a deep breath. "Thank you," she said.

I hadn't seen her since a few days before Tony had admitted that he killed Stevie and Tony and we had our little run in at the river. I'd been busy, and, in a way, avoiding her, because I wasn't sure she'd really want to have anything to do with me, seeing as I was the one who'd thrown her whole world into chaos.

Then she looked at me and gave that same sad, sweet smile I had seen on her face way back when it seemed everything had started, at Stevie's funeral. I knew instantly and with the deepest sense of relief that we'd be okay. I gave her a slight smile back. She was a remarkable woman.

It was good to see Jackie. The last time I'd seen her was after she'd patched me up at her office, and I'd dropped her off before going back to Stevie's place. It seemed like ages ago. She smiled at me. It was a nice smile.

I nodded hello to Ronald. He nodded back, matter-of-factly. His look was calm and composed, impossible to read.

"Mrs. Augustino, I'd like to ask you a few questions,

just to follow up on the report my trooper gave me. Would you like to go somewhere more private?" Captain Winters asked.

"No—except, girls," she said turning to each of her daughters, left and right. "Why don't you give Cherokee and Goldie a little exercise in the paddock?"

"Yes, Mom," each said.

They stood, bent over, and each gave their mother a hug, in turn, then walked over to their respective horses. We waited while they entered the stalls, put halters on the horses, attached the leads, and led the horses out of the stable.

"Are you sure you don't want do this alone?" Captain Winters asked again, once they were out of earshot.

"No, I'm fine. I'd rather Ronald and Jackie were here with me," she answered.

"What about him?" he asked, tilting his head in my direction.

Sue Ellen looked at me. Her smile turned warmer. "I'd like Wes to be here too," she said.

"Mrs. Augustino, it seems you were the last person to see your husband alive. You were with him twice last night, is that correct?" Winters asked.

"Yes, early in the evening we had dinner together. Then I left him to say goodnight to the girls, spend a little time with them. It's all been a little hard for them to understand. Then I came back to the study. We had…things to discuss," she answered.

"What was his mood? Was he agitated? Depressed?" Winters continued.

She took a moment to consider the question. "No, in fact, for the first time in a long time he seemed…I don't know…regular, not playing the big shot, if that makes sense," Sue Ellen said softly.

Chief Roark stepped forward to stand beside Captain Winters. "He was spending all his time in the study—his nights there. Was there animosity between the two of you?" she asked.

Sue Ellen stiffened and her eyes flared for a moment. "Animosity? He killed my brother, he put my daughters' future in jeopardy, we might lose everything, the dry cleaners—" She looked around at the stable. "—have to sell this, all the property. Would you blame me if there was animosity?"

"Yet you had dinner with him? Met with him alone later that night?" Chief Roark continued, ignoring her question.

Sue Ellen took a breath, a deep one. "As I said, we had things to discuss…our daughters' schooling this fall, where we'd be sending them after all this. He wanted to let me know what kind of deal he was going to make with you, or whoever he had to make a deal with, other things—and, despite how I felt, he was still my children's father. For their sake, I had to…had to…I don't know…accept things…" Sue Ellen said, her voice trailing off at the end.

I noticed that Chief Roark and Captain Winters shared a brief look.

"Your husband left a suicide note…" Captain Winters began.

"A note? May I see it? What did he write?" Sue Ellen asked.

"Our forensic team is looking at it," he continued. "You can have it shortly. But in it, your husband wrote that he 'put your daughters at risk.' That seems like an odd choice of words. You yourself used 'jeopardized.' Is there something we should know?"

Sue Ellen looked back over her shoulder at Ronald. He looked down at her and gave her a reassuring nod. She turned back to us. "There were threats, at the dry cleaners, at TSN, at the lawyer's office." She was wringing her hands. Her voice grew a little shaky, though she tried to control it. "They said that if Tony testified, made any kind of deal, not only would they kill him but all of us—my daughters." Her voice trembled. "They said they'd kill my daughters."

Chief Roark leaned her head close to Captain Winters. "The Crawfords," she said quietly.

Captain Winters nodded in agreement. "And how did Tony react to these threats?" he asked.

"At first, he was the old Tony, he just dismissed them. He said there was no way anyone could get to us, that they were just trying to scare him. Last night, like I said, he was…well, last night he brought the threats up and said he'd take care of it. I asked him how. He said I'd see. I assumed it was part of the deal he was making with you—or whoever," she answered.

Again, Captain Winters and Chief Roark looked at each other and nodded, seeming to be sharing the same thoughts.

"One last question. Doc Livingston suggested there's a possibility your husband had drugs in his system. Do you know anything about that?" Captain Winters asked.

"Drugs?" Sue Ellen said. She looked down at her hands for just a moment. "Um…I um…I got a prescription for Valium after…when…well, you know…I needed something. I told Tony and he asked me to give him a few, said he was having trouble sleeping. I didn't see the harm. I didn't give him that many."

"How many?" Chief Roark asked.

"In all, over the past few nights…five, maybe six," she answered.

"Did you see him take the Valium each time you gave it to him?" Chief Roark asked.

"No, he put them aside, said he'd wait until he was going to bed."

Captain Winters inhaled and let out a long puff of breath through his lips. He was silent for a few moments. He tapped the finger and thumb tips on each hand together in front of him. He looked at Ronald. "Mr. Wesley, besides Mrs. Augustino, you were the last person to see Mr. Augustino alive, when you came for the dishes. How did he look to you—his mood," he asked.

"Well, actually, I didn't see him. He was in the bathroom

when I went into the study," Ronald answered.

"How about before that then, when you brought him his meal."

"Seemed like the same old Mr. Augustino. He really never had much to say to me. Didn't last night. I just laid the food out on the table and left," Ronald replied.

"Okay. I think that's about it then," Captain Winters said. He looked at Chief Roark. She nodded. "At this time, there's no reason for us to suspect that your husband's death was anything but a suicide. We will keep a few men around the property for a few more days—have them escort you or your daughters if you need to go anywhere, considering the threats, but I think now that your husband is dead…well, I don't think you or your daughters are in danger anymore."

"Thank you, Captain," Sue Ellen replied. "What happens next—to Tony? I've got to—" Her voice broke, the first real sign of emotion she'd shown up to now. "—to begin making arrangements for his funeral."

"Doc Livingston will conduct a post-mortem examination of the body. I don't expect it will tell us much we don't already know—or suspect. The body will be released in a day or two."

"All right then. Again, thank you," Sue Ellen said.

"You're welcome, ma'am, and we are sorry," Captain Winters answered.

Chief Roark nodded solemnly. They both turned and walked out of the stables. I stayed.

We all stood quietly for a few moments.

Then I turned to Sue Ellen. "Okay, tell me what really happened," I said.

CHAPTER 56

"Wes, what are you—" Jackie said, a look of bewilderment on her face. "Didn't you just hear the police?"

"Jackie, do you mind if I speak to Sue Ellen and Ronald alone? I've got a few questions of my own to ask," I said.

Jackie stiffened and that sweet smile I'd seen only moments before evaporated.

"You're damn right I mind. Sue Ellen is my friend and her whole world has been torn apart the past few days. I'm not going to leave and let you ask your questions and poke and probe while she's vulnerable. Is this for some story? Part of your big comeback so you can go off to bigger and better worlds?"

Her words hurt. I didn't expect that from her, even though just hours before, I was contemplating making my comeback with the juicy job offers that were sure to come my way.

"It's okay, Jackie," Sue Ellen said, rising from her seat and crossing over to her. She gave Jackie a hug. "Wes is just being Wes, that's all. I guess questions are a lot like potato chips with him. Once he starts asking them, he just can't stop."

Jackie smiled at Sue Ellen. "Okay, I think I'll go check on the girls and the horses," she said. "I want to get a good look at Cherokee's leg in the sunlight." She started off and then she turned back to Sue Ellen, her back to me. "I'll stop back before I go. Give you a report," she said before she headed out of the stable.

I watched her go. All was quiet.

"Ronald, why don't you go see about lunch?" Sue Ellen said, turning to him.

"If it's all the same to you, Mrs. A, I'd like to stay," Ronald said.

"Actually, I would like to talk to both of you," I said.

"Do you mind, Ronald?" she asked.

"No, not at all," he said. He remained standing by her side.

"First off, Sue Ellen, I want you to know this is the last thing I wanted for you," I began. "You know I never liked Tony, but I never expected—"

"It's okay, Wes. I'm the one who asked you to find Stevie's killer, remember? It's actually a relief to know for sure—to know it's all over." She got up, walked over to me, and gave me a hug. "Thank you," she said softly into my ear. "You're such a good friend."

I put my hands on her shoulders and stepped back so I could look into her eyes. "Then tell me the truth about what happened with Tony."

She let her arms drop to her side, a slight look of surprise on her face. "What do you mean? You sound like you really don't believe that Tony committed suicide."

"Yeah, I heard the police, but..."

"But what?" she asked, her eyes searching mine.

"It just doesn't make sense, not with Tony. He always thought he was so much smarter than everyone else. He had to think he'd find a way to get out from under all this, have the last laugh, no matter how bad it looked. The police needed him if they wanted to get the Crawfords. He knew that. He would've squeezed them until they gave him anything he wanted. That's how he was."

"Maybe this time he put his family first," she said.

"And I saw the rope, the knots—the one tied around the beam and the other that made the noose," I said.

"So?" she asked.

I looked at Ronald. His face was as impassive as earlier, but he was looking me straight in the eyes.

"They were good, too good. The slip knot around the beam and the hangman's noose—I don't believe Tony could have tied them. But someone with experience tying knots, someone who'd been in the navy, say, where they tend to get a lot of practice—"

"Are you saying you think Ronald killed Tony?" Sue Ellen said.

I looked back at her. "Not just Ronald," I said.

"You mean me. You think I—"

"Sue Ellen, I know you. I remember when we were kids. Anyone messed with Stevie, you were there to stick up for him. No matter who it was, even if Stevie deserved it. He was family, and that's all that mattered."

She didn't say anything. She just stood there, looking at me, her breathing growing a little heavier.

"It wouldn't have been hard, not with the two of you working it. You—or Ronald—could have hidden the rope in the study during the day, when Tony went out for one of his walks under the supervision of the troopers and the study was unguarded. During dinner last night, you could have slipped ground up Valium into his food or into his drink. You never gave it to Tony during the last few nights. Then you left him alone to let the drug take effect. You came back an hour later, with Ronald. Tony was probably passed out by then, or at the least extremely groggy, especially with the alcohol I'm sure he drank with dinner. Ronald then must have thrown the one end of the rope over the exposed beam, tied the slip knot, and pulled it up tight. The hangman's noose was no doubt tied earlier. The two of you carried or walked Tony over to the stool, got him up on it, placed the noose around his neck and then kicked the stool aside. Ronald left with the dinner dishes, you stayed to watch Tony die."

Sue Ellen closed her eyes and bowed her head, her chin

touching the top of her chest. "Damn you, Wes. You just don't understand," she said quietly.

"You typed the suicide note, forged his signature. It probably wouldn't stand up under any hard scrutiny, but they won't look. It's what Tony accused me of, being a little lazy. The police have their theory, and they'll just fit all the pieces together just to make them work. Everyone just can't wait to blame the Crawfords," I said.

"Why are you doing this to her? You don't have any proof. It's all conjecture," Ronald said, stepping forward, his hands balled into fists. "Why don't you just get the hell out of here and let her be?"

"It's okay, Ronald. It's okay," Sue Ellen said, stopping him.

"Tony killed Stevie and you avenged his death. That's as simple as it all is. The part about the threats from the Crawfords—that was just smoke, and it all worked beautifully," I said.

Sue Ellen raised her head and looked me squarely in the eyes. "Oh, the threats were real. That was the final straw. What Tony did to Stevie was enough of a reason for me to kill him—you're right about that—but on top of everything else that son of a bitch had done, those bastards threatened to harm my babies, and he didn't even care. Not one bit. He said we could go into witness protection. The Crawfords would never find us. Like it was okay to just rip my daughters out of the only life they'd ever known, away from their friends, their school—everything. We'd spend the rest of our lives looking over our shoulders, no matter where we went. I told him this is where we live. He said that if I— we—didn't want to go into witness protection, then he'd go on his own, leave us. Said the Crawfords would forget. He acted like he didn't know that, as long as he was alive somewhere, they would never forget. We'd never be safe. He was such a coward."

She walked over to the gate to Cherokee's stall, looked around inside it, and gently kicked at the bottom of gate a few times. She turned back to me. "Wes, I want you to know that killing Tony was all my idea. Ronald had nothing to do with it."

"Except to tie the noose and help you put Tony's head through it," I said.

"Mrs. A, I can't let you take the blame," Ronald said, his hands no longer clenched, looking at Sue Ellen with obvious admiration. Then he faced me. "Wes, it was all my doing. I drugged his food, I tied the ropes, I strung him up. I was the one who went to Ferdie Crawford, made the deal."

"Wait. You what?" I asked, caught completely by surprise by the last bit of news. "You went to Ferdie? How? What kind of deal?"

"With the threats and all…well, it was obvious the Crawfords wanted Mr. Augustino dead. I went to him, asked him if I killed Mr. Augustino, would he leave Mrs. A and the girls alone. He agreed so I hung the bastard. Simple as that," Ronald said.

My look swung from Ronald to Sue Ellen to Ronald. It was just crazy enough to be true. I'd been wrong about so much up to now, why should this be different?

"But how did you get to Ferdie?" I asked.

Ronald let out a slight chuckle. "Wes, one thing about Hastings County. Everybody you know is going to know somebody that you might want to talk to."

I stood for a moment trying to decipher that Hastings County wisdom. Then it struck me. "Kenny!" I said. "Kenny put you in touch."

"I'm not getting anyone else involved," Ronald answered. He turned to Sue Ellen. "Mrs. A, I can't let you confess to this. You got your girls to look after. I know you'll help my wife look after mine. You go to jail, we all suffer."

"Oh, Ronald," Sue Ellen said. Her eyes had welled up with tears. "I can't. I can't let you." She faced me. "It was my idea. He only did what I asked, for me and my daughters." She smiled at Ronald. "You are such a good and loyal friend."

Tears had also begun to fill Ronald's eyes.

"Mrs. A, I—I—"

Sue Ellen again faced me. She wiped the tears from her eyes. She came over to me and took her hands in mine. "I want you to know—and I'm not telling you so you'll do anything that's not right—but I know Ferdie Crawford threatened Jackie—and you—because I got you into this."

I looked at Ronald. He had regained his composure. "Stacey told you. Damn him."

"The big guy likes you, Wes. He's gonna do what he thinks is best. He wanted me to help him go after Ferdie—me and him, on our own against that whole family—put an end to it," Ronald answered, shaking his head in respectful disbelief.

"I wasn't going to let anyone else get hurt. The deal I made with Ferdie Crawford," Sue Ellen continued. "I made him promise not to hurt Jackie, or you. He agreed, as far as this is all concerned."

"He wouldn't make no guarantees about the future, least as far as you're concerned," Ronald added quickly. "He wants you to stay out of his business from here on out."

A week earlier, it had all seemed so simple. A quick stop-over on my way to wherever the road took me, attend a funeral to pay my last respects to an old friend, have a few drinks with old buddies, one day, maybe two—tops—before I continued on my merry way toward...toward... well, oblivion in all likelihood.

"So, Wes," Sue Ellen said, still holding my hand, that sad, sweet smile on her face. "It looks like you got your story. Congratulations. Believe it or not, I'm happy for you. I could see how much you were hurting. Maybe now you can go on and get your life back."

I looked deeply into her eyes. "Why does everyone seem to think the only reason I came back here was for a story?" I asked.

"Wes, it's because you're a reporter. It's who you are. It's what makes you happy, isn't it?" she answered.

"Yeah? Well, maybe, but not every story has to be told."

"What are you saying?" Sue Ellen asked.

"I'm saying that this is all over. I'll let the police have their story. All-in-all, it's a good one. It actually works for me, and I think Hoppy will like it too."

"Oh, Wes," Sue Ellen cried, and she gave me a huge hug. "Are you sure? I don't want you—"

"Sue Ellen, let's leave it," I said, squeezing her hard. I stepped back. Her eyes had again teared up.

Ronald came over and took my hand, shaking it strongly, giving me a deep look of appreciation. "Thank you, Wes. It's a fine thing you're doing," he said.

"Yeah, well, like you said, I've got no proof and the last thing Hoppy would want is a libel suit coming his way over shoddy reporting. Speaking of which, I've got to get to the *Chronicle* and get some kind of article written, and I've got a few other things to discuss with Hoppy. You wouldn't possibly be able to give me a ride back to the state police barracks, could you? I need to get my car. I came here with Captain Winters and Chief Roark."

"Actually," Sue Ellen said, placing her arm through mine and walking me toward the stable door. "There's a million things I need Ronald to do around here. Maybe if you ask Jackie real nice…"

I smiled at her. "You think so? She didn't look too happy with me when she left a few moments ago."

"Oh, I'll put in a good word for you, and, Wes?"

"Yes, Sue Ellen?"

"I think it's okay if, from here on out, you start calling the old house your place."

"You know, I think I'd like that."

Arm in arm, we left the stable.

About the Author

Fascinated by the complexities of human nature, John Essick uses his vast experience as a writer to craft wonderful stories with a unique blend of crime, mystery, and humor. *Last Respects* is his first novel in the Wes Graham series. His screenplay for the short film *Wishing Well* won the Best Science Fiction Screenplay at the Indie Gathering International Film Festival. He currently lives in the Mid-Hudson Valley region of New York State with his wife, stage director June Prager.